Madras on Rainy Days

Farrar, Straus and Giroux
NEW YORK

Madras on Rainy Days

Samina Ali

FARRAR, STRAUS AND GIROUX
19 Union Square West, New York 10003

Distributed in Canada by Douglas & McIntyre Ltd.
Printed in the United States of America
First edition, 2004

Library of Congress Cataloging-in-Publication Data
Ali, Samina, 1969–
Madras on rainy days / Samina Ali.— 1st ed.
p. cm.
ISBN 0-374-19562-5 (hardcover : alk. paper)
1. East Indian American women—Fiction. 2. Children of immigrants—Fiction. 3. Americans—India—Fiction. 4. Arranged marriage—Fiction. 5. Culture conflict—Fiction. 6. Young women—Fiction. 7. India—Fiction. I. Title.

PS3601.L38M34 2004
813'.6—dc21

2003009233

Designed by Gretchen Achilles

www.fsgbooks.com

1 3 5 7 9 10 8 6 4 2

To Ammy and Daddy,

whose faith, light, and courage

carry me through

Madras on Rainy Days

PROLOGUE: ONE YEAR AGO

Mung'ni

SUFFERING QUIETLY IN a room not my own. The door locked. The wooden shutters pulled closed and bolted. No breeze out there, nothing to rustle the leaves of the mango or coconut trees. Only stillness. Early morning on a hot May day, the middle of the summer season in Hyderabad. It must be 104 outside. In here, it feels much hotter.

One of the wooden shutters is splintered and warped along the edge, allowing a single beam of sunlight to enter the room. I am lying at the center of my aunt's bed, the one she brought with her in dowry some twenty years earlier. For her wedding night, it had been draped with a pink mosquito net, ropes of jasmine and rose hanging from the four sides, filling the air with their scent. She saw my uncle's face for the first time that evening when he made love to her—not on the soft red velvet that covered the mattress for this celebration, but carefully positioned on top of the two-by-two-foot white sheet that would give more validity to this union than her wedding necklace or their vows. The next morning, he hung the red-spotted cloth on the clothesline and it fluttered in the wind for all to see, a white flag of her surrender and his victory. Then she, having proven herself worthy of him, began the long process of forgetting her own family to become integrated with my own. Now, the bed stands naked and bare, exposing itself to be nothing more than it actually is: a wooden platform layered with a two-inch cotton mattress that doesn't even provide comfort. I feel the wood press against the hard edges of my own body, the back of my head, my shoulder blades, my elbows, my heels. If a man were to lie on top of me now, I imagine I would break.

The narrow strip of sunlight falls across my lips, and as I feel them growing warmer, I think this is what red lipstick should feel like. Wedding red. Soon, though, I am uncomfortable, my neck and back sweaty, moistening the cotton sheet beneath me so I know that I am leaving an imprint.

But I don't move. In fact, I don't move for the rest of the day. As the sun crosses the closed-off sky, the band of light descends my body. It leaves my lips to slip across my throat, then slices my breasts, my stomach, my pelvis and thighs, and, finally, too weak, it retreats, crawling to the turquoise wall. With no other means, this is how I have clocked the passage of time. In the end, the dust particles in the air are no longer visible. Nor are the outlines of my own skin. Everything becomes blurry and enmeshed so that the curve of my arm might really be the folds of my shirt, and where I once clearly saw my big toe sticking straight up might now actually be the doorknob from across the room.

Everything is in shadows. Except this: my mother's voice on the other side of the locked door.

She is whimpering as she thrusts her forehead against the bedroom door, then pulls away, only to thrust it forward again. Each time she smashes her head, I hear the dull thud of wood and the door vibrates, and I fear it might give way under pressure. But I keep my eyes closed, trying to ignore these motions of suffering. Still, I cannot stop this grinding of my teeth, nor the way my fingernails are tearing stretches of skin on my thighs until I can feel the sticky warmth of my own blood right through the thin, polyester *shalwar.* Somehow, there is relief in our joint anguish.

"Your mother's heart is breaking. You are breaking your mother's heart. Devil's child, you will never be happy, you'll see." It is Amme's voice, though it no longer holds any semblance to the one I know. There seems to be another woman speaking out from her, cursing me, when we both know no curse clings better than that of mother to daughter, flesh and loam. Who is the devil's child, then, she or I?

On the other side of the shutters, leaves crunch and a twig breaks. My uncle is pacing, too apprehensive yet to intervene—not because he approves of my silent protest, but because he knows that it is for his sister and his wife, the women of this house, to convince me to assent to this suitor, the one they have all chosen for me to marry, then love. Yet I feel the burden of his presence and this, more than all the silly wailing, is enough to make me buckle.

My nanny and her daughter yank my mother away from the door. Their sandals shuffle and skid on the tiled floor. Amme begs that they leave her be. She says she knows what she is doing. This is ancient and stubborn poise.

"You are bleeding," my nanny says. "*Hai* Allah, what type of daughter is this? What have you borne, you unlucky mother?" The two take Amme away, their voices fading as they leave the hallway and enter the living room.

"I don't know what else to do," Amme sobs. "Her father is not here. He's never here. Is there no one who can help me? How can I do this alone?"

"Shhh . . ."

The room has shifted from shadows into darkness. My breathing grows shallow and I can smell my own sweat. Outside, more leaves crunch underfoot. This time, farther away. My uncle is retreating and I wonder where his wife is.

There are no sounds now, only the silence I know so well, and in the blackened room, I see floating images of Amme's bloody forehead and my bloodstained thighs merging and separating, becoming grotesque, and just when I tell myself I will not give in, not this time, Amme suddenly breaks free of my nanny. A chair scrapes along the floor as my nanny's old body falls against it. She screeches and Amme screeches and both tones pulsate and become one and the same before my nanny's stops short and Amme's continues. She is running back down the hall toward the bedroom, toward me, her ill-fated daughter, her voice growing louder and deeper as she comes closer.

"Whore!" she growls, pounding on the door. Fists and forehead. Fists and forehead. Bare feet. "Tell me who is your lover. Shameless whore! Just like your father. Who are you sleeping with that you can't marry another?" Of course there is no one, and I am exactly how she has raised me to be, innocent. But she condemns me and my femaleness, hoping to take control in the only way anyone can: through my body.

"I'll throw you out and you can prostitute yourself to stay alive." She has taken on my father's threats, something she has never done before. Then I hear my aunt's voice over my left shoulder, on the other side of the shutters, as she urges her husband to intervene, and my uncle sighs and steps forward, dry leaves shattering under his *chappals* as his knuckles knock hesitantly on the wood, "Come out, Beta," he says, meaning daughter, a loving title he uses only when provoked. "Your mother is right. You cannot build your happiness upon her ruins. All of this anger and filth is not good, not good for you, not good for anyone."

He walks away, toward the front gate, and it creaks as he opens and shuts it behind him, and my aunt walks in the other direction, back toward the entrance to the house, and I know she is headed for my mother, to lend her arm, to wrap it around Amme's trembling shoulders, to quiet the anger and filth because my nanny and her daughter are still crying in the living room, and the walls in this room are muttering, too softly for me to hear, yet I open my eyes and see the stillness of the overhead fan, its rounded blades disappearing into the darkened ceiling, but before I can think of the consequences of giving in, my mother smashes her head against the door, a final time, a bit too hard, and this last strike causes her to fall to the floor, a folding of her body then a thump, and the earth sighs, and I rise, finally, just another weed in this wretched soil.

Shai'tan

AMME AND I sat in the backseat of the Fiat, covered entirely with black chadors. Only our eyes showed, both brown, pear-shaped, and frightened. In her irises I saw my own face reflected back at me, featureless, a dark, oval mass, the ghost or the devil she already believed me to be. We were driving into the inner parts of the Old City to visit the *alim*. Amme was convinced the devil was inside me and she wanted the mystic to exorcise it. But I knew that when she looked into my eyes, she saw the same thing, her own face dark and formless.

My uncle sat in the front seat of the car in order to direct our driver, Ahmed. Amme didn't want anyone to know our destination, not even the driver. She worried word might reach Sameer, my fiancé, and he would break the engagement if he heard I was possessed. So Abu Uncle guided the young driver through the maze of these narrow back alleys that looked identical with their one- to two-room shacks as he searched for the *alim*'s house. The deeper we moved into the neighborhood, the fewer trees I saw. There were only cement walls here, one after the other, and alleys that led to more alleys, shooting off each other like veins, and I doubted we would find the *alim*. A few times we reached dead ends in the dirt road and had to backtrack.

"He'll take care of you," Amme whispered to me through the glistening polyester of her veil. But she was careful to sit close to the door, careful not to touch me. "Don't be worried. The dreams will stop. And the bleeding. You'll be better. It's not you, Layla, it's not." Her eyes searched me up and down as though she were looking for any signs of the devil. The more she behaved this way, the more I believed there really was something inside me. I stared at her without blinking, feeling silently powerful and mysterious, beyond any of them.

She glanced toward the front seat, at the slim and broad shoulders of Ahmed and Abu Uncle, then turned again to me. "The *alim*'s good," she continued to whisper. "Not like the others. Your uncle says this one is authentic—he doesn't take money." Her eyes grew bigger and smaller as she spoke. "Don't look at me like that," she said. "Your eyes scare me." She gazed out the window. Beneath her black veil, on her thigh, I saw the movement of her fist as she rolled her knuckles.

Outside, the Old City streets were becoming narrower and narrower, and the cement houses smaller. In these parts, not even motor-rickshaws passed, so at the sound of our slow-moving car, bare-legged kids jumped out of doorways and chased after it, some waving sticks. We grew silent in their shrill laughter. A light rain was coming down, though here and there the clouds broke and sun shone down as well. It was early July in India and the monsoons were just under way.

Despite the rain, my uncle had his window open and his thick arm placed outside, the black hair becoming wet and pressed into his chocolate skin. His other arm was thrown across the length of the seat back, his fingers lingering near Ahmed's thin shoulders. I watched the tips drum the vinyl car seat and waited to see if he would actually touch Ahmed. Men did that here, openly caressed one another, and no one was sure what those touches really meant, not even the men themselves . . . or their brides-to-be. On the streets, men held hands and wrapped arms around waists while they walked. Having been raised in both India and America, for me these differences in cultures, slight as they sometimes might be, had caused much confusion. Each time I arrived in India or the U.S., after spending a half year away, it was like turning a page and not knowing whether to begin reading the script from right to left or left to right, Urdu or English. Yet the direction I chose always made a difference.

"Here, here," Abu Uncle said, squeezing Ahmed's shoulder then pointing left toward an alleyway that looked like all the others. "Turn here."

By now Ahmed had turned on the wipers and they squeaked and scratched the windshield. He stopped the car and stuck his head out the window.

"I can't go in there, *sa'ab*," he said to Abu Uncle. "The car will get stuck."

"No, no, I think this will work. Go on, go on."

"I don't think so, *sa'ab*. Look how narrow the alley is. Even if the car goes in, how will any of you be able to get out?" He laughed. From behind, the hair of both was long and wavy, covering the sweaty napes of their necks.

Amme and I leaned forward. It was early morning on a Friday, the holy day for Muslims, so the streets were unusually empty, which made them visible in their entirety. I studied the narrow passageway that lay between two rows of tiny houses, but couldn't be certain if we would fit or not. The Fiat was smaller than the BMW I drove in Minneapolis, so I couldn't trust my judgment.

"Try to go in as far as you can, Ahmed," Amme said. "Get us in closer."

"I don't think it'll go," Ahmed said, turning to face her.

"I know what can fit and what can't, Ahmed. Just go in farther. I won't be caught walking these streets. What will people say if they see us?"

"But *memsa'ab* . . ."

"Do it," Abu Uncle ordered.

Ahmed sighed and turned the car. The kids snickered and yelled, then smacked the trunk with open palms. The metal echoed. Ahmed mumbled that no one could recognize Amme and me with our chadors on, and we pretended not to hear any of it. The street was cobblestone and I assumed it had been built during the time of Nizam.

Today, back alleys were nothing but dirt pathways. A sign of progress, indeed. The engine groaned but the car only inched forward as the kids pretended to push the Fiat from the sides and back. Ahmed drove us in about five feet then simply turned off the engine. The children's sneers grew louder.

On either side of us were white cement row houses, the roofs of corrugated sheet metal, the windows barred, the wooden shutters wide open to catch what air there might be back here. Every ten or so feet a different-colored door—blue, orange, pink, shades of yellow—each color representing a different house.

"I'll run the rest of the way and see if he's in," Abu Uncle offered. He had an angular face with thick eyebrows.

Amme nodded. My uncle gave me a quick glance then tried on a smile. I stared at him, knowing he couldn't see anything but my eyes, so I needn't force an expression. He opened the door, which hit against the wall of a house, and squeezed out. I watched his black-and-red checkered shirt disappear around a corner as he ran down the length of the curved passageway.

"They call this Elephant Alley," Ahmed said, turning toward us. His lips were dark from smoking. "It's famous because not even an elephant could get through. It got stuck up there." He pointed in the direction Abu Uncle had just gone down. "It took the men four hours to pull out the dumb animal."

"People here are always forcing things to happen," I said, scrutinizing the whitewashed walls for any signs of skin or blood. There was none. "It's only the show that counts. Poor animal."

"It happened because of a wedding," Ahmed explained.

"Everything here happens because of weddings," I mumbled.

The driver kept talking on, "The groom was riding the elephant to meet his bride at the mosque down the street. The entire wedding band was here, you see, and they were playing on their trumpets and banging on their drums as they led the groom. This way the bride and guests know the groom has arrived. You'll see in just two days at your . . ."

"Ahmed," I warned. I wasn't in the mood to discuss my wedding. "You always talk too much."

"Sorry, Layla-bebe," he said, smiling. I was sure he thought that I was behaving as a bride should, bashful, too mortified to talk about the upcoming event—for it meant the loss of virginity on the wedding night—and I let him think this.

The children continued to pound on the trunk, the sound of the reverberating metal bringing women to their doorways and windows. They wore old cotton saris and one had a baby in her arms, its eyes lined black with kohl so the child wouldn't catch the evil eye. They stood just outside our car and watched us. Amme and I clutched the smooth fabric against our faces, my mother so hidden inside her veil that only half her eyes showed.

"Cover up," she snapped to me, but I ignored her. What more could I hide?

The car jiggled as the kids pushed against it. My stomach began to cramp at even this slight motion and I turned and gave the brats a nasty look. They didn't see me. So I imagined using my demonic powers. Maybe my eyes would turn red as I stared at them. Maybe I could fling them away without even a touch. But these were just images I had picked up in American horror movies. What did it mean, then, in real life, to be possessed?

Amme began whispering prayers for my salvation, her eyes closed, the veil's fabric rippling against her lips, and I realized there was nothing she could now do to save me.

"MAKE THE KIDS go away," I told Ahmed. His dark cheeks were covered with pockmarks.

He stuck his head out the driver's window and screamed at them. They screamed back, then continued to shake the car.

"Such disgusting children," Amme said, her surahs finally completed. "These mothers have kids, then throw them to the streets. No discipline, no worry. Let whatever happens happen. Then they wonder why India is making no progress. Thoo!" She spat out the window to show the women her contempt. Then she quickly covered her face.

"Forget them, *memsa'ab*," Ahmed said, trying to console her. "They are only alley kids."

"I don't care about them," she said. "I'm worried about the car." She leaned out and yelled at the kids. "Get away from the car, you bastards!" They stopped moving at once. I turned and saw that three or four were actually sitting on the roof and sliding down the back window. Their skinny thighs were pressed flat against the glass. "Who's going to pay for the damages? Your father? Move away or I'll come out and use those sticks on you."

The children laughed. There must have been ten of them. By now, their nylon shirts had become drenched and their hair was flat on the crowns of their heads, making their ears stick out.

"Zaheer," one of the women called from her doorway. She rested her palms on the hood as she peered over the car at the children. "Do as the lady says and stop playing with the car."

There was silence, then the boy who must have been Zaheer ordered the others away. As the ones on the roof jumped off, the car bounced.

Amme moved back inside and sat satisfied against the seat. "*Ageeb log hai*," she said. "I have never seen such strange people."

"So listen," Ahmed began again. "The groom was so eager to get married, he leapt off the rear of the elephant and ran to the mosque—without the band! They were on the other side and didn't even see him go . . ."

"Ahmed, stop your babbling," Amme said. "You're making me more angry."

"I'm just telling a story. It's to calm Layla-bebe."

"Layla-bebe doesn't need calming. Why would you think that?"

"Of course she doesn't," he said and smiled.

So, he already knew it all. Servants always did. You couldn't keep any secrets from them. I glanced at Amme, but she hadn't noticed his smile. She had grown even more restless and was turning this way and that, looking behind us, then in front.

"When is he coming back?" she asked. "You can't trust anyone with anything. He knows we can't be seen out here. And still he takes his time."

"No one can recognize you under the veil," I said, trying to help. "Even I wouldn't be able to."

"Don't be so naive, Layla, everyone knows us," she snapped, knuckles once more turning on a thigh. She had been this way all morning, ever since I told her about my bleeding and suggested we cancel the wedding. "Someone might even recognize this car," she went on. "Or Ahmed. Ahmed!" She turned to him. "Stop looking around. Hide your face."

"*Ar're, memsa'ab*," he said, grinning. "No one will recognize me."

"If you don't stop arguing with me, Ahmed, I'll throw you out and get another driver. You're only one in a dozen. Don't forget that."

His face grew solemn and he dropped low behind the steering wheel. I was glad she had shut him up.

"And don't you tell me you wouldn't know your own mother," she said, turning her face away from me. "You have such a black tongue. So ungrateful—just like your father. Every day you grow more and more like him. No matter what I do, neither of you sees it. Conveniently blind. Both of you, the same."

I, too, slid down in my seat and looked absently out the front window to the narrowing alley beyond. Though I had done everything I could not to be like my father—including agreeing to this marriage—I could no longer say that she was wrong.

ABU UNCLE APPEARED around the corner, out of breath, and the women hid inside their houses so they wouldn't be seen by the unknown man. Just when they disappeared, the alley kids ran back to the car and began jumping on the trunk again. We shook inside. I held my stomach. It was round and hard. Abu Uncle leaned in through the passenger window. Ahmed sat up. "The *alim* is there," my uncle said. "He'll see us."

"How many other visitors does he have?" Amme asked.

"Only three people. He says he'll seat us in the bedroom until they leave, but we have to be quick. It's late already and getting time for his prayers."

"Let's go then," she said, turning to me.

I breathed in as I stepped out of the car. The kids laughed and ran away.

"Come on, come on. Quickly," Abu Uncle said, waving to me. Amme was already racing through the alley, her head down. A black ghost against the white walls. I followed my uncle. We passed several open doors and windows, and from behind the curtains, I saw half faces, eyes, watching us pass. I was thankful for the chador and how invisible I became inside it.

Behind us, Ahmed began yelling at the kids, while ahead, the alley curved, then led to the same monotony on the other side of the bend. Rows of concrete. The rain continued to fall. Hardly a breeze back here and only the stink of sharp urine and dull spices. The hem of my veil flapped against my ankles. Our sandals skidded on the wet cobblestones and echoed. Water pooled between rocks. One eye, half lips, stones. The rough heels of Abu Uncle's sandaled feet. That was all I saw. I quickly lost my breath, then my foot caught and I slipped. I fell forward and a hot cramp pierced through my stomach. Abu Uncle grabbed my arm. His thumbnail jabbed into my flesh and I shrugged him away.

"Sorry," I said through the chador. I pressed my palm against my abdomen to soothe it, thankful that neither he nor Amme could see me doing this.

"Careful," he said.

I nodded, and we rushed forward again. I didn't understand this rush. I felt simultaneously inside my body, dashing through this narrowing canyon, and outside it, looking at the three of us, our heads down, our faces serious, as we prayed that this *alim* could make the demon go away. Something about India, its collapse of walls between the spiritual and the material, the mundane and the profane, made anything seem possible. Even devils. Especially devils. Why else would I have done such things in Minneapolis—at the last minute, right before the wedding—when I had never been tempted to do them before? Secretly exposing forbidden skin. Being with an American man. Deliberately giving him what I'd always been warned didn't belong to me, but to my future husband. On the wedding night, when Sameer discovered what I'd done, certainly he would throw me out. The wedding had to be stopped before that could happen.

I ran forward and grabbed Amme's small hand. She gave me a startled look, but didn't let go. Together, we trailed behind Abu Uncle.

When we arrived at a blue door, my uncle knocked lightly and a woman immediately opened it. She wore a faded sari, its torn edge wrapped around her head as a scarf, the end tight between her teeth. Her lashes were straight and pointy, her hands wrinkled, blue veins branching through bony fingers. She led us inside. We entered an inner courtyard and I saw how large the homes were. They ran narrow and deep. The courtyard was also cobblestone, and a water well stood at its center, an empty bucket on its stone rim. Two mourning doves perched on the bucket and they tilted their heads to see us. On the opposite side of the doorway, the main house, designed like most old houses, with three walls only, the fourth side opening to this inner courtyard.

In the living room, a bearded old man sat on a *takat*, a wooden bed, his unblinking eyes staring off into the distance. On the floor around him sat three veiled women. They wore the old-style burkhas with mesh face coverings cast back to reveal their features, and not the more fashionable Iranian chadors that Amme and I did, so I guessed they were poor. One held a crying baby in her arms. The women turned our way, revealing kohl-lined eyes, their cheeks smudged black, and I knew they too had been crying. I stared back at them as I followed the old lady into a separate room. Inside, a simple bed and a wardrobe. A clock on the wall read a quarter to five, but the pendulum was not moving. Arbitrary time.

"I am Noor. When they have gone, I will call you in," the old woman said, standing by the door.

"Thank you," Abu Uncle and Amme said together.

"Would you like something to drink? Something cold or some hot tea?"

Abu Uncle asked for water, Amme for chai, and I declined, feeling it had been a strange offer to begin with. This wasn't, after all, a social visit.

MY UNCLE WHISPERED assurances to Amme and she nodded in response. Although her eyes looked worried, she wasn't crying. Ten years ago, she had locked herself in her room and mourned. A month later, she emerged, skinnier, her hands shaky, her eyelids dark, but she hadn't wept since. She no longer had reason to. For her, life was over. Now she sat hunched, nodding to Abu Uncle's words, and glanced at me every now and then—only to turn away when I met her gaze. Although we had come to various *alims* before, each time, in fact, when we returned from the U.S., those visits had been more ritual than sincere. This time, with my nightmares and steady menstrual bleeding, the visit was in earnest, and Amme understood this.

I watched the door, waiting for Noor to return and wishing I could see what was happening outside. I worried about the baby, hardly the length of my forearm, because I thought it must be ill. Sometimes, when a child became sick, villagers and poor mothers came to these mystics rather than seeking conventional doctors. *Alims* offered hope, so people sought them out. Faith healers, exorcists, practitioners of black magic, miracle workers, whatever we needed, the *alim* became, all you had to do was ask—and put forth some money. We all bought our dreams in different ways.

The old woman entered the room with a small bamboo tray. On it was a short glass of water and a white cup of steaming chai.

"You don't want anything?" she asked me.

"Nothing," I said, walking to the open door and peeking out from behind the curtain. The three women still sat in a semicircle around the old *alim*. One now held up the baby, her arms stretched and her elbows wrinkled, so the child hung crying under the man's nose. The *alim* stopped rocking, closed his eyes, and began sniffing the boy. The other two women wiped their faces, their sloped backs still shaking with sobs. The child's mother rested her head against one raised arm. Exhausted, I was sure, for this was the second time she had to give her baby life. Yet what real mother would let her baby die? Even Amme said she would rather kill herself than see me injured. Now that I was sick, she begged Allah to place in her own body what was inside mine. This was her way of blessing me.

The *alim* suddenly opened his eyes and looked my way. His one blue eye took me in while the other continued to stare at the child. I pulled the curtain shut and hurried back into the bedroom.

"Why do you look so scared?" Abu Uncle asked, smiling. He sat erect, palms on his thighs, and his stomach bulged, pushing against the shirt buttons.

I went to the *takat* and sat next to Amme. She had her face uncovered as she sipped her tea, and I saw again the straight nose and thin lips that were considered beautiful here, features I did not have. I resembled Dad, round in face, eyes, nose, and full lips. But, as he always said, as a man he carried his features well. I, on the other hand, would always be ugly.

"I think the *alim* saw me," I said.

Noor laughed. "The *alim* sees everyone. You don't need to be standing by the door for that." The servant stood with one hand on her hip, waiting to take away the empty dishes. She was thin and small, and her sari-*pallow* had fallen back some to expose gray hair. Below her blue nylon sari, she was wearing a white petticoat rather than a matching blue one, so the white background glared, making it hard to see the designs on the sari itself.

"He has blue eyes," I said.

"He's blind."

"Blind?"

"When he was a child, he was hit by a bus. He flew some twenty feet, they say, and landed on his head. It split open. Then he died for fifteen minutes." She paused, nodding emphatically. "When he came back to this world, he was blind. But he began to see in other ways, and, one day, he began to heal."

My mother and uncle were visibly impressed with the story, and Abu Uncle raised his hands and together they whispered, "*Alhum-du-illah*," Allah be praised. Then my uncle elbowed Amme and raised his brows, silently saying, Now aren't you glad I brought you to see him? Amme simply turned to Noor and said the *alim* had an enviable kismet, for she, too, would like to come back to life and begin healing.

I snorted. After all, when a person stops breathing for that long, if he returns it's with brain damage, not miraculous powers.

The old woman grinned. "You have come from far away?" she asked Amme. "Your daughter has an accent."

"America," Amme said.

"It's good she can speak Urdu at all. Most children who go there forget everything. Today, everyone wants to be modern."

"Not my daughter," Amme said. "We've taught her well."

"What's wrong with the baby?" I asked, interrupting them.

The servant looked at me strangely, her hand still on her hip. The empty tray was held flat against her leg. "The baby's sick," she finally said.

"They should take him to a doctor."

"They have already tried. Is your daughter a skeptic?" she asked Amme.

Amme smiled as she sipped her tea. Abu Uncle handed the empty glass back to Noor. She took it, two of her fingers inside the rim.

"She's just a child," Amme said. "What does she know?"

The old servant nodded but continued to scrutinize me. I became nervous and began to watch Amme drink her tea. Her lipstick had faded and vertical lines were etched on her lips. She was growing prematurely old and I blamed Dad for this. When she had finished, she handed the cup and saucer to the woman. The cup had a crescent moon on its rim from her lipstick. Noor placed these empty dishes back on her tray and walked to the door. Before she went out, she turned to me.

"A child in your position shouldn't doubt people who can help you," she said. "You may have come from America, but we backward people also know some things." She stood by the door, as though waiting for my mother or uncle to reprimand her. When neither did, she went on. "My name is Noor, which means light, you understand? I may not be able to see beyond what is visible, like my blind husband can, but I know many things. One thing I know, child, is that you doubt those people you can trust. And those who will betray you are your best friends. You see with only your eyes, child, so you see nothing. You are the blind one—as blind as your name tells us. Layla. Darkness. Learn to see with all of yourself, and from the eyes of those around you and those who came before you. Until then, you will always be misguided." She raised her chin and left.

"You're a good one," I said to Amme. "Why didn't you say anything to her?"

"What could I say?"

"I thought she was the servant," I said, shaking my head. "Why is she wearing such a shabby sari?"

"Why should she dress up to walk around the house?"

"Just forget it," Abu Uncle hushed us. "Both of you are just nervous. The *alim* will take care of everything, I promise." He set his hand on Amme's arm, softly reassuring her again, "The wedding will go on, Apa," Sister. "There is nothing to fear. What you have been praying for all these years is about to come true. Allah will reward you."

He looked at me, tilting his head, asking me to comfort her, too. I began pacing. The room was not longer than ten feet, with white cement walls, no windows, and the dead face of that damn clock reflecting my shadow, so I felt trapped, like a black fly buzzing away inside a clear jar, not knowing that everything it sees is actually outside the glass.

Noor's words had been incisive, as though she had intuited the real nature of my bleeding and the truth behind those nightmares. I had carried something across the ocean with me this time and kept it hidden from everyone—even from those to whom my condition would have mattered the most. I wondered now if I should come clean. But, in the end, I decided she was wrong. For I didn't think I could trust such people as *alims*. Indeed, I felt no one, Indian or American, healer or doctor, family or friend, could help me. All their responses seemed predictable. Amme would surely become desperate and unreasonable, locking herself inside a room again and, this time, not come out. My cousin and closest friend, Henna, would retreat even further, making me into a stranger. And Nate would say that now of all times I should be given the space to make my own decisions—as though I hadn't done so already.

And *alims* would use their sorcery—burning locks of my hair to check the smell, placing a lemon on top of my head to see which way it fell, advising me to sleep with unboiled eggs. Don't show hair, don't wear makeup, don't expose skin. I wasn't American, after all, so why act like them, why deprive the spirit of morals in such a cruel way? This only attracted demons—and America was full of them. A few prayers, a bath with a gold bangle inside the tub, and my body and spirit would be purified. Then the *alim* would unfold his brown palm, the lines deeply engraved and dusty, and ask for his fee.

How could I have faith in any of them?

PEEKING OUT AGAIN, I could see the women were now standing by the edge of the living room, slipping on their sandals. The little boy had cried himself to sleep and lay limp in his mother's arms, head dangling. He looked dead. Most likely typhoid or dysentery. Poor, innocent child.

The women straightened their burkhas, pulling the heavy net veil over their faces, and brought their right hands close to their noses and lips to salaam the *alim*. The *alim* salaamed back and I wondered how he had seen them make the gesture. He then began to rock, his hands folded under his crossed legs. The three walked across the courtyard to where Noor stood by the door, waiting to let them out. As they rounded the well, the doves flew away. Silently. When they came to Noor, each woman kissed her hand. The old woman ran her fingers through the child's hair, then shut the door behind them.

The mystic continued to rock, his lips moving quickly as he muttered, his white beard reaching his collarbone. His blank eyes wandered around the room, but mostly they were rolled up, as though digging their way back inside his skull. He wore white and, because his hand was shoved beneath his leg, the kurta's sleeve curled back and revealed a watch on his left wrist.

Noor leaned over his ear and whispered something. He nodded, but continued his silent chant. She kissed his forehead. He rocked. She turned his wrist and read the time. He placed it back under his foot. She smoothed out the fabric, covering the watch. Then she whispered something more. He nodded again. She now headed toward our room and I retreated.

"She's coming," I said.

Abu Uncle and Amme both rose.

"The *alim*'s very good," Abu Uncle said. "So don't be scared. Remember, you've been through this a dozen times before." He took a comb out from his side pocket and began combing, one palm patting down the heavier strands as the teeth passed through.

"I'm not worried," I said. "Are you sure he doesn't charge?"

Noor's footsteps approached from behind.

"Well," he said, hesitating. "It's customary to give him a donation. He doesn't have a flat fee. People just give him what they think is necessary. The rich give more, the poor less." He put the comb away.

"What if we don't give him anything?"

"Ar're!" He was surprised, even offended, as though he had cut himself a deal with the *alim*. A commission he would receive from our sale. Abu Uncle had done things like that in the past. "He's got to run this house," he said. "You can't just take his advice and leave. It doesn't look good."

"But I thought you said he's free?"

"He is."

Amme clucked. "What can we do now?" she asked, shaking her head. She looked disappointed in me. Then she sighed and said more tenderly, "Don't be worried about money, Layla. What matters is that he cures you. My money is not worth more than your well-being."

Money, as far as I could see, was all Amme had left, just dollars and the little freedom they offered her. Hearing her say this, I felt guilty and ashamed about what I had done in Minneapolis, and how it was causing my mother such misery. If Abu Uncle wasn't in the room, I would have confessed everything to her right then and willingly accepted her judgment of me. But he was there, as someone always seemed to be in India. Hardly any privacy. So I had no time to tell Amme the truth.

Noor pulled open the curtain, and I felt her against my back. For a moment, I didn't move. What if we just left? I wondered. If the *alim* was a fake, as I imagined him to be, then why spend the money when I already knew what ailed me? And, if by chance, he was authentic, why take the risk that he might detect the truth and give me away?

"Follow me," Noor said, talking over my shoulder. She placed her veiny hand on my waist to push me aside, but I resisted.

"Layla," Amme said, "move away and let Noor in. Why are you being so rude? She'll think I didn't raise you properly."

I didn't budge.

Amme gripped my arm and pulled me aside. Abu Uncle walked out. My mother followed.

"Amme," I called.

"Stop being such a child, Layla," she said.

"I'm no longer a child, Amme."

She stopped and looked strangely at me, the chador making her body formless and unrecognizable.

"If you have something to tell me, child, tell me now," she whispered. "I have been wondering. But I've been waiting for you to tell me yourself."

Amme always knew when I kept something hidden.

"Layla, what is it?" she asked.

She was shorter than me, and though enveloped in that monstrous chador, the way her eyes stared up at mine, she seemed entirely exposed. Her shoulders had tensed as she prepared herself to hear my perverse confession. It took all her strength.

In my family, the only things revealed and discussed were those things that didn't matter. This way, none of us got hurt by what another did. We hadn't always lived like this. It had only become this way in the past ten years, since Dad took on a second wife and Amme finally came out of the bedroom, skinnier, dried out, and no longer able to endure losing faith.

"Apa," Abu Uncle called. "The *alim* is waiting."

"Do you think I'm possessed, Amme?" I asked.

She shrugged. "I think there must be something over you. Otherwise you wouldn't behave the way you do."

"Apa," my uncle said again, extending his hand to her.

I pressed the veil against my face. The polyester smelled of sweat.

"*Chalu*," I said to Amme, let's go. We walked in a single line, Abu Uncle, Amme, me, then Noor. Light, she had said her name meant, Light. Why had she told me that? It meant nothing. None of these people could offer me anything useful now. If the *alim* wanted to slice lemons over my head, let him. If he wanted me to cover my face, hide my skin, not go out of the house, nor speak to any man other than a close relative, that was fine with me. After all, what did it matter in the end? There were many ways to harvest a woman's body. Eventually, she must learn to liberate herself.

Amme knew that. It was why, despite how hard it must have been for her, she had gathered herself together and held her breath as she waited for my confession. The truth was, I was no longer the girl others imagined me to be. I was not going to my future husband as a virgin. And the bleeding, it was not demonic. It was a dying baby. Nate's. I had gotten pregnant. An accident, conceived in haste . . . or in good times. Either way, I couldn't be caught this way now, not two days before the wedding, not unless I wanted to be banished from my family and everything I knew. So I went on taking the pill, silently killing this life inside me.

I was possessed, then, by this innocent, dying child.

HE DID HAVE blind eyes, and I could see them. He wore no glasses. A thick white film covered the entire eyeballs, and each stared off in a different direction.

Behind him, the three walls of the living room were covered almost entirely with rectangular mirrors, some older than others, but identical in dimension. Each one was the size of a poster board. All the frames were a simple two-inch-thick dull brass. The mirrors were hung in such a way as to reflect others. Mirrors inside mirrors, multiple reflections, refractions, and the original became lost, impossible to discern. Along the walls, in a few places, the turquoise paint revealed itself. Inside the mirrors, however, these bare spots were completely concealed.

Abu Uncle sat next to the *alim*, on the *takat*, while Amme and I sat on the tiled floor, facing the two men, just as I had seen the women before us do. The courtyard was behind me, and I heard the rain falling through branches and leaves, splattering on the ground. Noor stood next to her husband, her hands clutched before her, her head bowed. She was so quiet and reverent during our session that I soon forgot she was there.

When I sneaked a peek at the old man, I saw inside his nose and noticed long hair reaching out to curve around each nostril. Inch-long hair also poked out from behind the low-cut kurta and from below the wide pajama bottoms. I lowered my gaze, somehow feeling I had been improper to notice these things. Segregation between women and men had that effect on me. Since I was a child, my mother had tried to teach me correct behavior and I followed her wishes when she was watching—covering my hair, hiding my legs, draping a scarf over kurtas to conceal the curve of my breasts, muffling my laughter, whispering, averting my eyes. I always knew I had to do these things because man, as Islam said, was the weaker sex, so it was my responsibility to keep him from becoming aroused. All these precautions were taken to prevent intercourse or, as Amme would say, so I would not fall prey to a man's desires. Naturally, then, when I encountered any man, young or old, in the theater, on the bus, passing by our car, rather than feeling chaste, I felt more desire wrapped in the chador, more aware that I was a woman, and he, simply by the fate of his being a man, wanted me. So I sometimes met their curious gaze, sometimes let them brush against me as they walked by, and sometimes even followed them with my eyes, admiring their rounded shoulders, their rigid chins, their hairy chests and forearms, their hands. From what better place to notice a man's body than from behind a chador?

"You have come about the girl," the *alim* said to us. He kept his voice near a whisper, as though to create a confidence.

"Yes," Amme said. Neither of us looked directly at the *alim*. It was considered improper for men and women to look into each other's eyes, unless they were married. "My daughter."

"What is your relationship to the man sitting next to me?" he asked.

"He is my sister's husband."

The old man nodded. He smelled of sweat and betel nut. "Now," he said, "what is wrong with the girl?"

"The girl has been bleeding . . . like menses," Abu Uncle said, also quietly, "but longer, much much longer. And with it, she is having bad dreams." When the *alim* only nodded, he added, "My sister-in-law and her daughter have just arrived from America, where they live."

"I see," the *alim* said and rocked a while in silence.

I saw from his thoughtful expression that he was considering tactful ways to say what he believed. His eyes hovered just above my head and I could not help but stare into them, wanting to peel away the top coating with a pair of tweezers. Would they look normal beneath? And would he then be able to see?

"*Umrika* is not the best place to raise a daughter, my sister," he finally said to Amme.

"What can we do? The times are such. You know how difficult it is for Muslims in India. And her father and I are very strict with her." Amme said this to most anyone who raised doubts about her and Dad leaving their homeland.

"No matter. Children go there and get lost," he said.

Amme shrugged.

The *alim* continued his sermon, his eyes blindly staring over our heads, watching the rain. Amme grew more annoyed and gestured angrily at Abu Uncle, pointing at various times toward the old man. She didn't think it was necessary for my uncle to have revealed where we lived, especially since the *alim*'s reaction was predictable, and worse, despite his preaching, he would now expect more rupees from us, *dollar* rupees.

The truth was, nothing the *alim* or anyone else might say would convince my parents to return to India. After twenty years abroad, my parents considered America their home. They may have been born and raised in India, but their present life existed there—Dad's work, my schooling, other Indian friends. If caught in an honest moment, they would even admit that the quality of life in the U.S. was better because it was cleaner—the water, the air, the food, the streets. No religious riots. No military curfews. But they planned to retire here. Which is to say that for them, birth and death occurred in India, but not life.

My uncle shifted a few inches away from the *alim* and gestured back to Amme. He pointed at me several times then spread his palms, as if to say, "Come on, Apa, the *alim* has to know. America is the source of all Layla's problems."

I rolled my eyes. I had faced this all my life, the way each country held a moral stance over the other. It was as though each nation had its own uniform and I wore the shirt of one, the trousers of the other, and both sides were shooting at me. Oh, the way each culture condemned and complained. India was backward and primitive, exotic. America was morally bankrupt, a cultural colonizer. But I knew this chiding was really a flirtation. For below these criticisms, the truth was that each place held allure for the other, a fascination and curiosity, an attraction and longing. They exchanged hamburgers for chicken curry, combined Ayurvedic and modern medicine, and swapped yoga for aerobics. I had never witnessed such confused and beguiled lovers.

"Children begin to commit sins," the *alim* continued. Noor nodded in agreement, her eyes still closed. "They don't know better and do as their *Umrikan* friends. Drink alcohol. Go to dirty bars and dance with the opposite sex. I have heard that some of our girls are even wearing miniskirts and bikinis. *Tho-ba, tho-ba,*" he said, lightly slapping his cheeks to show repentance. "No shame left at all. This is all a sign the day of judgment is coming."

"Our daughter is not like that," Amme said, looking over the *alim*'s shoulder at the mirrors, then into the courtyard at the drizzle, then at her wristwatch. Even her voice sounded bored. "Her father is very strict with her. No phone calls from American friends, boys or girls. No going out of the house unless it is to attend classes. She's been very . . . isolated." She began to clean her toenails.

"Is this true, Beta?" he asked me.

"Very true," I said, for it was, and I had always resented my parents for it. Isolation to prevent assimilation. If I happened to stay out late one night or got a call from a boy, Dad would beat me to remind me of who I was.

"My sister-in-law brings her daughter home each summer," Abu Uncle said, nodding at Amme. He was making up to her now, noticing, I was sure, how the *alim* had not proceeded to connect my bleeding with America to offer me a simple cure. "Every year Apa leaves her home in the U.S. to bring her daughter to Hyderabad. Have you ever heard of such devotion, Alim-ji?"

Amme lowered her head and listened to my uncle's praise.

I heard raindrops patter into the empty steel bucket by the well and thought it strange that the doves sat in the rain.

Abu Uncle smiled wide, showing most of his yellow teeth, as he leaned over to look into the *alim*'s face. Then, reminded that the old man was blind, he withdrew. But, as he talked, he leaned forward again. And withdrew again.

The *alim* nodded, as though considering my uncle's words, but his expression did not change.

"Of course Layla isn't like the girls you've heard of, Alim-ji," my uncle was saying. "She's a decent girl. Her parents are very strict. Very, very strict. They wouldn't let Layla grow up American. *Ar're!* What a thing to say! Apa brings Layla back every year so the girl won't forget who she really is. Imagine the money it takes to travel back and forth every single year . . ."

Amme cleared her throat at the mention of money and Abu Uncle quieted.

"Good, good," the *alim* said. "But one thing still confuses me." He rocked silently again, his hands holding his ankles. The face of his watch peeped out and I glanced at Noor. Her head was down, eyes closed. No one seemed to notice it but me. "If all of this is true," the *alim* said, "then why have you come to me? What are these dreams you speak of? And what is the cause of this flowing blood?"

"We don't know why she's having these dreams," Amme said. She stared into her palms, as though questioning her own life decisions. "We wanted your help for that."

"I do not mean offense, my sister, but I must ask you one thing. I beg you to be honest with me. Are you quite sure, my sister, that your daughter was as secluded as you say?"

"Yes, yes, of course," Amme said, but when she glanced at me, I thought I saw doubt in her eyes.

I grew uncomfortable and slumped into my veil, trying to hide from her and the *alim*'s dead eyes. No one had ever thought to question this before and I felt exposed. In fact, I began to feel convinced that the *alim* knew everything, that he was, at that moment, conjuring up all the events of the previous month. As though on a movie screen, I visualized the images displayed on the back of his white eyes. As he watched, I, too, recalled.

There was Nate, dark haired, gray-green eyes, his camera knocking against his jeans, following me onto a college bus after our shared photography class. And there was I, elated and afraid, having never dated, but feeling I needed to now, boarding the wrong bus, already hiding my engagement ring. There we were, getting off at the first stop, then walking across campus, to my next class, and agreeing to meet for coffee. Now there I was, skipping classes to go sailing with him. There, wearing a bikini. Now, lying in the sun—as though I needed a tan. There, drinking beer. Now, returning home on time and complaining to my parents about the difficulty of college classes. Oh God, there I was, late at night, finding a way to get him inside the house. Now we're making love, one floor below my mother. Early in the morning, he quietly leaves, easily, through the patio door.

No, I hadn't the courage to sneak out of the house. But I had found someone willing to sneak in.

"DON'T BE ASHAMED, Layla," Amme said, poking my thigh. "He's like a doctor. Tell him about your dreams."

I shook my head no. I had described my dreams to one person, my mother, and only out of fear. Since I was a child she had been saying the devil was inside me, trying to take control. So when I began having these dreams, I wondered if she might, after all, be right. Now, if Amme wanted, she could inform him herself, just as she had Abu Uncle and his wife—and who knows how many others. Besides, if it was considered improper for me to look into a strange man's face, how then did she expect me to confide in that man about my sexual dreams?

"Go on and tell him," Amme urged.

I turned away from her.

"May I?" Abu Uncle jumped in. "In her dreams, Alim-ji," he whispered, "a man visits her. The dreams . . . how can I say this?" He grew uncomfortable and laughed. "I'm not sure what you will think, Alim-ji, but the dreams are sexual in nature."

"I see," the *alim* said. He cracked his knuckles, the noise like small thunder during monsoon showers. "What does this man look like?"

"She can't see his face," my uncle said.

"How long ago did this start?"

"She says a little over one month."

"What has changed in the past few weeks?"

No one spoke.

"Beta," the *alim* said, addressing me as Daughter. "What has changed in the past month?"

"In the past month?" I said, tracing a tile with my pinkie. "Very little has changed."

"But something must have happened to start these dreams."

"Like what?" I asked, laughing. But the other three only looked at me, even that blind *alim*, all their brows arched and foreheads lined. A bird flew into the mirrored living room and its black-and-red wings, its marble-sized head, were reflected over and over and over.

"I think there is a demon in her," Amme finally said. "When she was a child, only a year old, she would jump on the bed, screaming, '*Mai shai-tan hoon*—' " I am the devil. "All day long she jumped and screamed. I could not make her stop. And I knew then she was possessed. The moment we arrived in America it started. And now . . ." she shook her head and clucked in sadness. "Now that beast won't let my child get married. I have heard, Alim-ji, that when a demon takes a liking to a woman, he won't let her be happy with anyone else. I think this one is doing the same. He wants to keep Layla to himself." She raised her head to address his belly. "Can you do anything to remove him?" she asked.

"I would be happy to make the demon go away, my sister. I can see that you are very upset."

"She's my only daughter," Amme said. "My only child. I want her to be happy. Money is not an issue."

The *alim* put up a palm. "*Nai, nai*," he said. "Let's not talk about money. I am worried only about the child. She is bleeding and having nightmares. This does sound like a very serious case. But, tell me, my sister, why is it that you have not yet taken your daughter to see a lady doctor?"

"We thought of you, of course," Abu Uncle said, leaning toward the *alim*. "The girl is not sick, she needs the demon removed."

"Please, Alim-ji," Amme said. "The wedding begins the day after tomorrow. We need you to do something quick. We only just discovered this ourselves."

"My sister, you cannot marry your daughter in such a condition. It is not possible."

I straightened, almost smiling behind my chador. Perhaps there was a way out of this marriage? A reasonable way. Let the *alim* forbid it. None of my own objections had mattered, but if someone Amme revered protested, maybe she would listen. The *alim*'s words filled my head like a silly, catchy jingle I wanted to believe in, and in those few moments, I saw clearly how I was a ghost caught in these cultural ruins, not a ghost from the past, but one from the future, someone whose life had already been lived for her, not once, but a thousand times before, and there was nothing left for me to do but gaze at the scorched relics of my own existence.

"What are you saying?" Amme asked the *alim*. In her fear, she clutched the chador against her lips, and I saw her hand tremble. "Will this demon kill her if she weds?"

"No, no, you misunderstand me. What I am saying is that your child is not fit to marry. Are you, Beta?" He turned in my direction.

I wanted so badly to agree with him, but when the time came, I found myself thinking more about Amme's happiness than my own. Perhaps if I had not seen her trembling, I would have been courageous enough to reverse all that had come before.

"How would she know?" Amme asked. "You are the *alim*. You tell us. We have come to you for help and now you are giving us more strain. What kind of help is this?" She snorted. "*Ageeb admi hai*," she said under her breath, strange man.

"*Hahn*," Abu Uncle agreed. "What Apa says is true, Alim-ji. We cannot stop the wedding now. The invitations have been sent out. The chefs hired. The wedding hall rented. The date was set a year ago. *Ar're!* We are not playing a game here. This is a serious matter. This is a wedding. Layla's name has been linked with the boy's. No one else will marry her now. Tell us something we *can* do."

Amme nodded at Abu Uncle, silently praising him for standing up to the *alim*. My uncle nodded back, once, his lips downturned, confident.

The old man slumped in thought, his beard now reaching the hair on his chest. His brows were thick and overgrown, his blue irises shining through the white film. He folded and unfolded his hands as he rocked.

"Sister, if you do not mind," he finally said, "I must say you are rushing this marriage. Perhaps you could postpone it until your daughter is better suited to meet her husband?" He sighed, his fleshy belly rising, then sagging. Over his sloped shoulder, I saw the black bird sitting on a brass rung of a chandelier, tilting its head this way and that as it contemplated its own reflections. "But you are the mother of the child and you will do for her what you think is fitting. There is nothing I can say that will change your mind?" He paused, and Amme and Abu Uncle lowered their heads, remaining silent. The *alim* muttered something in Arabic and spit over his shoulder. Then he said, "Who is this young man she will marry?"

"The boy's name is Sameer," Amme said. Behind us, the rain fell heavily again. Monsoons were like that. An outpouring, then a retraction.

"And whose son is he?"

"Ibrahim Mohammed's."

"Ibrahim? Yes, I know the man. Very gentle. Very caring." The *alim* paused and played with his beard, the tips of his yellow fingernails poking through. Some strands were dyed red as though he had experimented with henna at some point, then decided to let the color fade and be natural. One eye turned toward Noor, who stood so quietly I wondered if she slept, and the other hung over my shoulder, to where the mourning doves perched. "I know the son well, too," he finally said.

"He's an engineer," Abu Uncle said quickly. Degrees were prized here, often put on the back of names, like a doctor's: Sameer Mohammed, Mechanical Engineer, Hyderabad University. My relatives touted Sameer's degree to let people know I was marrying an educated man. It raised family esteem.

"Yes, I last saw the boy when he was entering university. His mother brought him to me after Sameer broke his leg in that terrible accident." He clucked. "The leg never healed properly. I blame the mother for the boy's misfortune. She did not want to spend the money on an operation. Now the boy has a limp. The leg is shorter than the other. He is the one you are marrying, Beta? Yes, you are doing a good deed. Allah will bless you for it."

I didn't respond for a moment, surprised at what I'd heard. Then I changed positions, rising to sit on my heels, so that I could lessen the distance between the *alim* and me. White stubble grew on his reddish brown neck. My legs had fallen asleep and began to tingle. "I . . . I don't think that's the one," I said, stammering and staring at the wet circles under his arms. "I'm not doing any good deed. I think you must be thinking of someone else."

Abu Uncle moved away from the *alim*, half of his bottom hanging off the *takat*. Amme had forgotten her manners and stared directly at the old man's face. "The boy has never limped before us," she said. "Yes, you must be wrong."

"But I cannot be wrong. I know him well. He is the elder son of two. The boy was in an accident only six years earlier, when he was eighteen, and the mother brought him to me. Of course, I couldn't heal him. The boy just needed medical attention. I told the mother this. But she refused."

I didn't know Sameer's mother well, having met her only twice, briefly. Still, I couldn't imagine why a mother wouldn't heal her child. A year earlier when I had been engaged to Sameer, I hadn't noticed a limp either. But he had had some problems sitting cross-legged at the ceremony. And now, for the wedding, the groom's family had ordered chairs for the wedding stage, something that was uncustomary and perplexing, yet something that we had not asked to be explained. After all, the groom's family had the right to ask for what they wanted. And we, the bride's family, had not the right to ask why.

"What kind of accident was it?" I asked.

"A motorcycle accident. He broke his leg severely. Up by the thigh and hip. He couldn't walk for months. Somehow, without medical attention, he healed. A miracle! For even I, after my accident . . . But the boy did not tell you this himself?" Now the *alim* also appeared confused. "I am sure I am thinking of the right boy. His father, Ibrahim, still visits me. We are very close."

"In this community," Amme said, "there are many Ibrahims and many Sameers. How can we say they are the same? Certainly the family would have told us, Alim-ji. Why would they deceive us on such a big matter? You must be thinking of someone else."

"Yes, yes, of course, Sister," the *alim* said. "Of course you are right." He crossed his arms over his chest, bringing his shoulders in tight, and over them, I again saw the bird. Now it flew madly in the living room, smashing into mirrors, unable to find its way out. Each time I heard the dull thud of the small body as it hit glass, I cringed, wishing Noor would shoo it out with a broom. But she remained motionless, her hands cupped before her thighs.

Then the old man asked to see my hand, but by this time, our minds were on Sameer and what the *alim* had told us, so no one listened closely. After our visit, the *alim* refused any donations. He must have felt that he had told us something his other clients did not intend for us to know. More important, he knew that he had upset a situation that was going forward, and in India, weddings are not taken lightly. Careful scrutiny is taken of horoscopes, numerology, and the Qur'an that considers not only the groom's name and the bride's, the groom's birthday and the bride's, but also the parents' names and birth dates to see if the marriage will be Bad, Mixed, or Good. Sometimes, as in my case, the Qur'anic reading comes back as Better. Better, as in Better Than Average, Better Than Good, Better Go For It. Even specifics had been described: my husband and I would have two boys, one girl; we would travel; we would earn much money; we would be happy together; and Sameer would only take on one wife during his lifetime—

me. According to one palmist we consulted, the sex would also be Better.

When we heard about Sameer's broken and never-quite-healed right leg, my mother and uncle became understandably concerned. As did I. Surely if I was agreeing to marry a man of my mother's choice, then the least she could do was provide one who had two even legs. This was certainly unfair. We all thought this. Unfair. It was as though the word lingered between us, crowding us, choking us, and when we looked up and saw that poor, injured bird flying about the living room, trapped by its own reflections, unable to find its way out, we thought it again. Unfair. So when the *alim* felt my forehead and arm, when he placed his hand on my abdomen, then encouraged Amme to bring me to a "lady doctor as quickly as possible," Amme and Abu Uncle vaguely nodded in adherence, then rose unexpectedly.

I followed.

"No demons, then?" Abu Uncle asked, straightening his pants at the waist. He tucked his shirt in farther.

"Not ones I can chase away," the *alim* said.

"Good, good. Thank you. The mother has been very worried. Did you hear that, Apa? No demons."

Amme nodded again, but her eyes, the most expressive feature on her, resembled the *alim*'s as they darted about the room. I prayed she was finally seeing how there was no way to move forward with the wedding.

"Visit a doctor, Beta," the *alim* said to me. "I give you the same advice I gave your fiancé's mother."

"You are thinking of the wrong man, Alim-ji," Amme said suddenly. She stood over him, glaring into his face. "Who do you take us for? I would never marry my daughter to a man like that. What does my daughter not offer? She has everything. Everything. She has America. She could marry any man she wanted. I have known Ibrahim since I was a child so I chose his son for my daughter. The family would not have hidden such a big thing from us. I am sure they would not have."

The *alim* lowered his head. Noor looked away. Abu Uncle placed his arm around Amme to comfort her.

"Let us go, Apa. We'll talk about this later." He tried to guide her to the courtyard.

She flung his arm away before throwing a bundle of rupees next to the old man. Then she turned, the chador swirling around her legs, and walked off. "*Ageeb admi hai*," she muttered as she went.

Noor jumped ahead, racing to the gate. I looked at the mirrors on the wall again, some smudged by the colliding bird. It lay now on the tile floor, its small chest heaving.

"I keep the mirrors to trap demons," the *alim* said. "Once they are inside the mirrors, they can't get out." He must have sensed my astonishment, for he laughed. "Don't be scared of me, child. I am an old blind man. I have been this way for most of my life. In order to survive, I must be able to sense what is around me. I must be able to see what you see . . . and a little more." He paused. "I would never harm you," he said.

"Come on, Layla, stop talking to that useless man," Amme called from behind. "*Chalu!*" She was already annoyed. But it was not her fault. She had too much to think about. And right when she thought things were moving smoothly. It becomes difficult for some to trust in the good that happens in life when punishment trails so closely behind. Amme was like that, an angel of sorrow.

"Thank you," I said to the *alim*. He nodded once. I salaamed him and he salaamed back, his eyes roaming. Then a high beep sounded, tearing the air between us. He fumbled for his watch and turned off the alarm. "Time for prayers," he said, rising. He stood on top of the *takat*, and when I followed his movement up, I noticed, for the first time, that the ceiling, too, was covered with mirrors. In it, the entire room was displayed, upside down. The *alim* and I stood on our heads, my face elongated, our feet dangling, the black-and-white tile floor was now the sky, and on it, that bird, still puffing, black, the red-tipped wings twitching, once, twice, then motionless. Too sudden for me to understand.

I dashed across the courtyard, the rain feeling cool against my face. The way the chador rose behind me, I hoped that I would scare the doves into flight. But the two sat cooing on the bucket, their voices holding human sadness, yet without human meaning.

AS WE RACED back through Elephant Alley, the azan began, calling Muslims to the second prayer of the day. The three of us ran silently, not noticing this time the heavy rain, not the women in the doorways who reappeared at the echo of our footsteps, not seeing the cobblestones, not tripping, not holding hands, just rushing.

"Allah *ho Akbar*," Allah is great, the imam's deep voice rang through the loudspeaker.

We sprang from the alley's curve. The car was quiet, the driver's door open. Ahmed's feet dangled out. He was sleeping. The kids had finally let him alone.

"*Ashadan-la-illah-ha-illa-la*," there is no God but Allah.

Abu Uncle pounded on the hood. The cheap metal bowed under his fist. Ahmed shot up. His face was deep brown, the blood had drained into his head. Amme and I rounded the Fiat from either direction. Ahmed held open the back door for her.

"*Hai ya-lul-salah*," come to prayer.

The cushion dipped when we sat, more on Amme's side than on mine. We rolled down the windows and looked out. Rain sprinkled my right arm and thigh.

"You can't pray because of your bleeding," Amme said, then sighed. "I'll have to pray for you myself. All my life I've been praying for you."

"Where to?" Ahmed asked. The car reversed out of the alley.

"Home," Amme said.

"I thought you wanted to shop for the wedding?"

"Don't argue, Ahmed."

"Sorry, *memsa'ab*."

"*Hai ya-lul-falah*," come to success.

"Don't worry, Apa," Abu Uncle said. "They would not hide such a big thing from us."

Amme pursed her lips.

"I'll go over to find out if you want," he offered.

Still no answer.

"That's a good idea," I said.

He nodded.

The back streets were empty. The residents most certainly at the mosque. Even those brats.

"Such a big thing to hide," Amme said. "A cripple!"

"*Ar're!*" Abu Uncle said. He laughed. Uneasily. "He is not a cripple, Apa. Just an injury."

Ahmed looked in the rearview mirror at me. His eyes were round, big, and I knew he took it all in. Let him.

"*Kat ka mut tes salah,*" come to good deeds.

"No wonder they ordered chairs for the wedding," Amme said. "The boy can't sit. How could I have been so blind?"

"We don't know if it is him, Apa."

"Oh, shut up, Abu," she snapped. "Who else could it be? Our community is not big. There's only one Ibrahim with one son named Sameer. And only one cheap mother. Zeba. She doesn't bring her own son to the hospital. For what? Money! I have never seen such strange people!"

The car fell silent. Every minute or so, almost on cue, Amme let out a sigh. Deep. Guttural. It sat between us, edging me more and more toward the door. Even the wind coming through the open windows could not blow her moans away.

My story had gotten lost in his. What better twist of fate could I have asked for? I sat back in the seat. We wound our way out of the alleys, away from all fables about eager bridegrooms and trapped creatures.

"Allah *ho Akbar,*" the imam repeated, Allah is great.

I smiled, hidden by the chador. He certainly is, I thought.

Mehndi

DAWN. THE FIRST day of my wedding.

I was standing on the flat roof of my mother's great house in the old walled city, staring out at the dirt alleys and whitewashed houses, slim minarets rising all around, the neighborhood that was as much part of me as the tree-lined suburban streets, the Colonial-style homes in Minneapolis. Five times a day, from each of these corner mosques, a different azan sounded, filling the air with God's adoration, his greatness, humble words quickly evaporating, being replaced with the sounds of cocks crowing, goats bleating, a lone dog's howl. Even the lamb now tied to a guava tree in our house's inner courtyard, awaiting its own slaughter on the day of the *nik'kah*, four days from now, bayed along with the azan, as though itself praying for Allah's mercy.

Allah's mercy. It was what I, too, wanted, though coming in what form, I could no longer say. What was I feeling on this, the first day of my wedding? Indeed, like God's praise evaporating, leaving in its wake the noise one could not bear to hear, the noise of dirty animals, the soul transcending the body, plunging down to earth, so, too, had my dread, my apprehension, my small hope of escaping these marital ties vanished, and the emotion that took over was no emotion at all, just a dullness that matched the overhead skies, singing of a different kind of surrender.

DAD WAS SITTING on a bamboo chair in front of me. His chin was resting on a hand as one graceful finger stroked the skin below his fleshy lower lip. He was grinning at me, his light eyes filled with a playfulness, a tenderness, I'd not seen before . . . at least, not since he'd married Sabana. We were facing each other, our deep chairs shifted to stand just beneath the ceiling fan. Its wind blew back the collar of his white kurta, exposing fair skin still taut around the neck, under the eyes, though he was forty-nine and overworked, though he managed two families. Below the tunic, he wore the dark trousers he usually wore to the hospital, pressed down the center, and below that, deep brown patent leather shoes whose color had, in the two days since his arrival, grown even deeper from dirt and dust. I knew he'd end up giving them to Ahmed or Munir, the cook, before he returned to the U.S. A servant doing chores in shoes that cost more than a year's salary. The shoes were left untied and he wasn't wearing socks.

The finger moved to his dark mustache and smoothed it down. "Do you remember the song we used to sing when you were a little girl?" he asked. Before I could answer, he began singing it himself. "Early in the morning, just like me. You are eating breakfast, just like me. Dancing in the streets, just like me . . . !" He threw back his head and laughed, the roof of his mouth a healthy pink against his white teeth.

I gave him a smile. Yes, I remembered the song, though I did not remember singing it with him more than once. I must have been four then. We were in the U.S., in the first home my parents owned, a small two-bedroom rambler in south Minneapolis. We were sitting on the floor, Dad with his back against the sofa, long legs stretched before him. He was bouncing me on his lap as we sang together, my young voice rising to such a pitch it was really a scream. He had thrown his head back then, too, laughing. Then something happened—did Amme announce that I had again wet my bed, did a neighbor's son come over and ask if I could play?—and I was no longer on his lap but inside the dirty laundry basket, clothes piled on top, hiding me. The song's beat was now a fist's beat against walls and doors as he searched the house. It was the one time I had gotten away from him.

"Where were you hiding?" he now asked. "The first day of your wedding, and the *dul'han* herself is gone!"

"I wasn't hiding," I said. "I was on the roof. Someone's strung green flags up and down the alley. I don't remember that from previous years. They've even been tied to our house." Then I said, "The flag has a crescent moon on it, a star shining within its belly . . . like it's pregnant."

"Poverty makes people religious," he said, his gleeful eyes already wandering off to the inner courtyard. I couldn't tell if he was taking in his two young sons or, through the kitchen's latticework window, his second wife. Though it had been nearly ten years since the two had married, his light eyes still grew fiery when he looked at her. She was now in the middle of her third pregnancy.

The two boys, the older half my age, stood in the harsh sun in T-shirts and jeans, barefoot, using long sticks to poke the tender flesh of the lamb. The poor thing had wound its way around and around the thin trunk until it could do nothing but lay its head against the wood. It bayed.

Dad had arrived with his family two days ago, the same day we'd visited the blind *alim*. When we'd come back to the house, we'd found two fat taxis rolling away from the front boundary gate, one used to transport the family, the other the lamb Dad had bought on the way home from the airport. As the taxis drove off, I could see the animal's pale prints on the back windshield, where the scared creature must have kicked. The sacrifice was Dad's way of celebrating my wedding—though I would have preferred that he simply come by himself, without the animal, without his family.

"*Ar're*, leave it be!" Dad shouted to his sons, though he was still grinning, and I knew he didn't mean it. The boys continued to lunge and poke. The lamb jerked. Sabana sang a Hindi song as she cooked her family's breakfast, her voice high and off-tune. She told people she had been a great Hindi film actress, though, in truth, she'd been nothing more than a nameless face in the few movies she'd briefly appeared in. Maybe it was to be the leading lady that she'd cajoled Dad into divorcing Amme. For that was what he'd done, the reason my mother had locked herself in her room and cried for a month. He hadn't simply taken on a second wife, something Amme had been raised to prepare for, a man's right here by Old City laws, but he had done the unthinkable and abandoned her.

He now turned back to me, his slender fingers diving into his thick, wavy hair, arm hung in midair as he scrutinized me. He had long fingers and graceful wrists, hands molded for exactly what he did, heart surgery. It was hard to believe that the very hands that had signed the divorce deeds, that beat me, saved lives every day.

"I was searching for you because I have a gift," he said, calling out to Amme to bring it. She was in the bedroom, the one she had to share with Sabana, her own dowry furniture shifted to one side to fit that of the new wife's. Though he had divorced Amme, Dad continued to support us. In the U.S., we had separate houses; here, where men kept multiple families, where men did not divorce their wives, he kept us in the same place. No one in the Old City, not neighbors, not relatives, knew of the divorce.

Amme shuffled out with a thick envelope. She was wearing a cream-colored sari printed with blossoming pink roses and the festive pattern matched her own mood. She'd been in the bedroom all morning with my nanny, Nafiza, the two women giggling as they assembled the dowry onto silver trays: saris and jewels for me; jeans and corduroys, button-down oxfords for Sameer.

"Tell Nafiza to make me chai," Dad said as he took the envelope. He massaged his head. "This heat is giving me a headache."

"You know your wife won't let any of my servants into the kitchen," Amme said. Sabana was terrified that Amme would have them mix black magic herbs into Dad's food that would turn his affections back to us. It was the reason Sabana did all his cooking. "Besides, I need Nafiza to help me with the dowry. If you want chai, get up and tell your wife to make it. Look how much she cares for you—cooking even in this heat!" She grunted, then strolled back to her room as she stared across the courtyard at the kitchen. Already, her eyes had lost some of their gaiety. Since their divorce, Amme spoke to Dad with an irreverence she could never have shown if he had remained her husband. But that was the point, to never let him forget what he'd done. If he had kept her as his wife—even a cowife—she would have happily taken his request as an order and gone to stand next to Sabana, boiling the tea herself, two women jostling for one man's attention, for his one pleasure. It was the life Amme would have preferred.

"*Aie*, no one's happy," Dad said as he tossed the envelope onto my lap. "No matter what I do, no one's happy." He winked at me, trying to enlist me to take his side.

I opened the envelope and found two airline tickets for the U.S., one with my name, another with Sameer's. They expired in six months.

Dad crossed his other leg, a hand running down the front pleat to straighten it. Pale ankles peeked out. Shoelaces dragged on the tile floor. "I remember when I first got the call to go to the U.S.," he said, staring at something just beyond me. His mustache twitched. "You'd just been born. I told your mother, 'See how lucky my daughter is. Her footsteps into this house have blessed us.' I was so pleased, I took you both to Madras to get my visa." He nodded and his eyes closed briefly before they locked on me again. There was something other than tenderness in them now, another emotion I was more used to seeing, a hard resolve.

"Return as soon as you can," he ordered, "as soon as your husband gets his visa. You know how your mother's life is: she'll be alone there in that big house. You and Sameer can take an entire floor to yourselves, have all the privacy you need. No need to venture out. How would you pay for an apartment anyway? He'll come there, expecting to find a job, but no one will honor his degree. He'll have to take engineering classes over again, just as I had to take my medical exams. He'll have no job, other than one at McDonald's or as a taxi driver. He won't be able to support you. Live in the house, continue to take care of your mother. Don't forget all the sacrifices she's made for you. Remember, you're responsible for her."

I stared out into the courtyard. The two boys had gone into the alley to play with the local kids. July, the season for kites; I remembered that from my childhood here as well as I remembered singing that song with Dad in the U.S.

Sabana's shadow passed through the kitchen door and I saw the moment I had gone from being the lucky girl to the ill-fated daughter. Amme's sacrifices, the reason she had stayed on with Dad after he had cast her away, erasing her own future, was so she could give me the one thing she no longer possessed, a husband.

"Did Amme tell you about his leg?" I asked.

He shrugged as he rose from his chair. He was done with what he had to say.

He stuck a hand into a pocket, the shape of a fist. "The boy confessed," he said. "When your Abu Uncle went to his house, the boy didn't hide it. He confessed. That shows courage." Then he stared down at me and I watched him take in my round nose, the full lips, features he'd passed on to me as he'd later passed on responsibility for my mother. I knew what he was thinking, had even heard him remark on it once to his Bollywood wife. He thought I was ugly.

"Be grateful to have him, Layla. No one can detect the limp. You know how it is here when it comes to tying a marriage. The boy's degree, the girl's beauty. Nothing else matters."

Nothing? What about the one thing he would not name? Without a father, without a proper home, a girl could never think to enter a new one.

SOON AFTER BREAKFAST, the house began to transform, and I realized it didn't matter how much I had prepared myself, going over and over the upcoming events in my mind, for when it was actually happening, my body was still left shocked.

The green flags that someone had strung along the ground-floor balcony had been removed and, in their place, wedding lights went up. Strings of colorful lights now hung from each of the three floors, from the *chandni* I had been standing on this morning, gazing across at what seemed an unchanging city, and they twisted through the guava and coconut branches as women here wove floral strings through their hair. Two young women from the local beauty shop had come to the house and painted my hands and feet with intricate designs of henna. Then they'd put sugar water on top to keep the raw henna in place. The longer it stayed on, the deeper the red would be, and the more auspicious my marriage. Inside the delicate leaf painted on my right palm, within the fragile lines, Sameer's initials. That, too, was auspicious, his name seeping into blood and skin, becoming part of me. It was tradition here for the groom to search for his initials on the wedding night, a silly ritual perhaps intended to provide a natural way for the young couple to touch each other when they had never touched before.

Wedding musicians had arrived just as the sun was going down and were set up in the courtyard, not too far from the crying lamb. The cracked wood of the old *takat* they'd been seated on had been covered by a red *masnat*, its gold embroidery shaping into the pointy guava leaves shading the two men. Under the *shenai*'s plaintive call and the steady beat of the *dol*, I could hear the dull thud of pots and pans as the servants cooked the evening meal. Tonight, for the first wedding ceremony, *mun-jay*, the women of my family would begin to prepare me to meet my new husband.

Already, it was nearing time for them to arrive, so Amme had sent me to my room. Only when all the guests had gathered and the salon had been fully decorated would I be presented, splendid in my first wedding outfit, its sheer *duppatta* pulled down over my face, reaching my knees. Nafiza had dressed me moments earlier, covering my hands in pink plastic bags, cinched at the wrists by rubber bands to keep the henna from staining the fabric. Then she'd seated me at the center of my dowry bed, the headboard carved into the shape of a peacock's lean neck, the face turned sideways, beak parted in a silent cry. The footboard was the creature's regal tail feathers. She herself had taken a place on the stone floor, sewing the velvet pillowcases that matched the maroon velvet of the bedcover. On the morning of my wedding day, all the bedroom furniture would be moved to Sameer's house: the Godrej *almari* stuffed with the saris and jewels I was to wear in my new home; the dresser with the tall mirror now veiled by a sequined cloth to prevent me from seeing my reflection until the wedding night, when I was fully his bride; and, of course, this majestic bridal bed on which he would discover how I was unfit to be his wife.

"He fooled me with those black boots," I now said to my nanny through the thick mosquito netting. The bedroom's door and windows were closed to keep anyone from glimpsing me, and it softened the *dol*'s beating so that it could have been the surging of my own pulse. "Don't you remember, Nafiza-una, on each of those three dates you and I went on with him, he wore those thick-soled boots. They must be corrective."

She didn't look up from her sewing. She had spread a cloth underneath the pillow covers to protect them from soiling, but not underneath her own sari. She was barefoot, as she always was around the house, the pads of her feet thickly encrusted with dirt, as dark as her small eyes. Her hair was pulled up in its usual bun, and under the glare of the overhead light, I could see where she'd applied henna to her hair, asking the beauty shop women for a dab to cover her gray. Her hands were steady as she pushed and pulled the needle, though I had been the one with the sharp eye to thread it.

My nanny had come to work for my maternal grandfather when she was about four, a child who'd been born to villagers on Nana's land in distant Miryalgurda. During Partition, when the servants and villagers had risen up against my *nana*, using the chaotic time to claim his *haveli*, his land, as their own, she had been one of three servants to remain loyal to the family, fleeing with them to Nana's city cottage in Vijayanagar Colony. She was a year or two older than Amme and remembered no family of her own other than ours. After I'd been born, she had been the one to nurse me.

She now said, "You no married and already you sick of you husband. What happen, child? After you engagement, we go with him to Public Gardens and you let him hold you hand. I no stop you. I see you happy. Happy with him. He has pretty-pretty face, you tell me you-self. You ask me if he face more pretty than you, that maybe he no love you for this." She paused before repeating, "Tell me, child, what turn you against him?"

"No one wears boots in this heat," I said. "I should have known he was hiding something."

She stared at me, the skin on her cheeks dry and hardened, the dark lips parted to expose teeth stained red from betel nut. It was the same look she gave me whenever my cousin Henna slept in my bed. It seemed to say she knew what I was up to even as she asked it. An assertion and retraction. For that was our relationship. After all, the woman who had breast-fed me, who continued to bathe and dress me, and would do so even after I was married, was also the one who, as a servant, could not question my behavior.

Outside now, I could hear Amme greeting my aunts, laughter, the hum of excited conversation.

Nafiza said, "I raise you as me own, child. I no see difference between you and me daughter, Roshan. I know you no worry about you husband. I know you worry about you-self. The boy no hiding leg. You know about he leg. He tell you uncle he-self. But what *you* tell you husband when he find you blood? Who you go to when he throw you out?"

I didn't answer, for there was no answer to give. In all I had gone over in my mind, again and again, it was the one question I hadn't been able to confront. If he threw me out, it would mean that he had found me unsuitable. And an unsuitable wife here, by Old City laws, was a whore, so by those same laws, her father had the right to kill her. The man who had begun beating me at two, how far would he be driven to punish me now?

Nafiza clucked, muttering how she had not meant to frighten me. She tore the thread between her brittle front teeth, then rose, a hand resting on the new dresser to help her up. One of her legs was always giving her trouble, and she began pounding on it as she walked stiffly over to me, unable to fully bend the knee. She was short, my nanny, not fully five feet, but there was something about her face, her stature, that made her seem formidable. She parted the heavy mosquito netting, dark eyes narrowing onto my face. An opening of her presence. "I protect you, child, as I do when you little girl, running from you daddy . . ."

Amme pulled back the golden door curtain, the coconut hanging from the top of the door frame trembling, a sign of fertility. The *dol*'s beat grew intense, taking on a different rhythm inside me. From laughter, my mother's face had grown the deep red of the rubies she was wearing.

"*Chalu,*" she said, extending an arm to me, rings on every finger. "It's time for the bride to show herself."

THE WOMEN CHEERED as I emerged and gathered about me, hands clasping my arms, resting steadily on my back, guiding me to the center of the salon. From under the brocade veil, my head lowered in modesty, I could only make out thin and dark bare feet, toes glinting with silver toe rings like my own. I was seated on a low stool, its wood painted the same crimson red as the canopy hanging above. The women giggled and whispered to each other as they sat cross-legged on the white sheets that had been spread across the tile floor. They encircled me. Their voices were carried away by the long notes of the *shenai*.

We were all dressed in yellow. The Hyderabadi Muslim wedding lasts five days, each ceremony bearing its own ritual along with its own color. The first three days are the gold that promises fortune and fertility, the wedding *nik'kah* is the blood red of union, and the *walima* dinner that is given only upon a successful coupling is the green of Islam, of submission.

Silver trays were shuffled about and finally settled at my feet. They were loaded down with flowers strung into lush necklaces and bracelets, sweetmeats covered in thin sheets of edible silver, engraved bowls filled with turmeric and rosewater, a short flask of jasmine *itar*, almond oil, and even this, a bottle of hair removal cream.

My mother's sister-in-law, the matriarch, crouched before me first, her thin midriff covered entirely by her sari-*pallow*. Slender hands made frail by diabetes thrust past my veil and inside the layers of my silk kurta and up the bottoms of my *chooridar* to rub my skin with oils and perfumes. She fed me sweet *ladu*, rolled the floral bracelets over the pink plastic covering my hands, draped me in a floral rope. Finally, she leaned over and whispered into my ear.

"I'll tell you what I tell all my biology students," she said, though her voice did not hold its usual authority. Along with teaching girls at the local high school, Ameera Auntie had taught me to read and write Urdu. "Help him out so he knows what to do. You know your body better than him. These Indian boys come to marriage as inexperienced as you." Then she withdrew, kissing my cheek through the veil, her skin smelling of the mothballs she placed in the *almari* between her clothes. The *dol* took up a steady beat.

The women quibbled over who should go next, Amme or her younger sister, Asma Kala. Being the mother of the bride, by all rights, Amme should have blessed me now. But she was busy putting on a show of her own, feigning fear and reluctance to let her little girl leave the protection of her home, to go and become a woman. Ameera Auntie finally took on her commanding tone and told her to hurry it up.

My mother sat on the floor beside my feet, her hunched form so familiar to me that I could not believe I would no longer be seeing it. When Sameer threw me out, I would not dare return here. And, yet, if I took that airline ticket Dad had given me and returned to the U.S., where would I go? No money of my own, no college degree, and, most of all, no experience—no life ever lived—outside my mother's home, not even that night with Nate.

My mother stuffed my mouth with sweets, her touch rough and awkward; this a woman who had never fed me before. Just beyond her, against the far wall, I caught sight of Nafiza and Raga-be witnessing the rituals they could not be a part of. Both of the old servants were wearing yellow. Amme rose on her knees, laughing uncomfortably as she complained about the ancient customs. She was having the time of her life.

After she draped me in a floral rope, she opened a velvet box and took out a gold necklace. She clipped it on me. Then she opened another box and clipped a ruby one over the gold. Again and again, more and more jewelry until my neck was weighed down in flowers and gold, her own bangles clinking gently. When she was done, rather than whisper her advice to me, she turned to the women and announced, "My only daughter. My only child since . . ." she stopped herself from saying his name, the son she'd borne, the one who'd died soon after birth. His death, her unwillingness to have another child, were the reasons, Amme believed, Dad had taken a second wife.

She cleared her throat and said, "I've spent many years planning and preparing for this wedding. Nothing, absolutely nothing, shall go wrong!"

"*Inshal'lah!*" they all shouted together, then they began clapping to the tune of the *dol.* Someone started singing in a high voice like Sabana's, though I knew it was not her. Earlier, before the guests had arrived, she'd left the house with Dad and their two sons, not wanting or not being invited to take part.

Amme's sister finally came forth, her body so full and soft that others had to shuffle aside to make room. She seemed to have swallowed up the vivacity Ameera Auntie so desperately needed. Again, the same ritual with oils and sweetmeats, yet another floral necklace, bracelets, followed by more advice.

In the revelry and singing, the servants' children dancing in the background, she leaned into me, the scent of her hair reminding me of her daughter, Henna, and whispered, "Let him make all the moves . . . or he might suspect you've had experience." She edged back to stare intently at me through the brocade, and I knew what she was saying. His letters had arrived at her home, the address I'd given to Nate not only because Henna was my best friend, but because Asma Kala's husband, Abu Uncle, was the holder of our secrets.

She set her hand on mine, over the veil, over the plastic bag, before pulling back into the group of women, a blur of yellow. Nafiza's daughter, Roshan, sat before me, reading glasses too big for her thin face. She had been four when her mother began breast-feeding me. Later, she'd married a man who owned a chai shop, so she no longer was a servant and was welcome now to perform this ritual. To my nanny, we were like sisters, but it was her presence in this queue of women instead of Henna's that told me my cousin-sister had not attended the ceremony. In fact, I'd not seen her since I'd arrived in Hyderabad. Asma Kala told me that Henna was having a difficult pregnancy and couldn't get out of the house, but I believed that she was staying away because she knew about me. Knew what these women would still not see, even after the visit to the blind *alim*.

And that was when it occurred to me. Deny it, deny Nate, deny what we'd done. Indeed, in the Old City, where women were never alone with men outside of marriage, what I had done a floor beneath my mother's bedroom in Minneapolis was the very thing that was not possible.

Roshan presented me with a sari as she whispered how my husband wouldn't be able to resist me—two, three times a night he'd wake me—and I turned my face away. Like that, one by one, each woman scooted up and blessed me, and when there was no one left, hands came together, gripping my arms and waist, standing me up. Someone shouted for the servants to hold a cloth before the musicians' faces so the men wouldn't see the bride as she was taken across the courtyard to the hammam, and though I thought I now knew what to do on the wedding night, the room still blurred yellow and my legs buckled. I fell hard on the stool. The women gasped and there was a moment in which I could hear nothing but my own slow breathing, the soft swish of saris, the sound of *dol* pressing into my skin.

"She tripped on her *duppatta*," someone finally muttered, yanking it from under my feet.

There were exclamations to Allah, thanking him that it wasn't anything like a stomach parasite that I'd gotten in the past, making me swoon. Then the women rolled my veil around their wrists, raising it high behind me as they led me to the hammam. Someone had brought along the wooden stool and I was again seated on it. Hands came down and undressed me, then peeled off the plastic bags from over the dried henna. Turmeric was rubbed into my skin until the brown glinted gold. Then all the hair on my body was removed, making me appear to be what they all still believed I was, and what my husband was expecting, a girl.

DAWN. THE SECOND day of my wedding. *Sanchak*, the ceremony in which the women of the groom's family come to the bridal home, dressing her in the wedding clothes the groom's mother has chosen. Then the women pull off the bride's golden veil and throw on a crimson one of their own, and, in this way, begin taking possession.

Outside my window, in the courtyard, the lamb was baying along with the azan. Last night had been the first the creature had passed in peace, the commencement of my wedding somehow providing it solace. I had passed yet another sleepless night. I now rose and went into the salon, finally viewing the decorations I'd not been able to the night before from under the veil, flowers and gold and modesty keeping my head bowed. As usual, only the servants were awake, the azan their call to work.

Amme's old house was designed like most old homes in this part of the city: a central living space surrounded by bedrooms on three sides. The fourth side opened onto the verandah, which led into the courtyard, across from which stood the kitchen and hammam, and the servants' quarters. Over the years, Dad had added two more floors in the exact design as the first, intending to banish Amme to one of the upper levels. But she had refused to give up the master bedroom and he had no rights left to order her. After all, twenty years before, it had been the room she had entered as a new bride, her sari and veil blazing red. At that time, newly graduated from medical school and possessing little money to lay down as *mahr*, Dad had vowed in the marriage contract to give Amme his father's house if he ever divorced her. He probably never imagined it would come to that.

Now the house looked the same as it had when Amme had stepped into it as a young bride, and then, ten years later, when Sabana had entered it as a bride herself. She and Dad consummated their marriage on a bed facing the one he had once lain on with Amme. For my wedding, the cotton door curtains to all five bedrooms had been replaced with ones made of golden raw silk. As a symbol of fertility, small coconuts wrapped in gold and red tissue paper hung from the center of every doorway—the one that led into the bridal room, into the room the two boys shared, into the master bedroom where Amme slept alone, and, finally, into the small room across from mine, next to the one used for prayer, in which Dad and Sabana now slept, shutting the door on everyone, on Amme. During the day, their room became the *divan*, the place where guests were seated.

In the inner courtyard, the circular staircase leading up to the empty floors blinked colorful lights against the purple dawn. Above the *takat*, the black tarp that covered the Fiat each time we returned to the U.S. was suspended from the branches to shield the musicians who would soon arrive from the glare of the rising sun.

The furniture had been cleared from the large main area, and the servants had laid down long white sheets, covering the tiles from edge to edge. In the place where Dad and I had sat early yesterday morning, there was now that low stool I'd again be seated on for tonight's ceremony, this time surrounded by Sameer's family.

Raga-be came up the verandah steps, a stick broom in her wrinkled arm. She was thin and fit, her eyes thickly lined with *kajal*, and it was only her slightly hunched back that gave away her age to be older than my nanny's. It was her task to sweep the house each morning.

"Why you up so early, Bitea?" she asked me. One side of her mouth bulged from where she'd tucked tobacco. She placed the low stool against the wall and began sweeping the sheets of the rose petals.

She was the reason I was up before anyone else, and I quickly approached the old woman. "Raga-be," I began.

At once, she glanced into the courtyard and turned away from me, bending over the broom even more, one arm slung across her lower back. The palm was painted red with henna. She didn't stop sweeping.

I stared across the courtyard. Only the cook, Munir, was stirring about in the kitchen. "I know how you've helped women on the farm," I whispered to her back. "I know what you learned . . . *to do* when you were growing up on my grandfather's land." I was talking about the very thing Sabana feared, *jadu*, black magic.

"Me no know what you say, Bitea," she cried, louder than I wanted. The lamb jerked its head and bayed a final time as it nervously eyed us. "I no can help you!"

I looked at Amme's bedroom door. "You must know about the bleeding," I persisted. "You've got to make it stop. I know you can. I've heard about the things you can do . . ."

She turned and shook the stick broom at me and her eyes squinted into two lines of kohl. The inside of her mouth was filled with the red juice from the tobacco *paan*, and this forced her to tilt her head up as she spoke. "You no Indian," she said. "Chance me *jadu* go backwards. Then you mama throw me out." She stared at me awhile, willing me to go away, it seemed, but I stayed where I was, fighting an urge I'd never felt before. I wanted to grab that broom and shake it at her, maybe even whack her humped back until she understood my predicament, until she did what she was told.

I kept my voice steady. "I can deny everything," I said, "but I cannot deny the bleeding. Raga-be, if he throws *me* out, where will I go? Amme's right. I've got to make his home my home, it's the only way . . ."

"Shhaa, Bitea!" she cried as she gazed across the courtyard once more. Then her eyes locked onto mine before sliding back across the courtyard, and this time I followed her gaze. Just outside the kitchen door, almost hidden around the cement railing of the circular staircase, was my nanny, crouched on the ground, scrutinizing us with that same look she'd given me last night, suspicion, retraction. So this was what held the old woman's tongue. Indeed, in trying to protect me, Nafiza would certainly tattle to Amme, just as she'd done in the past.

"Me say again, Bitea. You no Indian. Me *jadu* no good for you." She stretched her eyes wide, the brown irises capturing my full form, then the lids clamped down on it.

I sighed and turned to go back to my room. Just then, I heard her whisper in what sounded like a strange hum, "No worry-worry, Bitea. I come when it time. I come me-self."

LATER THAT MORNING, I woke to silence.

I thought there must have been a fight between Amme and Dad, something so bad it had even stopped the musicians from taking up their instruments. I rose and rushed to the salon, only to find everyone eating, including the two old musicians on the *takat*, facing away from the salon, tea cups and glasses of water set next to their instruments. It was already noon. How was it possible that I had slept seven hours, right through the morning pounding and screaming of the *dol* and *shenai*, that damn bleating of the lamb?

Amme looked up from her plate and nodded at me without saying a word. One of the deep bamboo chairs had been brought out for her and set near the verandah. A plate of rice rested on her lap. Her small feet didn't reach the floor. She pushed stray hair back from her dark-circled eyes as she called across the courtyard to Nafiza to bring me food. She appeared relieved that I was finally up.

On the other side of the salon, a rectangular red cloth had been spread over the white sheets, a *dastar-khan*. Dad and his family sat around it to eat. Dad had his back resting against the wall, and every now and then, Sabana lifted a spoon and he leaned forward, extending his plate, and she served him. One time, as she was holding up the spoon, Dad and his eldest son, Farzad, brought their plates forward at the same time. Immediately, Dad snatched back his plate and when Sabana insisted on attending to him first, he took the spoon from her hand and filled his son's plate himself. The boy was ten, around the age I was when Dad remarried.

"So the *dul'han* is awake!" Dad called, then chuckled as his light eyes flitted beyond me to Amme. Since the wedding began, he'd been having fun calling me the bride to tease my mother, not me, because he knew my wedding was a fulfillment of *her* dreams.

Sabana glanced up at me and slowly took in the golden kurta-*chooridar* from last night's ceremony. After the women had bathed me by massaging my scalp and body with turmeric and oils, they had redressed me in my first wedding outfit and told me to wear it to sleep. Now that the wedding had started, there was never to be a moment when I was not to look like the bride.

Sabana herself was dressed in a yellow *shalwar-kameez*, though she had not attended the ceremony. Her lipstick had stained her teeth red and was also smudged on her chin. The kurta creased across her growing stomach. Her pregnancy was two months behind Henna's, five months ahead of my own. She now lifted a spoon and served Dad as she said, "All morning, your father has been stopping Nafiza from waking you, saying the bride needs her sleep. A father can spoil his children, but a husband will never spoil his wives. Look how I attend to your father, even in my pregnancy."

Was she telling me to emulate her actions, this woman who was sitting in my mother's house? I held my tongue, for speaking aloud such things was what led to trouble, beatings.

Dad pushed back against the wall while sucking the marrow from a bone. His lips and mustache glistened with the cooking oils as much as my own skin and hair glistened with the almond oil and perfumes. I had already become invisible to him, receding once more with Amme into his past life. His younger son, Ziad, curly haired like his mother, and with the same thin face, asked to be excused. He said he was tired of eating rice and curry. He wanted cereal. He wanted to go home. Sabana reminded him that they had come for my wedding. Ziad was four years younger than his brother. If my own brother had been alive, he would have been three years younger than me.

Nafiza hobbled up the verandah steps with my plate of food. Just beyond her, in the courtyard, Ahmed was waving to get my attention. He was holding one of the floral ropes from last night's ceremony. With exaggerated steps, he tiptoed over to the sleeping lamb and hung it around the creature's neck. The animal didn't start, as I thought it would. It simply opened one eye, and its moist nostrils curled back as it sniffed. It began eating the dried-up flowers. Ahmed roared and clapped his hands. I turned away.

Nafiza was glancing from the *dastar-khan* to Amme, wanting to know if she should seat me with Dad's family. Amme shook her head and told her to take me to the kitchen, to feed me there as she used to when I was a little girl.

HENNA FINALLY ARRIVED, two hours before the evening's ceremony. While my aunts and uncles were being seated on the verandah, Amme ordering the servants to serve chai and cold *sharbat*, I grabbed her hand, bloated with pregnancy, unrecognizable to me, and rushed her to the roof. On the climb up the three flights, she had to halt several times and grip her belly with both hands, out of breath. The last time we'd come up here, soon after my engagement, we'd raced each other, winding around and around the circular staircase, she winning. She had always been more courageous than me, not cautious, as I was, about where she placed her step, of how she might fall. Though a year younger, she'd done everything first, walking, riding a bike, starting her menses, and now this, getting married, having a child. It was to Henna I went for advice, as Amme went to Abu Uncle. Like her father, Henna's eyes were dark and deep-set, expressing the same mixture of kindness and understanding. The eyes promised redemption. So why was it that now, when I was finally alone with Henna, I could tell her nothing?

We were standing next to the cement railing that encircled the flat roof, staring west across the Old City, toward Mecca. Perhaps it was the view that kept my mouth closed. For before us was an image no postcard would show, yet the one I carried with me, defining my experience of India. A tangle of white structures crammed one next to the other, the monotony broken only by a sudden shooting green of tall ashoka and coconut trees. And the green, too, of those small flags with the crescent moon strung one next to the other on twine to hang up and down the streets, like clothes drying in the wind.

Surrounding the Old City was a six-mile-long stone wall. The last of its thirteen massive gates stood close behind Amme's house, its top now visible to us over the trees. It was through this Dabir Pura Gate the Fiat thrust each time I went to and from the airport, each time Ahmed drove me to Henna's house in Vijayanagar Colony, and, in two days, through which I would be taken to usher me to my husband's home.

I could not imagine a life in India that occurred outside these uneven stone walls and impressive double doors, where everything, including the day sliced neatly into five parts by the muezzin's call, did not hold distinction: *who you are, what you could amount to.* There was no defying limits here. This was a Muslim neighborhood, where women did not leave the house unveiled, not even girls as young as six, their bodies yet indistinguishable from boys'; and where the center of men's foreheads held a dark patch from the repeated bowing and resting of the face against the pressed dirt of the prayer *sujda-ga.* The largest mosque in India, Mecca Masjid, stood at the center of the Old City, its granite dome, in the distance, shimmering like glass in the setting sun, and near it, the four slender minarets of the Char Minar pointed to the four corners of the sky. These monuments had been built in the sixteenth century by the Muslim founders of Hyderabad, the Qutb Shahi kings, who had ruled the area for 170 years from Golconda Fort, ten kilometers west of the Old City. The fort's walls were so mighty that even when the great Mughal armies attacked, they found it impregnable. So, they besieged Golconda for eight months . . . until, finally, late one night, a traitor opened a door from inside, quietly, easily. And the enemy invaded.

I turned to Henna and, as though anticipating my confession, she held up Nate's letters. Four of them had arrived, spread before the globe of her belly like a fan. I didn't take them. Instead, I pushed aside the fabric of her golden sari and traced a dark, vertical line down her stomach that hadn't been there before.

"Why did you stop writing?" I asked. Henna had gotten married three months after my engagement, when I'd already returned to the U.S. Growing up, I'd always vowed to return for her wedding, yet after the engagement, I found I didn't want to come back to Hyderabad because I didn't want to see my fiancé. By the time of her wedding, I had already received twelve letters from Sameer, one for each week we'd been apart. If I had been unsure about him at first, then surprised at my own softening, his letters did nothing but push me away. Yet my absence from Henna's wedding must have hurt her enough to make her stop writing me herself. And my own guilt and embarrassment kept me from persisting. It was the only reason Henna didn't know about Nate.

She now set his letters before me on the railing and pulled her long hair up with both hands, twisting it into a high bun. Her fair cheeks had become fuller with the pregnancy, which made her eyes appear even more deep set. There were dark shadows under them I hadn't seen before. She was staring down the congested alleyway at the expanding houses. Like her husband, young men from the Old City were leaving to work in the Middle East, then sending back money to support their families, aging parents, young wives, and children who weren't allowed to join them. Rials converted generously into rupees, and soon the houses began to sprout up. When I was a child, Amme's place had been the largest in the neighborhood. Now nearly every one in the narrow alley had added a second level, and one down at the end was even laying bricks for a third.

"I was married and didn't have time to write," she said, and I thought I saw tears coming to her eyes. Very quickly, she blinked and turned to me and said, "I didn't know how to tell you. No," she corrected herself, "I didn't *want* to tell you. And I made sure no one else did, not while you were planning your wedding."

So she had come with a secret of her own, so painful that she had carried the burden alone in order to protect me.

"Do you remember, Layla, how we'd always dreamed about our weddings? Coming up here or climbing the neem tree in my courtyard and filling the whole day with our talk of how our wedding dresses would look, how our husbands would look—we planned our whole futures with them even before we had glimpsed their faces! *Hai* Allah, we were so young . . ." Her words ended with a sigh and she reached out and squeezed my face.

Were young? Henna was eighteen, the year at which most in the U.S. are just graduating high school and embarking on their futures, lives not yet begun.

"Henna," I said, and my voice broke.

"Look at you," she cried, putting on a smile. "You see why I didn't want to tell you. You're finally getting married. You should be rejoicing!"

She began to move away and I grabbed her hand and pressed my palm against hers. Life lines intersecting, the intricate lines of my henna designs weaving with her own. This was a gesture we'd been making since childhood, a sign that showed we were one, nothing between us.

She sighed and shut her eyes. Her full breasts pushed against her tight sari-blouse. The bottom three hooks had been left undone above the rise of her swelling belly. She spoke slowly without opening her eyes. "After Hanif left for Saudi, he wrote my father. He told him . . ." she bit her lower lip and her body grew very still. She took in a deep breath. "He told my father to take me home."

I clasped her hand and my gaze fell from her full face to Nate's letters. What was the use in reading them? What could they tell me that I didn't already know?

I said, "I don't believe you could have done anything to deserve being thrown out."

At last she opened her eyes and there was that promise of redemption. She pulled her hand from mine and placed it on her belly, then wrapped the sari-*pallow* over both. She gazed down at the expanding houses again. "These Saudi laws," she said, her voice firm and reasonable. "I can't join him, and he has to work for two years before he can take leave. Then he comes back for a month, and then returns again for another two years. How can a marriage survive? There was no reason for me to go on living with his parents . . . without him." She laughed and there was an edge of defiance in the sound, the courage she possessed at last presenting itself. "In all we'd dreamed, Layla, this kind of life—no, it's not a life at all! I prefer to be at home. I'll raise my child myself."

And so she would have to, alone. For if Saudi had its laws, so, too, did the Old City. No one would marry her now. Her life was over, even before it had fully begun. She was no better than Amme. And it was to avoid becoming my mother that I had gone on taking the pill, killing the life inside before it had a chance to swallow me whole. It wasn't a matter of courage, but of will.

We stood silent for a while, and the wedding music rose between us, the same tunes played over and over until I had them memorized. Yet from up here, they sounded distant and strange, the marriage announcement of some other girl. The announcement of some familiar and anticipated doom.

Finally Henna scowled at the view and said, "Everyone in the Old City knows. Wherever I go, women have questions or advice. They blame me or they pity me. It's become so hard, I don't want to leave the house." She grunted as she picked up Nate's letters and ran a finger over his name in the way I wanted to myself.

She said, "Your situation is different from mine, Layla. You'll be bringing your husband with you to the U.S. The two of you can make a life together, just like you would with an American." Then she said, "There is much more to a marriage than love."

So here was her advice. Forget Nate and what I'd done. Move forward with the wedding. Yet how could I tell her it wasn't what I had intended to ask? What I had wanted to know was how, with my pregnancy, I could make my husband believe I was still untouched.

When she pushed the letters at me again, I turned toward the view, unable to take them. I said, "What did your father do when you returned home?"

Her jaw stiffened, though her gaze remained steady on me. She said, "It was the reason he had his heart attack. He almost died."

Yes, the very fate I feared for Amme. I was like Dad, she always told me, and as his one deed had ended her life, mine could now kill her.

THE WEDDING MUSIC came to an abrupt end, and in its place, Nafiza's voice flew, asking us to come. It was time for the bride to get dressed for the evening's ceremony.

Henna took my hand and we walked slowly down the circular stairs, our steps sober and careful. As we neared the second floor, we could hear the men talking below. We stopped and peeked over the balcony. The bamboo chairs had been brought out to the verandah, where Dad and my two uncles were sitting in the cooling air, the day slowly collapsing into the purplish hues that it had blossomed in. On the table between them were empty cups of chai, and the three men were now enjoying sweet mango juice Munir had freshly prepared. July, the season for mangoes. When Henna and I were children, we'd each take a *rasala* mango and sit under the shade of her neem tree, squeezing the fruit, the yellow juice running down to our elbows. We would lick each other's arms.

The men were discussing the land my grandfather had once possessed in the jungles near Miryalgurda. Along with the *haveli* and fields, the lush acreage near the Krishna River had also been seized by his servants and workers, then later, by the local government. In 1966, close to twenty years after Partition, the world's largest masonry dam, NagarJuna Sagar, was constructed near his land, transforming the entire dense jungle, including what had been the family's private property, into a well-traveled tourist spot. Amme's older brother, Taqi Mamu, had been entangled in an eight-year court battle with the local government, hoping to receive monetary compensation. Only in the last few months had he finally located the deeds that proved he legally owned some of the site, and the case was about to be decided.

As we were climbing down the last flight, I glimpsed Dad wiping his brow with a cotton handkerchief. The other hand was again lost in his curly hair as the fingers pressed the scalp. It was hard to believe he had grown up in this heat.

"Ask twenty *crore*," he advised my uncle. "Do you know how much property values have gone up? Just look at this neighborhood, all these men going off to work in the Gulf, sending back money. In the last five years, this house itself has tripled in value. Inflation, Bhai, inflation."

Taqi Mamu shrugged before resting his square chin on a hand. He appeared to be considering Dad's suggestion, though I knew he was really trying to figure out a polite way of saying what he really believed.

Henna and I reached the bottom of the stairs and I saw the lamb gnawing on the guava trunk, its thick tail swatting flies. It finally had some peace, since my two half brothers, along with Sabana, had gone to stay at her mother's. They planned to return the morning of the *nik'kah*. In the kitchen, the musicians were squatting on the floor as they ate their dinner. Later tonight, when food was served to Sameer's family, the musicians would be back on the *takat*, reclining against velvet pillows as they performed, while I again became the heart of the gathering. Could I, the ill-fated daughter, the one with no real position in this household, rightfully belong at its center?

Taqi Mamu's gaze landed on us as we crossed the courtyard toward the house. Like Amme, he had wide, almond-shaped eyes, a straight nose that flared at the nostrils. He and Abu Uncle were sitting side by side, facing Dad across the bamboo table. None of the men were wearing yellow. I hadn't seen Taqi Mamu since I had locked myself into his bedroom a year before, in protest of the wedding, and I wondered if he would compliment me on my outfit. But he returned to their conversation with no sign of recognition, a hand lost in his own thick hair in imitation of Dad's gesture. He was not a man who worked for an income. He lived on his inheritance and his wife's teaching salary. This made him feel insecure before my father.

He now glanced at Abu Uncle before speaking his mind. "It's useless to ask the government for anything," he told Dad. "*Ar're*, just look at how our city is failing. This used to be one of the most beautiful cities in India, paved with gardens. Now when you cross Musi River to get into the Old City, it stinks of feces and urine. Hundreds of huts have gone up along its banks. People defecate in the water. They let their animals defecate in the water. Then they bathe in it. And it's the same water that runs into our homes. If the government won't give us clean drinking water, why will they give me twenty *crore* . . ."

"That is a different issue," Dad interrupted. He didn't have the patience for local complaints. Hyderabad, the landscape of his childhood, was now a place Dad visited two weeks a year. The concerns here, the Old City's limits, no longer hemmed him in. "We're talking about personal property, what rightfully belongs to you . . ."

Abu Uncle chuckled, palms flat on his thighs. He was wearing the jeans Amme had brought back for him. "Doctor *sa'ab* is right," he said to Taqi Mamu, calling Dad by the title he'd used for as long as I could remember. In a place where not many men were educated beyond high school or Islamic school, Dad's success was prized and honored. He said, "The water doesn't belong to you, even if it runs through your house's faucets. You have no right to say whether or not it should be clean. That's how our system works. But these people have taken your land. You've got the papers to prove it. Ask for thirty *crore*, fifty *crore*, who cares whether or not you'll get it. The point is, you finally have the right to ask the bastards for something!" Abu Uncle laughed as he nodded at Dad and his palms turned up in a gesture that said, Isn't that right, Doctor *sa'ab*? He was always trying to please someone.

Dad threw back his aching head to rest his neck against the top of the chair. He called Ahmed to come massage him, then closed his eyes. The conversation was over.

Henna and I stopped near the men and salaamed each. Across the salon, in Amme's room, I could see the flash of flowing saris as my mother and aunts carefully dressed themselves for the evening's ceremony. Though the two families had known each other for seven generations—Sameer's family had rented from Amme's up till Partition—what mattered tonight was a different, much older tradition. As the bride's family, the ones who were about to hand over a daughter to live in someone else's home, we were now the ones without the power. Every preparation made for the wedding was in hopes of impressing my in-laws.

Dad opened his eyes and stared up at us. Then his gaze wandered down to Henna's belly. He said, "After her husband died, my sister raised two children on her own. She's now forty and they're grown, yet the strangest thing just happened!" His light eyes widened to show his surprise, even disbelief. "She received a marriage proposal. The man is a Saudi. He's going to give her dowry and take her back with him. Customs are changing, Henna. These outsiders come in, they stir things up, they make things possible. These walls," he said as he spun a graceful hand in the air to indicate the city's stone walls, "sometimes the only way to build a life here is to get out."

Henna lowered her head as she hid her belly behind me. The only man in Saudi she wanted was her own husband. But how could Dad understand that, the man who had so easily swapped one family for another?

Taqi Mamu stuck a pinkie in the air to signal he had to run to the bathroom, but when he got to the center of the courtyard, he swerved left toward the alley, just as I knew he would. He'd gone out to smoke. Abu Uncle tapped his chest with his three middle fingers, and I realized it was his paunch that had prevented me from noticing before just how frail he had become, his shoulders slumping, the shirt that had been cut to his size now loose around his weakened form. He didn't look up at his daughter. I tugged her along to my room, where I knew Nafiza was waiting, my second wedding dress ironed and laid out.

Behind us, Abu Uncle was describing his heart attack and the medication he was required to take for life. He wanted to know if Dad agreed with the local doctor's assessment. And just as he had with Henna, Dad was once more giving counsel on how to mend a broken heart.

HENNA AND NAFIZA stood me in front of the dresser, its long glass still veiled behind the sequined cloth. They positioned themselves on either side of me, my nanny coming up to my shoulders, Henna eye-to-eye, her belly bumping up against my own hardened one. Together, they began to unzip and unhook, unwind and undo the layers of my kurta-*chooridar*. When they had me undressed, Nafiza dusted my hands and feet, my face and neck, those parts of my body that would be exposed to my in-laws, with powder two tones lighter than my natural color. She wanted me to look fair, which here meant she wanted me to look beautiful. As she was rubbing my stomach and thighs with scented oils, Henna wrapped Nate's letters in the previous night's wedding kurta then slid the bundle into a dresser drawer, neatly, quietly, Nafiza not noticing.

The two combed and plaited my hair, and when the imam began tapping the loudspeaker, ready to announce the evening azan, they draped a *duppatta* over my head before covering their own. The entire house went quiet, including the musicians. This was what my family did each time the azan rang through the skies, our single gesture of respect. No one headed to the prayer room or to the local mosque. When the azan concluded, another began from a different *masjid*, but it was enough to have honored one call. The musicians started up again, accompanying the lamb's singing. The men's voices resumed on the verandah. Henna and Nafiza carefully removed my second wedding dress from the *almari*, a short top embroidered with pearls along the collar and waist, a wide silk skirt, and a six-foot-long veil. If the first night's wedding dress had been a pale gold, shyly announcing the commencement of my wedding, this one was brighter and bolder, the evolution of a bride.

They dressed me carefully, zipping up and clipping on, hooking together the various fabrics. By the time they had lowered the veil over my face and Nafiza had reminded me to keep my head bowed in modesty, a car honked outside the gates. Amme's voice rang out, shrill over the music, shooing away the men. Wood scraped along the verandah tiles as the chairs were hauled away. The *dol* and *shenai* began rising in a crescendo. Nafiza slipped out of the room; Henna slid her arm through mine and led me to the center of the salon. The women from my side of the family passed hands over my veiled head, then cracked knuckles against their temples to do away with the evil eye. Henna seated me on the low stool before she slowly eased herself onto the floor beside me. Under the layers of the wedding dress, I held her hand.

The lights were put out and the courtyard glowed in celebration colors. Candles were lit and secured into brass holders, placed on the floor on top of the white sheets. I rested a cheek on my knees as I watched the proceedings through the veil.

The women from my family formed two lines on the verandah and raised their arms over their heads, red fabric held between them, a silk arch that flowed down the steps, into the courtyard. Nafiza opened the gate, and the women from Sameer's family entered: small girls followed by adolescents followed by women, the span of a life. Each one passed under the arch, as I would soon pass under the arched Dabir Pura Gate to reach my husband's house. They carried in silver trays filled with sweetmeats, perfumes and oils, jasmine and rose flowers, jewels, all the things I had seen last night, and then this: a shimmering red wedding dress, its gilded silk embroidered gold; and, finally, an emerald green sari threaded with silver, intended for me to wear the fifth night of the wedding, concluding the celebrations by announcing a successful union. Yet it was not the wedding adornments and dresses, but his relatives' faces, which I'd not seen since the engagement, that knocked up against the hard numbness and shock I had thus far been feeling and turned it into knowledge. I was getting married.

Sameer's mother, Zeba, stepped in last. The gold of her sari matched the gold of my wedding dress, and over it, she wore a black *duppatta* that covered her head and shoulders. Amme and she greeted each other, my mother's flashy sari and jewels glowing more brightly than the wedding lights. Zeba's only jewelry consisted of red glass bangles that encircled one wrist. Renter and landowner, childhood friends, and now this, fellow mothers-in-law. A strange formality erected itself between the two women, as palpable as the *dhan dhinak dhin* of the *dol*, and it took three clumsy attempts before they were able to embrace.

The lights switched back on. Amme led Zeba over to me and asked her to sit down. As my mother-in-law took her place before the short stool, Sameer's relatives encircled me, while my mother and aunts moved back against the walls to watch the celebrations from afar. That was how I glimpsed what it could be like for me in my new family: I might actually belong.

Before she began the ceremony, Zeba raised her palms and the women became silent, as we had earlier at the sound of the azan. Someone stopped the musicians and Zeba led everyone in prayer. Unlike Amme, who closed her eyes whenever she recited, Zeba's gaze, through my wedding veil, remained so focused on my face that I was reminded of her son, and it was I who closed my eyes, silently making a prayer of my own, the show of mercy I wanted finally taking form. The form of my husband: let him not cast me out.

The prayers completed, Zeba gently fed me *ladu* to sweeten my mouth, and the women shouted, "*Alhum-du-illah*." The musicians were asked not to play during the ceremony, and the women themselves remained quiet, attentive to Zeba, quickly handing her what she needed. With strong, steady movements, my mother-in-law performed the long ritual of applying oils and perfumes, draping me in flowers. Then she adorned me with the traditional Hyderabadi Muslim jewels: a pearl and emerald necklace of seven strands that hung to my navel, a matching pearl choker as wide as my wrist, diamond and pearl earrings so heavy I feared they would tear my lobes, ruby and emerald rings for each finger, silver ones for my toes, gold bracelets that clinked with each movement of the wrist, a pearl strand to cover the center of my hair part, and, finally, a nose loop ring as wide as my cheek, which Zeba had had the jeweler, specifically for me, mold into a clip-on. My mother-in-law's touch remained confident throughout, and with each additional motion of her hand, each jewel and oil that went on, I began to believe in this process of renewal. A girl transforming into a woman, a daughter into a wife, it was magical.

When she had made me into the image of a perfect bride, she leaned into me, as the women of my family had the previous night when they'd whispered their secrets.

Zeba said, "I have come here tonight not wearing any jewels, for I no longer have need for them. I have passed everything my mother-in-law gave to me on to you. You are now my only jewel, the jewel of my family."

She kissed my forehead through the veil, then asked Henna to join my family against the wall. Two women from Sameer's family rose and came to either side of me. Together, they lifted my yellow brocade veil and, in its place, Zeba draped a red one, pulling it down to my feet, claiming this new bride as her own.

HENNA SLOWLY UNWOUND her sari, letting it fall to the floor around her feet, a pool of shimmering gold. She slid open the slit of the thick mosquito netting and slipped inside, crawling up the bed to nestle next to me. She was wearing just her petticoat and tight sari-blouse, and her bare belly thrust into the curve of my lower back. The room was dark. The overhead fan lifeless on this cool night that promised monsoons. The dowry bed was pushed into a corner, beneath two windows, the shutters flung open to a view of the inner courtyard. The only sound came from the lamb munching on fallen guava leaves as it satisfied itself before the slaughter. The swollen moon filled a window frame. Its silver light reminded me of the *walima* sari, and I thought of how, in just under a week, the desperation I'd felt in wanting to cancel the wedding had become a desperation in wanting it to succeed.

Henna began unhooking the back of my wedding top. Her fingers glided inside and pushed the fabric aside as she made her way up to my breast. She passed a hand under my bra and cupped me, her body curling into itself, as much over the belly as possible, her nose poking into the back of my neck. When she spoke, I felt her breath tease my skin.

"I want to know what he felt when he touched me," she whispered.

I placed my hand over hers and squeezed it to let her feel the contours of my flesh, those parts I'd been told to keep hidden from all men but my husband. What had I been thinking to allow Nate to slip inside? Different worlds, and in each I was a different woman, unrecognizable even to myself. I was like the two faces of the moon, new and full, one always veiled behind the other.

And now, finally, I could feel the other woman in me stirring awake, alive to where she was, taking form inside her wedding dress. It was Zeba's steady touch that had called her forth. A daughter's only home is with her husband, that was what was believed here. And tonight, as I wore the jewels Zeba had once worn herself, I understood how that could be possible.

I squeezed into Henna even more as I asked her to tell me about her wedding night.

She drew her hand out from under mine and slid it down the long stretch of my body. She found my wrist and encircled it with her thumb and pinkie, then held my palm up to the moonlight. Fingertips stroked the mehndi designs from base to tips, slowly spreading the fingers open.

"My husband took a long time to find his initials . . . but I think he took his time on purpose. I remember his fingers gliding down my palm. Just that light touch . . ." she imitated the caress, and I thought of Nate. Not of the first time I had held his hand, but of the first time I had uttered his name. Out of respect, a woman here did not use a man's name, so it was this small gesture, his allowing me to say his name, his expecting it, and my doing so, in public, in the quiet of my bed, calling, whispering, sighing his name, that had made him a part of me long before he had slid inside.

"Are you scared?" she asked.

I closed my hand over hers and pressed it to my own swollen belly. "It was his letters," I said. "For a whole year, it's all he wrote about. The different ways in which he would . . . pornographic!"

She surprised me by laughing and tugged me close. A cramp shot through my stomach and I ignored it, as I was learning to do. "You've grown up in America, Layla, how could you not know such things! He's a man. You're the first woman he's had access to. What do you think is on his mind! A whole year? It's probably the only thing he's been thinking about for a whole ten years. Oh, Layla," she muttered as she buried her nose in my hair, still giggling. "Layla, Layla, do not be in the darkness, as your name suggests."

She was right, of course, and though I felt foolish before her for my reaction, I could not deny how his words, his descriptions, had caused me to draw away, repelled. It was how I had felt the past two mornings when I had entered the salon and found the door to Dad's room still shut, the image of what he and Sabana were doing inside floating up in me, forcing my eyes closed. I wanted nothing more to do with him.

"There are better ways to seduce a woman," I said, turning over. She spread her long hair over the velvet pillow, the rich strands glistening in the moonlight. She was beautiful, Henna, having the sort of beauty I didn't possess. She was fair with glinting black eyes, lips that were the bruised red of a pomegranate. Growing up, I had always longed to be like her, and eventually, it became a longing to be her, or, at least, be one with her. How could her husband have given her up? But that was territory I knew better than to explore, having never asked it even of my own mother. The only life left to us now, to dream about, as we used to when we were children, was my own. And, soon, even that might be over.

I rested my head on her chest. Above the rise of her breasts, her baby, now seven months along. I wrapped an arm over it, secretly claiming it as my own. She was carrying our child, the one I must not bear.

"Tell me about him," she said, referring to Nate. "In what way was he better?"

Better? I did not know Sameer well enough to say one man was better. It had been his gaze, steady and gentle, that stirred something awake inside—not a different self, as Zeba had done, but a feeling. I had to try on love, just once with the man I chose, before . . .

But that life *was* already over. In two nights, when the moon was full, on the fifteenth day of the Islamic month of Shaw'wal, the day the Qur'an and the astrologer had determined would be auspicious, I would begin a different phase of my life.

"You tell me about Sameer," I said. "Remind me how I felt for him," but even as I spoke, the image of my fiancé fluttered before my eyes. His dark gaze, piercing and unsettling, calling up that dull tug of attraction. He had a gap between his front two teeth and his tongue wiggled in and out of it, teasing. "Oh dear God," I cried, hiding my face in Henna's soft shoulder. "I pray I haven't made a mistake."

Henna stroked my hair before raising my face to her own. And there they were, those eyes, offering me redemption. Yet what could I confess, which life of mine, which choice, was in error?

"Layla," she whispered, her voice scared in a way I'd never heard. What stray thought had caused her courage to seep out? "Did you go too far with him, Layla? This bleeding . . . will your husband . . ."

"No," I said, staring at the shadows under her eyes. If, like Amme, she had carried her burden alone, so, too, could I. Perhaps this was part of becoming a woman.

She pressed her palm against mine, the mehndi lines telling a different tale than the ones that foretold our lives. She wanted the truth.

"No," I said again. "No."

AFTER HENNA HAD fallen asleep, I slowly pulled away from her and wrapped the long *duppatta* around me to hide my exposed back, the hooks undone.

I was going out in search of Raga-be. It was past midnight and I thought the house was asleep, but when I opened the bedroom door, the wood creaking, the coconuts swaying over my head, I saw Amme standing by the courtyard faucet. She was barefoot, her sari hitched up to her calves, her body lit bright in the moonlight. She was performing *wazu*. Her prayers for me were never recited during the day or in public, as Zeba's had been tonight, but in a private audience with God. Night salat was so appreciated by Allah, it was said, that he rewarded one night prayer as equal to praying a thousand years. The five prayers that punctuated each day could be uttered in five minutes. Night salat was so extensive, she would be reciting till dawn.

I hid behind the door curtain and watched as she passed her small hands under the sink, splashing the moonlight. Right hand. Left hand. God's hand, the devil's hand, they said. But in reality, just fragile, wrinkled hands that had, at one time, carried me. Now she passed water over her face, the part down the center of her head, and finally up her bare feet, each gesture, each motion cleansing her spirit of the waste of this world so she could stand pure before Allah. There was something about watching my mother like this, when she felt alone and unobserved except by God, that made her seem like an angel to me, and me like the real earthly waste she had to shed in order to return to her ethereal splendor.

DUSK. THE THIRD day of my wedding, mehndi.

I was lying alone in my wedding bed, the wooden shutters pulled open, the widening moon suspended in the window frame. Time was running out.

The women of my family had already left for Sameer's house, Ameera Auntie stuffing the musicians and their instruments into her Ambassador. This was the groom's ceremony. And just as the women from his family had come to Amme's house the previous night, bearing my wedding clothes, adorning me, so, tonight, did the women of my family journey to his home with silver trays displaying our gifts: jeans and corduroys, polo T-shirts and button-downs, an electric shaver and three cans of Gillette shaving cream, a leather wallet and a bottle of Ralph Lauren cologne, and finally, the gold wedding band, which Henna, representing me, would slip onto his finger.

Earlier, my aunts and cousins had once more gathered here to straighten each other's sari pleats, weave flowers through each other's braids, and come up with ideas on how to tease the groom. Unlike the ceremony his family had conducted, quiet and sober, my family intended to perform with full gaiety. The women had dug up old memories of his family and spun them into jokes, even as they invented clever ways to exaggerate my virtues. Henna was advised again and again to resist sliding on the wedding ring too quickly. All this was customary, a tussle, a play, meant to prove to the groom that his bride was worthy of him. Tomorrow night, games aside, he would find out for himself.

Dad's figure now crossed over the ripening moon, so dark against its luminescence that he could have been the demon risen from my dreams, the form without a face, mute. He called out to Munir to feed the lamb, not to fatten it up even more, but in hopes of quieting the creature. Munir was already gone. Dinner tonight would be served at Sameer's house, and our cook had seized the opportunity to take an early leave. Dad threw the animal three guavas that Ahmed had picked from the tree as he crossed the courtyard and slipped out the front gate, whistling. He was taking the motorcycle to his mother-in-law's house, and I thought how unfair it was that I had acted no differently from him, yet I would be the one punished. Arranged in marriage to one person, choosing another to love. What he did, by Old City laws, was natural for a man, even expected. Islam itself sanctioned four wives, just as it had sanctioned divorce. So easy for a man to release himself: *talak, talak, talak*, the one word pronounced thrice to undo an entire existence.

It was local custom that prevented Dad from fully abandoning us, and whatever deed Amme had made *him* sign after their divorce. A girl here went from her father's house to her husband's, from the protection of one man to the protection of another. A girl raised without a father, without a man's name shielding her reputation, might as well be illegitimate, might as well be a whore—the very thing I had become, according to those local customs, by sleeping with Nate. And the very thing Amme had tried to prevent by staying on with Dad even after their divorce.

Talak, talak, talak, each word punched out, as distinct as the heart's beating on an EKG. That year, he had returned from his two-week vacation to Hyderabad with two deeds: one he enacted to end Amme's life, one he signed to give her this house. Her tomb. She locked herself into the bedroom of her suburban house, one floor above mine, and mourned for a month. Ten days short of the forty Islam designates to grieve a death. For she hadn't fully died, nor had he fully died to her. Instead, a different arrangement had been made, one never pronounced aloud, never revealed to me, the daughter, as the divorce itself was never disclosed. This deed was written up by Amme and slid under the locked door, and only when he signed it did the door open.

Amme had emerged silent and dried up, yet it was the high-pitched wail I'd heard for a month, drifting down the vents, seeping through the walls and ceiling, that went on echoing inside me, becoming the loam of my loam, bone and flesh. The noise of a dying woman. Though it had been ten years, the sound was still as familiar to me as my own voice, and, like my voice, I heard that howl both within and without. The crying lamb, the long notes of the *shenai*, the breeze now tussling the guava leaves all sprang from the residue of that shriek.

Nafiza hobbled into the room, humming a song she had invented long ago about a girl who would one day find her way home. She sat at the edge of my bed, behind me, caressing my hair. A fruit bat flew across the surface of the moon, as black as my name.

"Henna's at Sameer's house right now," I said. "She even gets to see my future home before I do."

"You love she too much, child," Nafiza said, and I knew what she meant. My nanny didn't like Henna and me sleeping in the same bed, touching. A few years ago, Nafiza had gone to Amme and complained, asking my mother to keep us separated. Amme had simply laughed and accused the old woman of having a dirty mind, then referred to something my nanny had done on the farm when the two had been young women, and my nanny never brought it up again. Still, I could see the disapproval like a shadow across her face, her small eyes drawing closed, pulling in her presence.

"You said you would protect me, Nafiza, as you used to when I was a little girl. What will you do if he doesn't want me as his wife?" But even as I asked it, I knew there was nothing she could do. A woman, a servant, what power had she?

"When you mama come home tonight, we tell she about the *gora* boy. She no understand the bleeding. You mama only see Sameer. She only see you wedding."

Yes, tell my mother about Nate, just as Nafiza had told her about Henna. The dirty mind, the polluted body, and she, my mother, the angel splashing moonlight, what could even she do? When my father beat me, she stayed in the other room, attentive to the sound of wounded flesh. When I was four, hiding in the laundry basket, his heavy leather shoes shaking the ground beneath me, she had simply told him that if he continued searching, he would be late for his shift at the hospital. It was only because of work that he'd left, the one time I'd gotten away from him.

In truth, Amme couldn't stop him. She was not even allowed to utter his name, so how could she dare utter a word against his?

Prayer, it was the only power available, prayer to God, prayer to all invisible forces.

TWO HOURS BEFORE the call to prayer heralding my wedding day, Raga-be woke me.

Without warning, she stuffed a gold knife into my hand as she whispered, "You no safe at this hour. Time heavy with *djinns* and things that no sleep no more. Demon you dream of no real demon so even he no match for this." Then she turned and headed out of the room, the coconut swaying above her hunched form.

I slid out of the netting, the knife gripped tightly against my swollen belly. Nafiza was sleeping on the floor beside my bed, a sheet pulled over her entire body, even her head. It was how she protected herself from mosquitos. I carefully stepped over her and slipped out the door.

Raga-be was already in the courtyard, crouched in the moon shadows of the guava tree. With a short twig, she was writing on the dirt. The lamb jumped up and, though I was afraid it would begin calling, it simply wound its way around the trunk, hiding itself on the other side, and lay back down.

The doors to every room but one were open. Dad and his family were sleeping at his mother-in-law's. Henna had gone home with my aunts after the groom's ceremony, their houses so close to his in Vijayanagar Colony. Amme had returned alone, Ahmed carrying in the empty silver trays as he followed her steps into the house. My mother's face was as full as the moon's. Her daughter was finally getting married. Nothing, as she had announced at the *mun-jay*, nothing could now go wrong. Yet there she was, at it again, sequestered to the prayer room, a slender light visible from the crack beneath the door, incense fumes billowing out. What was she losing sleep over, what did she really know?

I joined Raga-be in the courtyard, the air cooler than I had expected, and I wrapped the *duppatta* around me as a scarf, still pressing the knife against my abdomen. On the dry earth, close to her bare toes, a script like none I had ever seen. *Alim*s, from the Arabic word for all-knowing, claimed to derive their power from Allah, their remedies his *rehmat*, grace. Raga-be channeled her knowledge from *djinn*s, beings that coexisted with us, hidden from the human eye. As humans were molded from clay, *djinn*s were created from fire; as our bodies were inalterable, they could shift shapes; as our eyes were limited, they saw all that had come before, all that was yet to come, all time inhabiting one moment. Raga-be was now chanting softly—or was she communicating with a *djinn* in a language I didn't understand? She wiped the dirt clean with a quick swipe of the hand, the red of the henna creating an illusion of fire.

She stood without any effort, so unlike my weakened nanny, and headed toward the circular stairs. There she stopped, and the moonlight cast a shadow of her bowed frame that crept up the stairs before we did. Without showing me her face, she said, "Bitea, you tie hair?"

"Yes," I said, feeling my braid through the *duppatta*. Even as I had resisted Sameer's letters and this marriage, I had grown my hair to the perfect length so that bridal flowers could be easily pinned through its plaits.

"Keep tie," Raga-be advised. "No want no evil to nest in hair."

We crept up to the second floor, quietly passing the balcony Henna and I had stood on together, arms slung around each other's waists, peeking down at the men, her father, my father, men who never seemed to see us . . . until we stepped outside our limits. What I was doing tonight, up here with Raga-be, reaching into the folds of darkness, into the unseen, was well within a woman's limits, not a regressive act, but one of two ways she could maneuver outside a man's grasp, regaining control of her body. If prayers to Allah ascended the stone walls of this neighborhood, prayers to *djinn*s dug beneath like tunnels.

At the center of the flat roof was an earthenware jug, fire shooting out of its tight lips. Before it lay an empty burlap rice sack she must have spread for us to sit on. Off to the side, a flat, round bowl with a raised edge that, at first, I thought was empty. But when I sat and peered inside, I saw a dark liquid reflecting the nearly perfect moon. The image wrinkled and straightened, and that was how I knew the liquid moved.

Rather than sit next to me, Raga-be squatted on the opposite side of the flames.

"Give me you knife," she said, holding open a red palm.

I pulled it out from under the *duppatta* and handed it to her. She set the knife over the round mouth of the jug and the flames curved around the blade, leaping red and blue. She picked up the flat bowl and smelled the liquid, her kohl-lined eyes closing, before she passed the wide bottom over the flames, heating it. After she had made the eleventh pass, she swirled the liquid, which crackled and spit like hot oil. She spoke in her language again and blew, and once it had settled, she set the bowl before me.

"You dip twenty nails. First hands. Second feet. First left. Second right. Then I cut them away. Important you do as I say."

I looked into the bowl again. "What is it?"

She stared at me awhile, the flames captured in her black eyes, trying to extend beyond them. "Blood of rooster. Fresh." Then she added, "I cut me-self." She gestured to the gold knife between us.

I turned away. Our roof was still the highest in the alley and the entire city's lights surrounded us. Where they came to an abrupt end and folded into darkness, there stood the stone walls, like the edges of a sky hemming in stars. And as with the stars, I knew if I stared at the lights long enough, I could make the shape of the knife appear in them, just as we make shapes appear in constellations—trying to give meaning to what we can't understand.

"I know what you think, Bitea. I know you no like up here. But you ask me you-self, you come to me, Bitea, I no come to you." She laughed, the meat of her tongue red from betel nut. "You more like you ayah than you think. When Nafiza you age, she come to me, too.

Right before she marry!" She leaned toward the fire, and her face lit up. Her eyes were spread wide, and behind the trapped flames, I saw a dark form I took to be me. I grunted.

"You no believe, ask she!"

She retreated into the darkness and her voice came out deeper than before, as though some *djinn* had already lodged inside. "You decide in hurry-hurry, Bitea. This no work if you no believe." Then she said, "You always like this, Bitea, always with a split tongue, saying two things, believing two things. When you stitch it together?"

Stitch my tongue together, stitch my body together, the two women jostling inside the one frame no longer tearing the skin by its seams—could she not see, this woman who, with the *djinn*'s help, could now see all, it was the very thing I wanted?

She flipped the knife over on the flames, and though I wondered what she was planning to do with it, I pushed the thought out of my mind, just as I'd been pushing away memories of Nate, my body's cramping and spitting blood. She was chanting again, the *kajal* across the lids of her closed eyes resembling the lines she'd drawn in the earth. Her body was rocking, the fire growing, and somewhere in it all, I thought I heard her say the name Nate.

Inside the flat bowl, the moon was widening and disappearing. Nate and Sameer, the one who had come to me in the darkness of the new moon, the one who would appear when it was at its brightest, the one who didn't exist, the only one who did.

I, too, closed my eyes, and the moon became the illuminated dome of Mecca Masjid, the flames the glowing minarets of the Char Minar. The blood was the passage below the earth, unseen. In the distance, a door opened, in the heart of night, and the invader was invited in. The enemies' guns had already broken a hole through a wall, but a paper facade had been painted and hung over the damage, fooling the conquerors into thinking the fort had remained untouched.

I sunk my fingers into the warm blood, staring at the old woman. "Make him believe I'm still a girl."

She snatched the knife from the fire and dropped it into the bowl. The blood hissed as it swallowed the blade.

DAD RAISED THE machete into the air, raindrops dripping off the steel blade, and swung it down, heaving. A practice strike.

What did it matter what time it was? It was my wedding day.

The first time the butcher had shown up at the house that morning, he'd arrived just as the last of the morning azans were ending, his tall, thick figure filling up the gate's door as he ducked to enter, his T-shirt a startling white against the gray dawn. Munir had let him in, walking sleepily across the courtyard, pushing up his thick glasses. Raga-be and I were making our way down the stairs, and when we heard the butcher calling his arrival, we stopped, hidden behind the cement railing, my legs feeling heavy. I had to sit on a step. The man was sent away. Dad wasn't home yet from his in-laws'.

When Munir had made his way back into the kitchen, Raga-be helped me up and, tightly gripping my arm, fingers pinching my skin, she guided me to my room. Nafiza was pulling off the bedsheets, the velvet blanket and pillows stacked on the maroon stool before the tall mirror. When she saw me with Raga-be, she straightened and her small eyes became smaller, her dark lips pursing. She wouldn't allow herself to say what she wanted. She took my other arm and shooed away the old servant. Then she looked about the room, unsure, as always, of where to seat me. The movers were scheduled to arrive to take the furniture. Finally, she brought me into the salon and shifted a bamboo chair under a ceiling fan. Then she went back to my room, back to what she'd been doing: preparing for my move to Sameer's.

I must have fallen asleep on that chair, for when I awoke again, it was to the sound of men's voices. They were calling to each other in Telugu as they carried the furniture down the verandah steps, past the lamb. A lorry had been backed into the courtyard, two skinny planks lowered, and the wood curved under each of the men's loads. Amme was standing at the edge of the salon, yelling at them to be more careful, then yelling because the headboard had slipped, dropping on the stairs. It was raining, the tiles slick, the men's hair pushed flat against their scalps, water dripping from their lashes, nose tips, earlobes. One met my gaze. I stretched and massaged a leg, then turned over in the deep chair.

When my eyes opened again, the day was still dark, as though it refused to begin. The men had vanished with my dowry. The lamb was pressed against the tree trunk to duck the rain, which fell so hard it made the sound that a leather sole makes when it slaps flesh. Nafiza was standing over me.

"Sleep, child," she said, not touching me. "Only sleep wears this off."

"You know, don't you?" I said.

She moved away.

Then, in her place, were the two boys, Dad's sons, small hands gripping the chair's arm, rising and falling from tiptoes.

"You don't look like a bride," the younger one, Ziad, said. He was dressed in a silky silver kurta-pajama. Farzad was wearing the same design in gold. Both had thick lashes that curled back to graze the eyelid.

The older one smiled at me, his lips as full as Dad's, as my own. He said, "My mother says it's raining on your wedding day because you licked pots when you were young."

I blinked at him, straightening in the chair. What had she done to me, what had she mixed into that rooster's blood to make me feel like this? I began pounding on a leg as I'd so often seen Nafiza do. "What does that mean?" I asked.

He lost his smile for a moment, then shot me an even wider one. He was missing two teeth. "It's just some stupid Indian saying," he said. "But I thought it was funny."

Sabana called them away to watch the slaughter, and the two boys scampered to either side of her. She flung a thick arm around each, nestling them against the sides of her expanding belly. They were standing at the edge of the verandah, where Amme had been that same morning, monitoring the movers, protected from the rain. Dad was in the courtyard, raising and lowering the machete. The butcher had returned.

I sat up in the chair. Behind me, I could hear Amme in her bedroom, telling Nafiza to accompany me to Sameer's house, where she would attend to me until I returned with my husband to the U.S. She was advising my nanny to pack her clothes as she gave her a month's salary in advance.

The butcher's white T-shirt was now spotted brownish-red from his morning slaughterings. He was lining up knives on the *takat* the musicians had been sitting on for the past three days. For a second, he ducked under the black tarp and wiped his face clean of the rain, then dived back out. His wet T-shirt was pressed to him, his shoulder blades jutting out. He nodded at Dad.

Dad called something out toward the kitchen. The legs of his dark trousers were flapping against his calves. He had taken a wide stance, the machete gripped in both his graceful hands, leather shoes digging into the mud. Over his thick, wavy hair, he'd slipped on the baseball cap that belonged to his older son. It was to keep the rain from his eyes. Water dripped in streams off the bill.

Munir and Ahmed rushed out of the kitchen, pant legs folded up, exposing bony ankles. Ahmed untied the lamb and dragged it out by the rope from where it had taken shelter. It bellowed and kicked and ran back under the branches, flattening its broad belly against the trunk. Ahmed grabbed the rope again, and this time, the butcher went behind the lamb and kicked it forward. This was work for him. Later, he'd have to attend to another slaughter.

Munir's glasses had steamed up and he took them off and slid them into his shirt pocket. The butcher wrapped the front paws with the rope, running the length of it down the center of the animal, where it got lost in the wool, then reappeared at the other end. He tied together the back legs before handing them to Munir. The cook and driver hauled the lamb out to the center of the courtyard, clear of branches and other obstructions. Dad kept raising and lowering the machete as he smiled up at his sons from under the baseball cap. Did he even notice me here, the bride for whom he was making this offering?

When the lamb was positioned, the two servants still gripping its legs, trying to hold it still, Dad stepped forward. Ziad hid his face in Sabana's belly, but she pinched his chin and straightened it.

"Watch your father," she ordered. "Learn from him."

So they were being taught, as I had been, how to survive here.

Dad raised the machete a final time, then heaved it toward the earth, slicing the lamb's neck. At once, the head fell forward, kicking legs going slack. Blood poured out the severed neck, creating a pool under the poor creature that washed away along with the rain, a gentle red stream flowing into the roots of the guava tree.

I rose unsteadily and made my way out to the courtyard and into the rain. I stumbled to the faucet where I'd watched Amme performing *wazu* and vomited.

His letters, the ones wrapped in my first wedding dress, slipped into the dresser drawer by Henna's agile hand, had gone with the rest of my wedding dowry, to my husband's house.

THE RAIN THRASHING the earth.

I was standing at the center of Amme's bedroom, her dowry bed and dresser, her *almari* on one side of me, Sabana's on the other. Dad was sitting with his family in the salon, around the red *dastar-khan*, enjoying fresh liver fried in garlic and ginger. His sons were hesitant to taste what they called the family pet, and Dad and Sabana were teasing them in order to get them to eat. Beyond the family, hanging from a clothesline in the courtyard, was the shorn wool. Despite the rain, flies were buzzing about the slaughter, the house stinking of blood and death.

I spread the golden curtain more fully across the door. Amme was laying out the sari and jewels she planned to wear to my *nik'kah*, the sari a brighter red than my own wedding dress, the tone matching my henna designs. As she moved about, her *pallow* kept falling, and she twisted it and draped it tightly across her chest, exposing the loose flesh of her belly, the long cesarean scar she'd gotten from my brother.

"Did you know Henna was returned?" I asked.

She unfolded the new sari and began admiring its bead work, not answering. Then she cast it aside and sat on her bed, staring into her palms. She said, "It was the reason she didn't attend the *mun-jay* ceremony. It would have been bad luck for a woman in her position to perform rituals meant to begin your wedding."

A woman in her position, one who'd been returned, abandoned. "But you performed the rituals," I said.

She looked up at me, blinking, as though trying to make out who I was. "It's time for you to bathe," she said. "I've asked Raga-be to help Nafiza prepare you. The wedding dress is elaborate. And, after you bathe, there are more rituals to scent your skin." She rose and snapped closed the velvet jewelry boxes. Keeping her back to me, she said, "Go now, child, go from here."

I pressed a thumb into my palm and tried to rub out his initials. I said, "If I'm returned, we can go back to the U.S. together . . . can't we?"

Her body straightened, loose hair falling out of her bun. For a moment, she was very still. Then she suddenly turned and walked past me to the door, where she twisted the fabric of the door curtain as she had her *pallow* and shoved it over the door. Outside, framed by the doorway, was Dad, sitting cross-legged on the ground, lips tugging back into a smile even as he ate, proud of his kill. He had changed out of his trousers into cotton pajamas, and the tie-string hung between his legs. His shoes, now caked with dirt and blood, were on the verandah, being washed clean by the rain. Across one pale ankle, lamb's blood.

She was using him as a threat, warning me to stay quiet, within my limits. There would be no returning with her—no returning *to* her.

"*Talak, talak, talak*," I said, aware of my legs growing weaker, barely keeping me up. "I was in my room when it happened. I heard everything."

She busied herself with folding the sari, spreading it open, then folding it again. She said, "In the U.S., people say you lose your independence when you get married. That's not true for you, Layla. Once you're married, you'll be free." She paused before adding, "No matter what he does, he doesn't see it as wrong."

"There are different laws in the U.S.," I said. "You can get alimony . . ."

"I don't want his money, Layla! What will I do with more of his money? I want my life back! Can he give me that? Can anyone?"

There, she had said the one thing she'd never said before, the one desire forever pulsing with her blood, and we stared at each other, both of us inadequate. Her hope to give me a home, my hope to let her give me one, each believing it would bring the other happiness, yet somehow now it just didn't seem enough.

I stepped toward her, finally able to say what I'd always wanted to myself. "I wasn't worth giving up your life for, Amme. I wasn't worth your sacrifices . . . This house, give it back to him, or tell him to leave with his family. After I'm gone, don't live like this anymore. Don't share this room . . ."

Dad stepped into the doorway and the light shining in from behind blackened his figure.

"What am I hearing in here?" he asked, his voice barely above a whisper. "What are you two talking about?" He moved in farther, his light eyes dark with anger. The demon in him coming out.

"What are you teaching your mother?" he asked, moving toward me even as his eyes darted about the room. He was searching for a tool, a weapon, something he could get his hands on, quickly, easily. There was no belt with the loose pajamas. The shoes were being rained on. His fingers curled into fists. "I send you back here each year so you'll learn who you are, and still I find you teaching your mother these ideas . . . these American ways. *Randi!* It's because of you she speaks to me with disrespect, in front of her relatives, in front of servants."

I began pounding on my legs. Useless, they were useless. How long ago had I learned I couldn't run away, couldn't escape, not him, not his laws.

"This is my house," he said, his voice still low, spit flying out of his mouth. "This will always be my house. Do you think it matters whose name it's in? Throw me out, throw my family out, out of my own house!" His voice began rising, knuckles grinding against a palm. "I'll throw *you* out and you can prostitute yourself to stay alive."

My legs buckled and I curled up on the floor, hiding those parts I knew he liked to beat, my belly and breasts, my thighs, between my legs, the woman in me. He wanted to break her.

He grabbed a silver tray from the dresser, one of those that had carried over Sameer's dowry gifts, and hurled it into the air, ready to strike. I closed my eyes and heard the rain thrashing the ground, his two sons playing in the salon. Amme threw her red sari over me, covering my body. She stepped before him, stepped between us, at last stopping him.

"She doesn't belong to you, not anymore!" she cried, arms flung wide to hide me even more. "You have no rights left. She is married."

He hesitated, glaring from her to me before he tossed the tray onto Amme's bed, a thick lip pulling up in disgust as he turned away.

So she had done it, after all. My mother may have lost one child, but somehow, she had managed to save the other.

Sus'ral

DHAK. DHAK. DHAK *dhinak dhin. Dhak. Dhak.*

I was naked, a towel concealing my damp body. Nafiza had just bathed me, as she had been doing since I was a child, washing away the night's impurities and the day's illness. Now she and Raga-be lugged two earthenware bowls into Amme's bedroom, where I was sitting at the edge of her bed. The doors and windows were bolted closed. These were a bride's private rituals.

Dhin dhin.

Thunder rumbled in the distance, the rain that had been tormenting the earth having at last ceased. In its place, the unmerciful glare of the sun. How would I put on the layers of silk and netting and jewels when my skin, at the touch of a cotton towel, was recoiling? The bath water that had been rolling down my neck and breasts was now shimmying sweat. The musicians had been moved into a sheltered corner of the verandah, protected from any further onslaught of rain, and the *shenai* raised a high-pitched note, rising even higher against the *dol*'s steady beating, then collapsed.

Dhinak dhin dhak.

Steam was swirling out of the narrow-mouthed jug Raga-be had by the neck, held away from her body, this ceremony more frightening to her, it would seem, than the *jadu* she'd performed last night. Nafiza placed the large, flat bowl at the center of the floor and Raga-be squatted next to it, turning over the jug. Hot coals tumbled out. Nafiza added what looked like small black stones. Fragrant fumes rose.

The women spread a white sheet on the floor and laid me on top, my head near the coals. Each took sections of my wet hair and dried it over the fumes, capturing the fragrance. Then they sat me up and passed my forearms and shoulders, thighs and feet over the bowl. They asked me to undo the towel and lean over it. My breasts hung low, nipples wide as quarters. After a moment, they pulled me up and told me to stand over the bowl. I placed a leg on either side. Fumes swelled up around me and pushed inside. Not the smell of jasmine, but the bitter scent of a brand-new bride.

Dhin. Dhin. Dhak.

THE RATTLE AND chaos of a brass band. The members were dressed in red uniforms with brass buttons, shiny black-and-white shoes, gold *shamlahs* on their heads that rivaled the groom's own. Two or three performers were drinking kerosene, spitting fire, lungs ablaze, then black, withering. The music was burning into my skin, taking root at the core, a sound I would forever carry, like the wedding *dol*, like Amme's wail from long ago. Each as much part of me as my beating heart, my gurgling innards. All this noise just to lead the bride to her new home.

The wedding car, a red Chevy Impala, was covered bumper-to-bumper in floral ropes, and inside, on the ivory backseat, I was squeezed between my new husband and my mother-in-law. In front sat Sameer's father, younger brother, Feroz, and the driver who had come with the rented car. A young man was marching with the band, recklessly close to a fire breather, the only one out there in a suit. The fabric was the color of his skin, the cut showing off his broad shoulders and thin face. When the band stopped, as it did every fifty or so feet, the men took up their instruments and the man danced for us, the bride and groom, to the music that was never meant for dancing.

My mother-in-law kept her face turned away from the spectacle, staring out the side window. Feroz clapped. Sameer peered at me through the veil, watching me watch the stranger. His hand was clutching mine under the layers of my *duppatta*, respectfully concealed from his mother, the rings biting into my skin. The man was dancing in front of the Chevy now, legs cut off by the long hood, his jacket swirling about, exposing his lean waist and narrow hips, the button that had come undone at his belly, flapping open and closed, the soft flesh beneath. Two fire breathers, one on either side of him, bent onto their knees and threw back their heads. In the scorched air, I saw him peering into the front windshield, eyes squinting against the headlights. His face was stern and unsmiling, though he was forcing his body to move.

Zeba tightened the black *duppatta* around her head, her face still turned away. She'd worn the veil to the *nik'kah*, just as she'd done to the *sanchak*, right over her fancy wedding clothes. "*Minas shai-tan e rajim*," she whispered, shooing away the devil, then began reciting Qur'anic prayers.

Sameer's hand tightened around mine, and the band resumed its slow march as the man stepped to the side of the road. He shook his jacket by the collar to straighten it, then rolled his neck. When the car caught up to him, he began walking in pace, just outside my husband's window.

SAMEER'S HOUSE WAS the last on the dead-end road, next to a field of tall grasses curled into themselves from the heat. It was a one-story structure with a flat roof, lit up by a thousand celebration lights. The marching band's racket had alerted everyone, and his women relatives stood outside the front gate, dressed in bright silk saris, flowers strung through their long braids, waiting for the car to pull up, the younger girls bouncing in excitement. Neighbors had also come to the street, Muslim women covered in veils standing next to Hindu women with red *surma* lining their hair parts, a sight I had never seen in the Old

City. I spotted my nanny off to the side, against the tall boundary wall, hands clasped at the thighs. She was dressed in the sari Amme had bought her for my wedding, her face closed against the surrounding happiness. She didn't know that Raga-be's *jadu* had made the bleeding stop.

When the car parked, the band played even louder, growing into a crescendo that cut through the heavy night sky, a cacophony of celebration that must have reached the dim stars. Doors were flung open and Sameer jumped out, the back of his long silk jacket creased and stained red by flowers. He disappeared into the crowd. Arms reached in, covered to the elbows in red glass bangles, and helped me out. My silk kurta and veils were straightened and pulled out from beneath my high heels, then, hunched under the weight of flowers, I was led into my new home. At the doorway, Sameer's father, Ibrahim, held the Qu'ran over my head, blessing my steps.

The women guided me into the bridal room. My dowry furniture had been set up, the red sequined cloth pulled off the tall mirror, the bed's mosquito netting draped from end to end with ropes of marigold. The peacock's beak had chipped in the move and been painted over in a pale white that did not match the original ivory. Outside, the band was leaving, and the growing quiet felt immense.

The women closed the bedroom door and stood me before the mirror. I was the image of a perfect bride. Wrapped in a six-foot-long *duppatta*, my face concealed behind two red wedding veils that hung to my waist, and underneath, strung around my neck, five pounds of flowers and ten pounds of gold. My wedding henna matched the red of the wedding dress. In the drawer before me, Nate's letters.

The women began unwinding the *duppatta* and pulling the pins from the veil, and like that, just as they had adorned me a couple of days before, they now stripped me of the jewels and clothes. I was left with only the silk skirt and a tight top that stopped just below my breasts. The only thing keeping it on was a gold thread that tied at the front; meant to be easily taken off. My face was wiped of sweat, fresh powder dusted on, the red wedding veil draped over me again.

Zeba, who had been standing apart, instructing, now drew keys hooked onto her sari by a silver key ring. She opened my *almari*, and the women placed the jewels and folded clothes inside.

The door to the mosquito net was parted. The mattress was covered by the maroon velvet blanket Amme had sent along and the pillows Nafiza had sewn together. The blanket was pulled back to reveal white bedsheets on top of which was another, smaller, white cloth. The women seated me at the center of the cloth and arranged the veil around me, bangles clinking gently. Then they withdrew and Zeba stepped forward. I could feel her staring at me through the netting.

"I prayed a long time for this day," she finally said, her voice trembling with emotion. "Allah, *tera shukar*," she said, thanking Allah for granting her wish. Then she whispered, "Beti," daughter, and left the room, the women following with the soft swish of flowing saris.

Certainly, she hadn't prayed for a daughter like me.

SAMEER WAS LYING across the foot of the bed, on top of the velvet blanket the women had folded back. His long legs were bent, head propped up on a hand. He was staring at me through the wedding veil, his gaze so intense I found myself doing what I had when we'd first met. Taking him in with quick glances, his fair skin and hard jaw line, his dark eyes and wavy hair, that space between his front two teeth, the tongue moving in and out. My handsome husband, foreign to me yet also the most intimate. And there it was, that familiar pull of attraction, opening something up inside.

I was still sitting on the white cloth with my chin resting on a knee, the way the women had positioned me. He seemed calm for a man who had just gotten married, nothing like a husband who'd found letters from his new wife's old lover.

In the living room, women were playing the *dol* and singing a popular Hindi song: "Eik, do, then, char, paanch . . ." One, two, three, four, five, they counted, all the way to thirteen, then sang, "*This is how I tallied the days waiting for you.*"

Sameer said, "So they've undressed you, taking off the flowers and jewels. Making it much easier for me . . . but, look! They forgot something." He reached out and touched my big toe. On it, a silver toe ring gleaming against the red henna designs. "Now why do you think they left this poor little thing?" he asked, smiling, the tip of his tongue red from the sweetmeats we'd been fed all night. "Do you think they meant for me to take it off?" He pulled my foot toward him and put my toe into his mouth, his tongue swirling around it. Then he looked up at me and said, "For lubrication," and I couldn't help but laugh and kicked him away. I hadn't expected to be enjoying this, not right away, so what was taking over? Or what, at last, was giving in?

He grabbed my foot again and yanked it back, now bounding up, the neckline of his sheer kurta falling low to expose his clean chest, the muscles that hadn't been there before. He pushed my leg into the air so that I fell onto my back, the veil flattening across my face, and stretched apart the silver. He snapped the band off and slipped it on his own thumb, cinching the metal together again. He licked my tendon.

"*This is how I tallied the days waiting for you . . .*"

"The guests were marveling at the ceremony," he whispered, sliding back my skirt. "They said it was like the elaborate stage of a Hindi film, you and I the stars."

I was aware of the rise and fall of my chest, the veil pressed to my skin, fluttering against my nostrils with each slow breath, and overhead, the canopy of yellow flowers seen through hazy vermilion silk. The stink, the overpowering stink of marigolds and sweat. His tongue, which I had so often seen pushing through his front two teeth, I had never imagined would now be pushing inside me.

"*Tallied the days, one two three.*"

"Oh God!"

"What?"

"Oh God!" He rose, turning his face away from me, his hands up, blocking it even more. He fumbled about for the netting's door, and when he couldn't find it, he swore and yanked the netting up from the foot of the bed. He tumbled out and into the adjoining bathroom.

"Sameer!"

Nothing but the sound of women singing, bangles clinking, the beat of the *dol.* After a moment, the song came to an end, and in the breath's pause between notes, I heard my husband retching.

HE WAS SITTING on the velvet stool that had come along with the dresser, his knees rising almost to his chest. Between them, his hands clutching my first wedding kurta, the pale silk one Henna had wrapped around Nate's letters.

The women had gone to sleep. Rain was steadily tapping the window shutters. My heart was unusually calm, as it had been the night I had let Nate into my room, my body tamed by its habitual surrenders.

Between my new husband and me, the dense mosquito netting, the ropes of marigold. It was the blood—my bleeding mixed in with his saliva—that had made him vomit. I was wrong that Raga-be's *jadu* had made it stop. For there it was, two small splotches of red on that white cloth. I explained it away by saying I had started the pill on the wrong day, nothing more than my menses coming earlier than expected, things I knew that he, as a man, wouldn't really understand.

"I threw the letters out," he said, head hanging low, shoulders slumped, knees at his belly. He could have been the child caught with some secret, when it was I who had been the one to behave without judgment. "But I read them. I shouldn't have read them, but I did." He twisted the kurta around his fists. "Now I'm haunted by them . . . possessed by him, your old lover. When I was touching you, it was him I saw touching you. Over and over, he writes about the night he came to you. Thoo!" he spat, then lurched up and stood very still, fists trembling over his face, my kurta the color of his flesh. Through his sheer *kameez*, I could see the heavy rise and fall of his chest. "You have made a fool of me . . ."

"No!"

"Yes, a fool. While I was writing to you, telling you how much I wanted to touch you, be with you, you were there . . . with him. Letting him into your room, letting him . . . *fuck* you. You, my fiancée, my wife! Jesus Christ, it is all I see, what *he* has done to you. After reading those letters, I tried to do what he . . . I didn't know I would feel so *repelled*!" He let out a long breath and fell back onto the stool.

"Do you want me to leave? If you want to . . . send me away, just call Nafiza—" my voice buckled.

He was silent, slowly unwinding the kurta. I folded the white cloth as tidily as the women had folded my wedding clothes. My hands were trembling. The rain was beating the wood. He came over to the mosquito netting and drew back the slit that served as the entrance. He sat beside me and took my hand, his thumb winding around the henna designs until he found his initials at the center. He crushed the painted leaf.

"You belong to me now," he said, eyes averted from my face. "How many times did I write that I would do anything to make you mine? I have, and now I will do anything to keep you." He threw the cloth on the floor. "My mother placed that in here. Such traditions are important to her. I've told you before, I'm not that kind of man, I don't believe as they do here. They're stuck in some past that no longer exists. And that is what we must remember, baby." His fingers curved up into my hair and he pulled me close, his forehead pressing into mine. His breath became the air I breathed. "What has happened in the past no longer matters. We must never raise it again. I make a promise on our first night together, to forgive you and not ask any more questions. But you must do the same. You must not ask about my past. What matters is the man before you. I swear to you, baby, I will do my best to be the man you want—that *I* want to be. Just give me time to get over . . . *this*. My God!" he said, tugging at my blouse's gold thread, my silver toe ring glinting on his thumb. "How can I make you understand? I want nothing more than to be able to touch you."

THAT NIGHT, OUR wedding night, he slept with his arms crossed over his chest. In the morning, by the time Nafiza awakened me to dress, he was already gone. I hadn't expected that he'd leave me alone on the first day of our marriage, but, of course, I'd done things he hadn't expected either. The shutters were pushed open, revealing the gray boundary wall, the smell of wet dirt mingling with the scent of dying flowers.

Nafiza bathed me as before, singing that song she had long ago invented about a girl who would one day find her way home. It was about me, of course, recounting how, at nearly a year old, I had walked out of the family compound and gotten lost. My mother, who had been packing suitcases for our move to the U.S.—tropical clothes, rice and ghee, betel nut leaves, what do you bring to a country you've never been to?—hadn't noticed or, if she had, had thought Nafiza was attending to me. My nanny assumed I was with my mother. By the time the family went out to search, I was nowhere in the neighborhood. It wasn't until the next day that someone brought me to the police station. Amme said Dad was so relieved to have me back, he threw a party for four hundred people—as large as my wedding. I have no memory of any of it.

Now I said, "But Nafiza-una, haven't I found my way home?"

She raised her voice over mine, singing even louder, the exertion causing her to cough so deeply that she had to stoop behind me, a hand resting heavily on my back for support. I reached over my shoulder and patted it, but she drew away, still angry, I was sure, about what I'd done with Raga-be. I finished bathing myself while she fetched a towel.

When I came into the bedroom with it around me, I was surprised to find my mother-in-law. She was standing at the foot of the bed, and the sunlight falling through the open window revealed the deep lines across her forehead and under her eyes, around her lips. Tears were running down her wide cheekbones, which she didn't wipe away. The black veil was still wrapped about her, making me feel exposed.

"Islam says that heaven lies at the mother's feet," Zeba said. "To please her is to enter heaven. Today, Layla . . . Beti . . . you have earned your place in heaven." She stepped forward and wrapped me in her arms, the black cloth swooping about like ravens' wings. She smelled of sweat and cooking spices, the jasmine oil she must have applied to her hair. When she pulled back and saw my confused face, her lips curved into a tight smile, three crescents on either side of her mouth. It was the strongest expression of happiness I had seen on her. "This morning, Sameer gave me the cloth. You are a virtuous wife, Layla. Your steps into this house have blessed us all." She kissed my forehead, as she had at the *sanchak* ceremony, and this time, I was left with the softness of her lips and not the scratchy feel of the brocade. "Dress her in green," she ordered Nafiza, not taking her eyes off me. "I want to see my daughter in green all day, not only at the *walima*. Allah *ka shukar*, this is not just a show."

After she had gone, I dressed as she'd asked, choosing a green of raw henna, then sat on the stool before the mirror. Nafiza stood behind me, plaiting my hair.

She said, "You papa, he once believe you feet bless him."

I gazed at her through the tall mirror, but she kept her focus on my hair. She had it parted into three sections and was winding each tightly around the other as she blended in the strand of white jasmine Zeba had sent Sameer's brother, Feroz, to get. My husband had still not returned from wherever he'd gone.

I said, "My going to Raga-be for help is no different from Amme taking me to all those *alims*. Nafiza, there's no reason for you . . ."

"The boy, he touch you?" she asked, speaking over me.

I took in the face that was as familiar to me as my mother's, the hardened skin across the cheeks and forehead, the thin lips as dark as the rest of her. No matter that she had helped raise me here, how much could the old servant really understand about me and my life?

"Throw out the marigolds," I said. "I'm getting a headache. Maybe there's a maid who can help you." There was no maid, I knew, this was a modest household.

"Throw out flowers. Throw out bloody rags. Everything stink," she said, slowly adding, "Stink, too, the white cloth the boy give his mama. Same stink as rags."

I ignored her.

"Boy who touch he wife no leave house in hurry-hurry," she went on. "Sun still meeting ground, not in sky yet, and he gone. Why he keep wife he running from? She what use to him?" She shook her head. "Bloody cloth is *jadu* he use to fool people. Make them believe what no there. Child, you tell he mama . . ."

"Tell his mother, tell my mother—Nafiza, you tell *me*, what good will it do?" Before she could answer, I added, "You yourself went to Raga-be before you got married, tucking away some secret. So you know there are times when not everything should be revealed."

She yanked a section of hair, tearing the thread stringing together the flowers. White petals fell into my lap and on the floor. She pulled a bobby pin from her gray bun and, squeezing a few stems onto it, pushed it through my braid. Her eyes, small pinholes in her face, closed even more. A drawing in of her presence.

"Better you tell he mama the truth," she repeated.

"One night means nothing, Nafiza. I won't tell anyone. Giving him away is giving myself away. Don't you see that?"

"You no tell she what no concern her. Only tell she about she child. He no do what he say he do." She sighed, and I could feel the heavy weight of her breasts against me. "No telling what the boy up to. Better you protect you-self."

Protect myself from Sameer? He was the one protecting me. And hadn't she, my nanny, offered the same thing only three days before?

"Nafiza, if you really want to protect me, don't tell his mother, don't make me return to that house. There is no home there for me, there is only my father. He will kill me, if not for this, then for something else; one day he will end up killing me."

She pursed her lips, hands going still. Then she suddenly looked up at me, yellow teeth revealing themselves through a smile, a thought having crossed her mind. "This Allah's work, no *jadu*," she said. "You no see, child, if you go home now, he no kill you. The boy say he touch you, but he no touch you. You return now, you save you-self. Only when boy touch you and return you he-self will you papa . . ."

she stopped, unable to utter what we both knew he would do to me, Nafiza's second daughter.

Finally, she said, "Me old woman, Layla-bebe. Me no know how to read and write, me no go to foreign schools like you. All life, I spend in you mama's house. I grow up there, I marry there, and, one day, I die there, like me husband die there. Me girl, Roshan, I give her same-same milk I give you. No difference in milk. No difference in love. Now me girl giving milk to her girl. But you no making milk, you making blood. What you think become of me when I see this?"

I bowed my head in shame. I hadn't thought about her.

She pulled on my braid, forcing me to raise my head again. She said, "But I still standing beside you," and pinched my kurta. "Take this off. I get different clothes. Me girl return home in honor."

"No, Nafiza, I can't. You see . . ." I slid my fingertips across the drawer in which he'd found those letters. "It's too late. Sameer already knows about me. And by *jadu* or by God, he's keeping me on as his wife. Just like you, he still accepts me. But he's my husband, Nafiza, he needs some time to get over this. It's why he couldn't touch me last night."

She turned down her dark lips and grunted. She hadn't been expecting that. But nor had I when it happened. Some hidden powers at work, indeed.

Then Nafiza said, "Maybe he fooling you? Using what you do to hide he-self." But she no longer seemed as sure of what she knew.

I plucked the jasmine from my lap and slid them into my braid. My hand was turned sideways, and in the mirror, I could see the reflection of my palm, the leaf drawn red, already beginning to fade.

"I have to go greet my new family," I said, rising, and though I wanted to call Zeba "Mother," I couldn't, and instead said, "Zeba Auntie must be waiting."

She lumbered to the bed, pounding on the leg that gave her pain, and began snapping off the floral ropes. As usual, she was dressed in one of Amme's old saris, the ghost of my mother hovering about. She spoke through a sigh, "One night he no touch you, you say you no care so I no care. One night, maybe it mean no-thing. But Layla-bebe," she said, looking up at me, her face fully open and drawing me in as palpably as a caress, so I knew what she said was not a threat but a gesture of maternal love, "if one night become two and three and four and five, if one night go on like this, I speak to he mama me-self. I tell she the truth." Her hand closed on a marigold, crushing it.

"That's fine, Nafiza," I said, not believing it would come to that.

THE LAST OF the five wedding days, *walima*.

Over a thousand guests were invited to the dinner Sameer's parents hosted to proudly announce he had consummated the marriage. The wedding hall, which had sweltered with four hundred people the previous night of the *nik'kah*—forcing the manager to set up standing fans as tall as a man every ten or so feet—now became unbearable, the air stinking of sweat and skin, betel nut and spices, flowers and bad breath. All the fans were turned on high but did little to stir the dead air.

Sameer and I sat on a square-shaped dais, ropes of white jasmine and red roses hanging down three sides of a maroon canopy. Through the side free of flowers, we gazed out at the wedding guests, perched on those high-backed chairs his family had ordered for the wedding. It was true, he could not properly fold his broken-and-not-properly-healed right leg to sit cross-legged on a velvet *masnat*, as was tradition.

But not much was traditional about this night, nor, I was learning, about my husband. Rather than wear the heavy silver *sherwani* with the Nehru-cut collar, he had chosen a blue Armani suit Amme had sent over on one of those gift trays. And below, in place of the colorful silk sandals, he had on the thick-soled black boots I had seen him in the first time we'd met, then each of the three times we went out with Nafiza-una, the ones with the corrective heels. Beside him, I was the glorious image of the virtuous wife: wrapped in the six-foot-long silver threaded green sari, my ears and fingers and neck gleaming with emeralds, bangles clinking up to my elbows, ankles heavy with gold chains, only the silver ring missing from my one toe. Despite the heat,

I still wore the floral garland his mother had draped each of us in to commence the event, though he had immediately removed his and cast it by his feet.

Before us, the brightly lit wedding hall was jammed from end to end with tables of assorted sizes. In the courtyard, a large tent had been hitched and more tables arranged. Still, some guests ate standing up. His family, my family, went about greeting people, giving up their tables for other guests. It had been decided, upon gauging the crowd, that the immediate family members would eat after the event, including the bride and groom. After all, the celebratory feeding of others was the only ritual of the *walima*, no application of oils and turmeric, sweetening of the mouth. Our marriage was now official.

As guests finished their meals, they came up to congratulate us in colorful clumps, and Sameer rose and shook hands with the men, accepting their good wishes, while I lowered my head even farther in modesty, accepting clumsy pats on my head, fingers brushing against my cheek, further smudging the makeup the heat had already creased across my face. After a while, though, the salutations began to be accompanied by the rumor that had been seeping through the gathering, whispered from guest to guest, and now boldly raised by the men to the new groom: the evening seemed hastily put together, they complained, not enough tables, not enough chairs, perhaps not even enough food to go around. Most of the guests had been invited that very day by Feroz, who had rushed to various houses in the Old City and Vijayanagar Colony on his bicycle to announce the *walima* would indeed be hosted, the bride had been accepted. The men asked my husband if he and his family had assumed there would not be a successful union, the bride being American.

If Sameer had seemed impatient before with this ceremony, tapping the silver ring against the chair's arm, hurriedly greeting and getting each guest off the stage, now, having to defend my honor again and again to the hundreds who came up in small knots of color and curiosity, titillation, appeared to have defeated him. By the time the last of the guests bounded onto the dais to greet us before leaving, he didn't stand to greet them. He simply nodded, the hand with the silver toe ring massaging his forehead, the three deep lines that had emerged across it. And when the wedding photographer tried to take a final photo, he turned his face away. We didn't speak.

When the guests had gone, two long tables were pushed next to each other, the tall fans shifted to surround us. The high-backed chairs were moved to the center of one table, the women of Sameer's family sitting to my right, the men to Sameer's left. The man who had danced to the brass wedding band, the one Sameer had explained to me late last night was one of his closest friends, Naveed, was not among them.

At the other table, my family. Sabana was busy fussing over her boys, loading up their plates with *biriyani* and chicken *tikka*, lamb kabobs, and yogurt, while Dad was laughing, his head thrown back at some remark. Over the head of his younger son, his light-colored eyes were fixed on Ameera Auntie, and she was smiling shyly at him, her mouth partly covered by her sari-*pallow*. Her thin cheeks were flushed in a way I'd never seen before, Dad's presence the cause of the healthy glow the disease had taken away. My two uncles were bent over their plates, eating rapidly—it was now close to midnight. Just beyond them, my mother was embracing her sister, Asma Kala, both their faces flushed with joy, the matching green of their saris seeming to roll the two women into one, and I glimpsed how they must have looked as children, and then imagined how Henna and I would appear years from now, when the child she was now carrying was getting married. My cousin was fanning herself with a napkin, a hand resting on her expanding belly. She caught my eye and smiled.

How was it possible that I was not among my family and the dramas I had grown to know and accept? This, my physical separation, more than if Sameer had actually consummated the marriage, made my union with my husband ever more believable. It was true, I now belonged to him.

I touched his thigh under the table. "Where's your friend Naveed?" I asked, hoping to take his mind off the evening's lies, the *walima*'s grand announcement of a chaste coupling, then his own repeated one to the late-invited wedding guests—"Of course my wife is virtuous," he had said again and again, a mantra I knew he himself wanted to believe. "My mother's caution is not a sign that we ever doubted Layla."

He now shrugged, sweat running in lines down his temples, glistening on his neck. He had taken the jacket off and rolled up the sleeves of his shirt, exposing wide wrists and tanned arms. I could not imagine how hot his feet must have been inside the leather boots.

"Maybe he came and went," he said. "It's hard to remember with so many people." Then he gave me that look from last night, the one that said I'd made him into a fool, and rather than seeing him on that high-backed chair, I saw him on the round stool, my light-colored kurta stretched taut between his fists. He squeezed my hand against his weaker thigh, speaking as he had to the scandalized guests, through tight lips, "Once more, Mum's prudence has shamed me."

Amme came over just then and, standing behind Sameer and me, twirled a few hundred rupees over our heads, once, twice, seven times, the gesture Raga-be had made with the rooster's blood. She was doing away with evil spirits and the envious eye. When she was done, she handed the notes to me, saying to give the money to those who were less fortunate than us, the homeless.

Despite my new husband's anguished face, as I watched my mother take her seat at my family's table, I knew I could never go back to that.

DAWN IN VIJAYANAGAR Colony broke much quieter than dawn in the Old City. There, loudspeakers mounted on each corner mosque ushered in the new day, one azan starting seconds before or after another, sometimes even minutes later, when *fajr namaz* at a different *masjid* might have already concluded. Hearing so many calls to prayer, each wave of adulation lapping over the other, was discomfiting, a cacophony, a chaos overhead that matched the chaos of life below. It seemed as though the imams were sparring in the skies, one raising his voice, the other matching then raising his own, inviting followers to worship in that particular mosque.

That first Friday in Vijayanagar Colony, I woke just before dawn, my body grown accustomed to these morning arousals as it had grown accustomed to the new clock and calendar, morning in America, night in India, July there, Ze'qad here. We had gotten married on the fourth of July, and it had not occurred to me until weeks later, when we were at the American Consulate in Madras, that the fireworks flaring over the wedding hall could have been an echo of the displays erupting across the U.S.

Overhead, three taps on a loudspeaker, a gentle clearing of the throat, then the gradual ascent of a single voice, unfamiliar to me from the Old City ones I'd come to recognize. From start to finish, his voice alone, so that I could follow the cadence in the Arabic and feel the words delicately beckoning the faithful out of bed, "Allah is great," "There is no god but God," "Time has come for good deeds," "Time has come for prayer."

When it ended, there was a soft rap at the bedroom door. Sameer was still sleeping, his back to me, so far at the edge of the bed that his face was pressed into the thick mosquito netting. I rose, wrapping a *duppatta* around my head as I had learned from Zeba to do even in the house, and opened it. It was the younger brother, Feroz, dressed in the loose pajama-*kameez* he wore to bed. The *kameez* had three tiny gold buttons, which were undone, the fabric flapping back to expose the edge of a scar on his chest, knotted and darker than the rest of him, a familiar sight in the Old City. Men had scars that ran the length of their backs or across their shoulders or were centered, like this, just above a breast. They had been inflicted by self-flagellation during the month of mourning to express deep love for Allah and our saints. It was a bravery I respected, though couldn't fathom. From Feroz's scar, I knew he'd sliced his flesh with a razor blade.

"Mummy wants Sameer Bhai to come and pray," he said in his

high, nasal voice. His eyes slanted up at the corners like his mother's, lined with the black *surma* some men wore here to pray.

I stepped aside so he could wake Sameer himself. He hesitated, then rushed in past me. As soon as he moved, I saw Ibrahim, Sameer's father, on the *takat* behind him. He was sitting with his legs thrown over the edge, running a flat palm round and round his bald head, his face and clothes crumpled from sleep. Cast about him were pillows and sheets. Zeba was already in the prayer room, the black cloth wrapped about her, lighting incense. I hadn't realized that the two slept in the main room, right outside our bedroom. I salaamed him and moved back inside, giving him privacy.

Feroz was gripping Sameer's foot through the netting and shaking it. "Hurry and come," he said. "Mummy says it's the first Friday of your marriage. On this day at least you should offer up prayers."

Sameer snatched his foot away, bending his long legs to his chest, and folded the pillow over his head. His voice came out muffled. "Tell her what the mullah said at the *nik'kah*. Simply by marrying, I've done half my duties to Allah. That is all I am willing to do to appease her . . . or her God."

Feroz called to him again, but Sameer squeezed the pillow over his ears, elbows jutting out, and his brother grunted and headed for the door.

"Bhabhi, it would please Mummy if he prayed," he said, using the formal title for sister-in-law, though I'd been surprised to learn we were the same age. With the way Feroz rushed to dress each morning for college while Zeba hand-fed him, I had thought there were at least four years between us, he being younger.

"Does she want me to come?" I asked.

He shot me a wry smile, almost condescending, and said, "As your husband has shown, it is up to you. Allah has given us free will."

After he left, Sameer reached through the netting door and grabbed my hand. It was the first time he'd touched me since the wedding night, three nights before. I knew Nafiza was tallying up the days.

"Don't leave me," he pleaded, bringing my hand to his mouth, his own bearing the silver toe ring. He licked the metal.

HIS FATHER STAYED home Friday mornings, not going into work until after the noon prayers. This one morning along with Sunday was his only time off. Evenings, when he finally arrived back by eight, having endured the four bus changes it took to get from Vijayanagar Colony to the edge of Hyderabad, then over the bridge to its twin city, Secunderabad, he was tired and quiet, and Zeba would send her sons and me away as she tended to him, heating up his bath water, laying out his clothes, setting up his dinner. She made sure the rest of us ate at seven so she could be ready for him when he walked through the door. As he ate, slumped over the plate, she would stand over him and fan him with the day's newspaper. He always dined alone, politely asking her about her day, their sons, and now, even me. It was Ibrahim, not Sameer, who nightly brought back bottled water for me to drink.

In the mornings, by the time I sat down for breakfast, he was already up and gone. The bus rides took well over an hour, and exhaustion showed on him as clearly as the loose skin on his hands and face from advancing age and the brown spots on his bald head from the biting sun. He was a rail engineer, and Sameer told me he would be up for retirement in four years but was hoping to cut it down to two.

That first Friday morning in my new house, it was his voice that drew me out of bed, after I'd gotten back in again with Sameer. My husband had pulled me to him merely to fall back asleep, on this, the first morning he'd not disappeared. I shed his heavy, slumbering grip and, wrapping the *duppatta* once more about me, went out. I found Ibrahim sitting alone at the dining table, dressed in a pressed cotton pajama-*kameez*, the newspaper opened before him. Zeba and Nafiza were in the kitchen, fussing over the morning meal. I could smell the *kitcherie* they were making and hear the sizzle of frying eggs. Before me, the four windows in the main room were flung wide, opening onto the vacant lot, the high weeds yellowed and bowed, surrendered to the heat. The *takat* was cleared of all the blankets and pillows, and the thick Pakistani rug was once more spread on top, the bright knots of color faded by the sun's harsh glare.

Ibrahim folded the newspaper and set it on the table. He looked over his shoulder at me, his reading glasses low on the bridge of his nose, the lenses a large oval. He smiled and pulled back the chair next to him, its legs scraping the stone floor.

"I was hoping you would come, Beta," he said, taking off the glasses. He tried to slide them into his shirt pocket, as he did in the button-downs he wore to work, then remembering he was wearing a *kameez*, set them on the table.

I went and sat beside him. It was the closest I had been to him, and I could see he had tiny brown spots speckling his broad forehead and hairline, on the backs of his hands. Liver spots, perhaps, not from the sun at all.

Beyond him, I could see the whole of the house. No one had bothered or thought to give me a tour, and, in truth, there was not much to show. It was a boxy structure with a flat roof, a more modern construction than Amme's house in the Old City. The square shape had been cut down the center, one side being the *divan* and master bedroom (my bedroom), and the other, the main area and dining room. The living area, where Zeba and Ibrahim slept, opened onto a smaller room that they had set up as the prayer space, which converted, at night, into Feroz's bedroom, and the dining room led to the kitchen and bathroom behind me.

"Why don't you and Zeba Auntie take my room?" I suggested to Ibrahim. It seemed obvious to me now that there was no extra room for the couple, but coming from houses that were always more empty than occupied, it hadn't occurred to me before.

Ibrahim's lips slowly drew back into a grin, their reddish-brown color matching that of his skin spots. He snapped back the arms of his glasses, then snapped them shut again. In the bath, Feroz was singing that counting song from the wedding night, while in the kitchen, Zeba was asking Nafiza to taste the mango relish I'd seen her prepare all week, first drying the slices under the sun, then sinking them into spicy oil.

"You're as innocent as my sister was," Ibrahim said, staring at the glasses before him. Through the lenses, the red tablecloth enlarged and widened. "When I look at you, I think of her. You have the same round face and round eyes, the same *bholi* look. She used to say things like that, too."

"Used to?"

He turned down the corners of his mouth. "She died a long time ago, Beta. When we were still just children. TB in the brain." He was silent a moment before saying, "Your presence in my house doesn't seem unfamiliar to me. It seems natural, as though you've been here all along. Your husband is in a rush to go to the U.S.," he said, gesturing back to the bedroom. "I told him to wait awhile, to not take you away from me so quickly, but he says he can't. Go, go, go. That child has always been like that, in a hurry to go from one thing to the next. He was even going to quit his tutoring so he could rush off to Madras this week to file for his visa, but I talked him into staying. Those kids are depending on him for their entrance exams. It wouldn't be good to drop them and run. You've got to be responsible and finish what you've started."

So he was tutoring. No wonder his mother hadn't questioned his early departures, his absence all day, as I had been fearing she would.

"And, Beta," Ibrahim was saying, tilting his head down to look up at me as though he still had on his glasses, "no matter what anyone says, it's never good to advance yourself while neglecting others, or worse, hurting them. I hope you agree."

"It's why I think you two should take the bedroom. This morning, you looked so uncomfortable."

"Not as uncomfortable as your husband would be if I took away his privacy. He's a new bridegroom, after all. Don't tell him," he said, lowering his voice in confidence. "I've got tickets for you—two first-class rail tickets—booked for the end of the month. As soon as his tutoring duties are finished, you two may go. I must confess," he said, putting his glasses back on and opening the paper again, "part of the reason I worked so hard to convince him to stay was so I could have you in my house for the month. After that, Beta, you'll return to the U.S. with your husband—when will I see you again? Let me enjoy a daughter's presence for a while."

AFTER BREAKFAST, ZEBA asked me to join her and Feroz in the prayer room to recite the Qur'an. Every Friday for eleven years, the two had been reciting together, a family tradition she now wanted me to share. I felt too embarrassed to tell her I didn't know how to read the Qur'an. My parents had never taught me, nor did they know Arabic themselves. It had been enough for them that I'd memorized the few Arabic surahs I needed to say during prayers. Indeed, Islam in their house consisted of not much more than occasional prayers, on important religious days, on days when Amme needed more comfort. They had never woken me at dawn to pray, and the only time they woke early themselves was during Ramadan, when they had to eat before sunrise. Even then, after Dad began staying with Sabana, Amme found it difficult to do the ritual by herself, and rather than encourage me to fast with her, she would dissuade me, saying the hunger and thirst would distract my attention from studies. I had never fasted more than four days of the required thirty. Nor read the Qur'an, as others did while observing the requirements of Ramadan.

Ibrahim must have sensed my unease, for he quickly sent Sameer and me out for a walk, scolding his wife for asking me to think about God at a time when any new bride would only be able to think about her groom—"Let them get their fill of one another, Zeba, before you begin snatching her away."

Zeba's grunt of disapproval followed Sameer and me out the front door, then Nafiza came limping to the boundary gate, scowling behind Sameer's back. Overhead, the sky was as gray as nails, the clouds low, compressing the heat.

Nafiza said, "When you think the clouds clear? Already so many days go by." And I knew what she was saying. She was ready to speak to Zeba.

I waited until Sameer was a safe distance away, then pretending to help her close the heavy gate, I whispered, "He's not escaping me, Nafiza-una, he tutors all day." I thought the news would please her, but she stared at me with that look of disappointment. I said, "When you went to Amme about Henna and me, what good came of it? She merely accused you of having a dirty mind—Zeba was on the farm, too, she might think the same thing."

She looked startled before she stepped away from the gate, and I latched it.

Outside, the streets were much calmer than I was used to. No stray dogs sniffing about, no goats rushing into the courtyard to eat fallen guavas, no peddlers pushing carts of bananas and tropical fruits, baskets filled with onions as small as the garlic, ginger twisted into itself. As we walked from the dead end out toward the main roads, as far as I could see stretched a clean line of yellow boundary walls higher than my head, then lush leaves of almond and ashoka trees, giving the squat houses, set back from the road, even more privacy. The sidewalk was constructed of rectangular stones cemented together, the curb painted in horizontal stripes of gold and black, forbidding cars to park. The rust-colored lampposts were encircled at the base by green grass and lilies, a wire mesh protecting the vegetation from passing goats. Here and there, in front of a private gate, a design on the sidewalk in chalk, a swastika or a triangle broken into diamonds, Hindu signs of peace and prosperity, good fortune. Off in the distance, I could see two cows, one on either side of the road, ambling on, white horns curved back into crescent moons, tails flicking flies.

Sameer bumped my side with his, a gesture I'd seen Dad make with Amme, the most affection a husband could show his wife in public. "Don't worry about Mum," he said. "You have to stay firm when she asks you to do something you don't want. You heard me this morning, I told her I wouldn't pray. She's not the bloody religion police!" He picked up a rock and pitched it at a telephone pole, missing.

Up ahead, a group of children dressed in blue school uniforms was slowly crossing the road, sharing treats, school bags thicker than backs.

"I would have joined her except . . . I don't know how to read the Qur'an."

He was stooping for another rock and gazed up at me, eyes squinting against the light. He was wearing the white T-shirt and jeans Amme had sent over on those silver wedding trays, those damn black boots, and, for a moment, peering down at him, I thought I was in the U.S. It was the way he looked and also this, the liberty to walk down the block. Never before in India had I taken a stroll, always in a car, always with a driver and ayah, always taken from one boundary gate to another. The freedom Amme had promised I would experience once I was married seemed to be coming true.

"You were learning more important things in the States. I myself am what you might call a lapsed Muslim."

"A lapsed Muslim!" I said, laughing.

He shot me a stern look, and I covered my mouth. He cast the stone at the pole again, this time smacking it and sending out the sound of a high clink.

"I'm sorry," I said, now bumping his side with mine. "Can you tell me what you mean?"

"I mean I have more meaningful beliefs."

"Like what?"

He shrugged, then felt the muscle of an arm, flexing it between his fingers, before choosing another stone. A scooter blared past, three men squeezed onto the seat. He was gazing up at a coconut, the tree rooted inside the boundary wall. He tossed the rock a few times in his hand, as though weighing it, before changing his mind and flinging it aside.

He glanced at his watch. "Do you want to turn back?"

Turn back? We hadn't even reached the end of the block! "Do you need to be someplace?" I asked. "Are you tutoring even today?"

He raised his thick brows, surprised, then slowly said, "Only Monday through Thursday." Then his shoulders slumped, reminding me of how frail his form had been at the time of our engagement. "Listen, Layla," he said, "I'm sorry I didn't tell you. I was embarrassed. My parents can't fund our trip to Madras, as yours . . . I've been working and saving for the expenses. Alone, I would have stayed in hostels, but with you . . ." He turned away.

I wanted to reach for his hand but couldn't in public. Just how much freedom did I really have here with my husband, other than my addressing him by his name—and that only upon Sameer's insistence? I said, "At your age, Sameer, my father was working and saving, too. He went to the U.S. with fifty dollars in his pocket."

"And now he drives a fifty-thousand-dollar car!" He shook his head in disgust at his father's income. "My house, it's so . . . it's not what you're used to. The crouching toilets and . . . I heard you talking to Papa about where they sleep. The truth is, they gave us their room, and they won't take it back, not until we've left for the U.S. You don't have to feel bad, it's not your fault. Mum sets aside an entire room for prayer, why not use that as their bedroom, make Feroz sleep in the *divan* or who cares where, he's just a boy!" He gazed about at the houses then quietly said, "Papa is close to retirement and he's still renting! I'm not going to be like him, Layla. I'm going to make something of myself! Not here, a man like me can't succeed here, but there!" His eyes widened, as though perceiving all his opportunities in America right here, among these gates and boundary walls. The lines on his forehead eased, and I thought he smiled faintly before he turned and headed up the road again, flinging his arm in the motion of pitching rocks. I followed, not knowing what to say nor knowing my husband well enough to lend my faith.

Finally, he stopped and waited for me, hands thrust deep inside his pockets. When I caught up, he said, "Your Nafiza, what did she want?"

"Just help with the gate."

He stared at me, taking in my veil and *shalwar-kameez* as though for the first time, his lashes so thick they appeared to line the lids. He was trying to judge if I was telling the truth. I took his elbow.

"Let's go to Henna's," I said, then joked, "I know they won't be praying!"

He didn't move. "Her house is too far."

"The wedding car passed their street on the way here. I saw it myself."

He let out a long breath, clasping his hands behind his back, and lowered his head. "I'm not ready to see your relatives just yet. They'll ask us if we're happy and how we enjoy being married, and I won't know what to say. It'll only remind me of . . ." he seemed about to say Nate, then changed his mind, ". . . of how we're not really together. The *walima* dinner was bad enough."

I nodded. Henna herself had told me how she didn't like answering questions about Hanif. And hadn't I been the one, seeing the groom's pained expression at the *walima*, the way he had shut his eyes and turned away from the video, to ask Zeba, who didn't approve of the cameras anyway, to get them turned off?

"Don't look so sad, baby," he said, gently straightening my veil. "I'm telling you, not just yet. It's only been three or four days, and I don't need much longer, I swear. Going to your relatives right now would be the wrong move. Trust me," he said, pinching my chin and raising my face to his, as I had seen a thousand film heroes lift their brides' faces on those fantasy wedding nights that now seemed truer than mine. "I have faith in things I can see and touch and feel," he said. "When I have you by my side, what reason do I have to believe in God? You will give me all I need. *Razzaq*," he said, provider, and one of the names of Allah.

SATURDAY EVENING, I climbed onto the back of his motorcycle and we took off, gliding through the streets I had seen only through the Fiat's window. The air pushed at us, thick and dull, heavy with diesel fumes. I kept the veil tight around my head to keep my hair in place. I was sitting with my legs thrown to one side, an arm wrapped about my husband, feeling the hardness of his chest as I had not before. He was leaned forward slightly, fingers curled around the handlebars, switching gears, revving the engine, my ring shimmering on his thumb. The bike was speeding and slowing, slowing and speeding, swerving about cars and lorries, buses moving too fast in this kind of traffic—more bicycles and mopeds, more pedestrians than people safely encased inside vehicles. But what a sensation to be out here, in the open, sliding through the darkening evening. I leaned my cheek against Sameer's back, jiggling with the bike's movements, and began to become a part of India as I had not been able to before.

We were headed to Tank Bund, the bridge between the twin cities of Hyderabad and Secunderabad, a popular place for couples. The one-and-a-half-mile bridge crossed over Hussein Sagar, a dam fed by the Musi Nade, which ran near Amme's house in the Old City. The dam, which must have been as large as Lake Calhoun in Minneapolis, separated the twin cities, while the bridge connected the two. During the time the Sagar was built by a Qutb Shahi king, it had provided drinking water to the residents; now the water was too polluted to swim in.

Over the years, during my every coming and going from India, I had had to cross this bridge to get to and from the airport. On almost every trip, Dad had halted the taxi along the side of the bridge, near one of the food carts, and ordered a round of sweet coconut milk. The peddler would hack off the coconut's crown with a machete, slide in a flimsy pink straw, and hand it to Dad through his rolled down window. Dad would pass the fruit back, one at a time, to Amme and me. After we were finished, we'd pass the shells back out in the same way. When my father remarried and ceased returning to India with us, my mother continued to stop the taxi along the Bund, this time the driver getting our milk. Those brief moments of gazing out through tinted windows was how I had experienced the bridge, during moments of heightened excitement, arrival and departure, new beginnings, here or there.

Along the extent of the bridge, cars parked against a cement divider, on the other side of which lay a wide promenade; at regular intervals, cement stairs led down to a lawn, the edge of the waters.

Sameer pulled into a spot, and we hopped off the bike, the warm air from passing traffic blowing back my long kurta. He wrapped his helmet straps onto the handlebar and we wove our way through parked cars to the other side of the divider. Dusk was giving way and the lights of Hyderabad flickered a dim yellow to my left, while on my right was the brighter blaze of Secunderabad. A large, five-star hotel had sprouted up since last year, capital letters spelling out VICEROY in a harsh white that dulled the stars. These twin cities stood on the high Deccan plateau, sloping down toward Madras to the south and the Bay of Bengal to the east. Most of the landscape before me was of the same flatness as the American Midwest, but for a rocky hill spotting the horizon here and there. On top of the highest was the magnificent glow of Birla Masjid, its white marble brighter even in the distance than the modern hotel lettering just behind me. Along the promenade, every fifty feet, stood a statue of a famous Indian—Nehru, Mahatma Gandhi, the Buddha. And near the end of the bridge, by Secunderabad, was an unknown grave, which was rumored to belong to the Sufi saint who protected Tank Bund. Hindu, Muslim, Buddhist—these religions had made Hyderabad.

Sameer slipped his hand into mine and pulled me against the railing overlooking the dam. The water was as dark now as the liquid inside Raga-be's bowl, and there was no sound of movement, the crashing waves I was used to hearing at the lakes. Along its periphery, the reflection of city lights.

Without a word, my husband slid his fingers inside the chador, right under my chin, and undid the hook. The fabric fell back, and he caught it and yanked the rest free. "If it was up to me," he said, "you'd be in jeans. This is to please Mum." He held up the veil, a loose ball in his fist, and I was reminded of the kurta he'd wrapped around his hand on the wedding night. "I'll go set it in the helmet," he said, springing away.

I watched him weave his way through the crowd, a tall figure in tan corduroys and a blue button-down he'd kept untucked. So familiar now in the clothes Amme had brought back. He jumped over the di-

vider to his bike and a pair of young women with braids to their waists eyed him as they moved past, steps behind their own husbands.

Husband—the word itself felt foreign, though it had come into my life long before Sameer had. Amme's imaginings of him inside me, a ghost of my future. *Your husband will be a doctor or an engineer. Your husband will come from a good family. Your husband will be Muslim. Your husband will be from India.* Now, here he was, exactly as she had described, and yet so different from what I had expected. What was it that had pushed me to Nate? Was it something in Sameer I had seen last year at the engagement, or something in me—my doubts, my second side that was convinced love did not emerge after marriage? Saturday night on Tank Bund, over the soundless Sagar joining the two cities, was beginning to feel like I imagined a first date.

Sameer strolled back with a string of flowers he'd bought from a peddler. Without asking me to turn around, he slung his arms over my shoulders, drawing me close, and pinned them to my hair. Jasmine, jasmine and sweat.

We stood like that awhile, turned away from the outraged stares we must have been receiving from passersby. His heart was beating inside my ear. Finally, when a group of men began hollering and whistling, Sameer pulled away and leaned his elbows onto the railing. Overhead, a jet tore through the sky, heading south toward Madras, red lights blinking on its wings.

He said, "Are St. Paul and Minneapolis connected by a bridge? When I researched the cities, I couldn't find much. New York and Chicago, California, yes, but not Minneapolis. Most of my friends haven't even heard of it."

"It's small, like Hyderabad. And it's connected to St. Paul through freeways." How to describe that? "Roads like on Tank Bund, where cars go very fast and there are no stoplights."

He smiled. "You're explaining freeways to an engineer, baby."

"Sorry." How could I say that I had not yet gotten used to him, my husband?

He stared at me, his mouth slightly open, his tongue moving be-

hind his upper teeth, jabbing into the space then slipping away. "Twin cities," he finally said. "You go from one twin city to another. Twins, like you."

"Like me?"

"Yes, like you. You, the American, you, the Indian. Same face, two people. So where is your home?"

I gazed out toward the farthest end of the Sagar, then along its edge toward Secunderabad. Somewhere out there was the airport I arrived at twice a year.

"I was supposed to inhabit America without being inhabited by it—that was what my parents wanted."

"But you're a modern woman. Surely you don't believe that's possible. Take a look around you, baby, your America has reached even here, the darkest part of India. Tandoori pizza, lamb hamburgers, listen to the Hindi film music. It's all disco and synthesizers. The next time we come to Tank Bund, there might even be a statue of the American president! Why not? Nothing goes uncorrupted . . . not even you."

No, not even me. And the memory of Nate, those letters, must have fluttered through his mind as well, for he blinked at the woman before him, the image he was suddenly seeing, before his gaze faltered and his head dropped between his shoulders. His thumb, the ring, began clanging against the metal railing.

He said, "Most Americans have probably never heard of Hyderabad or even know where it is, yet America is here. Merely a fashion statement today, a status symbol, something to eat and wear, but tomorrow, who knows what it will mean to be Indian? If it will mean anything anymore. You, who live there—and this is what I meant—if we are being corrupted halfway round the world, how could you, who live there, not be corrup— I mean, it would not be possible for you to remain . . . pure." He let out a long breath and slumped even farther onto the railing, shaking his head. He felt defeated, I could tell, his words, without his intending, coiling around Nate, what I had done, and from my husband's own lips, how my behavior might even be excused, explained away. Possessed, indeed, by the man who had entered me. It was not possible anymore for him to make even a broad statement about cultural invasion without thinking specifically about my body.

I ran my hand along the back of his head, feeling its shape and contours, the soft waves of his hair. My fingers slipped to his neck, under the collar of his shirt, the hard bone of his spinal cord, the scratchiness of the shirt's designer label. He shut his eyes, his lips curling up to show displeasure, but he didn't pull away. I traced his ear, his jaw line, finally getting to know my husband, who was as strange to me as he was familiar.

I whispered, "You and I are the same, Sameer. Same color, same language, same race. You understand parts of me no American ever will. I don't have to explain to you what the chador means; I don't have to . . . translate myself to you or feel misunderstood. You are more part of me than . . . than I had even realized myself." I opened up my palm to show him his initials, but even in the lamppost's frail light, I could see the henna had faded into an unattractive orange, parts of the design, the letters of his name, already seeped into skin and blood.

THAT NIGHT, HE slept closer to the center of the bed, closer to me, but in the morning, was again gone before I woke, the men of the house winding their way out of this dead-end road, while I was left behind with Zeba and Nafiza. The previous week, I had not known his presence well enough to miss it. Now, after three days of being with him, I was startled to find myself in Zeba's role, eagerly awaiting my husband's return.

I joined my mother-in-law later that morning, crawling up beside her on the *takat* she slept on at night. It was here, resting against three pillows she had embroidered herself, that she began preparations for the evening meal. Set before her now was a steel pot overflowing with green beans, more than I had ever seen Amme use for one curry. This, a woman who was accustomed to feeding three grown men. She was breaking off the ends and casting them on the cement floor, the *dup-patta* rising and falling with the heavy movement of her breath.

As I was reaching for the pot, she held up her hand to stop me, the black fabric falling low. "You are in a rush to begin housework. How many times must I tell you, your wedding henna hasn't completely faded. You are still a new bride. No need to hurry. *Inshal'lah*, you have a full life ahead of cooking and cleaning for your husband. Right now, you must rest. Your ayah is here to do your work." She motioned with her head toward the kitchen. Nafiza was inside, washing my breakfast dishes, the sound of splashing water and clanging plates mingling, every now and then, with a low cough.

"I am tired of resting," I said, grabbing a few green beans.

Without looking up at me, she said, "You are already restless without him."

I snapped off the ends, starting a pile by my knee, and we sat awhile in silence, the beans popping as they broke. I was suddenly aware of Zeba being his mother. It was her face he bore, the same wide forehead and thick brows, those lines etched on her face already showing up on his.

She said, "What did you do at home? Did you help your *amme*?"

Help her? I had spent my life helping her, it seemed, once Dad had left. Making the phone calls she needed even for the most minor of tasks, paying bills, getting an appliance fixed or the heater running again. Going with her on visits to the doctors, even the gynecologist, to ensure she understood—I understood—what was happening with her health, her depression that sprang out as anger. Rearranging my schedule, setting aside my work, making her my priority. She, the mother who had become my child.

I said, "Amme was often alone, especially at night after my father divo— because he was often at the hospital. She needed me. She never got used to living in America. She never even picked up English!"

Zeba's eyes wandered to my bedroom and, through the open door, she took in my ivory-painted bed. It was so big it hardly left any space to walk. Gaudy, compared to their simple furniture, ostentatious and gaudy. Zeba grunted, as though in agreement, her hands not once slowing in their task. "Your *amme* and I have always known different lives. Did she tell you we were childhood friends?"

"She said you went to school together in the village."

"My family rented from hers. For seven generations, that's how we lived in Miryalgurda, always the renters, and your family always the landowners. Of course we were children and none of that made sense to us. We were only interested in playing. In that village, there was no one else. Sometimes your *amme* and I would get so bored of each other, we'd have your grandfather order the servants' children to play with us. We measured and sold them dirt, pretending it was the rice and grain your *nana* grew. Your Nafiza hated being forced to be with us. She wanted to be running around in the jungle with the boys. She was always getting in trouble."

Trouble, the kind that must have led her to seek Raga-be's help. Yet there was no way to ask Zeba about it.

"Amme tells stories about the jungle. She says there were bears and tigers, even king cobras, where you played hide-and-seek. And scorpions would crawl into her bed, stinging her. She told me that once someone gave Taqi Mamu a pair of monkeys as pets." Fantastical tales, hers were, or at least that was how I had always heard them, bedtime stories as entertaining and hard to believe as those Bollywood movies she loved to watch.

Zeba snapped a bean. "We did mostly play outside, in your *nana*'s fields and in the jungle. Your *nani* didn't like us in the house. It was a huge *haveli*, and she said noise echoed." She let out a heavy sigh, the veil crumpling and folding with her body. "She suffered so long from that brain tumor. Allah *raheem*," God have mercy.

Nafiza hobbled in and sat on the floor beside us, her arm on the *takat* supporting her as she folded her legs. She was still having trouble with her knees. Zeba gave her a handful of beans, and my nanny gathered them in her lap, breaking two at a time.

Zeba said, "So here we are again, old woman, together like when we were children. Who would have imagined it, huh?"

Nafiza didn't say anything.

I quickly asked, "What happened to make you lose touch?"

Zeba turned to me with a look of surprise. "Partition, Beti! No one knew where anyone went. Some said your *nana* took the family to Pakistan. Others said the *haveli* had been attacked and your family was . . . *nauz-ibiil'lah*," she said, shaking her head. "I heard they'd all been killed. It was Allah's hidden work that we rented here, so close to your family. If your Taqi Mamu and my husband hadn't bumped into each other, we would never have heard about you."

"Kismet," I said, recalling the Qur'anic reading about my marriage. Better, it had forecast. Better for me to get married. This was already better than the life I'd once known.

"Enough about the past," Zeba said, adjusting the pillows behind her. "History was my favorite subject in school, so you must be careful of me. Tell me, Beti, what is your *amme*'s life like now in the States?"

What was there to tell? Zeba may not have owned her house, but at least she owned her husband. "She does what you do. She cooks and cleans." I didn't say that rather than pray, Amme watched Hindi movies.

"*She* cooks and cleans. You mean a servant . . ."

"We have no servants there."

"No servants! Your mother cooks!"

"Yes, she cooks."

And there was that smile again, the small tug at the corners of her lips, curving them like the upward slants of her eyes.

"*Hai* Allah, she has gone to America only to find a life like mine. What would your *nana* think of that? You know, he never let her near the kitchen."

Nafiza suddenly looked up, the sari-*pallow* draped over her head doing nothing to soften her face. Zeba had us all covering. "We cook with wood in the jungle. So much smoke. He no want he child to get *dhum*," asthma.

"*Dhum! Chalu*, Nafiza, the man was proud. Remember what happened when the village mutt mated with his *alshishan*? He brought out his rifle and killed it." She grunted, loosening the veil around her face and using the edge to wipe the sweat on her brow. "What good did it do? Rosy still had seven puppies by him. Your *nana* buried them alive," she said, turning to me. "I can still hear Rosy howling in grief, chained to the . . ."

"I've never seen Miryalgurda," I blurted.

"No need to see it," Nafiza said. "All gone, you *nana*'s land. Nothing left to see. Even his *haveli* burn down—*they* burn it down." She turned back to the beans, cursing the invaders under her breath.

"Your *amme* never liked it there, Beti. She was always scared. The *haveli* was big and dark. They didn't have electricity out there, only lanterns. And all night, your *nani* would scream in pain. Toward the end, she began hallucinating, seeing *shai'tan*s, even talking to them. Most nights, your *amme* would sleep at my house, in my bed." Her hands finally went still. "And now she's sent her daughter to my house," she said, looking at me with a tenderness I was not used to seeing on a mother's face, the same she'd shown me the morning after the wedding, when she'd called me her virtuous daughter. "Sameer tells me you don't know how to read the Qur'an," she said. "Don't look so surprised, Beti. Your husband did not tell me to betray you, but because he did not want me to . . . embarrass you again by asking you to read with me. A child not knowing the Qur'an is not her fault, but the mother's, so you should not feel ashamed. It is a mother's duty to teach Islam. The man's domain is outside, and the woman rules the house. Without the balance, children would be lost." Even as I was wondering if she was chastising Amme, she said, "I will not neglect my duty to teach you. You will find solace in the words of Allah, Beti. And the long hours before your husband returns will pass much quicker."

Even if I wanted, I couldn't recite the Qur'an or pray with her, not with the bleeding. But how could I tell her this?

Nafiza said, "The child no clean. She begin menses."

Zeba took in my damp hair, her wide cheeks squeezing into a

solemn face. She continued to believe Sameer and I were having sex, so expected me to come out for breakfast only after my cleansing bath. I had been showering every morning since my arrival. Now she said, "In this house, there is prayer, not sin, Allah, not *shai-tan*. My son should know better than to come to you when you are bleeding. Sickness comes from such acts, sickness and disease. I shall talk to him tonight, and if he cannot vow to control himself, then you, Beti, shall sleep by my side."

MY HUSBAND SLEPT with his father all week, the two sharing the *takat* in the main room. It was narrower than our bed, so father and son slept inches apart from one another, much closer than Sameer and I had ever lain.

Zeba stayed with me in the bedroom, our bodies enclosed by the thick mosquito netting, the bird's face turned away from us. She snored in her sleep, loudly, often catching her breath and startling awake, and as the nights wore on, I began to turn heavily in bed, pounding my legs against the mattress, to wake her. In the brief lull, I would try desperately to fall asleep. But, in truth, it was less her snoring than my own thoughts keeping me awake.

Over that week, I began to realize that it was those very nights of sleeping beside my husband, though we did not touch—because we did not touch—that were drawing me to him. His weight next to me, his steady breathing, his withdrawal. Not as complete as Dad's had been, but enough to make me yearn for him to beckon.

Now he was even farther away, barely visible through the bed's heavy netting, the darkness of the house, the diminishing moon. New moon. He had come to me on the new moon, sliding in through the back screen door, sliding into my bed, into me. Lying next to Sameer's mother, I found myself thinking about my lover, his touch becoming my husband's, and when I finally fell asleep, even the faceless demon who continued to visit me in dreams took on my husband's pretty form. In the heart of every night, we made love.

If Zeba could only see her daughter's dreams, she would know the *shai-tan* was already in her house.

FRIDAY AGAIN. THE first call to prayer.

In the next room, Zeba was leaning over Sameer, shaking him awake. He groaned his protest and she pinched his ear, pulling him out of bed.

"You use your leg as an excuse not to pray anymore," she said. "But, for one day, you can bear the pain—as I bear the pain each moment of your lack of faith. Now get up!"

He protested again, but soon enough, was standing beside her, offering up dawn prayers along with the rest of his family. That complete, she told him to perform two more, one *shuk'rana*, thanking Allah for our successful union, and one in repentance for coming to me while I was bleeding.

I was not asked to join them, being impure, and while the family prayed, I bathed, planning to tell Zeba it was my cleansing bath for menses, and my husband should be allowed back into our room.

When I came out, Sameer was standing by the foot of the bed, his trunk of clothes open before him. His cotton pajamas were so sheer that the light shining in the window bared the shape of his legs, the thickness of his thighs. He wasn't wearing a shirt, his broad chest clean of hair and scars. He was not one to take a blade to himself, aroused by religion. When he saw me wrapped in a towel, he straightened, his tongue swiping his upper lip, his eyes falling down my body, taking me in as even Nate had not been able to in the darkness. If I was seeing my husband's naked form for the first time, he was also seeing mine.

He stepped backward and closed the door. On his head, a white prayer cap embroidered with the same design as the pillows Zeba rested against. Those dark eyes took on a look God should never see. He came toward me and, without a word, pulled me against him, sucking the dampness from the hollow of my collarbone.

I closed my eyes. It was not enough anymore to be touched only in dreams.

"Why did you tell your mother you would make love to me during my menses? Why did you lie? Is it to keep yourself away?"

"Lie? I did not lie. I want nothing more than to be able to make love to you."

The bedroom door opened and she stepped inside, a black ghost against the white walls. He did not notice, his back to her, his hands pushing inside the towel. I tried to stop him, but he grabbed my arms and twisted them behind me, the towel falling away.

"Stop it now!" I cried.

He drew back, the look of bewilderment folding into anger. He said, "So, in the end, I'm not the man you want."

"Sameer!" It was his mother.

He spun around and I tightened the towel about me. The two stared at each other awhile, before Zeba lowered her gaze, as though she was the one ashamed.

She said, "Just minutes before, Beta, you bowed your head to Allah. And now, you are succumbing to *shai-tan*. It's as if you have two men inside you."

Sameer drew in a long breath, his back and shoulders widening. He said, "I do not believe in your scriptures. All these limitations you have put on me." He lunged forward and picked up his boots, shaking them at her. "Look at what you have done to your son!"

She shut her eyes.

"I do not believe!" he yelled, yanking off his prayer cap. He crumpled it and threw it at her feet.

She raised her chin, her lips curled into themselves, trembling.

He grabbed a T-shirt and tucked it under his arm along with the boots as he walked out. A few seconds later, we heard the sound of his motorcycle blazing down the street.

Zeba did not stir and I went and picked up the cap, smoothing it over a palm. She grabbed my hand, the embroidery's thread scratching at my skin.

"If he is like this here, what will he become when you take him to America?"

THE MUSLIM NEIGHBORS wanted to meet the new bride.

There were three other Muslim families on the block, one directly across the street, and two down the road, though in which of the squat houses, I couldn't be sure.

Only the women came, all veiled in lengthy *duppattas* like Zeba's, faces clean of makeup. It was another blazing day, and before Feroz and Ibrahim left for *juma* prayers at the mosque (then on to work and school), they dragged seven chairs out from the *divan* and set them in a circle in the courtyard. I sat in the shade of a lean ashoka tree, some of its pointy, long leaves turned yellow and brittle, scattered about the ground. Zeba sat beside me, more animated among the women than I had ever seen her, though whenever a motorcycle or scooter passed, her eyes flitted to the gates as quickly as mine. Both of us awaited Sameer's return. Above, *koyals* called to each other.

Nafiza set out chai and biscuits, fresh fruit, then sat on the steps of the house. I wished I were alone inside.

The woman from across the street picked up a cup of tea and scraped the bottom against the saucer. She was glancing down, a coy smile teasing her lips. "My son's match has been tied," she announced, suddenly gazing up at me and assessing this other bride. Her eyelids were as dark as Amme's. I turned away. "He's getting married at the end of Zil'hij."

One neighbor had brought along her two adolescent daughters, and the girls glanced at each other and bowed their heads, shyly anticipating their own marriages. Their veils were attractively draped about their fair faces, thick braids pulled out of the fabric, sliding down past their breasts, knotted with matching bows. A flamboyant and daring gesture, meant to catch the eye of men. How different Henna and I had been.

"*Mubarak, mubarak*, Zehra!" the three friends cried, congratulating her.

Then the plump one with the daughters pouted and said, "*Ar're*, I didn't even know you were looking. Why did you keep it a secret, huh, telling me you were going to wait until he finished college?"

Zehra did not answer, and neither girl looked disheartened, as though having pined for the son.

Zeba said, "The end of *Zil'hij*? That's right before Muhar'ram," the month of mourning. "Zehra, have you thought about how you will have to keep the two sleeping apart for the month?" She glanced at the gate and said, "Your son may become . . . cross with you. He will be a new groom, after all. Perhaps it would be better for all if you waited until after Muhar'ram."

Zehra kept her eyes on me. "They have the rest of their lives to have fun. Best to marry them as soon as the match is tied. Nowadays, these arrangements break so easily. *Ar're*, it's not like when we were young. Then, your parents found someone, you got married, and everyone learned to live together. Now . . ." her lips curled up into a sneer, her head shaking.

The woman beside her clucked. She was frail and tall, her eyelids covered with moles. She said, "In times like these, I feel blessed Allah did not grant me children."

"My daughters will marry whomever I tell them to," the mother said, staring sternly at the two girls. The two kept their heads lowered, one sliding her sandal back and forth in the dirt. Her nails were painted purple. The mother said, "They are virtuous girls. No one can say anything against them."

Zehra turned to her. "The truth is, Lubna, it would have been my great kismet to accept one of your daughters, but you see . . ." her voice faltered. She tried to take another sip of chai, but her hand was trembling too much. She set the cup heavily onto the table, the tea splashing out. Nafiza labored off the steps and wiped it with a rag.

Lubna leaned over the tall neighbor and clutched Zehra's hand. A leaf from the ashoka tree fluttered into my lap. I pressed it against my palm. Lubna said, "Allah *raheem*, what is the matter, Zehra?"

Zehra crumpled forward, a hand across her face, hiding it, her back shaking with sobs. The three women exchanged glances. The two girls smiled at each other, an adult's loss of control always a show for the young. I was as invisible to the group as Nafiza, my role in this drama undefined, no longer a girl, not yet among the women.

Zehra jerked away from Lubna and looked up at Zeba, her face moist. It was to my mother-in-law she spoke. "He wanted to marry a girl from college." She licked her lips before saying, "A Hindu! He has fallen in love."

Lubna immediately shifted back into her chair. Her eyes landed on her daughters with a solemn but flat expression.

Zeba nodded, showing no surprise.

The frail one slowly said, "They get these ideas from Hindi films. How many of our Muslim heroes play Hindus? They are never cast as Muslim and all their heroines are Hindu themselves. Then, if that is not enough, they go marry them in real life, forgetting who they are, confused by the parts they play. What kind of role models are they? How can we blame our children?"

There was silence, and in it, Nafiza's throaty cough, the breeze shaking the slim branches and passing a warm hand down my neck. I began tearing the leaf into small pieces.

Zeba said, "Have you met the girl? Maybe she is willing to convert."

"These Hindus never convert! There is no reason for me to meet her."

Zeba selected a biscuit and, dusting the bits of leaf from my palm, pushed it into my hand. I hadn't been able to eat breakfast after he'd left. "Islam runs through the man's blood," she said. "If he is Muslim, their children will be Muslim. That is what is important, that *he* is Muslim . . ."

"Their children! Zeba, I have tied his match to someone else. A distant cousin to him. He's a boy, what does he know? The other day, he even told me that he is the one who has to live with her, not me. *Ar're*, we all have to live with her, with each other, the girl's family and ours, how would that be possible?"

The frail one nodded in agreement. "You did right, Zehra. We are all Indian, that is true, but their culture, their way of life, is very different from ours. We cannot be joined. It is enough that we share the same neighborhood. You must wave and nod when you see them, but that is all, it cannot go any farther than this . . . friendship."

Zehra looked beyond her to Lubna. "It is possible he might hurt the girl, and I didn't want . . . you and I, we are friends and neighbors . . ."

"No, no, no," Lubna said, shaking a plump hand in the air. "There is no need . . . I fully understand." She was relieved for her daughters and, gathering them together, rose to leave.

At the gates, the older one turned back, a finger winding nervously through her hair. "Zeba Auntie," she said, smiling shyly, and I noticed her lips were gleaming with clear gloss. "I didn't see Sameer Bhai today. I thought Friday was his day off."

HE DIDN'T COME home until two in the morning.

Zeba was still sleeping in my bed. When I'd told her my menses had stopped, I saw the suspicion in her slanted eyes even before she told me she wanted to make sure and wait the full seven days. It was over her snoring that I heard his motorcycle turn the corner of our street, the only noise outside but for a lazily barking dog. He switched the engine off before he reached the house, coasting in the rest of the way. The gate creaked open, then the front door. Zeba had left it unlatched for him, not fearing, as we generally did, the threat of intruders.

I was rising from the bed to greet him when he dropped onto the *takat*. All four windows in that room were open, and in the frail night light, I could just make him out. He was sitting with his face in his hands, slumped forward, his back swaying to and fro, the rhythm Zeba and Feroz fell into while reciting the Qur'an. I stopped. It was hard to tell whether he was praying or crying, the sound of any groans washed away by his mother's snores. His head fell lower, all ten fingers scratching at it, then clutching his hair. He sat curled into himself a moment before he suddenly straightened and turned my way. I was sitting up in bed, but the room was dark and the netting heavy, so it was likely he did not see me. He pulled off his boots and T-shirt and slid onto the pillow next to his father.

In the morning, before the call to prayer, he was gone again.

I WAS SITTING under the shade of the ashoka tree, in the circle of chairs that remained in the front courtyard, when Nafiza came and squatted on the ground by my feet. She had been wearing the same sari for almost a week, the deep green of the ashoka leaves set against a maroon border, a print of mangoes. Just as I hadn't considered where Zeba and Ibrahim might sleep in the house, I hadn't thought, until now, where Nafiza would bathe. There were only two bathrooms here, one attached to my bedroom, one in the main area, which Sameer's parents and brother used. A modern structure, with bathrooms inside the house, unlike traditional houses with an inner courtyard, where, set against the back boundary wall, cement one-room structures with roofs of corrugated steel served as the servants' quarters, and where, next to the place they ate and slept, was their own hammam. Here, Nafiza slept in the kitchen.

"Why don't you go bathe in my bathroom, Nafiza? I'm going to be sitting out here for a while. I'm enjoying the peace. I think it's the first time I've been alone since I've come to Hyderabad."

She kept her face lowered, one knee pulled up to her chin, bare toes squashing an ant. Her high bun, coarse and thickly oiled, was almost fully gray, the henna she had applied during my wedding having faded.

"Even if boy here, child, he mama no let him by you side, not in night, not in day. She think boy *must-must*. No-thing stop him from claiming you." *Must* was the word used here to describe animals in heat.

"I'm not in the mood to go around that topic again. You yourself got him pushed out of my bed. Then you saw what happened when he tried to approach me."

"I no come about that, child. I come to ask other thing. Tomorrow Sunday. I go visit me daughter. After I help you *saas* with food, I take bus to me child's house. I miss she, miss me *na'wasi*," granddaughter. "Monday morning, clinic by Roshan's apartment open. I see doctor about me cough. Too many days go on. No-thing help."

"What have you been taking?"

"Herbs."

Herbs, no doubt the kind Raga-be provided. It was like those women who had brought the baby to the blind *alim*, hoping for a miracle when medicine would do. But if it was like them, it was also like me. All of us turned away from doctors, turned away from what we thought it better not to know.

I rose and went to my bedroom and unlocked the *almari*. I took out fifty rupees, then thought better and took out fifty more. A generous allowance, too generous, in fact, perhaps in it a bribe to keep her on my side. Keep my nanny on my side. Her affections for me, her loyalties, bought and paid for. If we were going on pretending nothing had altered between us, then it was simply because we were acting out what we had learned by heart.

I went to the courtyard and took up my chair again. She was sitting where I had left her, chin resting on a weakened knee.

"Get a toy for your *na'wasi*," I said, handing her the money. If she was surprised by the amount, she didn't show it. She simply counted the bills then tucked them into her blouse, against one of her heavy breasts.

THAT NIGHT, IBRAHIM rapped softly at my door and asked me to join him for dinner. Though he didn't say, I knew Zeba must have mentioned that I hadn't been eating well since Sameer's departure. How could I? A week ago, on Saturday night, I had been out with my husband, feeling like I was on a first date, exhilarated. Tonight, after dinner, I would sleep beside his mother, as I had next to my own for years. What kind of virtue was this?

At the table, I sat across from Ibrahim, in the seat I usually took during family meals, Friday mornings, Sundays. There was a plate set out for me and a bottle of the purified water Ibrahim had brought back. Zeba stood over her husband, fanning him with the newspaper, the creases on her face seeming to have deepened overnight. The light in the prayer room was on, Feroz studying inside. Nafiza was already gone.

Ibrahim looked tired, this, the end of his work week. His full cheeks were sunken, his jowls hanging low, his work shirt stained with some sort of grease. Beside his plate, two bottles of medicine to control his ulcer.

He picked up a wooden spoon and began to fill my plate, his own still empty. When I tried to stop him, he snatched the spoon out of my reach.

"There is no shame in first attending to my daughter, only joy. I will think back on this day for many months and, God forbid, maybe even years to come, when you and your husband are in the States. Please, grant me this pleasure." He smiled, and I saw it was Sameer's smile, the same sensuous curve of the lips. As he poured curry over the rice, Zeba quietly instructed him to add more meat, saying it would give me strength. When he was done, he sat back, and she attended to him, serving him food and water.

He raised his glass to mine, brows arched, the loose skin along his forehead crumpling into itself, folding the skin spots. One of his eyes was red and irritated. "To health," he said, taking a sip.

We ate in silence, the refuge of our minds not a threat to the other, and it felt as though I had known no other father. When I was finishing, he nodded his approval, then shook his medicine at me, the pills clattering like a child's rattle.

"Whatever is happening outside, Beta, you must not let it sink into your flesh. Do not punish your body for what it cannot control."

WITH NAFIZA GONE, I decided to help Zeba in the kitchen as she prepared the elaborate breakfast she made on Sundays, one of the two mornings her family was together. She was standing at the stove, too hesitant to let me near the kerosene, knowing I was used to electric burners.

I stood with my back to her, against the black counter, cutting onions with a dull knife. The kitchen had only one window for ventilation, and the cooking fumes and spices, the onions, quickly made me tear.

As I was dabbing my face with my *duppatta*, I said, "He comes in the middle of the night, close to two. He hasn't completely disappeared."

For a moment she was silent and I wondered if she had heard me over the sizzling oil. At last she said, "That boy is always looking for a reason to run out. A week, two weeks, one time he disappeared for a month. I thought he had died. Imagine a mother's heart! When he goes with you to the U.S., I know he will not return."

Not return, I could not imagine that. Six months out of every year spent here. Had my migrations finally come to an end? Of course they had, without my having even realized, the back and forth motions having accomplished exactly what my parents had hoped: launching me into this marriage, into this, my one and only true home, my husband's.

I said, "Where does he go all those days? Have you asked?"

She came over and gathered the sliced onions into a hand then slid them into the oil. It splattered, and she stepped back, covering her face with the black veil.

When I pressed her again, she said, "Beti, I have done my duties as his mother. The rest is between you two. As his wife, you have more power over him than I ever did. Do not forget that. Islam places the woman's role among the highest. It gives you rights to make demands of Sameer, in any capacity you find him failing as a husband and provider."

In the next room, Feroz began cheering and clapping as he had on the wedding night when we'd watched Naveed's strange dance. Zeba and I glanced at each other and went out. Father and son were sitting at the table, the newspaper they had been sharing set aside. They were turned in their chairs, toward the front door. Sameer was here, standing slumped just inside the entrance, his return his victory or surrender, I could not tell. His clothes were crumpled, his face as tired as Ibrahim's had looked last night, dark from stubble. Over his father's head, his eyes met mine, and there was a quick flash, the moment he had pulled me close. The memory sprang up between us, its actuality replacing, at last, what he had only imagined from Nate's letters.

Feroz welcomed his brother home and Sameer blinked, heading for the bedroom. He ducked under the doorway, not fully closing the door behind him. I moved to follow, but Zeba clutched my arm and stopped me.

"He has come back for you, that is enough for now. Let him sleep."

MONDAY NIGHT, SHE let him back into my bed.

Before he came into the room, I dressed in the silky silver nightdress Amme had bought for me, and which I hadn't thought I would ever wear, preparing myself for him in much the way he had, over the last year, prepared himself for me, giving shape to his form. Then I arranged myself on the bed, the netting's heavy curtain about me, a nervousness inside I had not even experienced on the wedding night . . . or the night Nate had slipped in.

He entered without a word and dimmed the lights. I watched him move to the window and bolt its heavy shutter, the hot air going still and flat. He pulled off his shirt and cast it across his clothes chest. The bed creaked as he set a knee on it, crawling inside. For a moment, we did nothing—could do nothing—but stare at one another, the flesh that had been forbidden for a week somehow grown more attractive.

We sat facing each other, as Henna and I had two nights before my wedding, and I suddenly understood I did not know what to do. Those few hours, almost two months ago, had taught me little about men, how it was they liked to be—should be—touched. Nate had not expected anything from me, the virgin, except my full surrender. Sameer, he expected me to provide, *razzaq*.

I reached out and pressed my palm against his, and his thick brows twitched, confused. Clumsy move, one belonging to a different life, to Henna and me, not suitable here, with him. I untied the knot of his loose pajamas and the fabric fell open, exposing his bare hips. Still, he did not stir, and I rose to my knees and maneuvered onto his thighs, squeezing myself against him. His face was smothered in my neck. He laughed and, in one quick motion, had me flat on my belly, his body gliding up the back of mine, weighing me down.

He whispered into my ear, "You did not read the letters I sent."

We were lying horizontally on the bed, his feet hanging out the netting's door, dangling over the edge. With his nose, he rolled the strap off my shoulder.

"Of course I read them." And I had, but none of what he had described he would do, none of that filth, felt like this.

"Do you remember what I want, what I have asked of you, my wife?" He was pulling up my dress, gripping my legs, easing them open. He guided my toes into a curve of the peacock's wings. These were not the awkward moves of a guileless lover. Indeed, if I had been expected to be innocent, so, too, had he.

He pushed himself against my buttocks, the first time I was feeling him, his flesh sticking to mine in the heat. I stiffened. He relaxed, slipping down to lick my lower back, cool saliva made cooler by the overhead fan. He tugged off the pajamas from around his ankles. I rolled over, hiding myself.

"Teach me how to touch you."

He gazed up at me, the tip of his tongue slicing through his front teeth. He brought his thumb to his mouth and wrapped his lips around the toe ring before sliding the entire thing inside. He sucked at it, releasing it slowly, the sound like a kiss as it glided out.

ZEBA BEGAN TEACHING me Arabic the next afternoon. The book she pulled out had once belonged to Sameer, his name written in a childish scrawl across the cover. Inside, all the spaces where he was to copy the Arabic letters were filled in. The alphabet was similar to the Urdu I had grown up learning, though shorter and having vowel accents, so it was as if I had always carried it inside, an echo of my own first language. Zeba was pleased, and within an hour, we were sitting on the ground in the prayer room, both enveloped in heavy *duppattas*, the Qur'an open before us. I felt guilty reading it with the bleeding not fully gone, but, of course, I'd acted out worse sins than this.

Incense was burning and the small room filled with gray smoke, reminding me of the bridal fumes that had risen up inside me on the wedding day, giving my old body new form. From a ghost I had materialized into this life.

"Alif, lam, ra."

The Arabic letters merged and cut each other short so that it was hard for me to tell where one ended and another began, or which letter it was I was reading—trying to read. In English, individual letters remained full and complete, unto themselves, recognizable even in cursive. If culture was language, this was how it would appear.

"These are the verses of the Glorious Book. We have revealed the Qur'an in the Arabic tongue so you may understand it."

Each page of the Qur'an was beautifully crafted, cream with a green border, the calligraphy etched in gold. On top, a design of leaves strung together, a vine running to the edge and continuing on the following page. Down the right side, a translation in Urdu to what we had just recited. The chapter on Joseph.

"In revealing this Qur'an We will recount to you the best of histories, though before We revealed it you were heedless of Our signs."

When the incense burned down, Zeba lit another, and when it, too, had burned away, a small pile of ash on the copper holder, she closed the book. We stood together and prayed the late afternoon salat.

When we were done, she turned to me and said, "My grandmother spoke and understood Arabic, now I read Arabic but need an Urdu translation. Tomorrow, your children will need an English translation. Every day we grow farther from our roots."

HE WAS LYING on his back, arms under his head as he stared up at the spinning ceiling fan. He had closed the shutters again, the canopy of the netting bowed under the pressure of the revolving air, none of it reaching us. I was on my side, head propped up on a hand, studying the body I was still not used to. His skin was various tones of brown, his stomach, his chest, the round muscles of his arms almost the color Nate had been, while his forearms, his neck, his face—those parts of him exposed to the sun—took on the deepness of the honey his mother fed Ibrahim, two pills for the ulcer, one spoon of honey, the elixir, according to Islam, against illness.

I had determined to ask him what was between him and his mother, though I had to ease my way into it, knowing he could draw himself closed, draw away.

I said, "Your mother began tutoring me in the Qur'an today. We used one of your old lesson books."

He took in a deep breath, hard ribs pushing out against his flesh. I followed the curve of one with a finger.

"Do you disapprove?"

He turned down his lips to show he didn't, but when he spoke, I could hear his voice growing rigid with tension. "Why should I disapprove? We each have our own beliefs. What is important is not to push your beliefs onto others."

"She hasn't pushed anything onto me. She's teaching me because she says it's her maternal duty, as she once taught you . . . and still tries."

"Still tries," he said, now fully stiffening with anger. "Yet, I'm no longer the boy who scribbled into that *Arabi* book, am I? I'm twenty-four. I have a college degree. Bloody hell, I have a wife! Her duties to me are complete, Layla. Even her Islam says parents must teach the tenets to their children, but if a child chooses differently, the sins belong to the child alone. If the Allah she worships provides me free will and personal responsibility, why can't she! Ask her that when she tutors you next!" He began to shift away and I pulled him back, resting my head on his shoulder to keep him in place. He closed his eyes, hands stiffly by his side, refusing to touch me. He must have thought I had joined up with his mother, against him. "Don't make the burden of your religion my burden, Layla. Don't become . . . intolerant."

Intolerant. Yet Zeba had been the one to advise the neighbor to let her son marry the Hindu girl.

"This is more than religion, isn't it, Sameer? What did she do that was so intolerant?"

He was silent and a muscle in his shoulder twitched against my cheek. Overhead, the fan creaked as it rotated, and, in the next room, his mother's abrasive snoring. Finally, he took my hand and guided it down to his pajamas, untying them. "See for yourself what she has done to me. The light is on. You can take a good look at your husband." His voice pitched with pain, an embarrassment I had not heard even the night he had confronted me about Nate.

I rose and sat by his waist. He continued to stare up at the overhead fan, jaw rigid, arms once more behind his head. When I tugged at the fabric, he raised his hips, letting me slide it down, and I realized I had not seen him fully naked before. Even last night, the room was so dim, we were but shadows of ourselves.

When I had taken the pajamas off, I understood even before he tapped his right leg that he was showing me his injury. There were no scars that I could see, no protrusions of any sort. Still, the entire thigh was weakened and frail, almost half the size of the other. Where there was a hard line of muscle nervously flexing in the left, there was nothing in the injured leg but soft flesh.

His eyes were on me, and I tried not to show any alarm.

"I don't understand. How could she . . ."

"How much do you know about the accident?"

"A bike injury when you were eighteen, nothing more."

He looked up at the ceiling again. "I was heading for the Dabir Pura Doors to get home, and there was this ox cart in front of me, moving so bloody slow I thought I would pass it on the left. I didn't see the Ambassador coming from the other direction. I faltered," he paused and licked his lips. "No, I lost control. *I* lost control," he repeated, as though that had been the true accident. Then he pointed up at the fan and his arm slowly imitated its rotation. "There's a big bolt at the center of the cart's wheel. It pierced into my thigh, then kept turning. It dragged me to the other side of the door, where I fell into a garbage heap. There's a *paan* stall there and the *paan-wala* got me into an auto-rickshaw and to Osmania Hospital. My muscle was chewed up, the femur cracked, but it could have been corrected, except Mum . . . except she . . ." His lips curled into themselves, the words refusing to come out. At last, he spat, "She refused to pay for anything. It's a bloody government hospital, it wouldn't have been much . . ." his words simply halted.

"I don't understand."

He smirked. "Faith, baby. Her faith. She said I'd become an infidel, and God punished infidels. The leg would always remind me of what I'd become."

"Those whom you serve besides Him are names which you and your fathers have invented and for which Allah has revealed no sanction. Judgment rests with Allah only . . . That is the true faith: yet most men do not know it."

That was what Zeba and I had read just that afternoon. Punishment and judgment are Allah's rights alone. How could a woman who, in every other way, had shown herself to me to be a true believer, have erred with her own child? It did not make sense, a follower turned into a god, a servant with the power to arbitrate. Yet here it was, as clearly as Amme had stayed on with Dad after he'd divorced her. Sins in any language.

I began kissing Sameer's thigh, and though at first he moaned in shame, trying to pull me away, at last, he drew my mouth to him, sighing, giving in.

ON WEDNESDAY, NAFIZA finally showed up, two days later than she'd vowed.

She returned wearing a fresh sari, her gray hair tight in a high bun and no longer slick with coconut oil. Zeba and I had just finished breakfast, and I thought my nanny had come in time to help with the afternoon meal. Then I heard a car pull up at the gates, the engine's groan deeper than Amme's Fiat, and just as familiar. A big Ambassador, the kind that had caused Sameer's accident. Taqi Mamu and his wife were here.

"I bring chai for guests," Nafiza said, avoiding my eye as she hurried to the kitchen, a flair of triumph about her. So she had gone and invited them, no doubt to confront me about Sameer. Now there was no way out of this.

Zeba took my arm and led me to the front gates to greet them. Ameera Auntie was still in the driver's seat, her head wrapped with the edge of the sari-*pallow*, the end gripped between her teeth. Taqi Mamu had wandered out and down to the dead end, where he stood smoking and staring into the empty field. Early this morning, as the imam was tapping the loudspeaker, there had also been the pattering of rain, though not enough to rescue the bowed grasses. He turned, sucking at the cigarette, and saw Zeba and me.

"*Ar're!*" he said, his large eyes growing wider in surprise, his hands spreading open. He quickly put out the cigarette and headed over, fingers passing through his thick hair. "We haven't even knocked, and you knew we were here! *Kamal ki baat hai*."

Ameera Auntie emerged from the car, her back wet with sweat. "I told the school my sugar was acting up," she said, "freeing myself to visit my favorite niece." She embraced me and I smelled the mothballs that she put in her *almari* on her skin and clothes. "Married for three weeks and not one visit. Have you forgotten about us?" she scolded, though I could tell she understood why I hadn't come. She pulled away to embrace Zeba, but her eyes still scrutinized me, at last landing on the *duppatta* I was now so used to wearing. "So married life has tamed you," she said as she winked and tugged at her own *pallow*.

Zeba asked the couple inside, and though I had thought she would lead them into the inner part of the house and seat them on the *takat* the family used during the day, she instead seated them in the *divan*, the room for guests. My mother-in-law and uncle had known each other since childhood, so I understood these formalities centered around me. The two were no longer old friends but new in-laws.

Nafiza served chai, then sat on the floor by the door, out of my sight, though I could feel her eagerly listening. Cockroaches, that was what servants were, moving about the walls of things, living off the muck of our lives. It was not in her capacity to understand she was doing me in.

Ameera Auntie leaned forward to peek into the main room, at Zeba and Ibrahim's *takat*, then shot me that coy smile I had seen her use with Dad at the *walima* dinner. I noticed her lips were tinted a blushing pink. "Where is your husband?" she asked me. "I haven't seen him since the wedding. He looked so handsome in his *shamlah*, I was surprised at myself for not having noticed before." She cleared her throat. "Noticed him, I mean."

Taqi Mamu was impatiently drumming his fingers against his cup, already staring out the window. He wanted to go. *Such matters were for the women of the house*, that was what he had said long ago when, in protest to this marriage, I had locked myself in their bedroom. Would I buckle again?

I said, "He tutors every day."

Her frail hand went to her breast. "Tutors! Does he know I teach? One day I'll have to talk to him about his tutoring. Students nowadays can be so difficult. There is this strange . . . dullness about them."

"Why should they study?" Taqi Mamu grumbled, not taking his eyes from the window. "What will it get them? Hindus get all the jobs, all the seats at colleges. Even a harijan is more valuable than a Muslim. This country is trying to erase us."

Ameera Auntie gently tapped his arm. "Remember why we have come," she whispered.

Zeba set her chai on the table and said, "Taqi Bhai, you look exactly like your father, but you could be no more different. What would he say if he could hear you speaking like that?"

Taqi Mamu turned to her, and his nostrils flared even more. "My father made a great mistake by not taking his family to Pakistan. We would have been much better off there. Look at us now. Elections are coming up, do you think it matters which party is elected? No one will bother about us. We're invisible." He mumbled something to his wife and rose, straightening his button-down shirt as he walked out. Through the window, I could see him standing by the front gates, his back to us as he smoked again.

"Ruling parties rule for themselves," Zeba said to Ameera Auntie. "They don't bother about the public, they just swindle as much money as possible in the five years of office—at least, that is what my husband says. Corruption and *rish'wat*," bribes. She smoothed her *duppatta* and stared up at the only thing that adorned this room, a round plaque with Allah Mohammed scrawled across the center. God, the only thing she was really sure of outside these walls.

Ameera Auntie set down her tea, then motioned for Nafiza to come fetch the empty cups. Nafiza didn't move. My aunt said, "You must forgive my husband. He's just returned from NagarJuna Sagar. He becomes like this every time he goes."

Taqi Mamu stuck his head through the window and spoke more forcefully than I had ever heard. "For eight years I have been fighting. It's my father's land, my land. *Ar're*, they go and build this immense dam there, it's like a corner of the sky has fallen into the Krishna River. And all these tourists picnicking on what rightfully belongs to me, and you know what they offer? Two *lakh*. Two *lakh* for five hundred acres of that land! The house we own in Vijayanagar is worth twice that. This plot next to your house, which is weeds, not a rich jungle, is worth more. They take me for a fool!"

"I'm telling him to take it," Ameera Auntie said. Then she turned to him and spoke as slowly as I imagined she would before a classroom, her hand tapping the chair's arm. "The money is not what matters. What matters is that they have acknowledged that it belongs to you. That is what is important."

Taqi Mamu grimaced before he ducked out the window again. "I'm walking home," he said over his shoulder as he unlocked the gates. "The largest masonry dam in the world," he called out, mocking whoever had told him, then went on to talk to himself in that way Ammie did. "*Ar're*, that's not a dam. It's Partition. That is what Partition looks like." His words grew fainter as he moved farther away from the house, the diminishing grumbling like Sameer's motorbike pulling away.

"Have you been there?" Ameera Auntie asked me. "They have cottages for honeymooners. It might help Sameer to relax."

So there it was, the opening to why she had come, like the head of a king cobra my uncle used to see in that very jungle, poking up from between tangled roots.

Zeba shook her head. "My daughter returning to her ancestral land as a tourist! Her grandfather wouldn't even approve."

"But she is a tourist here, in Hyderabad. She has not come here to live."

Zeba raised her chin in that way she had when Sameer threw down his prayer cap. She said, "Maybe she will stay this time, now that she has a home."

AMEERA AUNTIE ASKED me to walk her to the car, and when she noticed Nafiza tagging along, she stopped her in the courtyard and said, "There is no reason for you to come, Nafiza. You and I have already had our private talk."

"*Memsa'ab*," Nafiza said, startled, and even in the shade of the trees, I could see her small face growing darker. "You no taking child away in car?"

Ameera Auntie blinked at her, lashes short and pointy. "Go back to the house, Nafiza. Do the work you were sent here to do, nothing more."

"Yes, *memsa'ab*," my nanny said in her most formal tone. But as soon as Ameera Auntie turned for the gates, she grabbed my elbow and whispered, "I no tell she about you, Layla-bebe, only about the boy. I no betray you."

Ameera Auntie shooed her away and led me out to the street, closing the gates behind us. She leaned up against her car, arms crossed over her slender chest. Sick as she was, she was one of the only women I had ever seen driving here. She said, "Before I came, I did not know in what condition I would find you. I wondered if you had been the one to send Nafiza, asking through her to return home. Now, my heart is relieved. You seem happy here . . . in spite of all."

Happy, the one word could not contain how I felt. For so long, I had been unwanted in Amme's home, a *shai'tan* needing to be exorcised. Now, finally, I was a daughter, seen and touched, being urged to stay. My presence already missed. Why would I go back to being the ill-fated daughter?

"My in-laws don't call me Bahu," I said, Daughter-in-Law. "They say Beti," Daughter. "Feroz calls me Bhabhi. And I am, of course, Sameer's *bevi*. In this home, I have a place, I belong."

"A *bevi*," she repeated as she reached in through the open window for her sunglasses. She put them on, wide and thick and red, her face made more slim. "I am glad you know there is more than just *one* duty in being a wife. It is good to see you are no longer behaving as a child, Layla. You will better understand the decision we have made, see how it will benefit you. After Nafiza came to me, your *mamu* and I went to your Abu Uncle's and Asma Kala's. The four of us agree you have done right to stay on with Sameer—though we do regret you did not tell Zeba the truth. Still, we've decided not to tell your *amme* either, she already has so many . . . sorrows. And she may not fully understand, being married to a man like your father." Her gaze faltered and she cleared her throat, and I thought I saw a rush of blood rise up in her again, the memory of him at the *walima* dinner, his light eyes on her.

She began fingering her sari's pleats. "Remember what I told you at your *mun-jay* ceremony, Layla. You've got to help him out, and while he's learning, you've got to be patient. These young Indian boys, no matter how strong they look outside, inside they are scared. This is not America, where girls and boys interact and date, do everything before marriage then grow bored of each other by the time they are married. Here, we marry two young people and expect them to suddenly have emotions for one another. What no one tells you is that it takes time. I do not have to lecture you in biology, Layla, as though you were an innocent student of mine, but let me say that even for men, sometimes, it is a matter of feeling. Beta, he has probably not been with anyone else. To him, you are an American woman. He probably thinks he must be like . . . like Rambo! Do you see why he would feel nervous, even fear? Tell me," she said, leaning toward me, my face and torso caught in her lenses, looking so small. "Has he made no move toward you at all?"

He had made moves, and they weren't inexperienced, nor jittery and nervous. Indeed, if we hadn't had intercourse these past couple of nights, it was merely because he was too relaxed after I'd put him into my mouth—but how to explain that to my aunt, the trick I had learned to slowly uncoil my husband, luring him to me day by day. Just as a bride could slowly be possessed over the five wedding days, I was taking possession of my bridegroom in increments.

She looked toward the front gates to make sure no one was there before she whispered, "When you go to Madras, get him drunk. Don't laugh, Layla, this is a serious matter for men. Your Abu Uncle said that when he first got married, he couldn't go near your aunt for two months! Two months! Finally, she had a servant bring some *tadhi*." She grinned, not caring to hide behind her *pallow*, and it was the first time I had seen her entire face flush in enjoyment. She almost looked healthy. "He never left her alone after that. A taste of us, that's all they need."

Yes, a taste, but not of blood.

She patted my shoulder and got into the car, starting it up. I backed away to give her the space to turn the fat thing around, when she crooked her finger and invited me to come near. I leaned in through her window, noticing the thick smell of vinyl.

"The blind *alim* told your uncle the leg injury is up by the hip, is this true?"

I nodded. "The leg is . . . weaker than the other," I said, somehow feeling Sameer's shame myself.

She bit her lower lip. "Beta," she said, taking on the manner she did when she used to tutor me in Urdu. It meant there was only one way to correctly read what was before us. "If nothing changes in Madras, then we all agree he should be taken to a doctor. Your Abu Uncle thinks . . . well, you see, the injury is so close to his . . . you know what I am saying. Maybe it has made him . . . useless to women." She slapped her palms together, rotating them around in the gesture the eunuch *hijras* made.

THE FOLLOWING AFTERNOON, Zeba and I knelt side by side in the *ashur-khana*, each of us on a small velvet prayer rug, the incense smoke burning my eyes and making them water. I had to hold one shut as I tried to read the Qur'an. She was letting me recite alone, interfering only when I mixed up a letter—*kaf* for *ghaf*, *ra* for *zha*, just one strike here, one dot there made all the difference in the meaning of the word. She was a much more patient teacher than Ameera Auntie had ever been.

I was still making my way through the *surah*, chapter, on Joseph.

> *And when they took Joseph with them, they decided to cast him into a dark pit. We addressed him saying, "You shall tell them of all this when they will not know you."*

At nightfall they returned weeping to their father. They said: "We went racing and left Joseph with our goods. The wolf devoured him" . . .

And a caravan passed by, who sent their waterman to the pit. And when he had let down his pail, he cried: "Rejoice! A boy!"

They took Joseph and concealed him among their goods. But Allah knew what they did. They sold him for a trifling price, for a few pieces of silver. They cared nothing for him.

The Egyptian who brought him home said to his wife: "Use him kindly. He may prove useful to us, or we may adopt him as our son."

Zeba placed a hand over mine to stop me from going further. She read aloud the Urdu translation, then said, "What will it take to keep you here, in my home?"

She was staring up at the facing wall, three religious plaques one on top of the other. In the creases along her broad cheekbones, the glassy shine of tears. She seemed more in silent prayer with Allah than in conversation with me, and I could see from the stillness of her heavy chest, breath abated, that for her, to be granted what she was asking would be a miracle.

I said, "Growing up, it was always so confusing to be in both places. I would go to school there and all the kids would point and say, 'Hey, look, the Indian girl is back.' Then I'd suddenly be dropped into school here, and the girls would say, 'The American is back.' I never fit in. I could never make friends—I was different from everyone, and I would be leaving again in six months. Who wanted a friend like that? I told Amme to let me stay here, in one place. I told her that if she needed to return to the U.S., I could go live with Henna. Mummy," I said, surprising myself, though she did not even blink, our relationship, to her, no matter what I called her, remaining the same. "America seems very far away right now. I would be happy to go on living here."

She did not take her eyes from the plaques. "But it is your husband who must be convinced. They say, Beti, that for dawn prayer, the wife alone has the power to raise her husband from sleep, she the one lying by his side. I fear the call has come for you to awaken him." She closed her eyes, the lids shaped like Sameer's, like rose petals. "I had an alarming dream that week I was sleeping in your bed, Beti. Now, whenever I shut my eyes, I see it again. It will not let me rest."

So she had met my demon, after all.

"I dreamt you were pregnant, Beti, with a tiny little boy. He was fair and his eyes opened gray-blue; he looked like an American. He was crying. The fluid around him was not clear, it was red, like blood. He was dying." She opened her eyes again, muttering, "*La hol bil'la quwat*," to do away with evil and raised the Qur'an to her face and pressed her forehead against the prayers that had never changed.

"There is no future in America, Beti. Your grandfather was right: our home is here."

THAT NIGHT IN bed, while he lay relaxed beside me, his breathing growing deep and even, I told him about my parents' divorce.

I was lying sideways on the bed, my head resting on his stomach, feeling the gentle rise and fall of his belly. While I spoke, the creaking of the overhead fan, the sound of Zeba's snoring, even my husband's calm breath softened into the unbearable silence of my mother's suburban house. Three levels, six bedrooms, four bathrooms, just she and I living in it together, after he left us.

"When he was gone, I took over," I said, "trying to become her companion. I would take her to movies and restaurants, we would dress and go together to her friends' dinner parties. I'd watch her when we were there. She would always sit by herself, not really talking to anyone. Later, she would tell me they had nothing important to say. But she was like that with me, too. I'd come home from school so we could have dinner together, but she'd flip on some Hindi movie, and we'd eat in front of the TV. I think she was always looking for Sabana's face. She's all my mother ever talked about, and my own future wedding. She wanted to give me what she didn't have herself, a home."

He grunted, his hand smoothing back my hair. But he said nothing, not expressing surprise or disdain.

I said, "Sameer, she didn't come out of her room for a month, not until he signed some damn agreement she'd drawn up. I was ten and they think I have no memory of this. They think . . . they've always thought of me as a ghost."

I sat up and pressed my thumb into the center of my palm, where his initials had once been drawn red with henna. "Say something," I said. "Tell me—*vow* to me—that you'll give me a home. It's not enough what you said on the wedding night, that I belong to you. *You* must belong to me, too."

He raised himself on an elbow and finally looked at me with the surprise I'd been expecting all along. "Layla," he whispered, as his hand pushed into my hair. His fingers pressed into the back of my neck and drew my face close to his. When he spoke, I took in his breath. "I thought you understood. When I came back home the other day, I came back to you. Nothing has the power to drag me away, not anymore. *You* live inside of me." He brought my hand to his heart. "I swear to you, nothing—nobody—will ever take your place. Your home is with me, no matter where we are, your home is with me, safely, I swear."

NAFIZA'S DAUGHTER CAME to visit.

I did not know where to seat her, not because she was like my aunt and uncle, both an old and new relation, but because, growing up, I had known her as a servant. As such, like Nafiza, she had always taken a place on the floor. But, then, at sixteen, Roshan had fallen in love and married a man who owned a corner cafe, elevating herself out of servitude. Now, rather than living in my uncle's back quarters, she rented an apartment with her husband, one not much smaller, I guessed, than this place.

I gestured to the *divan* to show her she could sit anywhere. Let it be her decision, not mine, now that choices were open to her. She took a chair near the bamboo table, but when I offered chai, she declined. Not comfortable being waited on by her mother, or not comfortable around me in her elevated role (it had already been seven years), I could not tell. I sat across from her and wondered what it was she had come to say. No doubt, she, too, had been summoned here by my nanny, her mother.

She was wearing a bright red sari that made her dark skin appear even darker, and a thick braid swung at her waist. Her prescription glasses looked to have been passed on to her by Ameera Auntie.

"Where is your daughter?" I asked.

"My husband will watch her until three thirty, when he must go open the cafe again. He comes home every day for lunch." My aunt's tutoring had trained Roshan not to speak like her mother, but she was still unaccustomed to a chair. Even now, she was resting at the edge, hands clasped between her knees so that the sari's pleats dove between her thighs. An ungainly way to sit.

Nafiza carried in chai, holding a cup in either hand. For any other guest, she would have used a tray, as she had with my aunt and uncle. She set mine on the table before me, the cup clattering against the saucer. I noticed she handed Roshan a cup with a fine crack in it, the one she had reserved in this house for herself. It had no saucer. Roshan took the tea and nodded side to side at Nafiza, mother and daughter not addressing each other in any other way.

Without glancing at me, Nafiza left the room. Since my aunt's visit yesterday, she had been brusque with me, as though I had been the one who had secretly gone to my relatives and somehow turned them against her.

Roshan cleared her throat, then rested the cup on her knees. "My mother is worried about you," she said, her eyes flitting to the door behind Nafiza. After a moment, the two older women's voices came from the kitchen, too deep within the house to overhear us. "Amme is worried that your husband is fooling you. My mother has raised you as much as she has raised me. When she looks at you, she sees . . . well, she must see a girl like my own four-year-old. She wants to protect you."

"Yes, I know, but what I don't know is what she wants to protect me from, do you? Does she?"

She lowered her head and the glasses slid down her nose. "It was to see what he might be hiding from you that she asked my husband to follow him."

"Follow Sameer?"

"*Hahn, bebe*, to see where he goes all day."

Bebe. She was reverting back to her old role, calling me ma'am, and so telling me that, whether or not I approved, they had gone out of their way for my benefit, such was their allegiance to me.

"He goes tutoring, I already know that."

"In the afternoons, he tutors between eleven and four. His college is very far from here, in Banjara Hills, one hour by motorbike. My husband . . ."

"So where is he in the mornings?" I asked in spite of myself. "He leaves here close to six."

"He goes to the park."

"The park?"

"There is a park in the Old City, very close to your mother's house. It is where he goes to exercise. He runs and lifts heavy equipment."

"What else?"

"Nothing else. From the park, he goes to college."

What was she saying then? Had she ridden a bus all this way to tell me Sameer's schedule; that, in the end, her mother was wrong, he was doing nothing to fool me?

"Roshan, I'm not sure why you've come today. You made me anxious for no reason."

She set her cup on the table between us, not having taken a sip, and pushed up her glasses. "Just as my mother is your mother, your mother is like my own. She has always shown me love and given me money and clothes. She was the one who paid for Bisma's delivery. Layla," she said, then, "*bebe*, I know about the . . . *gora* man and your bleeding. There is a woman doctor by my house, the one who delivered Bisma. She is very good. Her clinic is open on Mondays and Wednesdays. I could go with you . . . while your husband is away. Layla . . . *bebe*, we have shared the same milk, there is nothing wrong with sharing secrets. We are like sisters."

WHEN NAFIZA WAS preparing my room for sleep, I went in behind her and shut the door. She was hunched over beside the bed, poking the stick broom underneath it, and a dried up marigold rolled out.

She said, "Why you say no to me daughter, child? She take you to doctor. Doctor clean you inside. Better for when you go home."

"Go home? Nafiza, after all you've done, you're lucky I'm not sending you home! Please don't make me remind you of who you are!"

"I no forget me-self, Layla-bebe. You husband, he forget. Look at he! Every day he dress in new *Umrikan* clothes, looking pretty-pretty. The woman across the street, she tell me today it look like you husband is *Umrikan* and you with *duppatta* around you, look like you from here. I tell she, 'No, no, me no care what me child look like, me no forget who she is. She forget, he forget, but no me.' " She coughed into her shoulder and it sounded thicker.

"Did you only run around confessing my problems, or did you visit a doctor about your own health?" Anger and concern mixed together; I was sounding like Amme.

"Me no worry-worry about me-self, child. Me have full life. When me time come, Allah take me, no medicine, no doctor can stop him. Me worry-worry about you. You young girl. You pretty, more pretty than he. No reason you waste life with man like him."

"Things have changed between us, Nafiza, that's what I've come to tell you. There is no reason anymore for you to go to Zeba, as you have to everyone else . . ."

"No-thing change, Layla-bebe. I clean you bed each morning, I see me-self. No-thing change. You think because you put *duppatta* around face and pray with he mama that everything change. No-thing change between you and you husband. Still, he man who no real man. Still, you wife who no real wife. This home no real home for you, child! *Tho!*" she spat to show her disgust, then quickly swept it up with the rest of the waste.

THE IMAM WAS tapping the loudspeaker, ready to start the azan.

I bit Sameer's ear. He stirred, eyes staying shut, though he was grinning, drawing me close. I passed a hand over his thighs, then squeezed between them, feeling him harden. Certainly not what Zeba had meant when she'd said that, in the morning, only a wife had the power to rouse her husband.

"Later," I promised, "if you come now and pray."

His eyes shot open. "What! Bloody hell, Layla, I knew this would happen." He turned away, the pillow once more bent over his head. I took his thumb into my mouth and sucked in the way he'd shown me, warm lips tugging and extracting the silver ring. He groaned, and an arm swept back and around my waist. He pulled me over him and flattened me against the wall, then rubbed himself against my buttocks.

"I'm doing this for you," he said, "not her, not her god."

So I got him to dress, and we joined the others in the prayer room. No one had knocked today in hope of waking us, and when Zeba saw Sameer by my side, her lips turned up in that small grin, the lines around her mouth, the corners of her eyes, deepening, lightening up her face. She handed me Sameer's prayer cap with its delicate embroidery, and I set it on my husband's head, and, in this way, she passed on to me what she had, till then, considered her responsibilities. She freed herself of her son.

We aligned ourselves in the small room, Sameer standing ahead of me as Ibrahim stood ahead of Zeba, Feroz by his father's side. Islamic prayer is a personal ritual, no loud sermons, no priest standing between

God and devotee, telling you how to approach him, read him, how to be forgiven, redemption. There is only you, and all of what you have done, and God's mercy.

I was looking to be pardoned for Nate, who had, from a man, taken the form of blood, then vomit from my husband's body. From desire had come revulsion. Repelled, Sameer had said on the wedding night, he had been repelled by me, by my flesh, a baby floating in blood, draining out. Now, every night I put him into my mouth, it was to uncoil him, yes, but also to prevent him from pushing into me, fingers, tongue, penis, prevent him from becoming repelled by the very flesh aching to open for him. A month-long punishment for a single night.

So I stood repentant before Allah, behind my husband, bowing, prostrating simultaneously, whispering prayers, my words lapping over his, his over mine, gaining strength, not a sparring at all, but a great union.

Allah *raheem.*

AT BREAKFAST, IBRAHIM presented Sameer with our rail tickets to Madras. We were scheduled to leave the following Friday, the morning after his tutoring duties came to an end.

Sameer rose from his seat and, rounding his brother at the end of the table, embraced his father. Zeba glanced at me. It was my responsibility now to ensure that her son, the one who carried her handsome face, had a future. And there was no future there.

Sameer spoke into his father's neck, hopes for a place he'd never seen. "When I get to the U.S., I'm going to work hard, Papa, I'm going to send back enough money for you to retire in two years. You've got to take care of your health."

Ibrahim patted him on the back. "First you take care of yourself and your wife. Then you think about taking care of others."

"And I'll bring Feroz over as soon as I can. You don't worry about him anymore. He's in my charge." As he was returning to his seat, he slapped his brother's head with the tickets. "Keep studying, huh. It may seem useless now, but you'll need a degree in the U.S. Can't get ahead without one."

Feroz grinned, his mouth full of *paratha*, and nodded his head side to side, eyes glistening with *surma*. I had never thought of him as wanting to come to America.

When Sameer was beside me again, he squeezed my hand under the table, then leaned over and kissed me, right in front of his family. I didn't pull away.

Zeba did not take her eyes from my face, my behavior unsettling her, making her see the other side of me, my twin, as Sameer had said. Indeed, if she had handed her son over to a woman who had led him to the prayer room, she had also handed him over to the woman who had the American passport to take him away. She said, "Elections are coming up. A young Muslim couple traveling alone. You hear stories. Rapes, killings. Maybe you should wait until it passes."

Sameer moved back into his chair, and his body stiffened as his presence withdrew. He spoke slowly, "Wait until what passes, Mum?"

"The tension between Hindus and Muslims."

"That would mean I could never go."

She finally turned to Sameer. "The limitations you accuse me of setting on you have always been meant to protect you, save you."

Ibrahim took Zeba's hand in both of his, a gesture of affection I'd never seen before between parents.

"I, too, do not want our children to leave us, Zeba, but it is not our decision to make. We are here only to facilitate their dreams." He turned to Sameer and me, one eye irritated and red, the way it looked when he returned from work. "Beta, going to Madras is only the first step in your lifelong journey together. As much as your mother and I are excited for you two, you must understand that we also have fears. We want you to be happy, we want you not to make mistakes." He sighed as he glanced at Zeba, and she nodded, urging him on.

"For many years, Sameer, you have spoken of going to America. You have worked hard at school not to find a job here, but determined to make your way there. Beta, America is a great place, and, *inshal'lah*, it will give you everything you have found lacking in your home. But America's opportunities will also expose you to a great many new freedoms. You will be tempted, I know, you may even forget yourself . . . lose yourself there."

He stopped and stared down at the table, the spots on his scalp the color of his kurta. "You and I have always held countering life philosophies. You have opposed me on many decisions, such as urging me to take *rish'wat* so that I could afford to buy a house and put inside it those things that you think make life more appealing, a color TV, a stereo and telephone, a car at the front gates. But you must remember, Beta, that possession, any possession, comes with a fee. It is like these politicians you are reading about each day in the papers. They take money from the public, but till today we have no clean drinking water, and day by day so much pollution thickens the air that I have to cover my face with a handkerchief the entire two hours to and from work! Still, look at my eye, always red. And look at what is happening to my skin, look at these spots. No doctor can tell me what they are. See, Beta, who is suffering? We are. Who is benefiting? Only a handful of people. In this way, do not place the good of yourself over the well-being of your family. Yes, work hard, get ahead in life, continue wearing all these flashy American clothes, but do not forget who you are inside. In the many things you will be leaving behind in India, do not entirely leave behind the person your mother and I have raised you to be, so driven by impulse that you become a man his own father cannot recognize . . . or his own wife!"

Sameer lowered his head and let out a long breath, his shoulders slumping. His lips were pursed, so I knew he was stopping himself from speaking, not wanting to oppose his father. The tickets began to bend in his grip.

Ibrahim set them on the table, then clasped Sameer's hand into mine. "No matter where you are, keep your life simple—that is all I am saying. Remember, a rich man is not one who has the most, but one who desires the least."

ZEBA ASKED ME if I still wanted to join Feroz and her in the prayer room to recite the Qur'an as the two had been doing every Friday for eleven years. We had talked about my doing so all week, ever since she started tutoring me and saw how many Arabic letters I could actually recognize and knot together. Guttural sounds, that was what I produced, a hum from deep within the throat, with no understandable meaning for me except that which was nonverbal, nonhuman.

But she was not asking the woman who had been praying with her all week, but the one who carried the American passport, the one who had openly kissed her husband at the breakfast table. What she had been blind to before was apparent to her now: the daughter who communicated with the mother in Urdu was the same who spoke to the husband in English, the daughter who covered herself in a *duppatta* similar to the mother's was the same who bared herself when out with the husband, out of her presence. She was seeing all now, what I had been exposed to—would expose her son to—when out of her house. Her limits had limits of their own.

Of course I would pray with her, as we had been discussing—as I had been looking forward to—all week. Family traditions, there were none in our house, save those ancient rites we had inherited, culture passed on along with the knobby bones of the spinal cord, erecting our existence: shaving my head at ten days as the Prophet had shaved the heads of his children; a *bismil'lah* ceremony at four years to declare I was Muslim; at twelve, the onset of menses celebrated with fireworks and the gathering of one hundred in front of whom I was showcased, marriageable age; at nineteen, the wedding. And there were those other traditions I had practiced, though not necessarily with my family: attaining a driver's license, getting drunk for the first time, sucking at my first joint, graduating high school, entering college, losing my virginity. What most any Muslim girl, most any American girl goes through, here, there. But what Feroz and Zeba were doing each Friday, voices mingling, backs swaying, this song, this lament, was not about who they were outside, joined with a larger community, but inside, joined together, mother and son. And now, mother and daughter. Sister and brother. Family.

Yes, I would join them, if they did not mind my halting breath.

I FOUND SAMEER in the courtyard. He was sprawled out in a chair, long legs stretched before him, head thrown back, eyes shut against the sun. I leaned over him and brushed my lips against his, my veil falling across his face. He reached up and pulled me into his lap, then clasped me in his arms. I rested my head against his chest, unbuttoned his shirt and slid a hand inside, his nipples as sensitive, I had learned, as my own.

"I spoke to your brother after we recited the Qur'an. He's very bright. Did you know that after his engineering classes he goes and takes other ones in computer languages? Something called CADD and dBASE III. He said you'd send him back money to study even more. He's really preparing himself to come."

His face was up to the sun again, and the way his neck rested on the back of the chair exposed the hard bone of his jaw. He turned down his lips and the skin wrinkled on his chin. "It'll take years to get him to America. I'll have to talk to him about going to the Middle East."

"But you just promised him and your father . . ."

"In due course, baby, in due course." He kissed my forehead, saying, "Don't tell me they've got my own wife thinking I'm corrupt," and I could hear the pain in his voice for what his father had gone and done.

"I'm sorry," I said. "I wish he had just given you the tickets."

He grunted. "Papa does nothing without giving advice. Not even a meal can be eaten without a moral, and none of what he says is practical. This country runs on *rish'wat*, yet he thinks that because I once took money from a student he has to save me from myself. Even something like corruption, baby, is a matter of perspective."

"You took money? For what?"

"Nothing that would hurt anyone, like he thinks. One of my students told me he was getting married and was desperate to get hired for this post way off in some bloody village I've never even heard of. To be considered, he had to have the highest marks. So I gave them to him. It was inconsequential, he had no chance of getting that job. You have two applicants, one Hindu, one Muslim, and even if both are equally qualified, the Hindu will be hired. That's our affirmative action, baby. Keep the dominant classes dominating."

"What did you do with the money?"

"I bought this bike," he said, opening a hand to the courtyard to indicate the blue Honda, eyes still closed. "I needed one after the accident."

Yes, those great Dabir Pura Doors. I was beginning to see their usefulness. During riots, during trouble, they could be closed up, protecting those inside. I said, "All this talk about Hindus and Muslims . . . you know, I've always stayed in the Old City, and you don't hear anything but the call to prayer, ten times a day! Sameer, *is* it dangerous for us go to Madras by ourselves?"

"Don't listen to my mother, Layla, it's just her way of trying to keep us here."

I traced his jawbone, then ran my finger down his throat before kissing his Adam's apple. How to ask this? "Would it be terrible for you to stay here?"

"Wouldn't it be for you?"

I didn't answer.

He scooted up in the chair, and his dark eyes narrowed on my face. He stared at me as though he didn't know me, that look Dad got whenever he was about to beat me. He pinched my veil. "Don't tell me this is the life you want, Layla, being stuck in the house with nothing to do but pray and cook and clean. Waiting for me all day, heating up my bath water. I've never objected before because there's nothing else for you to do here. It's just passing time. It's not a life, Layla, not one I want for us. And who you are here is not the woman I want, either. The woman I married attends university. She's heading toward a degree. She wears bikinis and she . . ." he licked his lips, hesitating, before he said, "she knows certain liberties."

THE FOLLOWING MORNING, I awoke to Sameer and Zeba arguing in the next room.

"I won't let you take her with you today," he was saying. "I don't care what you think or how important this is to you. She's my wife . . ."

"Let your wife choose how she wants to spend her day. Why should you decide for her? Let me ask her when she wakes up what she would like . . ."

"I've told you, she's my wife and she'll do as I say."

"You surprise me, Beta. You dress in those jeans and speak only in English with your wife, but when the time comes, you are no different from any other Muslim man I know."

"I am speaking to you in the only language you understand. I will say this once more. I do not want Layla in the kitchen with you anymore. I do not want to come home and find her sweating and stinking of onions and garlic. Her mother has sent Nafiza, use her. My wife is not your servant . . . or mine!"

"Learning how to care for her husband is not . . ."

"And no more Qur'an tutoring. I wish I had stopped it the day she told me. Papa convinces me to stay on with work, finish what I have begun, and look what happens while I'm away. Suddenly she wants to stay here, in India! She doesn't know anything about India. She doesn't know what she's asking. It's you filling her with your crazy ideas, taking advantage of her when she's alone here, when she has no one else. What kind of life do you think we'll have here, huh? This life, your life! Four more days, Mum, four more days of tutoring, then we're leaving for Madras. It is now up to you how you wish us to remember you. How you wish that time to be spent."

After a long silence, Zeba said, "Is it not enough that you are going, must you now vow to send for Feroz? Leading him there, corrupting him in the ways you've been corrupted . . ."

"Indians have corrupted me, Mum, Indians."

HE ASKED ME to put on my jeans, saying he was going to take me out for lunch, tandoori pizza. I'd never worn my American clothes in India, they were part of what I left behind each time I arrived. It was not merely a matter of blending in, belonging, but also a matter of what was appropriate.

When he caught me glancing toward the door, hesitant, he said, "Throw on your chador, she'll never know what you're wearing underneath. Oh, come on, baby!" he cried, when I didn't move. "Trust me. I'm not taking you to the Old City. Where we're going, no one will even blink at your clothes."

As I was changing, he sat at the edge of the bed, elbows on his thighs, both hands running through his hair. It was the way he had sat on the *takat* that week he was sleeping beside his father. I crouched on my knees before him and took his hands into mine, kissing them, just as I had wanted to that night.

"Why all this talk of corruption? Where do you go when you're not here?"

"I'm not cheating on you, Layla, if that's what you're concerned about."

No, he was not, Roshan had already confirmed that. "She said one time you were gone a month. You must . . ."

"That's in the past, Layla. You promised me not to bring up the past. The man I want you to know is the man before you . . . just as you are the woman before me."

The woman before him, of course, was the one he did not want to know. While the woman he wanted was one he had never seen or met.

"Listen," he said, "Mum is going to some shrine today. If you want to go with her . . . well, I won't stop you. It's your choice."

I ASKED HIM to fetch her a cycle-rickshaw while I finished dressing. The jeans had grown snug after weeks of sitting about the house—or did they just feel that way, my body grown used to loose *shalwars*? How frail the body's memory, how easily it adapted—could be coerced!—and this made me wonder if my husband was right: was I forgetting who I really was? How strange to think that, after years of reminding myself, and being reminded, that I truly was nothing other than an Indian Muslim.

When I heard Sameer's bike pull up, I threw on my chador and walked Zeba to the rickshaw, then helped her to climb in. Sameer remained on his motorcycle, revving the engine in impatience.

"I'm going to the shrine," Zeba said to me. "I want to pray about that dream I had. It's still haunting me." She stared at me awhile, her slanted eyes the only thing I could see from behind the *duppatta*. She was inviting me to join her.

I said, "I've asked Nafiza to prepare the evening meal, so you won't need to rush back."

Her chest rose in a deep sigh, the way Amme's did, not disappointment, but worse, she was saying she had expected as much. She turned and told the rickshaw driver where to go, then pulled up the vinyl hood, disappearing inside.

I hopped onto the back of Sameer's bike and we took off, passing her up quickly, though she kept her face averted. Toward the end of the block, I saw the Muslim neighbor's two daughters at their front gate, thick braids again pulled out from behind their veils; wearing matching lipstick, they smiled coyly at my husband.

THE PIZZA RESTAURANT was near his college, nearly an hour's drive from the house. We had to pass through the Old City on the way there, and I could not help but search for Amme's Fiat. Almost a month now, and she had not once visited.

Toward the newer parts of the city, the roads became wider and smoother, the traffic more orderly than the chaos we'd left behind. There were even stoplights, which, to my surprise, were obeyed. But everything else was the same, the same pastel-colored houses, the same high boundary walls and iron gates. The same crush of human life. Overhead, clouds were gathering, but it meant nothing. Each day they gathered, each day they dissipated, teasing skies.

At the restaurant, we sat next to a window in high-backed velvet chairs that reminded me of the ones at the *walima*. The restaurant was attached to a hotel, and we had a view of the swimming pool. On one of the fold-out chairs, I was surprised to see a woman in a bathing suit, lying out in the dimming sun as I had once thought it so brave of me to do in America, when I was rebelling against this very marriage. The woman's children and husband were splashing around in the water.

The pizza place itself could have been any around my own university campus, filled with students my age, girls and boys mixing together, laughing and joking, heavy bags of books cast about their feet. They were all wearing Western clothes, moving as easily between Urdu and English as I, the women with their hair cut to their shoulders, much shorter than mine. I had never seen this part of India before, and found myself, even in my American jeans, feeling much more restricted, confined, than they.

Sameer ordered a pizza, then took out a pack of cigarettes. He offered one to me, saying, "It's okay here. Anything goes."

It was true, even the women around me were smoking, and though I had smoked with Nate, there was something about smoking in Hyderabad, with my husband, that offended my sensibilities. He looked almost disappointed in me as he lit one for himself. He blew the smoke at the window, then stared at the woman in her bikini, and I felt a dull rise of jealousy. For the first time, I caught a glimpse of what he must have felt when he'd read Nate's letters, and I knew instantly that I could not be like Amme. I could not share my husband.

I spun the silver ring on his thumb, drawing him back to me. I said, "On the wedding night, you said you'd done everything you could to make me yours. What did you mean?"

He looked at me, surprised. "Mum, of course! She agreed to the match, but got nervous the moment you left for the U.S. Every day for a full year she came to me with something new: 'She's from America, Allah only knows what kind of character she has.' Or, 'When she takes you there, she'll make you live underground. I've heard these American houses have dark floors under the ground! How will my son live without light!' And of course she was always worried about what I would eat. Can you imagine, being concerned about my not being able to eat in America when I live in a place like this!" He shook his head, disgusted. "Mum did everything she could to convince me you weren't the right one." He paused, sucking at his cigarette, before saying, "She even tried to set me up with some girl down the street."

"One of those two sisters!"

"You've met them? Hey," he said, reaching across the table to touch my face, and the cigarette smoke burned my eyes. "Don't take it so seriously. You know Mum has fully accepted you. She has no regrets about the marriage. I'm her only regret. Her *shame*," he said, emphasizing the word and smiling to let me know he wasn't bothered by what she thought of him. I, on the other hand, had run my life according to Amme's wishes.

The pizza arrived, smaller than I had thought it would be, tomato sauce dripping off the sides. It was spicy, almost like eating curry with naan. No reason to tell him, though, when he was trying to show me the America he knew.

He glanced out the window again. He said, "What was it like for your father when he first went to the U.S.?"

So that was what was on his mind, not the woman at all, but the liberties that were almost in his reach. How to explain that it would not be as easy for him there as he thought? "My parents emigrated during the early seventies, during the brain drain, so there were a lot of Indian professionals going over, and they were able to build a community even in Minneapolis. My father used to say that at his hospital, people assumed he was Jewish: Khan, Kahn, there isn't much difference in the name. Growing up, I remember being invited to all the Jewish festivities at his colleagues' houses, and my parents just let them believe we were Jews from India."

He didn't see the humor in it, as I thought he would. He simply nodded. "They wouldn't have given him the job if they'd known he was Muslim," he said.

"No, my father said it was the first time he felt his name wasn't working against him. Sameer," I said, taking his hand again, "it's not so much religion there as color. You're not escaping discrimination by going there. You're just entering a different system."

His eyes took on that look from yesterday—his wife a stranger—not understanding or not willing to understand what I was saying.

I tried to explain. "In school, I was the only brown girl. The other kids didn't know what to do with me. I was always teased, and some took to calling me 'nigger lips.' Everywhere I go, I'm asked where I come from. Nigeria? Mexico? Egypt? When I say India, they say, 'Oh, yeah, I can hear the accent now.' Sameer, the only accent I have is midwestern. And my first semester at university, I was cornered by this man who accused me of getting accepted over some white student. He yelled at me for taking this student's spot and said I would go on to take that student's position at work. That's how you'll be seen there, as taking a place that legitimately belongs to someone else." *Who you are. What you could amount to.* Even the American dream held distinctions.

"Sameer, people are going to notice your accent. They will notice your skin and dark hair and eyes. It doesn't matter what clothes you wear or how educated you are or how good your English is, you will be considered different. You will not be seen for who you are."

He withdrew his hand and took out another cigarette, his eyes darting about the room, at the other students, his former life, all that he was leaving behind, none of it, no matter how westernized, preparing him for what he would encounter next. Was he seeing this? He turned down his lips. "I'm going to make it in America, Layla. I'm going to be as successful as your father. Nothing is going to hold me back, not Mum, not religion, and not . . ." he waved a hand, smoke swirling before his face.

AS WE WERE winding our way through the narrow back alleys, heading for the great Dabir Pura Doors, it began to shower, the air filling with the stink of gas fumes and urine, dust, then, at last, a new freshness. I covered my face with my chador and tried to duck from the rain behind Sameer's back. He sped up, hoping to get us home. But by the time we passed the Vijayanagar Jail-*khanna*, reaching the hill that dropped into the colony, it had turned into a torrential downpour, slanted rain, thick and heavy, pellets against the flesh. It was hard to keep the eyes open. The back wheel skidded, and thinking of his accident, I asked him to pull over. He drove off the road and into a thicket of trees. We huddled against a trunk, his bike parked against another nearby, water dripping from the seat, steam rising from the hot engine. His clothes were soaked through, sticking to him. He was shivering. I undid my chador and wrapped us both inside. We stared out through the lines of rain.

This part of the road was mostly uninhabited, only an old *haveli* across the way, which had, since I could remember, been abandoned. I had always assumed a homeless family would take up residence, but none had, just as no huts had gone up in the woods around us. A dirt path led deeper into the trees behind me, seeming to go nowhere.

I gazed up at Sameer, water rolling off the tip of his nose, dark lashes clumped. Since I'd told him my experience of America, he had turned solemn and distant, as though I had become his mother, the one who set limits.

I pushed back hair from his face, the broad forehead, the firm jaw line. Nothing, nothing about the way he looked I would change, not even that damn leg. "I'll be there for you," I promised. "I'll help you navigate. You're not on your own, not anymore." Words I wished to hear myself.

He looked at me in relief, the coldness about him so quickly shattering, and he pressed his forehead against mine. I rose on tiptoes, my sandals squishing into the wet ground, and stuck my tongue between the gap in his two front teeth. This was what I wanted now, it was not enough what we'd been doing, no matter what he might find, no matter his reaction.

He understood and pressed me against the trunk, then kneeled before me, hidden by the chador, his mouth on my navel.

"Not like this, not here, are you crazy!"

He didn't stop, my words lost in the thunderous downpour.

I tried to pull away. "Sameer, we're almost home. The house is empty." Nafiza, of course, but wouldn't my nanny be relieved?

"What?"

"Not here, not like this, please."

He seemed almost surprised at my protest before he stood and unwound the chador from around us. It was a wet rag.

"Wait," he said and ran to a nearby coconut palm, where he leapt up and tore one of its long fronds. He hauled it back and thrust it over my head, a tropical umbrella.

We jumped onto the bike, and now I rode with my legs on either side, thrust up against him. After a while, I let the palm leaf blow into the wind and wrapped my arms around him, then I dug my way into his shirt, unbuttoned it, pulled it up from his jeans, uncovered his back and licked it, the taste of sweat and rain. I heard men hollering, teasing as they rode by, but could not stop myself, and he didn't stop me. This was the woman he had married. Enough of these limits.

When he pulled into the front gates, we both hopped off, giggling, laughing, and he was calling me "*budhmash*" for behaving the way I had, but he had his fingers stuck inside my jeans and was walking toward me, undoing them easily, while I was walking backward, fumbling with his. I stumbled on the stairs, falling, and he pulled me straight, right up against him, and we were kissing, and I finally rolled off his shirt. Nothing, nothing to hold us back today.

Then I heard clapping, a male voice. Was Feroz not at college?

"*Wa! Wa!* This is a better love scene than any I've seen in films. The directors should take pointers from you two." It was Naveed, sitting in the *divan*, waiting for his friend, no doubt, and what an entrance we had made. A cigarette was stuck between his lips, reflecting sunglasses pushed up into his pile of hair. He started clapping again.

Sameer picked up his shirt from the floor and wrapped it around me. "Go change," he said, his dark eyes locked on his friend. He didn't move toward Naveed in greeting, but stayed where he was, trying to stick his hands down his wet pockets. His skin was glistening.

I quickly salaamed his friend and made my way to the inner part of the house. As I was doing so, I heard Sameer behind me.

"Bloody hell, what are you doing here?" he said. Angry, I suspected, like I was, for having been interrupted like this.

"*Ar're, yaar,* I haven't seen you since the wedding and this is how you greet me? I thought I was your closest friend! If I didn't know better, I'd say you were avoiding me, not wanting your beautiful wife to meet your *yaar*." He laughed, clapping again. "Great show, great show . . . just like the *walima* dinner."

WE WERE CROWDED around the bamboo table, the two friends on either side of me. Nafiza had served us chai and guavas sliced down the center, the pink flesh sprinkled with lemon and pepper, stinging the tongue.

"Okay, this is what I don't understand, Bhabhi," Naveed was saying to me, calling me sister-in-law as Feroz did. He pushed a guava piece into his mouth and his slim cheek puffed out. He spoke as he chewed. "You are beautiful, I see that now. I mean, *hahn*, you looked beautiful on the wedding day itself, but you know, with this old tradition of flowers and veils, man, you can't see a damn thing. But now I see why Sameer has been absent for the whole month," he winked as he gestured to the open door. The rain was falling furiously, wetting the stone floor around it, while pools of water grew wider in the courtyard. The sky captured inside was as dark as the wet dirt. He lowered his voice and leaned into me, "Tell me, Bhabhi, has it been this passionate since he married you?"

Sameer kicked him under the table. He was still in his wet jeans, refusing my urges to go and change. Finally, I'd dug into his trunk and brought back a blue shirt that I admired on him. Those creases he'd inherited from his mother now ran deep across his forehead, a sign I had begun associating with strain, but he was smiling. He said, "Watch yourself, or I'll make you walk to the *chow-rasta* to catch an auto-rickshaw," he meant the highway near the jailhouse.

"*Ar're*, Layla is an American. She can handle sexy talk," Naveed protested, but then waved a hand in dismissal. "Anyway, you are right, I am missing my own point. What I was going to ask, Bhabhi, is this. Here you are, an American, with an American passport, an American education, so why did you come back and get married in such a way? You know what I mean, *arranged*. This is so backward. Your husband and I used to talk about this very thing in college. All the time, we would say, 'No, no, not us. We will never succumb to our parents' arranging our marriage. We will marry whomever we love, Hindu, Muslim, Sikh, it doesn't matter, as long as it is our own choice.' Of course, we are in India, and when you have a mother like Sameer's, it is not always possible to do what you want. But you, Layla, you are from America. Don't you see this system like . . . like . . . *ar're*, *yaar*, what did we used to call it?" He ran his hand through his thick hair, knocking off his glasses. They clinked on the floor.

"Pagan sacrifice," Sameer said.

"*Hahn!* Right! Pagan sacrifice." He picked up his glasses and pointed them at Sameer. "You've always had the better mind, *yaar*, even in classes you never struggled."

"Did you also study engineering?" I asked. "Is that how you met?"

Naveed gulped down his chai while he watched Sameer over the cup's rim with a look I could not read. Blue hollows shadowed his light eyes, flecks of gold in them as I'd never seen before.

"The park," Sameer finally said. "We met at the park where I go exercising. A long time ago, *hahn*, Naveed? Seven, eight years."

"Seven," Naveed said. "I still remember the exact day."

The two stared at each other a moment, before Sameer took my hand and brought it to his lips. "We're leaving for Madras this Friday," he said. "Then off to the U.S. A different life for me, Naveed, one I choose."

Naveed laughed. "Oh, yes, the modern arrangement. Passport for degree. I am telling you, *yaar*, India is changing, you don't have any reason to run away. Just look at these marriage rites, *hahn*, the very thing that defines India. It used to be two people came together over commonalities, religion, family status, wealth," he counted by pressing his thumb into the three joints of his pinkie. "Now, these very ideas of family status and wealth are obsolete, replaced by passports and degrees, all the dowry cartable in a single purse or pocket. Who cares who you are and what you were, let us only see what you can change into! I am telling you, *yaar*, America's influence is here. It won't be long before even the idea of marriage is obsolete. Or, if marriage must continue, it won't matter who marries whom." He sucked in air before saying, "Please, *yaar*, there is no reason to run off to the U.S. when the U.S. is coming to your very doorstep."

Nafiza entered the room and asked if Naveed was staying for dinner. She looked especially tired, the dark skin of her neck and jowls taking on the yellowish hue I sometimes saw on people here, jaundice from the water and food. I would have to force her to the doctor, much as she was trying to force me.

Sameer jumped up and peeled the wet jeans from around his weaker thigh, hiding its form behind the thick denim. If Naveed hadn't been there, I would have gone to my husband and taken his hands in mine, stopping him from such embarrassment.

He excused Nafiza by saying, "Naveed has to get back to open his repair shop." She limped out, and he turned to me. "I'll just take him to an auto-rickshaw."

Without meaning to, I stared at his wounded leg. "In this rain!" I cried. "No, no, no, I won't let you go!" Limits to keep him safe, Zeba had said, even this, a broken-and-not-properly-healed right leg to keep her son from venturing too far. From mother to wife, duties to Sameer had been passed on, along with, it seemed, those same fears that he might not return home. "Your motorcycle was skidding, Sameer, please, don't go."

He grabbed ahold of the two arms of my chair and leaned into me, whispering into my ear, "I was losing control because of you, baby."

"Tomorrow is Sunday," Naveed said. "The shop is closed. Let me take you two out somewhere, as a wedding gift. A Hindi film? You know, *Chandni* is currently the biggest hit. *Ah-ha*, Sri Devi, what a star!"

Sameer was running his lips up and down my neck and didn't answer. The front of his shirt ballooned down to expose his clean chest.

"*Ar're, yaar,* stop this show. You tell me not to talk to your wife about such things and then you . . . Bhabhi, this is my closest friend, Bhabhi, you have no idea how much he means to me. I'm begging you, please do not take him so far away without letting him spend one last day with me. Please, I am asking you for just one day. You have him for the rest of your life."

NAVEED CAME UP with the idea of going to Golconda Fort, a two-hour journey from here. Though I could sense my husband's reluctance, I readily agreed: the excursion was a good way to see Henna, my closest friend, the one *I* wanted to spend a day with before my return to the U.S. The road to the fort was narrow, lorries overtaking lorries, overtaking smaller vehicles, the drivers reckless and drunk, and Sameer insisted he wouldn't bring me by motorbike. We had no car at our disposal. For a moment, it seemed the whole thing would be called off. Then Naveed said he would rent a car, on whatever little money he must have earned at the TV repair shop, and Sameer didn't offer to pitch in. Wedding gift.

Early Sunday morning, Naveed showed up in a flashy red Maruti that reminded me of a VW Golf, hip and urban, the newest arrival to India's car market of lumbering Fiats and Ambassadors, and yet another of the country's latest gestures toward the West. It had tinted windows and a tape recorder, *Chandni* playing so loudly I couldn't hear what the two friends were talking about in front. I rolled down my window and got lost in the hum, my husband's low voice and the auto-rickshaws puttering along, the woman on the cassette singing her regrets—no, she would not leave her parents' home to go to her in-laws'. An outdated lament.

We picked up Henna, and I knew from the moment I saw her face that something was wrong. I hadn't seen her since the wedding, and I quickly sidled up next to her and took her hand in mine. In just under a month, her belly had swelled so much that I could make out the shape of her belly button right through the kurta, which was stretched taut about her.

We took off again and, under the music, I asked Henna what was wrong. She shook her head while eyeing the two men, and I understood she wanted to wait until we were by ourselves. I flattened my palm against hers to let her know we were one.

We fell into silence, unable to banter as the two friends up front, and after about an hour, Sameer turned in his seat and took my other hand. He stared into my face in that way of his, trying to perceive what I was seeing. Though he did not say it, I could see the question in his eyes: Why are you so quiet, when you had been the one to insist on this adventure?

For a moment, gripping both his and Henna's hands, I felt a surge of happiness I'd not known before, and I gave him a smile.

Henna cried, "Sameer Bhai, you're wearing a toe ring! Why did you take off that gold band?" The one she had put on, representing me in marriage.

Sameer looked from her to me and his gaze fell down my body even as his tongue pushed through his front teeth, so unabashed in what he was revealing. No longer the man who did not want to confront my relatives, be confronted by them.

Henna released my hand and began fumbling with her kurta. I knew she felt as though she'd come between a husband and wife, and I laid my head against her soft shoulder, taking her hand again and not letting go of Sameer's.

WE WERE INSIDE the great walls of Golconda Fort, standing on what seemed a stone verandah up at its highest point, overlooking the citadel. The fort had been built on a granite hill, and we had parked in a lot filled with tour buses and cars, the spot where the Mughal armies had camped for eight months, besieging the impregnable fort. The door that had at last been opened, allowing the enemy to slip inside, easily, finally, I could not find. But on the way up to the terrace, climbing hundreds of steep stone steps, we had passed an ancient well inside which, I overheard a guide saying, the women of the harem, the women of the Qutb Shahi family, had drowned themselves, unwilling to let their bodies also be invaded. This was the heritage I carried.

Off in the distance, beyond one of the twisting masonry walls, the rolling grasses and stone outcroppings led naturally to the Qutb Shahi tombs. Seven majestic domes were all I could make out from here, out of perhaps thirteen, a denseness of bushy green trees huddled about each, a lushness I did not find elsewhere on the high plateau. The wind was cool against my skin, clean of diesel fumes, offering respite from the city's heat. The sun was fierce, the ground having greedily swallowed up yesterday's storm.

Sameer asked me to go with him to the top of the Darbar. It was a two-story structure with tall arches, inside of which was the stone *takht*. The steps leading up to the throne were narrow and winding, pulsing with visitors. Henna had already been complaining about the climb, and seeing it as a chance to finally be alone with her, I stayed behind. Naveed and Sameer went together, lighting cigarettes the moment they stepped away. Naveed wore jeans that were baggy around the waist and thighs, as though cut for someone else. Behind the large lenses of his sunglasses, I couldn't make out his eyes, those flecks of gold that had caught my attention. Sameer, as always, was in the clothes Amme had brought back for him, his heavy boots clicking on the stone floor, and guides kept rushing up and touching his arm, speaking the few English words they knew. They thought he had dollars. Henna and I in our Indian dresses were left in peace.

As soon as the two had disappeared inside the building, Henna grabbed my hand and said, "Hanif is coming home. He's coming back, Layla, to me."

"What! Henna, why then do you look so sad?" I could not help but take her face in my hands, the flesh plump and full of water. I began laughing in relief, and her eyes filled with tears. "My God, Henna," I said, "do you not want your husband anymore?"

She nodded, her tears warm on my skin. "It is all I have prayed for. He has arranged to come before the delivery. Layla," she whispered, gazing about. Who could be here to overhear this, save the wind and the ghosts still presiding over Golconda? "He hasn't told his parents, no one from his family. He's quitting his job. They wouldn't let him, you see. But we can't be apart anymore. He's going to live with me. My parents are readying my room. They're so happy!"

"But why aren't you?"

She tried to pull away, but I kept ahold of her. *Kajal* was smudging black at the corner of an eye. The dark circles I'd first seen during the wedding days had deepened. She said, "I don't understand it myself. All this time, it's all I've wanted, for him to be here with me. I'm having his baby!" She held onto her belly with both arms, as though already clutching the child. "But now that he's coming . . . I don't like the way he's coming. Slipping into this country, invisible. It makes me feel that something will go wrong, no, something *is* going to go wrong. I'm scared, Layla, I'm so scared something is going to happen, to him, to me, to the baby, I don't know to whom, but I can't sleep anymore. It's all I think about." She wiped her face with her *duppatta*. People walking by gazed at us, always moving so close that I could feel their fingers or clothes swipe at me. Too many people in India, too many differences in culture.

I tried to lead her to another corner when, from above, Sameer began calling my name. I found him standing at the edge of the Darbar's first floor, framed by an arch, waving. Naveed was nowhere in sight.

"I love you!" he suddenly called, surprising me, and his voice echoed through the walls. Those beside him stopped and stared down at me. A tour guide behind him was clapping to show the visitors how the sound carried all the way to the front of the fort, by the Grand Portico, though it could be heard nowhere else. So brilliantly had the acoustics been designed for signaling. When I said nothing, he shouted it again, words we had not yet uttered to each other, "I love you!" Once more, the echo, seeming to raise up all the ruins about me so that I could see what it had been like here before, the stables, the palaces, the gardens, the life. Not just survival, but a way of existence, it was possible here.

A group of young men yanked Sameer away from the arch, and I laughed and dragged Henna far from the view of tombs. I felt guilty being happy when she felt so sad, but these fears she was describing, this premonition, were nothing more than disguised excitement. I told her as much, her turn to confess, my turn to give courage.

"When you've wanted one thing for so long, Henna, and it finally is happening, it feels . . . it feels like this baby. A gift you don't want to lose. It feels fragile, but it's not, it has a force of its own, beyond us. I swear, we're all going to remain safe and happy. Nothing is going to go wrong. Henna, our lives are just beginning!"

"There you are!" Sameer called, bounding toward me. Naveed strolled behind him, hands thrust deep in his jean pockets as he whistled the song from *Chandni*. I passed my fingers through my husband's hand as I released Henna's, letting him know that I would be walking back with him. Related or not, Naveed could accompany my cousin.

When we had climbed down the winding steps and were nearing the imposing Balahisar Gate, twenty-five feet tall and covered in spikes to keep elephants from charging, I heard Naveed's voice from behind. "*Wa wa*, Henna Apa, that's a great idea! *Ar're, yaar*," he called, and

Sameer and I shuffled to the side to let others pass as the two came up. In his dark glasses, our reflection, smiling and content, the image of a newly married couple. "Henna Apa is right," he said. "With elections so soon, it is not safe for you two to travel alone to Madras. It is better if I come along."

THAT NIGHT IN bed, I told him I loved him, too. The words came out easily, even with some relief, the first time I had said them to anyone. And I knew, the instant I heard them aloud, just how long I'd been waiting for this moment, this sensation to take over me, as strong as any demon, though, I prayed, not as fickle. Let it forever possess me.

I was lying with my head on his chest, a hand flat on his belly feeling the steady pulse within, against my fingers, against my temple, matching my own rhythm. Around us, the maroon walls of the mosquito netting, the whir of the ceiling fan above, Zeba's distant snoring. I couldn't imagine my life in any other way. How to make him understand? Perhaps in increments.

"I wasn't able to attend Henna's wedding," I began, "but I'd like to be here for the delivery. She told me today that Hanif is returning. He's going to live with her. They're so close to our house, Sameer, just like that, we're already part of a small community. And you have Naveed. He cares so much for you. Renting that car must have cost him so much. For you, he did it for you."

He sucked in air then blew it out of his mouth, and my hair tickled my face. "Did you ask your cousin to invite Naveed to Madras?"

"On our honeymoon! Of course not. She's just scared, like your mother. I think it must be because she's so close to delivering. Besides, he took it well, he understands, he's not coming."

He was silent, still brooding over what had become, for him, an awkward situation. Turning away a close friend in what would be considered here, where honeymoons did not really exist—another import from the West—a generous offer.

"Listen, Sameer," I said as I slid a hand under his pajama bottoms, "by the time we get the visa and arrive in Minneapolis, it'll be November, right when it's getting cold. With wind chill, it can drop to seventy below; you can't know what that feels like. Then, it just keeps getting colder. If we waited six months—I'm used to being here, remember—we could go in spring. If we go back now, there's nothing, no job for you, and my semester will already be under way. My dad says you'll even have to take your engineering classes over again. Until you have an income, we'll be stuck inside my mother's house." Right back where I've always been. No future there, Zeba was right.

He shoved my hand aside and turned away to face the wall. I latched onto his back. Draw away, draw closed, but I would say it this time.

"It can't all be about getting ahead and building your career, Sameer. You keep talking about my father, but what good did making all that money do for my family? What you and your family have here is so much better. Your father may not have given your mother a house, but he did give her a life. If you could only have known me there, you would see how different I am with you, in India, in your home. Sameer, you've given me what you promised, please don't take it away so soon . . ."

"You cannot know what you're asking . . ."

"I do know, Sameer, I'm not as ignorant of India as you think. I've spent half my life here. It's where I've always felt more comfortable. I'm part of something here, I'm not just gazing out." I fell onto my back and stared up at the mosquito canopy, the fan's wind hardly reaching us. I could taste the salt of my own sweat on my lips. "What do you know about the U.S., Sameer? I mean other than what you've read or seen in film. What do you really know about what *you're* asking?"

He rose and fumbled out of the mosquito netting, then threw on a shirt. From a dresser drawer, he grabbed his pack of cigarettes and stuffed them into his pocket. He wouldn't look at me. "I promised to give you a home, Layla, and I will, *there*. I'll find a job, any job, and we'll move out of your mother's house. Two weeks, three weeks, that's all. We'll start our lives over, new lives, both of us, away from your past, away from my past." He stopped and hung his head, as though hating what he was about to say, the right he possessed to exert his power over me, his wife. "On Friday, we're going to Madras . . . alone! As soon as I get my visa, we're off to the U.S. That's it. Don't talk to me about this anymore."

SHE WOULD HAVE known by her own sense of intuition, the slightest stir in the air, that her son had disappeared again, but she didn't ask, nor did she provide me comfort, as I had been hoping she would. She was done with her duties to her son. The rest was between us, husband and wife.

After breakfast, when I took my usual spot on the *takat*, against one of her embroidered pillows, and tried to assist with the preparations for the evening meal, she stopped me, her voice sharp in a way I'd not heard before. Her son's prohibition, not hers, the one who wanted me to have a place in her home as much as I wanted it myself. I knew better than to try to press her: no matter that Sameer did not follow her mandates, she had to follow his, for her son was, before all else, a man like any other.

As I was scooting off the *takat*, there came a woman's voice from the front door, calling to see if anyone was home. She spoke a halting Urdu, so I knew it was not her first language.

"The *tho-bun* is here," Zeba said, then set aside the ginger she'd been peeling and adjusted the *duppatta* around her heavy chest. "Can you ask her inside?"

The laundry woman was a *lambarni* from the woods off the main highway—the place where Sameer and I had gotten caught in the rain—the lonesome dirt road I had seen probably leading to her hut, her village. She was wearing a wide skirt and a tight top that stopped just below her breasts to expose her tight belly and full back; the reds and maroons and purples of the skirt fabric were covered in tiny mirrors that sent shimmering circles dancing across the walls. The laundered clothes were in a large bundle balanced on her head, wrapped inside the fabric of an old plaid lungi. She plopped onto the floor next to the *takat*, her bottom wide and arched, as though having been molded by these habitual seatings.

Zeba got out a notebook from her *almari* and, as the woman presented each shirt and trouser, each sari and blouse, each bra and underwear, ticked it off in her ledger. Her writing was small and meticulous. Nothing miscalculated, nothing missing. When they were done, Zeba began loading her with this week's laundry, counting it up again, carefully jotting it down, and without telling her, I took Sameer's clean clothes and brought them to the bedroom and shut the door behind me.

Where does he go when he flees from here? It was to answer that question that I began to dig around in his trunk, pushing past clothes, sliding a hand into corners, while the pile of clean shirts and trousers sat neatly on the floor beside me. Whatever I was hoping to find—a photograph, a letter, what were those things Amme had overlooked before Dad had abandoned her?—I did not think I would discover what I actually did.

A plastic bag, crisp and crinkly, cool, against my fingertips when everything else was soft cloth. It was hidden between clothes he didn't wear anymore, the polyester-cotton blend shirts and trousers cut and stitched to fit him snugly, in the style often worn here, and what he himself had dressed in when he had come to propose. It was the image of his slim body in those unbecoming clothes that had caused Amme to buy him as many outfits as she'd done, her attempt, as the one who had arranged this marriage, to make him at least appear to be the kind of man she thought I would be amenable to marrying.

Inside the bag, I found articles ripped out of magazines, each one stapled, stacked one inch thick. Though I had never seen these condensed pages, I had already read the words, disguised as his to me in the letters he'd written, over and over, those sexual fantasies that were really pornography. In copying them down, he had changed nothing but the names, the generic American ones—Jeff, John, Sylvia, Jen—

becoming our own, Sameer, Layla. Why had he thought his fiancée, a woman largely unknown to him, would have appreciated such vulgar language and description, coming from her future husband? How could he not have guessed it would degrade me and push me away, making me feel like a whore?

A whore. And there they were, the letters he had told me he'd thrown away, Nate's to me, bundled up with the articles, as though, to Sameer, there was no difference, both describing the same thing. And, at first, because I had pushed that distant night so deep within, regretting it, ashamed of it, repenting, I, too, saw no difference. But then the words fell away, becoming images, and the images sound and feeling. The moonless night, the scent of jasmine, the bitter scent of his skin. No, he had not taken it lightly, he wrote, my having given up my virginity to him; he had understood what he was doing, what it would mean for me, before he had agreed to slip through the door, slip inside. If, in this way, he was proclaiming his love, the understanding of it for me had come too late.

The door opened and the boots came into view, tied up under his white pajamas; most likely he'd returned to change before tutoring. There was no reason to look up at his face when I could feel the heavy weight of his gaze. His trunk was open, the pile of newly pressed clothes was by now toppled onto the floor, and, scattered about, Nate's letters to me, the articles that had inspired his own letters.

THERE WAS NO show of anger, no cursing, no yelling, no accusations, just a complete withdrawal. The silence I had grown up knowing with Dad.

He simply chose fresh trousers from the pile on the floor and put them on, leaving for his afternoon tutoring. At dinner that night, he sat across the table from me, in the chair his father occupied on Friday and Sunday mornings, when the family ate together. Feroz and Zeba glanced at each other but said nothing. At eight, when Zeba ushered us all away so she could reheat the dinner for her exhausted husband

and take up the newspaper to fan him, Sameer did not leave as I thought he would. He instead followed me into the bedroom and lay on the bed, squeezed onto the far side, flattened against the wall, his back to me. The way this had all begun.

If he expected me to provide something, an explanation, an apology, I did not. Could not. My head was overcrowded with words, English and Urdu, the letters running into each other, from right and left.

When Nafiza came in to sweep for the night, Sameer did not rise, and, unable to go to her and confess what I had found, I crumpled onto the velvet stool, my head falling into my hands. She gave a heavy sigh before sweeping the floor about me.

Far into the night, his words came through the darkness. "You're an American woman, I didn't know what to say to you, what to write, you must understand. Your freedoms, what you have been exposed to, *there* . . . it was only to impress you, make you mine."

Yes, the man who had done everything he could to win over his own fiancée.

"Your words didn't create intimacy," I whispered. "I was repelled." The way he had been by my blood.

He groaned, and the bed creaked as he came to me and rested his head on my navel. His cheeks felt wet. "I'm so stupid," he said. "I'm so bloody stupid. Can you forgive me?"

"Why have you kept . . . everything?"

"I'll throw it out, I swear to you, baby, I'll throw it all out first thing in the morning. We've come so far together, let us not . . . it is in the past, it is in the past." He buried his face in my belly, arms cinching me.

In the morning, he rose earlier than usual and, through the dense mosquito netting, I watched him dig out the packet of letters and articles. He threw it into the canvas bag along with the engineering books he carried to and from tutoring. Before he left, he came and sat next to me, in the slit that served as the netting's door. One of his eyes was red and watering, as his father's got at the end of the day. He folded his hands in his lap and stared down at them.

"Did you want to return, now that you've read . . . did you want to go back? Maybe he is a better fit . . . maybe you think he is a better man . . ." his voice buckled.

"I told you I loved you," I said, though, in truth, the words did not come out as easily as they had the other night. But if my husband had behaved badly, hadn't I behaved worse, and he had been able to forgive me.

When the roar of his motorcycle was fading down the street, Nafiza walked into the room with Zeba. Even before I rose from bed and parted the netting, I knew Zeba was crying from how still she held her body. The window shutters were closed, the room dim, but I could make out the tears running down her broad cheekbones, getting caught in the deep creases before zigzagging past. The black *duppatta* had fallen from her head to expose thin hair, the gray at the parting dyed maroon with henna.

Without covering herself, she said, "Beti?" Daughter, but it was a question, all of her questions in the one word. Then she glanced at the bed behind me, and, in her slanted eyes, I could see her envisioning the spotted cloth Sameer had given her, the *walima* dinner, her asking Nafiza to dress me in green.

Not a show, she had said, thank Allah this was not just a show.

I ORDERED MY nanny to leave the house.

"You have forgotten yourself," I said, my voice surprisingly calm. "Whether you have breast-fed me or not, you will always be my servant, nothing more."

She flinched at the word, but her face did not close to me. In the next room, Zeba had shut herself inside the *ashur-khana* to pray. I hoped to get Nafiza out of the house before Zeba emerged. No more chance of the two talking again.

My nanny tried to grasp my hand, but I pulled away and opened my *almari*. How much did servants get compensated for being kicked out?

Behind me, I could hear her smacking the aching leg as she said, "He no show he-self to you, Layla-bebe. He demon, he no man. He take on pretty-pretty face so you no see he. This *jadu* worse than Raga-be do, make you stay here, with him, when this no good home for you."

"What is a good home for me, Nafiza-una, the one Dad provided?"

She spoke on, as though not having heard what I'd said. "Me you mama, no care what you say, me no servant to you. Me give you me milk, me bathe you, me carry you with me two hands. You me child. I no want to see you harm. What me say when me know about you *gora-wallah*? Me say, me no care. This me child. No matter what she do."

I tried to hand her a full month's salary, though I knew she would simply return to Amme's, and, after my mother went back to the U.S., to Taqi Mamu's.

She put up a hand, refusing it.

I said, "Of course you accepted me even after what I'd done. What choice do you have, what power over me?"

"You me child, like Roshan . . ."

"Take the money, Nafiza, and go."

Never before had I seen her eyes fill with tears. Very quickly, she blinked them back, refusing to cry before me. "Listen, child," she said, then cleared her throat. "Me know you no see right. This *jadu* he done to you with he pretty face and pretty words. When you see right, you come to me. You no feel shame for what you do today. I forgive you." She tightened the sari-*pallow* around her shoulders and tucked the edge into the sari blouse. It was the same blue sari she'd worn the day she'd returned from her trip away, over a week before. Her hair was oily again, strands rising here and there at the crown and from the bun. She had the bitter scent of sickness, and though I had determined to force her to the doctor's, I didn't say anything.

As she bundled her clothes and *paan-dan* together, tying it all inside an old torn sari, in the fashion the *tho-bun* had carried our laundry, I heard her humming that song from long ago, about a lost girl who would one day find her way home.

THE NEXT MORNING, Amme arrived at the house.

I had been standing with Zeba in the kitchen, against the black counter, as she washed our breakfast plates, a task usually given to Nafiza. She wouldn't let me help, and from behind, I watched the steady rise and fall of her shoulders, the stretching and creasing of the black *duppatta* as she sighed, then sighed again. When she was done, she began heating milk for chai. She didn't look at me, pretending I wasn't in the kitchen disobeying her son.

At last, I said, "I've been trying to convince Sameer to stay here a few extra months, as you and I talked about."

She stared at me in disbelief, not doubting my efforts, it seemed, but my sway. Limits she hadn't counted on.

Then she said, "Your mother is here," and only then did I hear the familiar groan of the Fiat's engine. Zeba checked the clock, saying, "Exactly on time. This is the hour your *nana* used to arrive each month at my parents' house, asking for his rent."

Zeba seated my mother on a chair she shifted just inside the living area, opposite her *takat*. My mother not fully a guest, yet not fully a member of this household.

Amme didn't sit right away. She stood framed by the doorway, enveloped in her shiny chador, her almond-shaped eyes studying the room: its simple furniture, the low fridge, the Pakistani rug on which Zeba and I sat, three cups of steaming chai on the silver tray beside us. My mother kept her eyes averted from my face, and I was reminded of what it had been like to be the ill-fated daughter. I wanted so badly for her to see me, if only to recognize what she had accomplished by pushing me into this marriage: at last, she had brought me to life.

Amme said, "Much has changed since I was here last, for your son's *sanchak* ceremony. There was much laughter and singing that night . . . much hope."

Zeba offered Amme a cup of tea, saying, "There is always hope when we place our faith in Allah."

Amme declined by explaining that she'd just eaten *paan*. But I knew what she really meant. For her, this was not a social call.

She unwrapped the layers of the chador, and a yellow sari emerged with a black border and crimson threads throughout. Gold, high-heeled sandals. It was as though she'd dressed for that very wedding ceremony. But, in truth, it was the way Amme always dressed, as though for some occasion, and despite the dark shadows under her eyes, she had a noble air, while, before her, Zeba appeared simple and old, the creases on her face speaking of hardships very different from my mother's. The renters, the landowners, their history, it was all revealed.

Amme draped the chador over the chair before she finally sat down. She stared at her palms, their lifelines showing the decisions she'd made. She was ready to announce the reason for this visit.

Zeba must have recognized the gesture, too, for she quickly said, "Your husband's sister has recently married, I have heard. For the second time. *Mubarak*. Allah willing, this marriage will last. Divorce is always more difficult for women. No matter the circumstance, they are the ones who are blamed. Men go on with their lives, marrying again, a second time, a third time, a fourth time, no one tallies up how many women they've been with. Women carry the burden. Once a woman's name is tied to a man's, she is seen as tainted, no matter the circumstance." She stopped to take a slow sip of her tea before adding, "Your sister-in-law has a good kismet. Most divorced women must spend the rest of their lives alone."

Amme was twirling an earring, gold molded into a rose, impatient for Zeba to finish. When she did, Amme finally said, "My husband and I are leaving in two days for the U.S. He would like . . ." she hesitated and cleared her throat, "he would like to see his daughter before we go." A lie, of course. She was just using Dad, a man, to legitimize this transaction between women. Though Zeba did not see it, my mother was up to something.

"Your husband?" Zeba cried, and the cup clattered onto its saucer. "You and I have watched each other grow up, and now we are watching each other grow old. *Meri sumdum*," she said, my fellow mother-in-law, "I know your situation. I know the sacrifices you have made for your daughter. There is no need to conceal the truth from me."

She was referring to my mother's divorce, and I could only think that Sameer had told Zeba, thus betraying me again. Would I be able to forgive this?

Amme didn't flinch, her face fixed as I'd seen before, so accustomed she was to these sudden announcements, this loss of faith. If she thought it was I, her daughter, who had exposed her, she didn't let on, her eyes still not turning to me.

Zeba reached across and patted Amme's hand. My mother pulled it back and hid both under her sari's pleats.

"You mustn't be ashamed," Zeba said. "You have shown great courage and resolve. A mother must do all she can to protect her child. If you hadn't stayed on in his home, kept his protection, where would you be now? Where would Layla be? In this world, a woman's only possession is her reputation, and you have kept ahold of yours." She passed a hand over my head, a gesture I could not remember Amme ever making. "Your daughter is now my daughter. She has a home here. If she has sent Nafiza away, then you must see it as her saying that she, too, would like to make this her home . . . no matter the present circumstance. It has only been a month. Allah will reward you for the sacrifices you've made for your daughter. He will provide." She raised her hands up to her chest, the *duppatta* stretched between them, a beggar asking for the wealth of his compassion.

Amme finally turned and looked at me, taking in the *duppatta* around my head, my wrists and neck as clean of jewelry as Zeba's. "It is true, what you are saying, the child does seem to have found a place here," she said. "But I must still ask to take her for the day, her father is waiting. I assure you, I will bring her back."

Zeba grew uncomfortable and said, "I was surprised when you sent Nafiza to my home. I knew she would make trouble. Don't you remember the trouble she caused when we were children? Your father had taken her into his home and raised her with such care, and what did she do? She seduced your own brother, Taqi! Chasing him around in the woods, swimming with him in the river. You and I are of the same age, don't you remember the adults whispering about it? It's how we first encountered . . ." she glanced in my direction, ". . . these intimacies that occur between a man and woman. What a shock we'd felt after they had told us such things did not happen in Islam. Then, there they were, happening under the very roof of your house. Your father was smart to force her to marry his driver, Moosa. No telling how far she would have gone, what she might have done, to become a legitimate daughter!"

So there it was, the reason my nanny had needed Raga-be's help, and, no doubt, one of the reasons she continued to accept me as her own. For along with her milk, my nanny seemed to have passed on to me her very legacy.

"I see you still enjoy speaking about the past," Amme said. "I assure you, Nafiza has learned from her mistakes. She is committed to Layla's well-being and wants only for the child to have a proper home." With that, she stood and wrapped the chador about her again. With her chin, she gestured for me to go into my room and change. When I rose, Zeba grabbed my hand, showing a desperation I had not seen in her before. This, the true mother asking for her daughter back.

She said, "Your family and mine have known each other for seven generations. There was no need for you to ask around about Sameer's character, his behavior, his past life, like others do before they marry their children. Nor did I make inquiries about Layla, her life in the U.S. We entered this marriage in good faith. Marium," she said, using my mother's name, which no one used anymore. Like me, she was a *bevi*, wife, *bhabhi*, sister-in-law, then also *apa*, sister, *amme*, and even *sauken*, the other woman. Defined, as most women were here, by how she was related to others. Indeed, a woman could not be on her own, her dependency constructed even in language.

"Marium, no matter what you think of my son, he has provided

Layla with a home. If you take her from here, she will not even have that . . . remember, there was the *walima* dinner announcing a successful union. No man will marry her now, not unless he takes her for a second or third wife. Did you sacrifice your life to make her into a woman no better than the one who stole your husband? I'm asking you, let the two have a chance. They will come together, *inshal'lah*."

MY MOTHER TOOK me to the OB by Roshan's house, finally heeding the blind *alim*'s advice to get me healed.

On the way, she kept herself pressed against the car's side door, face turned out the window. Only her eyes showed from behind the chador, her most expressive feature gone flat.

The Fiat, after winding its way out of the dead-end road, had not taken a left, toward the Old City, but a right, toward the outskirts of Vijayanagar Colony, and that was how I knew where we were headed. Amme had not directed Ahmed, nor had he asked where to go. He simply drove, the whole thing planned beforehand.

The farther we moved away from the center of town, the wider the road became, though there were fewer cars and buses. Even the puttering of auto-rickshaws was soon replaced by the creaking wheels of oxcarts, stacked high with long grasses, the farmer resting on top, a whip perched in a hand. Buildings fell away, opening to wild, uncultivated fields. Small ponds free of birds shimmered like sheets of glass under the noonday sun. The air stank of dung. I was aware of Ahmed's eyes on me, through the rearview mirror, nervous and blinking. He told no tales this time as he had of Elephant Alley to provide a moral for what was happening.

Off in the distance, new buildings had sprouted up from the infertile ground, the walls painted the harsh yellow of the sun. Ahmed stuck his arm out the window, wiggling his fingers to indicate that we were pulling over. He stopped before a two-story structure, apartments on top, storefronts below. A vegetable market, a pharmacy, the OB clinic, all a woman's needs in one place.

Over the entrance to the clinic was a rectangular board, the doctor's name written in clean block letters painted blue. It stated that she had been trained both here and in England, and this somehow made me feel I'd come to the right place: at last a healer who could understand me and my position. The front door was left open to catch whatever breeze was out here, and I glimpsed other patients on aluminum folding chairs, all hidden behind burkhas, making it hard to tell who was pregnant and who not. Another door led to the private exam area, covered by a thick curtain.

Amme made no move to get out of the car. She kept the chador pressed against her lips, and on her thigh, underneath the veil, her knuckles were rolling.

I glanced at Ahmed, wondering what I should—could—say, when Amme spoke with the frankness she had on my wedding day.

"If you had to do something, child, why didn't you come to me? You know better than to believe in *jadu*. *Ar're*, if it worked, wouldn't I be dead by now? Don't you think Sabana has tried numerous times to kill me?" She grunted. "Stealing my husband was not enough for that woman."

"I told you about the bleeding, Amme, and you brought me to the blind *alim* . . ."

She glared at me. "How could I have guessed about your . . . internal problems? My daughter," she said, looking me up and down with what appeared contempt. She pushed herself closer to the door, farther away from me, and gathered the loose folds of her chador onto her lap. "When Nafiza told me what you . . ." she stopped in midsentence, her lips still parted, unable to speak the unimaginable. She shook her head and said, "No matter what I did, you still turned out to be like your father."

"I didn't tell Zeba Auntie about the divorce," I said, careful, before Amme, not to refer to Zeba as my mother.

Her gaze flitted to Ahmed's back then out the window. He had lowered his tall figure as far as he could, hanging his head between his shoulders, level with the steering wheel.

Outside Amme's window, a cycle-rickshaw was passing, overloaded with schoolchildren in blue uniforms, girls with two braids each, looped around to look like nooses.

I said, "When you locked yourself into your room, there was no one to look after me. I went to school and pretended you weren't crying at home and pretended Dad wasn't going to the hospital, as though he'd done nothing, changed nothing. Every night, I ordered pizza. When you finally came out, you carried on as before; you never asked me how I'd survived the month nor once expressed pride that I did. Amme, I was only ten."

Her knuckles suddenly went still, but she said nothing.

I went on, still speaking to her averted face, "It's been a month since I've been at my husband's, don't you want to know what it's been like for me? Don't you want to hear how I've managed . . ."

"You manage as we all manage," she said, turning to meet my eyes, and there was an emptiness in hers that I had first seen when she'd emerged from her locked room. "What choice do any of us have but to make do?" Her gaze fell to my belly before she closed her eyes and took in a deep breath, the veil sucked into her nostrils. "If I made a mistake by forcing you into this marriage, I did so believing it was the best for you. Layla, at least one of my two children should have a life, at least to one I could give a home . . . my poor son, Abbas. You can't imagine what it was like. Feeling him kicking inside me, feeling him hiccuping after I ate curry. And when I could finally hold him . . . no movement at all." Her eyes filled with tears as I had not seen since Dad divorced her, and I reached out to my mother, but she drew away and wrapped the chador more fully about her.

With a corner, she dabbed her eyes as she said, "Your *saas* is right. No one will marry you now, not here, not from the Old City. That man who married your father's sister, he was some old Saudi, and she became his fourth wife. Allah only knows what kind of life she'll have with him. But that's not for you, Layla. Nor is coming back with me to your father's home. I've gotten you out, I've given you a life—don't you see how lucky you are? Nafiza says your husband knows what you've done, and still he let you stay in his home. He gave you dignity. If he was anything like your father, he would have killed you on the wedding night, and no one would have stopped him or thrown him in jail, not here. They would have said he was justified." She stared at me until I lowered my head, assenting to what she'd said. "When your uncle confronted him about the leg, he came out with it. The boy has shown no intention to deceive. And I don't believe he's hiding anything now, do you?"

"No," I said, thinking about Nate's letters and the articles. "Not anymore."

"If anything," she said, speaking over me, "the boy has acted with utmost honor, saving us all our shame." With that, she drew from her purse a bundle of rupees still stapled from the bank, three inches thick. A payoff like I'd tried to give to Nafiza before throwing her out. It seemed I wouldn't be seeing my mother again.

"What about you?" I asked. "What's going to become of you now that I'm finally gone? Are you really returning to the U.S. with Dad?"

She sighed, long and exhausted, as though the last breath of life was moving out of her . . . or was she just now embarking on a new existence? "Your father asked me to go home with him," she said, studying her palms. "Sabana is staying here till her eighth month. She wants to be with her mother. The children have to return to school. They need someone to watch them. Your father is busy at the hospital."

And so revealed, the life she had accepted for herself, the role of wife and mother dissolving into its most basic form, the role of caregiver. She had become no better than my nanny, this, the daughter of a nawab. If I had failed as a daughter, maybe even as a woman, so, in the end, had she.

"*Chalu*," she said, reaching forward to tap Ahmed's shoulder. He bounded out of the Fiat and opened her door.

I joined my mother at the steps to the clinic and grasped her hand a last time. She squeezed mine briefly before letting go.

Aysh

HE WAS SITTING on the bunk across from mine, smoking, appearing to be staring out the window, though I could sense his eyes on me through the reflection of the glass. We were in the air-conditioned compartment of the Madras Express, winding our way through rice paddies stretched flat under the darkening sky. Not even four yet, but we'd had to turn on the overhead lights, and the window cast back our image in such a way that the landscape of our bodies appeared more clearly than the one passing outside. In the AC car, which was a class above first, all the windows were bolted shut to trap the cold, artificial air, and with the dimming natural light, if I moved just a bit this way or that, I could see the external world mapped across my face, making me feel even more cut off from it. Indeed, the sensation I'd had riding on the back of Sameer's motorcycle, merging with the chaos and life about me, had retreated once more, and I felt as I had in the backseat of the Fiat, watching it all from a distance. India was my father, the two of us made of the same clay and pulsings of blood, yet severed.

And severed, at last, was Nate, the form he had taken up inside me, the blood, the bloated, cramping belly. The doctor had asked no questions, though I had gone to her prepared to confess it all. After a swift internal exam, she'd performed a D & C, which had been less painful, less invasive than I'd imagined. Still, I left the clinic feeling clean and dirty at once, as though she'd turned me inside out.

At home, I kept my distance from Sameer. What I had once believed would bring me closer to him, a purified body, had, in the end, become yet another betrayal. Draw away, draw closed, I was doing it this time. *Just like your father,* Amme had said, dropping me off at my husband's house, her last words to me, *just like your father.*

In the glass, his face looked like the demon's who continued to visit me in dreams, a charcoal sketch with features not fully drawn in. Except the dark eyes, ever watchful in that way of his, trying to pierce my skull to see what I was thinking. I stared past them to the green paddies, dotted here and there by grazing water buffaloes. The outlying trees were short and scrubby, the hills in the distance like low-lying clouds. At the center of one field, there was a group of farmers and workers with lungis folded up to midthigh, knee-deep in mud. They were harvesting, long shoots of rice stalk tied into small bundles and set behind them as they moved from the center out, in no particular order. One shirtless worker was entirely covered in muck, his chest and arms, his neck and face, only the whites of his eyeballs showing clear. He was leading a water buffalo by a short rope. No one looked up when the train hissed past, just another snake stirring in these parts.

He snubbed out the cigarette under the thick heel of a boot and leaned forward, elbows on his knees, eyes locking onto my face. He owned no warm clothes and was still dressed in a white T-shirt, the round muscles of his arms flexing as he brought his hands together, fingers pressed to his lips. What was intended to be luxurious comfort was really just frigid, and I had wrapped myself in the chador he didn't like me wearing, not offering, as I'd done that day we'd been caught in the rain, to enfold him inside. The lines across his forehead appeared carved into his flesh.

He said, "I have been looking forward to our going to Madras for some time now, Layla. I had never imagined I would be . . . so distressed. Nothing has been right since you found those letters. What is it you are keeping from me? Mum says you threw Nafiza out because she . . ." his gaze faltered, ". . . because she knew about . . . not consummating . . . yet, not yet." His boot tapped the floor, twice, stressing how it was just a matter of time, nothing more. He met my eyes again. "When I came home that day and you were gone—you'd never been gone before, you've always been there, waiting for me—I realized how much I need you, Layla! Then Mum told me you'd left with your *amme*, and I thought you wouldn't come back to me, but you did . . . in a way. Now you won't let me touch you. Is it those letters? Are you thinking about him, him touching you . . . ?"

"No, I told you, I don't want him. I came to India, I married you. I could have run away with him, I could have stayed there. You read yourself what he wrote. He was surprised I'd left him. He thought I'd stay."

He pushed himself back on the bunk and rested his head against the cool metal wall, the rise and fall of his Adam's apple. Exactly a week before I had found him like this in the courtyard, sprawled out in a chair under the warm sun. I'd gone to him then, gone and kissed the pulse in his neck. "*I am closer to you than your own jugular vein.*" That was what I had read in the Qur'an that same morning, Allah speaking to us, his faithful, and that was how I had felt with my husband, more intimate with him than I'd ever been with anyone else. It didn't matter that we hadn't had sex . . . *yet.*

Still, what seemed not to have mattered in the beginning, our betrayals—his lying to his mother about the white cloth, my lying to him about the bleeding—were now like cracks that might appear in the great dam Taqi Mamu grumbled about, the one built by our ancestral land in distant NagarJuna Sagar. Each one caused another to erupt and appear, weakening the whole structure. The truth was, the past could not so easily be left behind. But would my husband be able to understand that when I confessed the truth to him?

"Are you trying to purposely hurt me, bringing up what your . . . *lover* said?" He kept his eyes closed, face turned up to the ceiling, the fluorescent lights. "Do you think the words don't echo in my own ears?" With the movement of the train, his head bounced against the wall, a dull thudding sound.

He was right, I was punishing him, not liking the image I was seeing of my own self in the glass, the round features that belonged to my father. I rose and went to him, cradling his head in my arms. He stretched my leg across his lap so that I was straddling him. I pressed my face into his neck. I was crying.

"You told your mother about my parents' divorce. I told you not to do that. How could you betray me? I thought we wouldn't do that to each other. I thought we wouldn't be like them."

"What are you talking about, we're not like them, baby . . ."

"We are if we do things behind each other's backs. Don't you see? I don't care about those damn letters. I don't care what he says. What matters to me is you, you are my husband; don't speak to me anymore about wanting to become like my dad. My dad abandoned my mother and me, he went on to build a life on lies. Do you really want to be like him?"

"Oh God, Layla, no! You must understand how that is the very thing I do not want. It's so I don't have to continue living a lie that I want so desperately to go with you to the U.S." He gripped my face in both of his hands. "Listen to me, Layla, listen carefully. I cannot be who I am, here. In India, in Hyderabad, I am the firstborn son, I am a Muslim man even if I don't believe, and now I am a husband and am expected to one day be a father. I have responsibilities to everyone but myself. Each face I look into reminds me of who I should be, and who I can never be, here. And that is the lie, to me, that is the lie. Sometimes I think I worked so hard and accomplished so much at college because I never felt good enough. Baby, I don't think I have it in me to be what everyone else wants."

Roles that were too big and awkward, like oversized garments. Who else to better understand than me? I wrapped my arms about him, saying, "You can be yourself with me, Sameer. I'm not expecting anything from you as my husband but honesty. Please, we're going to

Madras, we're going to be leaving soon for the U.S., let's come out to each other about what we've done and start fresh . . ."

"Yes, start fresh in the U.S., it's all I want. It'll be like . . . like resetting my image. You have given me that, Layla. You have freed me." He grabbed my face and began kissing me. "I'm not your father, Layla, I'll never abandon you." He flipped me over, onto the bunk, crouching on the ground before me. He was trying to peel away the chador. The train began jerking as it came to yet another stop. Out the window, I could see the front cars curving round a bend, arms and heads sticking out of open windows, and what looked to be a man sitting on top of the engine, wrapped in a wool shawl. It had started to rain, light drops sliding down the window. I pulled away and walked over to the door. He looked at me, surprised, even hurt.

"Layla, what . . . ? Is this about your mother still? Are you still holding a grudge? Listen, baby," he stood and walked over to where I was standing and set his arms on either side of me, locking me in place. The train hollered. A little boy sat beside the tracks, his back turned to the train, defecating. He bowed his head before me in shame. "I felt exposed when you found those letters," he whispered. "I felt . . . you hated me. But it was me, Layla, I hated myself for what I'd done." He flattened himself against me, lifting up my kurta.

Yet another stop at some unknown village, its name scrawled in black lettering across the back cement wall of what served as the rail station. The Hindi letters that I was used to seeing now replaced by an unfamiliar Tamil. People were jumping off to stretch and smoke, drink chai from a seller who handed it out in small earthenware cups, passed from this person to the next. A tall woman in a black burkha that was much too short for her, face covered entirely by its netting, was walking about alone, ducking behind this person and the next, as though searching for somebody, a lost child, an old lover. Things that could not be left behind.

"My mother took me to the doctor," I whispered. "An OB. The bleeding, on the wedding night, all these days I've been putting you in my mouth . . . I'm telling you so we can start over, so there are no lies between us . . . I went there behind your back, and now I'm filled with shame. I should have come to you, I should have told you, right then, on the wedding night, but I was too scared. And now, now it's gone so far . . ."

He pulled back, trying to read my face even as he was shaking his head. He knew what I had to tell him. "What are you talking about? Layla, what are you . . . *talking about*?"

"I should have been on the pill a month . . . it had only been a couple of weeks, maybe less . . ."

"Don't tell me any more, I don't want to hear any more . . ."

"I had started them planning for the wedding night, not . . ."

"I'm telling you to stop!"

"I got pregnant, Sameer, oh God, I got pregnant."

He closed his eyes and his body went limp and still. After a moment, he spoke so quietly I could hardly hear him over the laughter and chaos outside. "All this time you've known, living in my house, sleeping in my bed?"

"Yes, yes."

There was nothing left to say.

THAT NIGHT, HE slept alone on the bunk across from mine, refusing my touches, any gestures of reconciliation, even apologies. What else could I provide?

At daybreak, when the train pulled into Central Station, the rain was thick and the sky still so dark there appeared to be no change between the night we had passed so uncomfortably and the new day, which brought no promises of relief. No calls to prayer here, at least none I could hear beyond the shrieking metal of the train, its final wheeze as it came to a full stop, an animal hunkering down on its belly to rest.

He had dressed himself sometime during the night, while I'd been asleep. Yell at me, curse me, even hit me, I was used to it all, had gotten used to it from Dad, who had started to beat me when I was two and only stopped the day of my wedding. Though Sameer did not know it, he had himself freed me.

Nevertheless, it was the beatings I preferred to the silence. The beatings were like the stretches between the train's village stops; I never knew when the next would suddenly be upon me, I was never able to fully be at ease. And this: when he was beating me, at least I knew he saw me, at least I knew I was alive. Submission, not to Allah, but to Dad, and the only way he knew how to touch me. Love, in my mind, at that time, could express itself from the visage of hate.

When I pulled out a fresh outfit to wear, Sameer stood before the window, gazing out, as though to hide me from view, though I knew he was really turning away from the body that had for this long deceived him. He had been right: on the wedding night, without intending to, I had made a fool of my husband.

The train had burrowed underground, and we had to make our way out by pushing through the crush of passengers then filing up the steep steps. Sameer carried our bags, the small one with his immigration papers and our passports strapped over his shoulder, the suitcase passed from one hand to the other as he strode through the crowd, plowing through in a way I had not yet learned to do. Too polite, always too scared. Before long, he was half a yard before me, easily spotted in his American clothes and fair skin, his height. Tamils appeared generally darker, their skin tight and smooth around their faces, the women's exposed bellies not the flapping flesh I was used to seeing on the women in the Old City, on my own Asma Kala, cloistered women whose only physical exertion was to get to and from the kitchen. And there she was, that tall woman in the burkha that was too short, shiny loose *shalwar*-pajamas exposed from shin down, masculine sandals. She was alone, as I had not known women could travel here, that child or lover she'd been searching for at the village stop never recovered. She kept pace with Sameer, as though she were his wife and not I. In his effort to flee the train station, flee me, he didn't notice her.

Outside, he set our suitcase under a cement overhang and lit a cigarette as he waited for me to catch up. The air was thickly humid in the way Hyderabad didn't get, the dry heat of the high plateau. We had journeyed down the sloping earth to the Bay of Bengal, its salt carried in the rain, tasted on my lips. Sameer's skin, if he would only let me kiss it, must have held the same flavor. His T-shirt was sticking to him.

When I caught up, he said, "Stay with the bags. I'll just run and hire a taxi." For a moment, he stared out into the rain, the kind of torrential storm Hyderabad hadn't yet experienced, the monsoons rising up from the south. Taxis were lined along the curb of the sidewalk, some distance away, and we had brought no umbrella, not preparing for anything but the Consulate.

I reached out and touched his back, running my hand down the center, along the ridges of his spine, and he turned and shot me that look he'd first given me when I'd suggested we stay on in India. He didn't know who his wife was.

"Sameer, please," I began, but he lurched away, his boots sloshing through the pools of water, and I watched him duck his head into a taxi window, his clothes and hair pinched down with water. As he was trying to get into the backseat, that woman in the burkha came up to him and said something, and he pointed down the road, before jumping into the taxi. She got into another one by herself. The taxi pulled up as close to me as possible, and Sameer and the driver, a short man wearing what looked to be a black plastic bag, cut out around his face, came running over. They grabbed the bags, and I scampered behind them to the car.

The hotel was just off Mount Road, a wide street filled mostly with cars and taxis. I didn't see any cycle-rickshaws here, everything looking cleaner, sharper, more in order. Stoplights that were heeded, a center divide between us and oncoming traffic, underground subways. I saw foreigners hiking about with overloaded backpacks, parka hoods tied tightly under their chins, their white skin startling to me, making Nate seem even more alien. The taxi pulled into the U-shaped driveway of Hotel Sri Lenka, dropping us right in front of the doors, and the bellman, dressed in red, his head shaved in some penitence, raced to the car and got our bags. As we were heading in, I saw a line of monks walking by, dressed in orange robes, heads shaved like the bellman's. They were holding brass bowls, fragrant fumes rising up and out, the gentle tinkling of temple bells. They did not seem to notice the rain.

The room was not like what I had expected, nothing like a honeymoon suite. It was on the second floor, just two twin beds pushed together to make a queen, a crouching toilet, a water heater for baths, a heavy floral curtain over the glass door blocking out the dim light. The bellman pushed it back and slid open the door to a narrow balcony, the rain wetting the carpet. Coconut trees outside, terra-cotta roof tiles of the building next door. When I peeked into the alley below, I saw a man reading a newspaper in the doorway of what looked to be his apartment. He was sitting cross-legged on the top step, shielded from the slanted rain, his arms cut off at the elbows. He would lick a stump and use it to flip a page.

The bellman left and Sameer peeled off his wet T-shirt. He stood before me a moment, wiping his chest with it, before saying he was going to take a bath. When he went inside, I heard him lock the door.

WHAT COULD WE do in this rain? Where could we go?

There was a cafe across the street that made foot-long masala *dosas*, and we ordered breakfast from there. Sameer paid the bellman to pick up the food for us. Then he sat at the round table by the door with the immigration forms I had brought back with me from the U.S. I watched him run the pen over the same question again and again, trying to read it. Finally, his face fell into his hands.

When the *dosas* arrived, I fed him myself, like Nafiza used to feed me. As he chewed, he stared at me with glistening, pained eyes. "*I am more intimate to you than your own jugular vein.*" How could he not see this?

I set the dish down and crouched before him, taking his hands in mine, that silver toe ring denting the flesh around his thumb. I kissed it. "I want you to make love to me."

He blinked at me, but said nothing.

"I want you to make love to me, Sameer," I repeated. "I don't want to wait anymore. I am clean now, I am entirely yours."

He pushed his chair away from me and rose, fingers on his forehead. "We seem to be living in two different worlds, Layla. I seem to recall you telling me that you'd gone to some bloody clinic, days before our honeymoon, to get rid of some other man's filth." His voice was rising in a way I'd never heard, spit spewing from his mouth.

I stepped toward him, and he angled away, then pushed to the other side of the room. He stumbled over the suitcase. Suddenly he was racing back to the door, and I stepped before it. He stopped, grimacing.

"I love you," I said. "I told you because I love you. Do you think I told anyone else—not even him!" Even as I was saying it, I heard how it must have sounded to him, twisted. Yet it was the truth. I had confessed to Sameer, exposing not simply what I had done, but who I was, my faults, my mistakes. In exchange, I wanted his forgiveness, his acceptance. "I want the fulfillment of my love, Sameer. I want you to make love to me."

"Are you mad? Have you gone out of your bloody mind?" He jabbed at his own head. "Make love to you? Do you think I'm just some . . . some bloody, I don't know, machine, that can just get it up and do it, fuck you, lie in bed with you, like you've been lying in my bed, lying to me, fucking me over. No, I can't, and I won't! I won't touch you . . . not now."

"Not now, not now," I said, mimicking him, the anger in me rising, taking full control, an intensity of feeling I'd never known before, a demon stronger than lust or love, and I picked up the ashtray from the table, intending to hit him, and he watched me, arms crossed over his chest, tongue pushing through his front teeth, daring me in that way I sometimes dared Dad, removed from all emotion, all physical pain. It was the opposite of prayer, where the spirit rises, soaring above the prison of our bodies; here, whenever Dad struck me, I hid inside the tendrils and gut of my own flesh, between the beating of the quickened heart, no sensation reaching me.

I set down the ashtray, whispering, "It is our honeymoon."

"Yes, it is," he said, then stepped onto the balcony and lit a cigarette. In the dark day, his figure was a darker shadow.

SO WE STAYED in the room all day, in this tropical paradise, the air suffused with the scent of the bay. I imagined that other couples on their honeymoon, even when it was sultry and inviting, chose to stay inside, providing each other the pleasure that no day, no matter how lush, ever could. Here, now, I had planted myself in the chair by the round table, close to the door, forbidding my husband to leave.

He was lying on the bed, on top of the covers, arms behind his head, staring up at the ceiling. No rotating fan here, just the ocean's wind coming through the glass sliding door, the kind Nate had pushed open to slip inside. The rain had dampened the floral curtain, half-drawn to keep the wetness out, and water dripped onto the carpet, a growing darkness that looked as though someone had urinated. I was now smoking his cigarettes, the ashtray nearly full. Night, day, there was no difference here, one rolling into the next without respite. I had seen nothing of Madras, but I already hated it.

"Would you have preferred I not tell you?"

He rolled onto his side, his back to me. "Please, give me some peace."

"I have been thinking these past few days—I guess ever since I found those articles—how strange it is . . . you know, it almost seems as though you prepared me for some incredible sexual adventure, yet you've given me nothing. I mean, yes, I've been taking you in my mouth, but you weren't prepared to do more even back then, when you didn't know about . . . what was happening inside me. You've not made a move in a month. I mean, it's not like I've been holding you back, like you've wanted to make love to me and I've . . . been holding you back. You have been perfectly satisfied with the way it is. I'm the one who wants more. You could go on like this, couldn't you? Honestly—and we are being honest with each other, ever since we got onto that damn train, we've been perfectly honest with each other—so, honestly, Sameer, what you do and what those articles describe are so very different, because really, *honestly*, you've not made a move, I mean, you've not once touched me, not really, you've not once, for instance, touched my breasts. I thought . . . well, I thought men liked that kind of thing." I sucked at the cigarette and noticed my hand was trembling. The room stank of sea salt and mildew and stale smoke.

He folded the pillow over his head. I was now the noise he did not want penetrating his skull, breaking into whatever it was he believed. "You want to talk about letters, baby, what about the ones you wrote to me, huh? Remember how you would describe your *amme*, always talking talking, driving you mad. That's what you're doing now, talking in circles, driving me bloody mad. You can't tell me what you did, then expect me to . . . to . . . bloody hell, I don't even know what you want from me anymore."

I snuffed out the cigarette and went to him, my knee falling into the crack between the two single mattresses and getting caught. I yanked it free and straddled his hips so that he fell onto his back. I began undoing his belt. How could he not know what I wanted when I had exposed myself in the severest way?

"Make love to me, please, just once," I pleaded.

He pried my hands away. "I'm warning you, Layla, I'm barely keeping control of myself. Don't do this, don't throw me over the edge."

I unzipped his trousers. "Is it me, Sameer? Do you not find me attractive? Is it my round features, my darker skin? Everyone at the wedding whispering how much more beautiful the groom is than the bride. Is that it, am I too ugly to fuck?"

He rose, gripping my hands behind my back, and stared at me in surprise, then, finally, in some recognition. "This isn't about me, is it, Layla? This is about you, this is about your bloody father! I told you,

I'm not him. I don't care what he told you about the way you look, nor what those fools said at the wedding. In India, it's about skin color, that's all. If you had skin like mine, they'd all say you were beautiful, but no one's looking at *you*, Layla. No one sees you, not here . . ."

"That's right, Sameer, no one sees me, not even you. Somehow, I'm not enough for you, am I? What is it about me that you *really* find . . . repelling?"

The word he had chosen when he had tasted me on the wedding night was still reverberating inside, a noise like Amme's wail from the other side of the locked door. She had been rejected, she had been cast out, not just herself but her entire femaleness humiliated, spurned. Of no use to the one man who, in this world, could be her lover.

Sameer closed his eyes, head sinking in apology for what he'd said, and his grip loosened around my wrists. I passed my fingers through his thick hair, kissing him. We fell sideways on the bed, the slit between the two mattresses passing under my back, widening. He fumbled with my kurta, raising it, digging his hand inside, finding my breast, but I knew he was merely being the dutiful husband, the one who had responsibilities to everyone but himself.

I released him, though I didn't want to, and after a moment, sensing my body had gone still, his face fell into the curve of my neck. Which of us was defeated?

"Listen, Layla, to me, making love is communication, it's connection. If my heart is feeling love for you, if my lips are telling you so, then my body will follow. It's just another language you and I can speak to each other, just one more way of coming together. But I've got to first hear that love in my heart . . . otherwise—well, since you've asked me to be honest—I can't get hard. I don't know what sex is to you, but that's what it is to me. If there is no love, there is no expression of love."

"Are you saying you don't love me?"

He sighed as he rose off my body and zipped up his trousers. "I'm saying I'm really confused. The things you've done have really hurt me.

You don't seem to understand how much it took out of me to forgive your . . . infidelity. You were always impatient about it, never once apologizing, just requiring that I move on as though nothing had happened. And now you're doing the same thing, except worse. Look at the demands you are making. It's like you're suddenly a little girl, an unreasonable little girl. You have lost all sense of yourself."

From the suitcase, he dug out that blue button-down I so admired on him.

"Let me go with you," I said. "Don't leave me, please."

He changed by keeping his body turned from me, as though hiding himself away. "I don't like leaving you, Layla, believe me, I've been wanting to go on this trip all month, you know that. I hate it there, in my parents' house, I hate that they're just outside the door, able to hear everything we do. I've wanted nothing more than to get out of there, to come here with you. Bloody hell, didn't I work till two days ago, saving up for this trip? But, now, there's no peace with you, either."

"I won't talk about it anymore. I promise."

He paused a moment and scratched roughly at his head with both hands. The lines were thick across his forehead. "Baby, it wouldn't be good if I stayed. As I said, I'm barely keeping control of myself."

He went over to the table and found the packet of cigarettes empty. He crumpled it before casting it on the floor. "I'll be back before too long."

DAWN, THE HOUR at which I'd grown accustomed to rising. My favorite time in India, when the roads were empty and quiet, and the sky filled with blessings. A lazy breeze was stirring the heavy curtain, the clouds cleared up, the early morning wrapped in gray-blue shadows. In the distance, wooden temple bells, then, farther away, metal ones, the sound as comforting to hear as the azan in Hyderabad, stirring the faithful awake. Sameer had still not returned.

During the night, another visit from the demon, his touches accentuating the rift between my husband and me. Though he continued to hide his face, this time he had actually spoken. *He'll never touch you,* he'd told me, laughing, *that boy will never touch you.*

That boy, he had said it as though he himself were some older man, my ancient lover, an intimacy in his tone laying claim to me in a way no one had before, not Nate, not my husband. And I was reminded of what Amme had said to the blind *alim* when describing my dreams: once a demon takes a liking to a woman, he won't let any man, not even her own husband, inhabit her.

THERE WERE THREE boys playing in the surf, all slender and curly haired, shirtless. Two were still wearing dark trousers, wet and clinging to their thin legs, one pair having dropped so low as to expose the bones of the boy's pelvis, a black string knotted around his slim waist with a silver amulet to ward off demonic possession, the very protection I needed. Off in the distance, beyond the third boy in his white briefs, were two smudges against the horizon, ships moving in and out of the bay. The sky was a hue darker than the blue water.

Sameer had returned not much earlier and had raced straight to the shower without a word to me. Again, the metallic click of the bolt. When he came out, he had a dingy white towel wrapped about his waist, hair flat across his crown and forehead. His damp feet left prints on the carpet. He crouched before the suitcase and dug around. When I saw he was trying to put on my jeans, I took them from him and slipped them on myself. I told him I wanted him to take me to Marina Beach.

It was close enough to walk to, and leading from the main road down to the water were makeshift stalls selling seashells constructed in every design I could think of: strung together with silver wire to make earrings and gaudy necklaces, bracelets; large conch shells turned over to form ash trays and pen holders, paper weights with Allah or Ganesh or Shiva inked in; boxes adorned with penny-colored shells. The air stank of fish, though when we came upon the beach, the only boats I saw were no larger than canoes, the wood warped and cracked, dilapidated, so I knew they hadn't been used in some time. The real fishing boats had probably gone out at dawn, when I had been just rising from sleep.

I took up a piece of driftwood and scrawled Sameer's name in the sand, remembering, against my will, how Raga-be had written in the dirt before bringing me up to the roof. He hadn't said a word to me since he'd returned. He kept his hands dug inside his pockets, head bowed, eyes averted. I could have been walking alone.

"Do you know someone in Madras?" I asked, crossing out his name.

He finally turned to me, surprised. "What are you talking about?"

"You were gone all night. In Hyderabad, it's one thing, you've got relatives and friends all over. Here, where did you go?"

"There is no other woman, Layla, I assure you of that. You needn't fear any such digressions, I swear."

"Yes, you told me that before—" and Roshan had confirmed it, park, school, home, such was his trajectory, "—but I can't help but wonder . . ."

"Listen to me," he said, then shielded himself behind me to light another cigarette. He'd been smoking one after another since we'd left the hotel, right through breakfast, his *dosa* left untouched. "When I left the room last night, I was just intending to go get more cigarettes, maybe take a walk or something. But I ran into a friend of mine . . . I didn't know he was here. I was just trying to figure out what he was doing here . . . It got late, I hardly slept on the train, and I was tired. We'd been fighting so much! I fell asleep there, at his place, with him." After a moment, he said, "See, baby, you have no reason to worry," and kissed my forehead. He walked off before I could ask any questions, his black boots splashing through the waves, the thick soles caked with sand. Overhead, gulls called each other as they followed him, then swooped down to peck at the cigarette butt he cast in the water.

I was carrying my sandals in one hand, jeans rolled up to my knees, the freest I'd been in India. I was growing tired of being confined to limits, especially those involving my husband. I threw the driftwood into the waves and watched it plummet out of sight, then resurface. The gulls squawked and blew off. A jumbo jet was leaving a white streak across the pale sky, and I thought how, eighteen years before, my parents had been here with me, getting their visas, planning their future, together. If they had remained in India, my father might have still taken on another wife, but he would never have thought to divorce my mother. Standing now where the two must have strolled, the water licking my feet, though at that time I must have been cradled in my parents' arms, I saw the long stretch of time compressed into the straight line of the horizon before me and felt the heavy weight of abandoned hopes, of lives lived in ways we never imagined for ourselves.

I felt his gaze on me before he reached my side. The cigarette smoke mingled with the scent of salt and fish.

I said, "My mother returned to the U.S. with my father. They went back the same day we came here. She denies to me that she wants him back as her husband, but he's the only thing she craves. Now she's going to watch his sons. The surrogate mother, the surrogate wife, without Sabana there—without *me* there—she's going to finally live out the fantasy of how her family should have been." I smirked, adding, "I can't believe she still loves him."

He was standing very close, facing me as I faced the bay, his chest against my arm. "How did you know you didn't love him? You left, even after your . . . night together. He's right, why didn't you stay with him, you gave him your virginity for God's sake, that's not a small thing, not for a Muslim woman!" His voice was agitated and rising and he stopped himself and blew smoke over my head. He pressed his forehead against my head so that his lips brushed the top of my ear. "Did you leave him only because he was forbidden to you, being an American man, or did you know—*how* did you know you didn't love him?"

Because he couldn't provide me what I needed, a life. And now, even the little he had provided me that night seemed to be ending the one I had tried so desperately to make with my husband.

"The more you stay away, Sameer, the more I think about that night. It's beginning to take on a significance it hadn't . . . *he's* the only one who's ever touched me."

Sameer threw his cigarette aside, then his thumb dove into the waist of my jeans as he pulled me close. "Let's go back to the hotel room right now. I want to . . . I *need* to make love to you, Layla . . . right away."

HE WAS LYING on top of me, crying.

The curtains were half drawn, not against the rain today, but the bitter sun. He had tried to force his body to perform, much like Naveed had tried to perform to the music of the brass band that was not meant for dancing. Cold, mechanical touches that made me think of those pornographic articles he'd sent me, written in his own hand. The body's functions, not the heart's, though his lips kept insisting he loved me, that he would do anything to keep me. In the end, he could not do the one thing I wanted.

He rolled off me and sat on the side of the bed, hands raking his scalp. He was bent over, the knobby ridges of his spine like a snake trapped inside his flesh. "You must know this isn't about you," he said, his voice barely over a whisper. "This is . . . I cannot tell you how much I needed to make love to you today, for me. Bloody hell, for *me*! You should not feel ashamed, you should not feel there is anything . . . lacking in you. There is something severely lacking in me, or so I am beginning to think." He threw his head up to the ceiling and his cheek glistened with tears. "I am afraid that maybe I cannot go on being your husband."

I sat up and stared at the back of him. When I said I loved him, it was to say that I believed the clay that had been used to mold him had been split down the center to shape me, his wife. "What are you talking about, Sameer? You promised you would never abandon me."

He sat as he was, back hunched, head turned up, letting the tears run down his face as freely as his mother did. "I tried to make love to you, I sincerely did. But when I touch you," he raised his hands before him and stared at them as though they were alien to his body, "there is something holding me back, something I cannot push past, some sort of invisible wall between us. I wish I could explain to you . . . or even to myself." He bowed his head in defeat. "I want nothing more than to be able to make love to you, Layla . . . even now. Please understand I am not a man given to faith, but I did have faith in this marriage. I did have faith that I would be able to make you happy."

I wrapped my arms about his waist and pressed myself to him. "This is my fault, Sameer. I shouldn't have pushed you, not right after telling you about the pregnancy. I thought that maybe if you made love to me then it would be your way of forgiving me. I didn't think you . . . I just didn't think. I'm sorry. Please . . ."

He jerked away and stood before me naked. His nails scratched at his head again. "No, Layla, you are not listening. I'm telling you, this has nothing to do with you. There is a wall that you cannot see—that I did not see till now—that is between us. You are so beautiful, Layla. You are . . . you read yourself what Nate had to say. Men are attracted to you, but I . . . I am afraid of what's happening here. I still don't believe . . . but how else can I explain . . ." He dropped on his knees before me and gripped my face, the muscles of his arms and chest flexing. His eyes were wild in a way I'd not seen before, unhinged. The loss of control he so feared. Spit flew from his mouth as he spoke. "Look at me, Layla, look at me. Do I not look like a man to you? Do I not look like I can satisfy . . . *whomever* I please? So tell me why I can't touch you—what is keeping me from touching you, Layla! Tell me!"

ONCE MORE THOSE back alleys, this time rushing through them with my husband.

Nothing had changed. Not the road, so narrow the taxi had to drop us off at the head, and not me, hidden in a black veil, and not those darting eyes. His now, not Amme's.

I was surprised he had agreed to come along on this journey, but perhaps my husband felt there was nothing left to lose. He was, after all, the same man who had no patience for Allah and his scriptures, his expectations of us. And without Allah there is no demon, just as there is no darkness without light. *Alim*, the Arabic word for all-knowing, and one of the ninety-nine names of Allah. Seeking one out now, on our honeymoon, was like seeking out a marriage therapist. Counsel and insight, healing, not exorcism, was what we wanted. Desperation that leads one to count on a stranger, come what may.

Sameer stopped at a slim door and compared the house numbers to those scribbled in blue ink across the fine lines of his palm. A *mol'lana* from Thousand Lights Mosque had told us where to find him. Zakir was his name, the *alim*'s, and I realized the moment the *mol'lana* had said it that I had never known the name of any other *alim*.

Sameer gripped my arms and stared into my face with those piercing eyes. "Are you sure about those dreams? Are you sure he said he'd never let me touch you?"

I reached up and caressed his handsome face. "I want nothing more than for us to be happy, don't you understand?"

He sighed before rapping on the door. Immediately, it opened and a frail child stood before us. She was wearing a Western-style dress, the hem of which came down to her knees, exposing ankles as thin as her wrists.

Sameer stared beyond her a moment, but there was no one else in the small stone foyer, so he crouched before her and gently said, "We have come in search of the *alim*."

But she didn't seem to hear him. She was gazing up at me with frightened eyes, as though I were some sort of demon, and I released the fabric of the chador from around my face and smiled at her.

A woman's voice called from one of the inside rooms. "Haven't I told you not to keep opening the door, Sadia? You know I can see what you're doing from here. I can see you no matter where you are."

The child did not move from the door. "A woman has come, looking for Bhabha."

"Another woman? See, I told you not to keep opening the door.

Aie, since you've been born, you've given me no peace. Ill-fated girl."

Sadia hung her head.

I edged back into the alley. It was as though I had entered my own past.

She grabbed my hand and pulled me in, saying, "Amma, should I let her inside?"

"Now that you've opened the door, Sadia, she must be let in, mustn't she? Tell her to wait in the *angan* while your *bhabha* finishes his prayers. Don't invite her inside the house, Sadia. Tell her I can hear her footsteps so I'll know if she tries to sneak in where she's not invited. Remember that, Sadia, never invite them into the house or they'll become real."

The girl released my hand and walked to the center of the foyer. Sameer closed the door behind us and came to stand by my side. Beyond Sadia were two more doors, both covered in green curtains, and to my right was a curved staircase that led to the second floor. She stopped in the middle of one of the square stones and squeezed the sides of her feet together. Her hair was parted down the center and braided into two loops. Around her neck was a thin gold necklace. I expected a small pendant to read Allah, but there was nothing on it at all, just a thin gold line that might have been a stray strand of hair.

"Amma says you are to wait here while Bhabha finishes his prayers. She says she is happy you are visiting because we have not had visitors for many months, not since she changed the house numbers to confuse the demons." She leaned toward us, her small feet remaining squeezed together, and whispered, "But the demons are inside." She tapped her head before fleeing into one of the inner rooms.

HE WAS YOUNGER than I had expected. Not much beyond his early thirties, though with his heavy beard it was hard to tell for sure.

He did not invite us inside the house, nor to the room on the second floor, from where he had just emerged. He kept us standing in the stone foyer, while he sat on the bottom step, his long kurta draped over his knees, legs pulled in to his wide chest. From deep in the house, I could hear Sadia, sometimes screaming, sometimes laughing, and the mother singing the same tune over and over.

"What kind of help have you come seeking?" he asked, digging his fingers around inside his beard.

Sameer glanced at me. I shook my head. I had never been the one to reveal myself to an *alim*.

After a moment, Sameer stepped closer to Zakir and stooped down to him, then rose up again. Finally, he said, "We are having trouble with intimacy. No matter how much I want, I cannot get close to my wife. A wall," he said, his hands rising to show this, but then they clasped together, unable to explain. "What I am saying, Zakir *sa'ab*, is that I need your help. You must show us a way through this . . . difficult situation."

So there it was, our problems confessed without apology, and without all the hesitation and reluctance, the back and forth I was so used to. The abruptness embarrassed me further, and I stared at Sameer's boots as I waited for the *alim*'s response. Certainly he would now want to know my part in all this, what I had done to push my husband away—*repelled*.

But Zakir remained silent, and, after a while, I glanced over at him and, without intending to, met his gaze. He didn't avert his eyes. There was something about the way he watched me that I found very familiar, not my husband's hypnotic, penetrating stare, but something I had been desperate to see for some time now. A look of tenderness that had drawn me to Nate, making me single him out. I covered my face with the veil.

Still, he kept his eyes on mine as he turned his palms up and began reciting prayers in Arabic, ones I had not heard before. When they came to an end, he took in a deep breath as though to begin others, but merely sighed and shook his head, his lips turned down over some regret. "I am sorry you two have come all this way, but this is not a case . . ." He stopped and turned to Sameer. "My powers are of no use; I think you know this."

Sameer was quiet a moment. Finally, his head dropped and a hand rose up to massage his forehead, as though to smooth out the deep lines. "Let us go, Layla," he said.

I stepped toward the *alim*, staring into his eyes as intently as I had into Nate's. "You must help us, please, this is our honeymoon." Then I remembered the money Amme had handed me at the clinic, some of which I had brought along, and added, "I will give you whatever you want."

HE CAME TO our hotel room that night, arriving exactly when he said he would. Outside, the mild showers had turned into another torrential downpour, though he came into the room completely dry, not even carrying an umbrella. For all I knew, he could have been in the lobby for hours, waiting for this instant.

Just as I, up here, had been waiting for his arrival with an impatience I used to feel with Nate, wondering why it took him so long to follow me, onto the bus, into my room. When I was finally sure he would come, I had dressed for him, choosing what I wore with as much care as I did tonight for Zakir. What was it I was feeling, this strange collapse of time? Stepping back into my past, indeed, right into the very night I had for so long been driving away. The time had come for me to face my demon, drive *him* away.

Zakir showed up entirely clean-shaven, the skin on his face radiant, and I hid a smile behind my *duppatta*. So he, too, had done some primping for this meeting. Now he looked even younger than I had originally thought, perhaps only in his late twenties.

Without glancing at me, he set the green bag he was carrying onto the round table and asked where I had last seen the demon. I was sitting on the bed, facing his back, the nape of his neck, and I wanted nothing more than to see those eyes, that tenderness.

"I think you may have misunderstood, Zakir *sa'ab*," Sameer said, using his most formal Urdu. He kept himself by the balcony door, blowing smoke out into the wet night, and I could not help but think he was keeping as far from the *alim* as possible, perhaps wondering how he'd let me convince him of this in the first place. "The demon Layla sees," he went on, "is one of the mind—perhaps even of her own making, her imagination. He visits her only in dreams."

Zakir turned to him and crossed his arms over his chest. The collar of his loose kurta ran down the center of his chest and it opened slightly to expose dark hair. Hair on Nate's chest, too, which I'd run my fingers through, memorizing him, our first and last night together. The *alim* said, "Demons don't appear out of nowhere, do they, Sameer Bhai?"

Sameer's gaze faltered, and he flicked the cigarette out the balcony door. Just the pounding of rain, no thunder at all. "No, they don't," he finally said, the lamppost behind him shedding a sickly yellow light that reminded me of Nafiza, the jaundice that was rising up her flesh.

I said, "I went to a lady doctor before we came to Madras. I thought that would make the dreams go away, but . . ." I stopped and shook my head, lips turned down in defeat. "When he came into this room, it was from that door." I gestured to the one behind Zakir, which led to the hallway.

He went and placed both palms on the wood and moved them in tight circles, the breeze from the cool night gently stirring the bottoms of his long kurta. I watched him feel the entire door, crouching low then reaching up beyond the door frame. He knocked on the wood, then placed an ear against it, listening, grunting, as though hearing some strange tale. Then he turned and stared at Sameer's boots. "*Djinns*," he said. "They reveal everything."

Sameer stuffed his hands into his trouser pockets and shook the fabric loose, and I knew he was trying to hide his weak thigh, feeling exposed. I stood and went to him, then dug his hands out and folded them into mine.

"Baby, I'm not sure about this," he whispered in English. "I'm a rational man, and this is . . ."

"The dreams started that same night," I said, then added what I thought would make sense to him, a reasonable way to look at this.

"I've read that when some experience really shakes the body, it yearns to go back and make sense of the event. If I can begin to accept that night as part of who I am, even here, then maybe . . ."

The *alim* interrupted, raising his voice over mine. "If you do not have any objections, Layla, I am going to ask your husband to leave the room." He paused before adding, "And I need your permission, too, Sameer Bhai. Without it, I cannot touch your wife."

"What!" Sameer stared at him, incredulous, and I passed a thumb over his forehead, easing the lines.

"It's okay," I reassured him. "I've done this a thousand times."

Indeed, a thousand times, and with each new *alim* came a new ritual. Only one thing remained constant: faith in its power to mend the body.

ONCE THE DOOR was shut, he changed entirely, gazing into my eyes so fiercely that I had to turn away. I suddenly became uncomfortable with my body, not knowing what to do with it, and I went and sat on the bed again.

As he walked toward me, his kurta swayed in the salty breeze coming in from the balcony door, the long slits pushed back to give away the lines of his firm thighs filling the pajamas. The fabric was the color of his skin, so that I felt I was seeing the whole flesh of him. He surprised me by sitting next to me, the mattress curving under us, and I didn't move away. He was turned toward me, examining my face, slowly taking it in, and I let him.

"So you have gone to a lady doctor, and yet your husband has not touched you?"

"Yes."

"And the dreams began . . ."

"Two months ago." I glanced at the sliding glass door. "They have grown stronger. The other night, he even spoke to me."

"The demon spoke to you?" He sounded surprised. "What did he say?"

"That my husband won't ever touch me. My mother says that when a demon takes a liking to a woman, he won't let another man near her. Is this true?"

"We shall soon find out," he said, cocking his head to stare at me full in the face. The overhead light splashed across his nose to cast his features in shadow. I filled them in. The hair in back was just long enough to pass a hand through and have the fingers become immersed, lost to me. There was already gray in it. "Tell me, Layla, how much do you know about your new husband?"

"On the wedding night, we vowed not to bring up the past. You see, I have done things I now regret, things that would push . . . any man away."

"I'm sorry. I did not mean to hurt you."

"I did not mean to hurt my husband. I want to make it better, I want . . . this demon to go away." I looked into his eyes. "I thought the *djinns* told you everything."

He laughed. "Do you really believe you are possessed, Layla?"

I felt the pressure of his body next to mine and turned to examine his wrist, the width of it, the tan skin tanned further by the sun, the dark hair. It was the wrist I loved the most. Then the hand. The fingers so able to manipulate, to caress or slap, to express emotion. "I can convince myself of anything."

He did not seem surprised this time by what he'd heard. He simply watched me, quietly, before saying, "I don't encounter these sorts of cases very often. But every now and then . . . such a pity. Always so much anguish on the wife's face. The pain and the confusion are always the same. Women are quick to blame themselves. It's because they don't know better. All their lives they've been protected. Were you protected, Layla?"

No one had ever asked me this before, not even him. "I was guarded. My movements restricted. Is that what you mean by protection?"

He sighed, letting out one long breath, letting out the life in him. I inhaled it, and we sat for a while, inhaling, exhaling, breathing in each other. I was about to say his name when the *alim* rose and rounded the bed to the top. He patted the pillow.

"Will you lie here for me?"

I glanced at the pillow then his hand on it. I crawled up the mattress and lay on my back on top of the covers, one hand over the other on my stomach. He went to the table and began rummaging in his bag. I was curious to know what he might take out, but he only removed three candles and three sticks of incense. "Three is an Islamic number," he said. "So are five, seven, and eleven." Then he went around the room, lighting the candles as he did. He placed one on the dresser, and when he saw it reflecting an image of itself in the mirror, he removed it, heated the end once more, and now set it at a corner. He placed another on the floor by the balcony, then closed the door and because it was dark outside, the glass captured what was inside, some of what I knew and some of what I didn't. The diminishing moon was hidden behind clouds, the night as dark as that on a new moon. He drew the shade over the lamppost's light.

Then he returned to the bed with the third candle, shielding the frail flame with a protective palm, and placed it on the night stand next to me. Bending down, he reached inside the lampshade and clicked off the light. Everything was obscured, and I could smell his bitter sweat.

He stood over me and spoke. "To re-create when he comes to you. As I told your husband, demons do not pop up out of nowhere. We must root them out." He struck a match. A trembling hand lit a stick of incense. He used jasmine. "I need for you to lift up your kurta."

I pulled it from around me and raised it above my belly.

"Higher."

I pulled it to just below my breasts.

He sat next to me. The mattress dipped, and I felt my body sinking toward him.

He set a palm on my rib cage. One slender finger on one slender rib. A perfect fit. He followed the bones up to my left breast. The hand closed in on itself, becoming a fist. The knuckles pressed back the breast while a thumb pushed away the underwire of the bra. "This may hurt."

"I've suffered through worse," I said, meaning Dad's beatings. Now why did I want him to know about those?

Or perhaps he already did—those *djinns* telling all—for he didn't ask what I meant. He simply lowered the burning tip of the incense and dug it into the soft underside of my breast. My jaw clenched. His knuckles relaxed. He was chanting. Then he blew on the burn, sending his healing words.

"When he comes to you in dreams, he touches you everywhere?"

"When he came to me that night, yes, everywhere."

He withdrew his hand, but left the touch with me.

Another match. I followed its light to the incense and tried to see beyond it, to his face. As though he had caught me, he lowered the match, bringing it next to my chin. He kept himself hidden even as he took me in. He liked to do that. Observe me when I wasn't aware, from a place hidden. He said he got his best photographs that way. When no one saw what he was doing. No one had ever seen him with me. He might never have been there.

When he spoke, the blaze flickered against the air of his breath. "You are a beautiful woman, Layla. It is such a shame about your husband, it is such a waste."

The match neared its end and he shook it out. He spoke in the dim candlelight, moving in and out of shadows. "When my wife was your age, she was very pretty, too. I was beguiled by her beauty. It is a weakness of mine. Looking back, I think I married her in that state of trance. Now she concerns herself with the girl. Sometimes I feel as though I've disappeared." He paused before adding, "Sadia's ill."

I whispered, "I know what it's like to disappear. To be the ghost or the demon to your family."

"I see you."

Yes, he had seen me from the beginning, even before I had noticed those gray-blue eyes, my shape taking form in them.

He lit another match. For a second, both it and the incense burned together. He blew them out with one breath. He placed his palm where he had just burned me, and I thought he'd burn me there again. Instead, he raked the fingertips across my chest to my right breast. The hand rolled into a knuckle. Again, he pressed up the flesh, lifting up the cup of the bra with a thumb, and pushed the stick into me.

I cried out and shoved his hand away.

He leaned closer so I could see his eyes in the candlelight. That look of concern and tenderness I so longed to see on my husband's face. "You said you were prepared. Should I stop?"

"Just be more gentle."

He receded once more into shadows. Next to me, the soft click of the stick being set down. He picked up a second one.

"You speak Urdu well, but I still hear the accent."

"In the U.S., I am told my English has an accent."

"Your husband tries to be someone he's not. When I first saw him, I thought he was the foreigner and you . . ." he stopped.

"And me?"

"And you his pretty, but naive bride. He's beguiled you. I do not blame you, of course. As I've said, I myself become blinded by beauty. It is my one weakness. Human weakness." He lit the incense. Lips curled and were brought close to blow it out. He curved an arm over my body, pressing the palm onto the mattress. He pushed himself down on the bed, the tan sleeve gliding against my skin. He sat by my thighs, away from even the far reaches of candlelight, enclosed in darkness. A hand tugged at my *shalwar.* "Will you undo this for me?"

I stared at the point of red hovering between us.

"Are you scared?"

"Yes."

"I promise to be gentle. I don't want to hurt you, but . . ."

"No, I'm ready. I want to go through with this. I have already decided that."

"Are you sure?"

I untied my pajamas and rolled them down to my knees. His hand closed on my thigh and parted my legs. I drew in air.

"It will be easier if you relax."

He had told me this before. I loosened my muscles.

His thumb pushed back the fabric of my panty. The red eye drew near and pushed into the skin on my pelvis. I flinched.

"Just once more on the other side." As he lifted his hand to get the matches, I felt it graze my vagina. I didn't say anything. Then the match was lit and the incense burned. And before I could see his face, both were blown out. He gripped my other thigh and squeezed the soft inner flesh, the thumb moving up and down. Then he slid it inside my panty. It got lost in the hair. He sighed, a long ache of breath lifting out of his body.

"You mustn't be beguiled by what is before you." He whispered it through clenched teeth as he pushed the stick deep into the folds of skin.

I stifled a cry, and felt my body thrust into the mattress, away from him. He whispered again, now chanting or reciting, and blew cool breath at the burn. Then he remained humped over me.

The rain pattered against the glass, the sound like my fast beating heart. It was over. I would never see him again. By the first stirring of morning light, this night, his touch, would be nothing better than a dream.

Without a word, he straightened and pulled up my pajamas, retying them as though I were still a girl. After a moment, he stood with some effort, coming up next to me. I felt his gaze on my face, my belly, my breasts. He pulled down my kurta, covering me.

"Shut your eyes."

I placed my hands over my lids. He flipped on the light. I saw the glow outlining my fingers. The darkness within. I removed my hands, and the *alim* was standing before me, just next to the nightstand, prying a candle off the surface. He enclosed it in his palm, and there was wax left on the table, and a ring where the candle had been. He went to the dresser and balcony, blowing out each candle before he collected it. He pulled back the curtain, then returned and picked up the three sticks of incense, the third still unused. He shoved everything back in his bag, then stood next to the round table with his profile to me, staring at the carpet. I sensed he wanted to say something, but didn't know how.

"What is wrong with Sadia?" I asked.

He continued to stare at the carpet, lips parted. "Tumor in the brain. It makes her hallucinate. She, too, sees demons. But I cannot do anything to save her. It's why my wife has grown to hate me." He paused, then added, "She has not much life left in her, I can feel this." He held up his hands, and I knew what he meant. He had placed his palms on her head, as he had that wooden door, and seen all there was to know.

I stared out the balcony. Nothing but the stale light of the street lamp, the shade over the bulb dripping old rainwater or its own sweat. It dribbled off slowly, then fell as quickly as the water from the sky. The genuine and the disingenuous. You couldn't tell them apart. Such was the calamity of our existence.

"Layla, as an *alim*, I cannot tell you what you do not already know. But I will say that as much as your husband hides himself, he has also revealed himself to you." He turned and met my gaze. "Sometimes we must let go of the very thing we desire the most. Allah tests us in the severest of ways."

"I thought you understood," I said, rising to get the money from my purse. "I have already endured that test."

"No, Layla, your test is yet to come. Remember what I said. You must root out the demon." When he saw the money, he grimaced and turned away. "I did not come here for that," he said, zipping up his bag. "I thought *you* understood."

I placed a hand on his. "This is for your daughter," I said. "Take her to a good doctor. Get her cured."

FIVE ROWS OF aluminum chairs. We sat somewhere in the middle, surrounded by all the others who hoped to get out, young and old alike, male and female, the dream of a better life surging equally through everyone, not holding any distinctions. The nondescript, square room of the Consulate stank as much of that dream's sticky-sweetness as it did of betel nut and sweat. America's freedom, from religious riots and curfews, from tainted water and hiring practices, and from whatever personal demon each was escaping. Raga-be had once told me that *jadu* worked only within the confines of a country, its powers evaporating across cold waters. In that way, did these people hope to shake free what was haunting them? Emigration as exorcism.

Sameer was bent over the immigration forms, rushing to complete them before the overhead monitor clicked our number in red. July fourth, he had scribbled in, stating when we had gotten married. That was what they wanted at the Embassy, not the Islamic date, which was nothing but a number existing underneath the real one, like the narrative of my one life almost invisible underneath the other, palimpsest. He hadn't asked about the *alim*.

I said, "My father went over first. He got a job, he rented an apartment, then he sent for my mother. There was a moment, apparently, during his layover in Bombay, when he almost got up and came back to Hyderabad. He suddenly became scared. Where was he headed? He didn't know anything about America or its people. He didn't have a place to live or a job. He didn't even own a winter coat—or know that he should! His pockets were stuffed with rupees. But then he went, leaving behind his family and friends, his country, everything he'd grown to know." I shook my head, amazed, as I was each time I thought of him boarding that plane to America. "There's no turning back when you do something like that," I said. "It takes so much courage. I don't think I would be able to . . . pass that test."

Sameer crossed his arms over his chest and grinned at me. "I think that's the first time I've heard you say anything good about your father. See, Layla, if you let go of that personal drama, you can see what the rest of us see in him."

Yes, one narrative on top of the other, it merely depended on which one you followed.

"I didn't have that dream last night," I said. "Do you think it actually worked, what that *alim* did?"

He brought his hand to his forehead and sighed, a drawing in of his presence. Of course he did not believe it worked. If he had allowed me—indulged me—to get exorcised, he had done so in the same spirit he'd allowed me to pray with his mother. My belief in invisible forces, not his, and maybe he even knew them to be in the realm of a woman's beliefs, her only way to control her world. I should have stuck to talking about my father.

"Listen, Layla, last night, when I left you with the *alim*, I went to the train station and changed our tickets. We're leaving for Hyderabad today, right after the Embassy. This whole trip . . . this bloody honeymoon." He shut his eyes, shaking his head. "We still have some weeks left before the visa comes through, maybe we'll go to Ooty. We'll do this properly." He grunted in disgust—at me, at this whole journey, I could not tell—and returned to the forms.

"But I'm saying I didn't have that dream last night. Maybe we could try again, tonight."

He stuck his finger to his lips, shushing me, as he glanced about at the others, then he threw an arm around my shoulders and pulled me close. His voice was edgy and hard. "Are you going to trust me, your husband, or some bloody *alim*, who you've never met before and who doesn't know a damn thing about us? Now I'm telling you what I need. I need to get away from Madras. I need that moment your father had at the Bombay airport to leave everything behind, *everything*." He drew back, tongue pushing through the front gap, lines thick across his forehead. Though he would not say it, his eyes did: tangible forces, the ones that mattered, belonged to him, my husband. And just as he had let me exercise my powers, now I would need to let him exercise his. A wife did as she was told, even a wife who had gotten her husband past the iron bars of the American Consulate and would soon get him through the immigration line at JFK airport. Her life nearly invisible under his.

Our number was called.

WE WERE ARGUING as we got off the elevator to the second floor of the hotel, so we didn't see that tall figure in the burkha right away. He was denying believing in Old City values—a *man's* value over a woman's—claiming that such archaic beliefs were part of what he was emigrating from. Still, he remained single-minded about leaving Madras that very day.

He saw her before I did and his words halted in midsentence, his dark eyes squinting in that way of his, trying to perceive what was not readily visible. Down the narrow hallway, she was hovering against our room's door, a black ghost against white walls, looking like the demon emerging from my dreams. Our steps slowed at the same time.

"Who is that?" Sameer muttered. His fingers closed around my wrist and he drew me behind him. A simple gesture—was this what Zakir had meant when he'd asked if I'd ever been protected, or was this a motion of love?

"She was on the train," I said, but he didn't hear me. He was digging out our room key while asking her who she was looking for.

She didn't answer. She didn't stir. Below the hem of her burkha, gray slacks, brown leather sandals. But what did that mean when I, myself, was in jeans?

We stopped a few feet from her, Sameer still gripping my hand. "That's our room," he told her in formal Urdu, being respectful. He pointed to the door with the sheaf of immigration papers we'd just turned in, copied for him on his request—he wouldn't take the chance of anything getting misplaced. "The person you're looking for is not here," he said, now trying to communicate in English. "I'm sorry, but . . ."

She began unhooking her burkha, up the side slit, then around her face. "How could you go to the Consulate today?" she asked, but it was not a woman's voice at all. "After Saturday night, after what happened between us, I thought you would stay here with me. I thought you understood this was not some game, some time-pass. I thought you loved me."

Nate's words to me, written in those letters, over and over, and now, finally, spoken out loud, but by someone else, and to my husband. That hollow echo of pain, that stunned disbelief, that tangled betrayal. A lover's heart, not silenced by limits we imposed, convention, taboo, denial. Indeed, love was prayer, rising out of the body, what did it matter in which direction you bowed?

He had come here to say as much, followed us on our honeymoon even after my husband had ordered his friend—lover—not to, using that same tone of authority, of finality, he'd used with me earlier, at the Consulate: *my place to give orders, your place not to ask why.*

He let the burkha drop to the floor, a black pool around his brown feet. Hair on his toes. Sameer's head fell low, as though watching the fabric's descent, his mouth agape, no sound at all—no mandates left to give—just a quick breath, out, out, out, no air going in.

His turn now to speak, to make visible what Sameer would not see, what the rest of us refused to see, the blue hollows under his eyes expressing an anguish that was familiar to me, an age-long suffering, abandonment. Tears had welled up. "How can you continue to go on with this? Before, yes, you could deny, to me, to yourself. Believe what everyone else says: men do not love men, not here, not in India, not in Islam. Oh, what shame, even Allah forbids our sinful bodies to be buried into this earth, though he formed us of that same dirt. Outcasts, *hijras*, our own parents will cast us out, say we are dead to them, to the world. People are so scared of us they scare us into being like them. Marry, have kids, do what is expected of you and not what you want . . ." he stopped, his lips moist, tears running down his face, but his voice was steady, ". . . and not what you *know* you are meant to do. They tell us we do not exist, and we believe them—*believed* them. Now you know, Sameer—at least that was what I was thinking—already you have had your chance . . . with her. On your honeymoon, it was me you found, me you returned to, me you love. After a month away from each other, was the lovemaking not better than before? How can you now deny what this means? How can you still go to America, go on with this other life, this betrayal?" He stepped toward my husband. "See, I have taken off the burkha. I am not scared anymore. Do not hate me, *yaar*, for doing this—is this not what you said, that I had come to Madras to ruin your life? Ruin your life! *Yaar*, I have come here to save you!"

Sameer continued to stare at his own boots, mouth wide open, head shaking. His tongue was wriggling about, useless. He was unrecognizable to me, my husband, more foreign than even I realized.

I pried my hand from his and backed into the room's door, out from between the two friends, the two lovers, the real couple. Bewilderment, anger, jealousy. What was I to feel when I had never prepared myself to be involved in such a predicament? Abandonment, yes, divorce, American-style. And even those Old City values, second wife, third wife, fourth wife. I had married a Muslim man, there were certain rights that belonged to him, things against which I could only pray. But how could I have prepared for this: the friend he had run into, the friend he had not known was here, was the one he had then made love to—yes, made love, communication, another language, another script—made love to him, Naveed—not a friend, but a beloved—while I had waited for him, my new husband, the one to whom I had confessed my sins, asking forgiveness, begging acceptance, fulfillment, that first night of our honeymoon. And this: letters copied from magazines not because he did not know what to write to an American woman, but because he did not know how to make love, even on paper, communicate love, to *any* woman, least of all his own future wife. In one instant, the walls of my world that had taken centuries to construct came crumbling down, my real loss of innocence.

"Look at me, *yaar*, please, look at me like you used to, as you did the other night. Let me see your eyes, your love. Do you not understand, now that she knows, now that someone else knows about us, about our love, you are free! There is no going back."

Going to America to escape lies, he had told me, vowing not to be like my father, when in fact, just like him, my husband had been faithful to nothing but a lie.

"Oh my God," I whispered, "oh my God."

Sameer glanced up at me, blinking, his fierce gaze gone flat. He fumbled with the room key, gave up, turned toward his friend, lover.

"Hello, Naveed," he said, reaching out to shake his hand, as he had that day we'd gone to Golconda, in greeting, in good-bye.

I grabbed the keys from him and locked myself into the room. He began knocking on the door, begging me to open it. He was screaming my name. I sat on the bed and watched the wood shudder, knowing it would give way under pressure. Amme was screaming on the other side of the locked door, calling me her ill-fated daughter, calling me a whore for not wanting to marry the one she had chosen for me to love, make love to. Then she was the one locked inside the room, refusing to come out, days leaking into weeks, into a month, the same wail, the same anguish, the same word: whore, this time, Sabana, the one who had taken her husband, her life, my life, though my mother went on believing she could save me, and in the pattern of the wood, some evil peering out at me, the face of my demon, so painlessly had he risen out from my sleeping body, as my soul would, when I died, snake through the shaft of my jugular vein. The beckoning smile, the light-colored eyes. So it was my father.

Love, why did we all confuse that emotion for what this really was, a desperate loneliness, a greed for human touch.

The door burst open and he strode in, papers gripped in a hand, folding into themselves, the bellman in red by his side, Naveed coming to rest against the door frame.

Two deeds. Hers to draw up the contract and slide it under the door, his to sign it.

She had sold me to him, to the man who would never love me.

My-Ka

I WENT TO Taqi Mamu's in search of Nafiza, the one who, like me, had been raised in a family in which she'd never belong.

I had left my husband in Madras with his lover and taken the Char Minar Express back to Hyderabad, traveling alone as I never thought I would in India, hidden and safe under my chador, being reminded, against my will, of the first time I saw Naveed in the burkha, at that remote village outside Madras, searching through the crowd, looking—though I wasn't aware at that time—for my own husband. Demons rooting *us* out, it didn't matter where you took refuge, in what scriptures, in whose arms.

Without my husband, without everything I had grown to know, it didn't seem possible that the outside world could look exactly the same, but it did, the same emerald rice paddies, the same grazing water buffaloes, the same farm workers, though, in truth, it was now mysterious, withholding. I was beginning to understand that for all I saw, there was something I was blind to, for all revealed, there was something concealed, shadow and light, demons and Allah, though not even that simple. If I had undertaken this journey believing I was cleansed, ready to consummate love, I was returning with a better comprehension of love than I had even bargained for; a carnal knowledge like a seed implanted in my womb. In the end, my husband had taken my innocence in a way Nate never had, nor Sameer himself could have if he had simply had sex with me, performing his duties as my husband.

When the taxi pulled up at my uncle's house, I found it strangely quiet. I knew Ameera Auntie was off teaching but had expected to find Taqi Mamu, who, since Nana had died, had not left the house but to fight the government over that ancestral piece of land (now tourist spot) that I had never seen, nor that he, I was sure, had much memory of. Even if he had been awarded the land's worth, to whom would he have passed on such an inheritance? He and Ameera Auntie had been unable to conceive, and there were no sons in this house to carry on the nawabi bloodline, only Henna and me, women brought up knowing we would be sold and looking forward to it.

Down the side yard, I could see the cement structure of the servants' quarters, the corrugated roof sending off a stiff glare under the hot sun. I had come back up to Hyderabad so quickly, I had beaten the rising monsoons. The door to my nanny's room was shut, the outside bolt drawn, so I knew she wasn't there. Though certainly, with Amme back in the U.S., Nafiza would have resumed working for my uncle, the two always home together, better companions than Taqi Mamu and his own wife.

I went to the front door, which was kept open during the day. Deep within the house, wood creaked, *chappals* skidded on the tile floor. From the verandah steps, I watched my uncle combing back his thick hair with a hand as he approached, walking with slow, sleepy steps down the long hallway. I waited for him, suddenly unsure of what to say. How could you speak of something that didn't exist?

If he was surprised to see me, returned to his house from my honeymoon, returned without my husband, he didn't show it. He simply ordered the driver to set my suitcase in the guest room, the one I used each time I visited and which they had reserved for a baby that never came.

When the driver had passed into the house, my uncle stepped

more fully into the door frame, his thick figure filling it. He didn't ask me in.

"Nafiza is not here, Beta," he said. "She's not working anymore. She's sick. In hospital. You'll have to see her there."

A NURSE AT the hospital had to ask two others before she could inform me that my nanny was in the general ward. Then she quickly left, hands full of green glass bottles and shiny steel trays shaped like kidneys, and I had to stop a doctor to ask how to get there. At first, he walked right past me, as though I hadn't spoken at all. Invisible. I would take no more of such an existence, and I yelled out to him in English, complaining of the hospital's inefficiency, and he paused a moment before returning. It was the American woman they saw here.

We spoke in English, and I noted that he had an English accent.

"How is this patient related to you?" he asked, his arms full of files. He was on his rounds.

I wanted to tell him that Nafiza was my mother. I had in fact called her "Amme" until my family had emigrated to the U.S., as a child not knowing any better or not seeing any difference. At what age did the divisions we saw around us begin to draw themselves inside?

"She's my ayah," I said, too ashamed of myself to call her mother. College fees, private schools, BMW, an *almari* full of jewelry, two airline tickets back to America, that was how Dad had paid for me; I should have known better than to think devotion came with duties.

The doctor took me in with a quick glance, the tight jeans and crumpled T-shirt I'd worn to the Consulate, mapping a future with my husband; then losing him. I must have looked as raw as his patients, scars on the body that no medicine of his could heal.

I thought he would simply tell me where to find Nafiza, but he surprised me by telling me about her case, right there, in the middle of the cement hallway with its stink of Dettol and murmuring of other doctors and patients. I had thought such intimacies required another sort of ritual, the discreet, indifferent walls of some office.

"She has hepatitis," he said, "the type that leads to liver failure. Death." He raised his thick brows, lines forming across his forehead like Sameer's, and I wondered if I would forever see my husband's face in other men's. "Such a disease is sometimes caused by . . . promiscuous behavior. What do you think of that?"

I could sense his condemnation of her and of her kind, his insinuation that such activities could only be committed by a shameless woman, a whore. What would *he* think of the knowledge of love I now carried inside?

"She's a widow, Doctor, with a grown daughter, who has a young daughter of her own. If she has this disease, her own husband must have given it to her. As I recall, he, too, died suddenly of liver failure. But the doctor, at that time, said it was from his drinking. Tell me, is it common practice here to hide things that might save a woman's life?"

IN THE GENERAL ward, hospital beds were lined up one alongside the other, wall to wall. On the far side, sunlight fell through tall, rectangular windows and cast a healthy glow on some of the patients. Every bed was occupied, a few with small groups huddled about. I didn't know how I would find her.

I was heading toward one of the patients by the window, a lone woman sitting up in bed, when I heard my name being called. It was a man's voice, coming from behind me, and I thought it must have been the doctor again, wanting to tell me something more I didn't want to hear. But then I saw Nafiza's son-in-law, Sammy, waving to me from a dark corner of the room. Roshan was sitting on an aluminum fold-out chair beside him, their sleeping daughter in her arms.

I made my way through the narrow aisle toward them, trying to see beyond Sammy to Nafiza's face. She had told me, that day I'd thrown her out, that I should come to her when I could see right again, and the *jadu* of Sameer's pretty-pretty face no longer beguiled me. Though, in truth, I had beguiled myself. As Amme said, *jadu*'s powers were not confined by the borders of a country, but by the borders of our own flesh. You had to believe in the power of something for it to take hold of you.

When I was upon the couple, Sammy salaamed me deeply, and Roshan stood with some effort to embrace me, her sleeping daughter squeezed between us. As she held me close, she whispered how happy our mother would be to see me. But even as she was saying it, over her shoulder, I could see my nanny. Her eyes were closed, her skin flushed yellow. One of her hands was set across her bloated belly, and it was only from its slight motion that I knew she was still breathing.

Here she was, my mother, already in a place beyond my reach.

"THE DOCTOR SAYS she'll be fine. *Irkan, ba,* everyone gets it." It was Sammy, speaking to me with a nervous laugh and a dismissive wave of his hand.

I wasn't sure if he said this because he had been misled by the doctor, or if he was trying to mislead me in an attempt to console. I didn't tell them I already knew it was not jaundice. Jaundice was merely a symptom of her hepatitis.

I looked about for a chair. Sammy slid me his, then stood at Nafiza's feet, hands gripping each other behind his slim back. He was much darker than Roshan, nearly black, the whites of his eyes startling, bloodshot. He had been a Christian when the two had first met, converting to Islam out of his love for her, only to later fall in love with Allah and become a true believer. Roshan had taught him how to pray, as Ameera Auntie had once taught her.

When I sat, I found myself at eye level with Nafiza's distended belly, covered up in a white blanket and two white sheets, though the air was stifling, and I thought of Henna. For there it was, looking exactly the same, the way our bodies carried life and death.

"How long has she been here?" I asked.

They both turned down their lips and shrugged.

Sammy said, "In the hospital, time stands still, *ba*," though I knew if Nafiza woke right then, she would disagree. Her body now winding down.

"We can track it by your mother," Roshan said. "The day before she left for the U.S."

The day after my D & C. Two days after I'd cast her out of the house. For so many years, I had been afraid that some single act of mine would kill my mother, as Dad had ended her life, and now I felt I had done just that.

"This is my fault," I said, my eyes tearing up. "I thought she was spoiling it for me. I hurt her, I rejected her for . . ."

Roshan quickly shook her head. But then she said, "Your mother is a generous woman. It's the reason Sabana's *jadu* does not effect her. She receives so many blessings." Holding her daughter's head to her chest, she bent and picked up her purse. She handed it to me. Inside, there were the reading glasses Ameera Auntie had passed on to Roshan and a bundle of rupees. The staples had been pulled apart to extract notes, but I knew if they were all there, it would equal what Amme had given me. More money would be spent on Nafiza's death than had ever been spent on her life.

I clasped the purse shut and set it against the foot of her chair.

"For the hospital bills," Roshan explained.

For what else could it be? Doctor bills, *alim* bills, even that blank check she had once tried to force on Sabana, hoping to bribe her into leaving. All this use of Dad's money, his power, to try to buy back what was already lost.

SAMMY PACED THE small space between Nafiza's bed and the next, hands so tightly clasped behind his back they were shaking.

He stopped and spoke over Nafiza's belly. "I have to go, *ba*! Roshan, *teik hai, na*? *Chalu*. It's almost four. Got to go make chai. We'll return in the morning." He passed a hand over his face, guilty for having to go run his cafe, go on running a life.

"I'll drop her off at the house," I offered.

Roshan glanced at me, and I nodded side to side. Her eyes narrowed into dark holes, my nanny looking out at me.

She turned to her husband. "You better go alone."

He glanced at me before nodding and raised a hand in good-bye, telling Roshan when he'd be home that night. We watched him go, his slender figure receding into the sunlight that was tumbling onto the floors in wide beams. His thin legs became scissors that cut his way out.

Roshan turned to me, and I knew she was about to ask where my husband was, and, in this way, unravel the details of my drama. And though I had asked her to stay so I could tell her, I suddenly felt there was nothing to say about such an old tale, this, the falling apart of a union, when Nafiza lay like this before me. Her still body speaking of tragedies more irreversible than mine.

So I said, "She's very yellow."

Roshan swallowed and stuck her nose into her daughter's hair. Bisma was facing her, chest to chest, plump legs straddling Roshan's hips, mouth parted in sleep. Drool was wetting Roshan's sari-blouse. Bisma was four years old, the age Roshan had been when her mother began nursing me.

She wiped her eyes with a delicate wrist. "She's changed so much, I don't recognize her. How can anyone say this is my mother?"

I followed her gaze to Nafiza's face and saw sunken eyes sunken further in sickness, as though already receding into the depths of death. Everything else about her was swollen by her own body's waste. The cheeks so full they were rising to envelop the nose, the dark skin like earth, the nose something buried. A miniature grave, a self-suffocation. A foretelling of what was to come.

"Have you tried other remedies?"

Roshan ran a hand up and down Bisma's back. "Raga-be came Friday night. She brought . . ." She paused and bit her lower lip, the skin as dark as mine—could be mine, flesh of the same flesh, just as her name was the shadow of my name: Roshan, Illuminate. She gestured with a chin at the pillow. She wanted me to see for myself what she found so unspeakable.

I rose and felt about under the pillow, the weight of my ayah's head on my hand, strands of coarse hair falling across my wrist. Her own hand was resting neatly on her pregnant belly, the skin dark and parched, the knuckles wrinkled, the nails still clumped with dirt from her daily chores—a life of servitude, to God, master, husband, and child.

A sharp, cool blade stabbed at my palm, and I understood what Raga-be had done. She'd brought that damn knife she'd tried to use on the roof to cut out my baby. Now she was hoping to cut out a sickness that could not be borne.

I had meant a different type of remedy, herbal, homeopathic, but who was I to judge? At such times, we saw not with our eyes, but with hope.

Without a word, I moved back to my chair and began examining my palms. The air stank of Dettol.

I TOLD HER as a way of telling Nafiza, letting my nanny know what she had been trying to tell me all along, how my husband had been fooling everyone, fooling me, the white cloth from our wedding night hiding his shame as much as mine.

When I was done, Roshan lowered her head into her daughter's crown and sighed, not seeming as surprised as I'd thought she'd be. When she finally spoke, strands of Bisma's hair flew back, as thick and coarse as Nafiza's. "You should leave him, of course. It's a sin to live with such a man. Islam prohibits it."

Yes, I knew, but what he had done to me seemed a greater sin. I said, "I fell in love with him."

"Of course you did, he's your husband."

"No, not like that. You know what I mean, Roshan, like you fell in love with Sammy, then married him. I don't know when it happened, but it began to feel like *I'd* chosen him, not Amme." I rolled my knuckles against my temples. "My mind is so quiet. It won't let me think about anything."

She watched me make the motion as she said, "Your mother did the best she could for you, you mustn't blame her. He's so strong and handsome. How could she have known, how could anyone . . . such things are not considered here." She tightened her arms around Bisma and swayed as she spoke. "People will blame you, Layla-bebe. They will even say you made him into the man he is, that you weren't enough to satisfy him so he was forced the other way. Whatever you do now, you must be careful to look compassionate. You're a woman. And no matter what Islam says about such men, it's still your reputation that will get harmed."

She was right, of course, and we both turned and gazed at Nafiza, as though waiting for her to agree or to give some advice of her own.

Finally I said, "You mustn't call me Layla-bebe. No one owns you anymore."

But she didn't hear me. Bisma was stirring, trying to throw off her mother's firm grip. Roshan immediately began bouncing her legs to get her back to sleep. The child pitched her head and mumbled something, calling out to her mother or grandmother. Roshan smoothed her hair and began singing that song Nafiza used to sing while bathing me, about a little girl who would one day find her way home. So my experience had become a lullaby in the same way Amme's memories of childhood had remained, for so long, bedtime stories. We all became our own myths.

When Bisma was dozing once more, Roshan said, "He must have believed he would be able to touch you . . . until he found he couldn't."

THAT EVENING, WHEN I returned to Taqi Mamu's house, it was as silent and deserted as it had been that morning. Twilight was slowly seeping through the skies, and a servant I didn't recognize was rushing about, turning on the courtyard lights. When I was passing him to get to the front doors, he stopped me and questioned who I was and where I was headed. This unsettled me, making me feel like an intruder sneaking into a place I didn't belong.

The long hallway to the back of the house was yet unlit, but I made my way without stumbling. How many times, since childhood, had I run up and down this same hallway, chased by Henna or Nafiza? And, of course, there was that time, a year ago, right before my engagement, when I had finally unlocked the bedroom door and found my mother lying right here, where my feet were now passing, encircled by mourning women, her forehead stained with blood. It was the last visit she had allowed me to make to this house.

I rounded a curve and could now make out a frail light at the end of the hallway, inside the dining room. But I didn't hear any voices so was surprised to find my aunt and uncle, joined by Abu Uncle, dining. A plate was set out for me, facedown, and I sat and said a quick salaam. Abu Uncle shot me that same look he had when Amme had reported my bleeding to him, both knowing and concealing.

My aunt had served a simple meal. Nothing more than green bean curry and rice, dal that needed more salt. After a full day of teaching and her severe diabetes, I knew she could not manage more. For the six months we visited India, Nafiza resumed her duties as my nanny, stopping her work for my aunt and uncle as cook. The two always had trouble finding a replacement for her—since Independence, fewer people were willing to do domestic work—and I wondered how they would manage now that Nafiza was gone.

I said, "Nafiza's unconscious. I spoke with the doctor, and I don't think he expects her to come out."

No one responded, and I realized they must have been speaking about me when I showed up, the reason they had become so quiet.

Finally, Ameera Auntie sighed and spoke in her measured manner. "I have a student who has offered one of her family servants to . . ." her eyes flickered toward her husband, ". . . to replace Nafiza. As you know, I am too sick myself to carry on . . ."

Taqi Mamu thrust away from the table and stood, his chair shrieking in the way I wanted to myself. His eyes darted about until they fell upon the back window, which opened onto the servants' quarters. "How many times must I tell you?" he cried. "Nafiza is more than hired help. She is . . . she cannot be replaced."

He shoved his unfinished plate away, and I noticed, for the first time, his trembling hands, his greasy hair, his crumpled shirt. He looked like me.

AFTER DINNER, ABU Uncle and I took our chai to the side yard and strolled back and forth, slipping in and out of the long shadows of the almond and guava trees, our elbows brushing at times. The windows to the master bedroom were open and fluorescent light tumbled out, forming rectangles on the dirt that reminded me of Nafiza, alone in a journey that hundreds of others were also making. One of the servants was preparing the bed for the night, the one Ameera Auntie had brought with her in dowry some twenty years earlier, and on which I'd lain, locked inside that very room in protest of this marriage.

I told Abu Uncle the same tale I'd just revealed to Roshan, and he listened without interruption as he nodded and stared at the path before us, at our footprints moving away then back, as though unsure of which way they were headed, lost in the darkness, seen again.

When I got to the end, he was silent for a while, as though searching out the moral. There was none, of course, so I stopped and let him walk ahead without me. He was wearing jeans and a blue T-shirt, my mother's gifts from the U.S., and the cologne he used overwhelmed all of nature's scents. I set the empty cup and saucer into the curve of a branch and heard a bat moving about the guavas. He turned where I knew he would, where we had thus far been turning, just at the stoop of Nafiza's lonely quarters. What could he say that I didn't already know, Islam's strict prohibition against such men, my own reputation as a woman, society's concerns, not mine.

He came and stopped before me, nodding at the ground. "Your stories are the same. So I feel there is hope. Maybe there's just been a misunderstanding."

"Whose stories?"

"*Ar're*, who else's! Yours and your husband's."

"He's back?"

"He got back late this afternoon. *Bechara*, he had to use his entire tutoring money to buy a plane ticket—he said he'd missed the train in all the commotion. That poor boy came straight from the airport to me. He didn't even go home! That's how concerned he is about this marriage."

His lip curled up in what appeared a sneer before he moved toward the property's boundary wall. Halfway there, he turned and gestured for me to join him. When I shook my head, he came back, gripped my elbow and dragged me to the front gates. I had seen him behave this way before with Henna, whenever he found his daughter playing with the neighborhood boys on the streets. We now stood next to an ancient coconut tree, its roots on both sides of the boundary wall.

He searched about to make sure we were alone before digging into his jeans pockets and pulling out envelopes. They were folded in half, one on top of the other and even before he flattened them, flashing the handwriting at me, his name and return address, I knew who they were from.

"These have been arriving for you at my house!" he said. "One after another. *Ar're*, what kind of shameless behavior is this! I have a married girl at home, her husband is soon coming to live with us, what if they came across this filth, how would we explain your behavior? Married to one man, getting . . ." he paused and licked his lips, ". . . getting letters like these from another. *Ar're!* This is not what our women do. This is not America. Do you know, if I had found something like this happening with my wife—I know Asma is your mother's sister—but if I had found anything like this . . ." he turned down his lips and shook his head, meaning, he would have killed her.

I lowered my gaze, hoping that if I seemed repentant, he would do as I said. "Amme gave me some money before she left. It's in the *almari* at Sameer's house. If you could please go get it for me . . ."

"What! Are you not listening to me? Layla, I have brought you out here to talk some sense into you. *Ar're*, you cannot leave the boy over such a small thing! So what if he had . . . recreational sex? What else was he to do? Look at him, he's handsome, he's fit, he must have desires, tremendous desires. Where can a man go in a society such as this, women segregated from men, women hidden behind veils. Who was he to turn to? This isn't America, he never had the freedom you did. And he's a man! Men have desires. Men need release. We are not as strong as women—some women—who can control themselves, save themselves till they are married. Men like Sameer, young men, strong men, virile men, they must seek . . . companionship. That park he goes to, I know that park, all men know about that park. You go there, you find someone, you have release. That's it. Recreational sex, nothing more. So what if some fool got carried away and thought he had fallen in love with Sameer, huh! What matters is that your husband says he is not in love with him. Your husband says he is in love with you . . . no matter what *you've* done." He gripped my arms and bent his knees to peer into my face. Concern, chastisement, it was too dark to read his features. "I will advise you exactly what I advised your husband! Forget about these things, Layla. Keep the past in the past. Don't speak of it again. Don't even think of it. Look toward your future, your future with Sameer. Now, tell me, doesn't it feel good to know your husband wants you back home, that he still accepts you as his wife?"

"I want to talk to Ameera Auntie."

He drew away and pushed the letters back into his pocket, before tapping his chest, as though reminding me of his heart attack or warning me of the disasters I could bring onto my family. "No one wants a daughter to return home—especially not under these circumstances. *Ar're*, think about your father. Are you going to be like him, deserting your spouse, ruining your reputation? Spread what you want about your husband, Layla, everyone will say you left a decent man to return to your . . . *Umrikan* lover. It is what your husband will spread about *you*, what any man would. So you see, there is no need to talk to Ameera Auntie or to your Asma Kala. You will not get the support of women here. We all agree this is just a marital spat, nothing out of the ordinary. With Nafiza dying, this is already a sad time, no one wants to be thinking about this . . . *filth*. You're married, Layla, that's it. You're married."

THEY LET ME stay at the house for three days, and each morning I dressed and went to the hospital to sit with Nafiza. Roshan would bring us lunch from her husband's cafe and we'd eat in silence. I never told her what Abu Uncle had said, not believing my family could ever send me back to Sameer.

Then, on the third night, as I was finishing another simple dinner with my aunt and uncle, I heard his motorcycle pull up, followed by the low rumbling of the car I knew to be Abu Uncle's. I was fleeing down the hallway to my room when I heard Taqi Mamu call from behind me, "Please, Beta, don't do this again, not here, not in my home."

Then he was before me, his tall figure in the narrow hallway, looking like he did on the wedding night, someone I didn't know, someone most intimate to me.

Abu Uncle came up behind him, wearing that checkered shirt he'd worn to the blind *alim*'s, and I realized that this man who had always tried to save me believed he was once more doing the same.

Sameer stopped short when he saw me, his face darkened by stubble, shadows under his eyes. His hair was standing up from his hands running through it, running through it.

"Tell her why you've come," my uncle urged him from behind, his head just reaching my husband's shoulders.

Sameer continued to gaze at me without a word, though his mouth fell open in that manner it had in the hallway of our hotel. Without knowing it, he was blocking the way into my room.

Abu Uncle squeezed in next to him and the two filled the entire space. He said, "You have tested your husband's patience, Layla. He now demands that you return with him."

I felt the pressure of footsteps behind me and turned to find Taqi Mamu and his wife. Ameera Auntie was standing a foot behind my uncle, hands cupped before her, eyes teared up. There was nothing she could do for me.

I tried to slip into her room, as I'd done that day so long ago, but Taqi Mamu stuck his foot inside and prevented me from fully shutting the door. "Not here, not again," he repeated, shaking his head. His thick hair was slick with grease, and I realized he had not once visited Nafiza in the hospital.

He said, "You are my sister's daughter, Layla, so you are my daughter, too, a child I was never blessed with. I am telling you for your own good. What you know of life is very little. So it is our duty, as your elders, to protect you, to make sure you don't make irreversible mistakes. Now, please," he said, kissing the air twice in the way he used to when I was a child, Henna and I fighting over some small thing, "make up with your husband and go home. There is already enough suffering and loss in this house."

Suffering and loss, indeed. "You all know about Amme's divorce, don't you?" I asked, then turned to Abu Uncle. "That blind *alim* said it. The Muslim community here is small, everyone knows what's happening with everyone else. No one talks about it, but we all know each other's secrets. So here you two are, brother and brother-in-law, two men who could have done something, yet you let my mother suffer alone all these years. Without a single protest, you let my father do whatever he wanted to her, to *us*. And now you want me to submit to the same existence. He is *incapable* of making me his wife—you know that, *all* of you!" I gazed at my aunt, silently pleading with her, and she finally stepped forward and patted her husband's arm, urging him to think through what he was doing—a young girl's life was at stake—but he jerked away from her.

"He is in love with Naveed!" I yelled.

"I demand that you return with me right now!" Sameer suddenly shouted, spit flying from his mouth. "I am your husband and you will do as I say."

I stared at him in disbelief. He *would* do anything to keep me as his. I said, "You who do not believe in Old City values, what is this now? How dare you, when we both know the truth? Husband who is no real husband," I said, repeating what Nafiza had so aptly observed.

"I will take no more of this!" Abu Uncle cried, as though I had insulted him. He lurched forward and grabbed me, throwing me over his shoulder and taking me to his car. I beat at his back and kicked the air, screaming out in Urdu, in English. Then I glimpsed Ameera Auntie trying to come to me, skinny arms reaching out, yelling something, but Taqi Mamu held her in place. Sameer was trailing behind with my suitcase, fingers pressed to his forehead, eyes averted, as though he was the one being forced against his will.

They left his motorcycle there, and the three of us squeezed into Abu Uncle's car, me in the middle of the two men, a homecoming very different from the one when I'd arrived at my husband's home in full bridal regalia. But there they were again, wedding lights on the house, this time dressing up the squat structure across from Sameer's. The Muslim son being forced into marriage with a distant cousin, no one able to recognize his chosen love.

The lights to Sameer's house were on, Zeba and Ibrahim sitting erectly on the *takat*, awaiting my return. Sameer dragged me past them and into the room, then slammed the door shut and bolted it. Then he pressed his back against the wood and slid down, elbows on his knees, hands covering his face. I sat on the bed. I'd thought I'd never see this place again.

"As soon as I get a chance, I'm leaving," I said. "You can't make me stay here, with you—why would you even want that?" Then I said, "I really loved you. You let me love you. How could you?"

He crawled over to me on his hands and knees and buried his face in my lap, arms cinching around my hips, squeezing me. "Oh God," he whispered, as though not able to believe himself what had just happened, what he had been able to pull off. "Oh God."

FRIDAY MORNING. DAWN azan. Just under the imam's call, the pattering of rain.

I'd lost track of how much time had passed since I'd come back to Hyderabad, my husband's house. Each new day slowly leaking into the next. Things I had not noticed—the essentials of America that were not essentials here—suddenly became apparent, wildly missed: a telephone, a car, even a bicycle. The life I had considered so constricted now seemed so free.

He had taken up a chair in the *divan* to monitor the door and prevent me from leaving, in the same way I'd stopped him from going out of our hotel room. His father and brother at work and school, unavailable to me. His mother in the kitchen, shooing me out, not wanting to listen, still following her son's mandates.

Now I cornered her in the prayer room, just as she and Feroz were beginning to recite the Qur'an, their eleven-year-old custom that I was about to break. I took my usual spot beside her and wrapped my hair in a *duppatta*. She didn't glance at me, but up at the Arabic plaques, and I knew her silent prayer: strength to face what she must have known I had come to say. No one had knocked on my door that morning.

Mother and son had the Qur'an open to a surah much farther along in the book, but when I joined them, Zeba paged back to the chapter on Joseph, remembering where she and I had left off. Without any urgings, I began to recite:

> *When she heard of their intrigue, she invited the city women to a banquet at her house. To each she gave a knife, and ordered Joseph to present himself before them. When they saw him, they were amazed at his beauty and cut their hands, exclaiming: "Allah preserve us! This is no mortal, but a gracious angel."*
>
> *"This is the man," she said, "on whose account you reproached*

me. I sought to seduce him, but he was unyielding. If he declines to do my bidding, he shall be thrown in prison and held in scorn."

Despite the evidence they had seen, the Egyptians thought it right to jail him.

When she had come to the end of the Urdu translation, her voice trembling, stumbling over words, I placed a hand on hers to stop her from going on. She told Feroz to leave the room.

I said, "You didn't invite anyone to the *walima* dinner until the very day; then you invited more than a thousand guests when you had only invited a hundred to the *nik'kah*. The announcement you were making was about your son, not about the union. You've known all along about Sameer."

She kept her eyes on the book before us, and a finger traced the Arabic letters, one flowing into the next.

"You call me your daughter," I went on. "Yet you've ruined my life."

Her lips curled into themselves and the deep lines appeared at the edges, along the broad cheekbones. "He has been misled . . . by this *friend* of his. No man would choose to be with another man when he has a woman available to him. I have told you. You must make your demands clear to him, as his wife. You have the power in you to bring him back to the straight path."

"He does not love me, Zeba Auntie. I have watched him this past month. He has tried to be my husband, he has even wanted it, but it is not in him. Please, let me go. I'll return to America alone, you needn't worry anymore about him coming. He'll stay here with you, your guidance, *your* demands."

She shook her head. "A wife stays with her husband . . . no matter what."

No matter what. So this was what she had meant that day when Amme had visited. As a woman, I had but one option: to spend my life with my husband, untouched, uncomplaining. These were Old City ethics. Die for not being a virgin, die for marrying the wrong kind of man. Pagan rituals of sacrifice, Sameer was right.

"Islam prohibits what you are doing," I said. "Even my *nik'kah* to him has automatically become void. He is unrelated to me now, to sleep in his bed is a sin, against me and against you for forcing me—*imprisoning* me. How can you sit here and pray!"

She raised her chin as she had that day Sameer had thrown his prayer cap at her feet, then stormed out of the house. My sin, she seemed to be saying, not hers, now that she'd passed on her duties to me.

"You told me you are afraid of what he'll do once he gets to the U.S.," I said, approaching her now through her fears, her imaginings of America. "You are right to be afraid. He'll have more freedom to behave like this. Devils, demons, people have no control over themselves. Even Amme brings me to an *alim* each time I return. People do whatever they like there, men and women both, there is no shame. If Sameer cannot stop himself here, imagine what he'll do in America, where there are no taboos, no limits."

She continued following the Arabic letters with her finger, as though reading some invisible guidelines. "It is better that he goes to the U.S. Here, if he stays and you are not with him, everyone will know. He is handsome, he is strong, he is young, what reason would a wife have to leave such a man? They will scorn him, scorn me and my family. We will be ostracized, hated. I have to think of Feroz, his wedding—who will marry him if they hear of this? Shall I have lost both my sons? No, you take him to America. He is dead to me." She closed the book and stared up at the plaques again, her eyes dry of tears, this a worn grief. "Islam says that when a man mounts another man, the throne of Allah shakes. Imagine the tremblings of a mother's heart. I have cursed him, cursed my own son. That day I was told of his motorcycle accident, I rejoiced. I prayed a *shukran namaz*," a prayer of thanksgiving, "before I went to the hospital. I was prepared *that* day to see his dead face. It was Allah's punishment. He was coming back from that park, from doing what he does there, when he got into that accident. I thought Allah had finally answered my prayers." She turned down her lips in regret and her heavy chest rose in a deep sigh, the black *duppatta* quivering. "But he was still alive. Why should I fix that leg? Let him walk with a limp. Let him be ashamed of it, ashamed of himself. He should always know he is not a complete man."

TWO MORNINGS LATER, Ibrahim's voice drew me out of bed. I found him sitting alone at the breakfast table, reading the newspaper. Zeba was in the kitchen, humming as she slowly prepared the elaborate breakfast she made on Sundays. Feroz was studying in the *divan*, his books scattered across the bamboo table I had sat around with my husband and his lover as we planned a trip to Golconda, not aware of the real reason behind Sameer's open kisses. What a show, Naveed had said when he'd found us stumbling through the door, snatching at each other's clothes, when the two of them, Naveed and Sameer, were the true performers. Made him into a fool, my husband had accused me, when he had done that very thing to me.

"I was hoping you would come, Beta," Ibrahim now said.

I sat in the chair beside him, and he folded the paper and set it on the table, the reading glasses placed on top, next to his ulcer medicine and the honey Zeba fed him each day.

"The elections have suddenly been moved up," he said. "This isn't a good sign. I am afraid of trouble, riots. Allah *ka shukar*, you and Sameer returned early from Madras. Now that you are here, I do not think it is wise for you two to go about together. Stay in the house. A young couple," he paused, his eyes drifting away, his fingers tapping the table, "a young couple is always a good target for these gangs. They symbolize hope to a community; killing them is like putting out a candle flame."

So he was aware of the calamities happening outside, but not of the ones under his very roof. How was that possible when even the youngest son of the house, the one who was not yet married, was sitting in the *divan*, where he'd never studied before, just so he could watch over me while his older brother slept?

"I did not mean to frighten you, Beta," he said, examining my face. He began scratching his arm, and I noticed brown spots had appeared there, matching the ones across his scalp and forehead. "Listen to this," he said and tried on a smile to console me as he picked up the paper again. He adjusted his glasses over his eyes. "This election season there will be 122 different candidates," he read, then lowered his head to stare at me above the lenses. "And your husband is under the impression that this country can offer him no choices!"

Yes, always choices here about who would represent us, politician, god, ancestor, parent, even Henna sliding on Sameer's wedding ring for me, but no choice in how we could represent ourselves. That, in the end, was the lie Sameer was escaping by fleeing to the U.S.

"Papa," I said, "do you remember telling me that we shouldn't get ahead while hurting others?"

"Yes, of course, Beta, that is a general rule of proper ethics, something I would never forget." He flattened the newspaper onto the table and turned to me. "Tell me, what is wrong, Beta, what has happened?"

I hesitated, not knowing how to tell him. Finally, I said, "Do you know why Nafiza isn't here anymore? Why Sameer and I came home early from Madras?"

"Because your ayah is sick, because she is now in hospital." He squinted at me, his forehead creasing, and I realized the faint spots there had darkened. "Is there something more? What is it, Beta, what have you come to tell me? I am your father, please do not hesitate. I will do whatever I can to help you."

My turn now to tap the table with my fingertips as I figured out how to say the unimaginable. "I think Sameer is coming to America seeking more than just employment. What I mean is, I think what he really wants is freedom, the kind he can't get here." He was still staring at me from above the lenses, his scalp looking so tender. Sameer's hope to send home money so his father could retire. I sighed. "Papa, your son has tried to will himself to love me, but he can't. He is . . ." gay, what did that word mean here, a different culture, a different context, words that did not translate, ". . . he is not attracted to me, not to any women at all." The words were coming out slowly, each a beat in what felt like a dying heart. "I discovered this on the honeymoon. His friend

Naveed followed us. They love each other. It is why I came back. I did not know Nafiza was ill."

So there it was, a confession like none I had made before. I felt the weight of some dense form sliding out of me and spreading onto the floor by my feet, then rising to erect itself between us. A wall like the kind Sameer had described. For the second time in my life, I had lost my father.

"I want to go from here," I said, stopping myself from calling him Papa. "If not for my sake, could you not help me in memory of your dead sister, the one I remind you of?"

He moved back into his chair, head tilted up, and blinked at the ceiling, hardly breathing, his slumped chest frail below the sheer kurta. After a long time, he shook his head, as though freeing himself from thoughts, images that did not belong—do not let what is happening outside sink into your flesh, he had advised me. He set his glasses down even as he picked up the paper, unable to see the announcement of doom.

"My son," he whispered, his voice breaking, anguished. "My son," he repeated, before clearing his throat. He turned away from me and said, "As his wife, you must warn my son of what I have just told you. No one leaves the house."

JUST AS SAMEER had taken to sitting in the *divan*, preventing me from leaving the house, I now took to sleeping at the corner of the bed, turned away from him.

No words now between us, not during the day when I kept away from him, shut up inside the bedroom or prayer room, and not at night, when we were alone together, the door and window closed and bolted, his parents and brother right outside, the peacock's face turned away from the spectacle.

He slept close behind me, his form stretched out a wrist's-width from mine, the mattress dipping under his weight, making me feel like I was tumbling toward him, the heat of his flesh. I pretended he wasn't there.

Then, one night, I woke to him pressing into me, his hardness against my soft thighs, my buttocks, only the sheer cloth of my *shalwar* between us, the demon who no longer appeared in my dreams now materializing into my husband, and I thought of how many times I had taken him into my mouth, the same part of him that dug into Naveed's flesh.

I shoved aside the netting and stumbled into the bathroom, retching.

THE FOLLOWING MORNING, while he was bathing, I snuck out of the bedroom and slowly made my way into the *divan*. I thought Ibrahim and Feroz had already left for the day, though I could hear Zeba's voice coming from the prayer room, where Feroz slept on the floor at night. Without a sound, I crossed the courtyard and slid open the metal lock on the front gates. It creaked, giving me away. Everything in this house against me.

Feroz's face flattened against the iron bars of his window, then his slanted eyes turned up even farther in surprise. He began shouting, "Mummy, she's leaving. Bhabhi is leaving the house!" There was scurrying inside.

But it was too late, I was already out, running down the ashoka-lined street I had strolled with my husband. On the road intersecting this one, an auto-rickshaw puttered past and I screamed for the driver to halt, but he didn't hear me. Then my *duppatta* got caught in a neighbor's gate and I thrust it off and raced past the lamppost Sameer had stood near, casting stones, and was reaching the end of the block when Feroz grabbed my arm from behind and yanked me. I stumbled and fell onto the stone sidewalk, and I picked up a handful of rocks and threw them at him. He blocked his face with his hands, twisting away his shoulders, but as soon as I was standing, he had me by the elbows and began tugging me back to the house.

"You are making a spectacle of yourself, Bhabhi," he said, his voice calm, condescending in that way it was when he corrected my Arabic. "People are going to think my brother's wife is mad."

All down the street, women had gathered at the front gates, watching, even those two young girls with their thick braids, the older one who wanted to marry Sameer. I called out for help. One by one, each slid inside again, vanishing. Zeba caught up to us, and she and Feroz dragged me back down the dead-end road and shoved me into the bedroom, then shut the door and locked it from outside.

Sameer was standing by his trunk, a towel wrapped around his waist, his clean chest still damp. He came over to me and slid his fingers around my neck, his thumb with my silver toe ring gliding across my lips. "You're mine," he said softly, a lover's voice like I'd not heard from him before, "and I'm going to do everything I can to keep you."

DAYS LEAKING INTO nights into days. Arbitrary time.

Then, one afternoon, Zeba did not sit at her usual place on the *takat*, against her hand-embroidered pillows, preparing the evening meal. Instead, she spread a silk sari across the colorful Pakistani rug and stood over it, ironing. It was the same red sari she'd worn on my wedding day, her head and chest covered by the black *duppatta*. The boy across the street was getting married tonight.

She did not ask me to dress, and that was how I knew I was not invited. She understood I'd make another scene, try once more to escape, adding to the chaos of this forced wedding, to the groom's own agitation. It was better for all that I stay in the house with my husband, and I wondered what excuse she would make for my absence.

By nightfall, I could hear the clamor of guests, cars pulling into the dead-end road, parking in the abandoned lot. The *dol* began beating a tune familiar to me, from my own wedding days, the sound like a quickened heart, anticipation, fear and dread, the announcement of emerging life. I did not know who to pity more, the boy being forced to become a bridegroom or the bride who would never be loved.

Through the bedroom door, from where I lay on that fancy bed, Amme's dreams for me—for herself—I could see Zeba sitting at the edge of her *takat*, now fully dressed, hands open in her lap as she stared up at the clock. Ibrahim was late.

"Just go, Mum," Sameer said from the *divan*. The rattle and boom of the brass band suddenly sounded in the distance and sent up laughter and clapping at the wedding house. The band would lead the groom to the wedding hall, then guide him back with his wife.

"I won't go without him," Zeba said, adding, "The man is never late. *Inshal'lah*, nothing has happened to him."

"I'll send Papa over as soon as he gets here," Sameer said, exasperated. "You're just crossing the street!"

Feroz emerged from his room, dressed in a silver pajama-kurta, the collar falling open to expose his chest, a patch of skin darkened and rough from the razor blade he'd taken up in the past to mourn our martyred saints. His eyes were thickly lined with black *surma*. Zeba nodded her head side to side, approvingly, before she sighed and grasped his hand, standing. She would go without her husband, after all. As she was leaving, her gaze flitted to the bedroom and met mine. She hesitated before dropping Feroz's arm and stepping forward; she kept herself just outside the door frame.

"I'm going to tell them you are too sick to come," she said as she tightened the *duppatta* about her round face. "Let them believe you are pregnant. You two will be off to the U.S. soon; they'll never know . . . anything."

I closed the door on her.

Soon there was nothing but the sound of the brass band, that noise played over and over, a hundred times a day, different grooms, different brides, same wedding. I folded the pillow over my head. It was covered in the maroon velvet case Nafiza had sewn for me.

Then, just like that, the music stopped. A lone shriek sliced the silence, followed by a different kind of commotion. I went out to the front gates, where Sameer was standing with his arms spread across the small opening, his shoulder blades jutting out, and when I ducked under an arm, he slung it about me and kept me from moving farther. A woman was in the middle of the street, the groom's mother, Zehra. She was unveiled, her sequined sari glittering in the night, against the house's celebration lights. She had her hair clutched in two fists and was looking this way and that, searching. Slowly, other women poured out from the gates and surrounded her, braids woven with jasmine, the scent filling the air. They tried to lead her back into the house.

She walked with them a few steps, then broke away, shrieking again, head pitched, clawing at her own face. Her legs buckled and she dropped onto her knees. "What have I borne? From my own womb, the *shai'tan*! Allah, why did you not kill me before showing me this day?" The women slowly gathered around her again and hid her shame. I did not see Zeba among them.

Lined on top of the squat house, on the flat roof, the men, silent, heads bowed, the blinking celebration lights casting festive hues across their silk pajamas. The band had broken up, the members huddled here and there along the sidewalk, mute instruments dangling from loose arms. The wedding car, a red Chevy Impala like the kind that had driven me here, sat empty at the end of the cul-de-sac, covered bumper-to-bumper in ropes of marigold.

The group of women helped Zehra to her feet and began guiding her to the house. At the front gates, she shrieked a last time, then swung away from the others and whacked her wrists against the stone boundary wall, shards of colorful glass from her bangles flying about. Then she tried to break her bones.

"I have done this with my own hands!" she cried. "I have brought this misery on my own house!" The women could not placate her.

Finally, her husband called down from the roof, his voice unwavering, strong. "Enough, Zehra. You have grieved enough. Now there is no more reason to grieve. We have no son."

Zehra folded in half and fell onto her back, her head thudding on the cement sidewalk. The women hauled her inside. The gates closed. Slowly, the band members began drifting away. As they went up the street, under the light of the lamppost, I spotted Ibrahim quickly heading toward us, weaving his way through the red-uniformed crowd, not seeming to notice them.

He stopped before Sameer and me, both eyes red and irritated, a hand passing over his face. Large circles of sweat had formed under his arms, glistened across his forehead and scalp.

"The groom ran away," Sameer said, tightening his hold on me. "There is no wedding for you to attend. He ran off with that Hindu girl he loves."

Ibrahim stared at him with that look Sameer used to give me, the one I now shot at him, his family. His son a stranger, not making any sense.

"I saw Taqi," Ibrahim said, turning to me. "I was coming off the bus just now . . . Beta," he said, placing a hand on my head in comfort, and I knew even before he said it what he had to tell me. Something so unimaginable that he had to call me daughter, an endearment he'd not used since the day I'd told him about his son. "Nafiza died, Beta. Nafiza . . ." he repeated, his hand passing over his face again, then rubbing his eyes. "Taqi and I used to run with her in the jungles. How can this be?"

I stared up past his anguished face to the celebration lights and up past those to the night sky, the diminishing moon. It had taken the shape of her nails, clumped with dirt. Soon her body would disappear into that very dirt as the moon would in the sky, reappearing not only to herald the Islamic month of Muhar'ram, but also the beginning of a new Islamic year. According to this calendar, I had been born on new year's day, the first dawn of the month of mourning, the reason, Amme said, I was so ill-fated. It was Nafiza, not Dad, who had accompanied Amme to the hospital. And it was to Nafiza I had been passed on, cut from the umbilical cord. Nafiza, who had pressed my naked flesh to hers, unhooking her sari-blouse.

My first touch, my first sip of life.

Ghum

WE OPEN EACH Islamic year in Muhar'ram, so we commence each new year in *ghum*, mourning. Muhar'ram is the month when, fourteen hundred years ago, the Prophet's grandson, Hussein, and his family were massacred on the plains of Kerbala. On camels and horses, they had been passing through the desert on their way to safety, when Caliph Yezid's troops stopped them, demanding, once more, their oath of loyalty. But the Prophet's family, the Imams, refused to be faithful to anyone but Allah.

So a battle ensued. The troops on horses, Imam Hussein's family—men and women and children and sick—encamped in tents. Under the desert sun, water supplies diminished, parched tongues shriveled black. Weakened and outnumbered, the men still went out, one by one, to overcome the troops, and, one by one, were overcome themselves. A slaughtering. A martyrdom. Then, on the tenth day of Muhar'ram, the darkest day, Hussein himself was slain, his severed head carried on the point of a javelin by order of Yezid.

And all in his remaining camp fell silent. While in the distance, Yezid's troops beat drums in victory.

We mourn the fate of our saints all month, dressing in no color but black, the women wiping off makeup, stowing away jewels, sometimes even shoes, and the men not shaving. At daily gatherings called *manjalises*, we come together for unified grief, singing dirges and beating breasts. For to us, the believers, the disgrace, the torture, the martyrdom did not happen just once, lifetimes ago, but was happening again now, conjured up before our very eyes by the *mol'lana*'s oral history.

Like this, each new year, each new birthday, I was caught up in those lives grander than my own, reminded of all that had given me rise.

MANJALISES WERE HELD in the Old City, and each afternoon at five, Zeba and I rode into the walled *sha-hare* by cycle-rickshaw, Sameer trailing behind on motorbike. What took ten minutes by car and motorcycle stretched into thirty, the poor rickshaw driver pumping vigorously out the dead-end road, then having to step off the bike and haul his rickety rickshaw and two grown women up the steep hill that led to the jail-*khanna*, and past that, to the great Dabir Pura Doors. Alongside that hill were the woods in which Sameer and I had taken shelter during the rainstorm, this main highway the road on which I'd peeled off his wet shirt, not confined, at last, to limits. It was that image I forced myself to see each day, each time the rickshaw slowed here, not my husband's deception, not his lover waiting for us at home, but my own sense of freedom.

Nafiza had been buried on the first day of Muhar'ram, on my birthday, and though my own relatives had been the ones to force me back to my husband's house, and there was no fear they would help me out now, Zeba refused to let me attend, accusing my nanny of having incited the kind of trouble in this house as she had at my *nana*'s. Ibrahim went alone, then returned well before Zeba took me to the first *manjalis* to knock at my bedroom door. I was lying in bed and didn't rise to answer it. He came in anyway and sat by my feet. Without a word, he began massaging them, a woman's gesture, her service to men, husband, son, father. I didn't stop him. Before long, he was weeping, first crying over Nafiza, then over his own son, who, he said, could have no life here. Finally, he set his forehead on my ankles, as the grieving workers used to before a nawab, and begged me for mercy. Take his son to America.

That evening, at the gathering meant only for *zanana*, women, I searched about for Henna and my aunts, Asma and Ameera. For seven generations the two families had acted as one, moving in and out of each other's *manjalises* as they had, as children, run in and out of each other's homes, the bond of faith as thick as blood. But, to my surprise, I couldn't find them, not at that first gathering, not at the next four. Was it Sameer, who sat outside each house, waiting for the dirges to end, who was sending them away, or had they decided themselves not to attend, perhaps not having anything left to say to me, perhaps following orders given by their own husbands?

Whatever it was, the union of marriage had revealed borders I had not known to exist.

THE WOMEN AT the gatherings, ones I recognized from my wedding, others I didn't know, kept their distance from me. And on the second night, I noticed that upon my arrival, they quieted and began pointing as they whispered to each other, unabashed. Only when it was time to sing the first dirge did they turn away, a wall of black, and I was reminded of what Henna had said about the looks of pity and scorn that had kept her from venturing out. She, the pregnant daughter returned home. So what had Zeba gone and spread about me?

Then, on the fifth night of Muhar'ram, two of Sameer's cousins came and sat beside me after the *manjalis*. They were young women my age, both attractive and unmarried, still attending college as I should have been myself. The last time I had seen them was on my wedding night, when the two had helped to arrange me enticingly on the marital bed, the red veil covering me head to foot. Then they had withdrawn into the living room with the other women and sung, "*One, two, three . . . this is how I tallied the days . . .*" Earlier tonight, at their mother's house, the two had sat at the center of the gathering, facing Mecca, chronicling the Imams' plight, "*I have fallen on burning earth, my body maimed and shattered . . . ,*" their thin faces not stained with powder and lipstick, as I had seen before, but with tears.

I told them their voices carried pathos, and the younger sister, Asma, looked about the gathering before whispering that her voice had trembled during her singing of the dirge because the words seemed to be foretelling what could happen again now, the abrupt and brutal end of our own lives.

This year, the tenth day of Muhar'ram, the pitch of Islam's grief, was coinciding with the tenth day of Ganpati, the height of the Ganesh festivities.

For Ganpati, Hindu followers celebrated elephant-headed Ganesh by producing model images of him in all sizes. The smaller of these were kept in homes for one and a half, five, seven, or ten days. The largest images of him—those I had seen sprouting up in the colony and sitting on makeshift stages at the center of town, taller than me—were among those models saved for the tenth day. At that time, Ganesh would be ceremoniously taken out of homes and neighborhoods and paraded, a thousand times over from a thousand different points of the city, to Tank Bund, the bridge that connected Hyderabad to its twin city, Secunderabad (the place I'd had my first date with my husband), and from there, he would be cast into the waters of Hussain Sagar. Around him, people would sing and drink and dance: "*Ganpati, bappa morya, agle baras tu jaldi aa,*" Father Ganpati, next year come quickly. He was the god of learning and protection, the remover of obstacles.

Alongside the Ganesh parades would be our own solemn procession, weaving its way through the narrow Old City streets to the *Imambara*, the House of Saints, at its center. At times, the procession would halt and the men taking part in it, naked to the waist, would self-flagellate with swords or razors or a bundle of sharp blades, blood rolling down fronts and backs, glistening under the noonday sun. Then they'd pick up and march on, trampling through each other's blood. This in commemoration of Hussein and his kin, our saints of protection and mercy.

Grief and celebration. Laments and revelry. And underneath it, politics. For India itself was mere weeks from election. The names of the candidates and their parties had been painted on the massive boundary wall encompassing the Chow-Rasta Jail-*khanna* and shouted out to those traveling the crossroads. Next to each, a drawing. A scale. A growling tiger. A bull. Icons of the parties shaped for the illiterate masses.

All this had materialized in the small stretch of time between my return from Madras and my first Muhar'ram outing. Even the last time I had passed the boundary walls of the jail, the last time I had visited Nafiza in the hospital, the painted slogans were those announcing the latest Telugu or Hindi movies. And the drawings were the competing images of the newest, hottest stars.

"BUT YOU ARE safe here," I told the sisters, repeating what I'd heard my parents often say. "Riots never happen in the Old City. The walls and doors will protect you."

"That's what I keep telling her," Zenath said as she made a gesture of annoyance at her younger sister. "But she doesn't listen. *Boli hai, na,*" she's naive.

"*Boli!*" Asma cried, and was quickly silenced by the women around us, stern looks reminding her not to forget the sad occasion. When they had turned away, Asma leaned into me and quietly said, "Maybe you do not know this, Bhabhi, but government and religion do not mix—these are the very things that lead to riots, killings! I'm telling you, for these first five days of Muhar'ram, I have prayed only for our safety."

Zenath hid a smile behind a hand, even the slightest pleasure not to be worn among the mourners. She said, "You don't understand the sacrifice she's making, Bhabhi. Usually, Asma only prays for a good husband."

"*Hul!*" Asma hissed and slapped her sister's thigh. "She makes jokes now, Bhabhi, because we're surrounded by women. But when everyone leaves and the house is quiet, then you should hear her. She cannot sleep because she hears a leaf falling in the courtyard or a bat flying in the guava branches and suddenly she starts screaming, 'Baba, Baba, wake up, someone has jumped over the boundary wall, ready to kill us!' "

Zenath bowed her head in embarrassment.

"But you must have lived through these things before," I said. "Even I have, two or three times. Riots happen, then curfews, the military goes out into the streets, and the people withdraw into their houses. It's not much different from other times, except now, the men are confined, too."

The sisters shrugged, unconvinced, and we turned and watched two women spread a red cloth down the center of the long room, dividing it in half. On it, they laid platters of *biriyani* and yogurt, and the mourners sidled up on both sides, sitting elbow to elbow, damp handkerchiefs crushed inside palms. The youngest of the three sisters, Shaheen, began moving about the circle of women, one step at a time, serving sweetened rosewater. She had a jug of it in one hand, a short glass in the other. When she came upon a woman, she poured a sip, and the two said, "Salaam," peace, to one another, before the woman drank it up. Then Shaheen stepped sideways to the next woman and offered up the same glass.

THE COUSINS WENT and got plates of food, bringing one back for me. When we were all sitting again, steel plates balanced on open palms, I asked if Hanif had arrived yet from Saudi, and, in this way, moved the discussion to what was most grieving me, the whereabouts of my family.

The sisters exchanged a quick glance. In age, the two were fourteen months apart, but with their matching black *shalwar-kameez*es and waist-length braids, their thin faces, they appeared to be twins. They now turned to me together, but it was the older sister who spoke.

"Haven't you heard, Bhabhi? All the women here are shocked. It's all they talk about, politics and Ganesh and . . ." she lowered her gaze, embarrassed, " . . . and Henna." And me, of course, though she wouldn't say it. "Since her husband's return," she went on, "the two have not once left your uncle's house. People are saying your uncle is letting them sleep in the same bed—at this holy time!"

"*Hahn*, Bhabhi," Asma broke in. "Hanif did not even tell his own mother he was returning, so for three days, she kept asking where her *bahu* was, and finally, someone told her, 'Open your eyes, Kosar! Your *bahu* is not with you because she is with your son. What they are doing together in sin keeps her from attending a sacred gathering!' His mother was so ashamed she left right then, and she's not showed her face since."

I set my plate down between us. "And what do you two think about what Henna's doing?"

Asma covered her face with her *duppatta*, shoulders quaking in a silent giggle, this, the one who prayed for a good husband. "Who cares what the women say, Bhabhi! They come and sing dirges, they beat their breasts, they cry, then afterward, they all pretend we're at some social function, every woman examining the young girls, choosing one for her son. You know, Bhabhi, this is when all marriages are arranged! Your cousin is doing the very thing these women have in mind, yet they blame her."

Yes, her and not Hanif. But even Islam said man was the weaker sex, easily seduced, misled. A wife's duties to keep him straight.

I stared at the two cousins, now wondering what they had come over to say when all others were keeping their distance. "And what do they blame me for?" I asked.

They both bowed their heads, though they did not appear surprised by the question. Their hands hung loosely above their plates, rice balls stuck between fingers.

I spoke to Asma, "What if the husband you pray for turns out to be like mine? What would you do then?" I turned to Zenath. "Would you not help your sister out?"

Zenath rested her wrist on her plate, unable to finish eating. I watched her gaze about the room until she found Zeba. My mother-in-law kept herself far from me at these gatherings, sequestered to some distant wall, surrounded by sadly clucking women. Zenath tried on a smile, not caring this time who among the mourners saw. She spoke louder than she had been, her words not meant solely for me, but to let others know she had fulfilled her mission. "Bhabhi, when we heard Sameer Bhai was here, we could not believe it until we peeked out the front window and saw him with our own eyes. You know, he has never come to these gatherings before. Always during Muhar'ram, he has disappeared. You cannot imagine the pain it has caused Zeba Auntie." She turned down her lips in sorrow for her aunt. "People say that on the tenth of Muhar'ram, he could be found in the movie theater. Imagine that, Bhabhi, imagine such sin!" She shook her head and whispered, "*Tho-ba, tho-ba*," as she lightly slapped her own cheeks in repentance.

"Yes, Bhabhi," Asma said, taking up her sister's song. "Look at how much his love for you has already changed him! You must keep trying . . . especially since he has come to you once, isn't that right, isn't that what Zeba Auntie has said, that she did not put on a show with the *walima* dinner, that he is capable," she lowered her voice and gazed up at me, "that she saw in a dream that you are pregnant. No, Bhabhi, no, the family must remain together, it is the only right way, the child with his father, husband and wife . . . look at your sister-cousin, Henna, is she not together with her husband again, is she not now happier? It is as Allah says: Peace is better."

ONCE AGAIN, I was sleeping beside his mother while he slept on the *takat* with Ibrahim. This time, no faceless demon invaded my sleep to make me restless. Now I was relieved he had been ordered away, by his mother again, during these days of mourning when contact between husband and wife was prohibited. Certainly, there was no threat of such an intimacy, this was just a show put on by his mother.

At night, now, it was not Zeba's snoring keeping me awake, but drums beating in different parts of the neighborhood, celebrating Ganesh. As the tenth of Muhar'ram grew nearer and our mourning intensified, so, too, did the jovial pounding. What had once been a faint sound springing up here and there, most often heard while we were rickshawing to the Old City, was now insistent, all-encompassing, drums beating on top of drums with no pause, the Imams' martyrdom, Yezid's victory, seeming to come to life.

At dawn on the seventh day of Muhar'ram, of Ganpati, the muezzin's voice struggled over this other calling. The family rose from bed and, following tradition, shed our black clothes to don green, the color of Islam, of submission. The color of that *walima* dinner. I went into the drawing room and waited for Sameer's family to gather so we could pray, becoming—at least in appearance—what this seventh day ordained: fakirs before Allah, surrendering our will to his, accepting our fates without complaint.

Sameer, of course, was dressed in his Western clothes, refusing his mother's insistence to throw on a green shirt just as he had refused to wear black all week. He was still lying where he now slept on the *takat*, reading the newspaper, and his long legs reached just beyond the edge so his feet dangled. I did not ask him to join us in prayer. Still, when the family had finally come together, they waited for me to invite him, father, mother, and younger son huddled at the entrance of the prayer room. At last, Ibrahim cleared his throat and Sameer looked up. For a moment, he seemed not to recognize his own family, then he blinked, and the newspaper fell from his hands.

He turned away from this image, eyes shutting tight. He shook his head and jumped up on the *takat*, his scalp perilously close to the rotating blades of the ceiling fan. Zeba gasped and yelled out that he could get killed. He ignored her and, without glancing at me, pushed on his black boots and raced for the front door. Zeba began chasing him, her black *duppatta* replaced by a green one I'd never seen. She stopped in the middle of the *divan*, one arm stretched toward Sameer as he mounted his bike, pleading for him not to leave, the other reaching back toward Feroz, wiggling fingers bidding him to help. I wondered if she and Feroz would actually drag my husband back into the house as they had me.

Just as Feroz was stepping toward her, Ibrahim gripped his arm, shaking his head.

"But, Papa," Feroz protested, the *surma* around his eyes growing heavier with each passing day of mourning, a sign, like the razor's scars on his chest, exhibiting his faith, "who will accompany Mummy to the *manjalis*?"

What he meant, of course, was who would guard over me?

WHILE WE PRAYED, the drums beat into our skin, trying to get in, more apparent than Allah's silent glory.

When we were done, Ibrahim announced that we would stay home that day and hold a family *manjalis*. Each year, Ibrahim was awarded twenty days of holiday, and he took them all during religious occasions. So the entire week, he and Feroz had been traveling to the Old City together, leaving before noon prayers and arriving home past midnight. Unlike the women's *manjalis*es, men's gatherings happened throughout the day and night, the beating of chests as persistent, in that part of the city, as the beating of drums was here.

"As I once told Layla," he explained, rubbing his bald scalp in tight circles, "it is not safe for people to travel at such a time. Before, I had mentioned to her the dangers for a young couple, and now I will say that two women alone are even more vulnerable. It is true that the four of us could go together to the Old City, but once there, we would have to separate, attend different *manjalis*es. There is no guarantee we would be able to find each other again. There is such chaos, and everyone is dressed in black, women are hard to find . . ." he stopped and glanced at me, his fingers tapping the prayer rug. Once more, the consideration of how to utter the unimaginable, rape, murder, the methods to put out the light of a community. "That main highway is deserted," he finally said, "and I will not take the chance of two women coming back by themselves . . . in the dark."

So it was resolved, the other threat left unspoken: my freeing myself of Zeba's grip and escaping. Zeba rolled up her prayer rug and disappeared into the kitchen to start breakfast, while Feroz clapped at what he said was a wise decision.

The day passed as any other, except Feroz now took up his brother's chair in the *divan.* As usual, I kept myself confined to the bedroom with nothing to do but lie in bed and reassure myself that I would find a way out. I kept the door closed against them.

That evening, about the time Zeba and I used to set out for the Old City, she came and knocked on my bedroom door. A clean sheet had been spread on the *takat,* on top of the Pakistani rug, and before it, the door to the prayer room was open, candles and incense emanating fragrant fumes. She had already set the table, plates covering the rice and curry, the food we would later eat in honor of our Imams.

We gathered on the sheet as we did in the prayer room, Feroz beside his father, I beside Zeba. The three took turns reciting dirges (my parents hadn't trained me in their melody), and when it was Zeba's turn, her voice rising high and off-tune, fully confident, a motorcycle pulled up at the front gates. Her voice broke and her eyes glanced up at the Arabic plaques in the prayer room—a silent thanks to Allah—before she began reading again. She must have assumed as I did, as the rest of us did, that it was Sameer. But right when it was time to join her in chorus, singing about our saints falling from horseback, slain by the enemy troops, an unfamiliar voice called over the boundary wall, intruding on this ancient grief. Ibrahim gestured for us to continue, and he rose unsteadily and went out. We finished the dirge without him, gazes wandering from the prayer room to the front door. Finally, Feroz got up and left. Zeba and I sat in silence, the men's voices not reaching us. After a while, she closed the book of hymns and tightened the *duppatta* around me.

"They say our Imams attend every *manjalis,* invisible to us," she said. "This can only be the devil."

THE THREE MUSLIM families that had once gathered in our courtyard to meet the new bride were now gathered together to meet the new stranger in our midst. This time, the husbands had come along, as frail and aged as Ibrahim, making Feroz the strongest one among us, this, the one whom I had once mistaken for being younger than me. Everyone was wearing green, except the stranger, who was in orange: a follower of Ganesh. He was like the flower, the nectar, that we, a flock of mynahs, had flown to for sustenance.

He called himself a friend. A friend of peace, a friend of someone who knew this family, a good person to whom he owed this favor. And, in this way, a friend to us. He had come bearing a warning: that night, our block, our houses, our families had been targeted. By whom? For what reason? For what benefit? There was no reason to ask such questions when all our lives we had been reading about these incidents in newspapers, swapping stories with each other: neighborhoods burned, houses looted, everyone murdered. The history of the Indian streets as much part of us as the history of our Imams. We knew better than to complain that such an ill fate could not be ours. Indeed, for all I had reassured Asma and Zenath about the safety of the Old City walls, I had overlooked, being as imprisoned as I was, how I was still out in the open. Only four Muslim families in this neighborhood. Outnumbered.

The plump mother of the two daughters crossed her arms over her chest, as though cuddling her breasts. She had left the girls at home, anticipating, as Zeba had, what this new friend of ours had come to say, and so protecting them in the only way left to her.

GANGS USUALLY CONTAINED ten members. All young men. All able-bodied. All bearing weapons.

Before jumping back on his motorcycle, our friend ran his pinkie across one of Feroz's eyelids, then held it up for us, the skin smudged black with *surma*.

"Lock yourselves in your houses and pray," he said. "Your lives are now in the hands of the one who created them." He rode away in the frail evening light, the single beam of his headlamp an obscure path to safety that receded in his wake.

For a while, no one spoke. The street was strangely quiet, deserted—where were all those women and men who had come out to watch this new bride exiting her red wedding car, the ones who later witnessed the brass band breaking up and leaving, Zehra's son having run off with his Hindu beloved? Did they know what misery was about to befall us now, would they later come out and watch the spectacle? Don't trust them!

Them? Us and Them.

Already my mind was working in the way these culprits had wanted, seeing only the divisions, even between the very people we had thus far been living next to in peace.

The plump mother shrieked and covered her face with her green *duppatta*.

"Our own houses our tombs," Zehra said, looking about at the squat structures. Then she met her husband's eyes. "It is good our son fled. It is good he is not here. At least now, he will survive, he will not . . ." her voice trembled and broke.

"My daughters!" the mother yelled as she tightened the *duppatta* over her face, as though trying to suffocate herself. Her husband bowed his head.

Lubna, the tall one with moles on her eyelids, repeated what she had the last time she'd come over. "Allah blessed me by not giving me children. What could I explain to them of this world?"

US. THEM.

The mother began demanding that we leave.

The father said, Where would we go? We cannot go. We have no car. It's dark. Who's going to travel alone on a moped to find an auto-rickshaw? Twenty minutes there. Twenty minutes back. And what if that person doesn't come back? It's better to stay together.

Yes, it's better for us to continue to remain as one.

So it was decided. The women would stay inside the houses. Each to her own home. Better to be separated. Better chance, that way, of some of us escaping. Surviving. Of not being raped. Stay in the innermost room. Lock all doors that lead to it. Bolt shut the windows. Be thankful for the iron bars.

Should we get the police?

The Chow-Rasta Jail-*khanna* is on a lonely highway. Near a wooded area.

Does no one have a phone? Do you think one of our . . . neighbors might?

Who would you call? Who can help us? No one's going to come here.

The police . . .

The police are conspirators. Why do you think these things go on and on? And now it's come to us.

Yes, it will be easier for all if we accept that it is now our time.

Fakirs before Allah.

The men, we agreed, would stay together. Take shifts sleeping. All of them, all five of them, four old, one young, would crowd on top of the roof of the house that belonged to the family who lived down the street, the first house these culprits would get to, the one with the two pretty daughters. And the house from where our men could spot them the soonest.

We had no weapons. Just knives. One or two wooden sticks. A walking cane.

WE LOCKED OURSELVES in my room, Zeba and I, first locking the front door, then the inner *divan* door, then the bedroom door. We could not help but feel we were locking our men out. So we bolted one shutter, left one ajar. To listen. The men had promised that, as *gorkhas* used to, they would strike a stick against the roof at each hour, informing us, in this way, that all was still okay.

It did not seem possible that we would hear such a strike.

"How will we know if they come?"

"It's a noise like no other—not their motorcycles and hollering, but the beating of our own hearts. It always knows when it is about to die. Now put on your jeans. No, not like that. Under your *shalwar*. Protect yourself as much as you can."

I slid them on and found they no longer fit. Too many days of lying about, sequestered to this very room. How was it that my prison had become my only refuge? I rummaged through a drawer. It wasn't on rollers and the wood kept thudding onto wood, sounding too much like the noise I expected to hear any minute, so I pulled the whole thing out. It crashed onto the floor. I found a safety pin and pulled it through the buttonhole and pinned the jeans together.

When I looked up, she was shaking her head at me, tears running down her face. She sat on the bed, just under the window, the open shutter letting in silence. She adjusted her green *duppatta* and opened the Qur'an—the only thing she'd grabbed before we'd locked ourselves inside, the dinner she had set out on the table, intending for us to eat just after our family *manjalis*, growing cold.

I crawled to the other side of her, to where her son usually slept. I lay down, sat up, then moved against the wall and pressed my back to the hard cement, letting it hold me up. The mosquito netting stretched, pulled by my weight, the peacock's head creaking in protest. The chip across its beak, which had been painted over in a tone lighter than the ivory, made the thing look like it was gagged. Though it was hot, we kept the fan turned off. Kept it from whining as it spun. We wanted to hear what was happening outside. And what was the use of sitting refreshed and cool, awaiting our killers?

The strike of wood. Eleven o'clock. We had seven hours to go until dawn. Nothing to do but sit. Sit and wait.

"I JUST REALIZED, the drumming has stopped. They know. *They* know! Yet, no one is coming to help us!"

Her head was bowed over the Qur'an, back swaying as she read. She had not asked me to join her.

After a while, I said, "What if Sameer is on his way back? What if he runs into that gang? You've not once shown concern for him. Yes, you've thanked your husband for keeping us here tonight—otherwise *we* would have been returning when this . . . this gang . . . but you've not once expressed concern for him, your son!"

She continued reciting, switching back and forth from Arabic to Urdu, her voice steady. It was the chapter called "Man," the verses describing what believers should expect after death, the promises of heaven.

"They shall be served with silver dishes, and beakers as large as goblets; . . . and cups filled with ginger-flavored water from the Fountain of Selsabil. They shall be attended by boys graced with eternal youth . . ."

I broke in again, "He's with Naveed, his lover, while I am trapped here. He's safe. He imprisoned me, then he abandoned me, here, to be raped and killed. If he's on his way back, he'll be returning from his lover's, just like that day he got into the accident. Are you secretly praying that he runs into the gang, that he dies tonight?" Or was it the very thing I myself was praying for?

She finally looked up at me and her heavy chest rose in a deep sigh. "Do not pester me anymore, child. The time has come for each to weigh her own soul. Tally up your sins. You might soon be facing your creator!"

THE WOODEN STICK struck twice. Two o'clock.

My head was folded into my arms. I couldn't stop crying.

She said, "I have been thinking about my childhood. Your mother and I used to walk to school together, both of us in our blue uniforms, except I wore *chappals*, while she wore shoes. Your *nana* wouldn't tolerate his children wearing *chappals*; he said they would make their feet flat, the toes all spread out. He wanted them to have perfectly shaped feet." She giggled like a girl.

I looked up at her. She was sitting against the headboard, right next to the open shutter. The Qur'an was closed, the *duppatta* flung off to expose her thin braid, gray died maroon with henna. The last time I had seen her uncovered was when she had confronted me about Sameer and our failed union. She now had a hand cupped over her lips, her usual tight smile replaced with an openmouthed grin.

"We didn't get a good education," she said, "but your mother and I didn't care. We were attending school to admire our teachers. They were all so young, just out of school themselves. Teaching in our village was their first post. They'd come only for two or three months, until they could get a transfer. Then we would be left with no teacher for two to three months, and finally someone would show up again and all the kids in the village would be rounded up." She lowered her eyes in modesty, though the wide smile remained visible behind her hand. "We fell in love with every teacher. It's all she and I talked about, marrying one, leaving the village. We would stroll home through the woods inventing our lives." She shook her head and grunted. "Now our lives have come to an end. At this age, the only dreaming left to do is for the children, their futures. That is the limitation of being human. No matter what, we have to be able to envision our lives continuing, in some form. Otherwise . . ." she turned and gazed at my face, the tears that were running freely.

"Your mother was much younger than you when this happened to her. The workers suddenly rose up against your *nana* and looted his *manzil*, then burned everything, including the saris because the fabric was lined with gold and silver. I was told they made balls of gold and carried them off to wherever they went. Her family had been warned, too. One of your *nana*'s friends told them to flee. Another friend had already been shot with a rifle. And, of course, they shot and killed your *nana*'s dog. But your *nana* was too proud. He wouldn't go. He's lucky they didn't kill the whole family." She rested her head against the curves of the peacock's wings, and the overhead light splashed across her sweaty face, baring the lines on the broad cheekbones, the corners of her mouth.

"WE'RE SAFE."

"What?"

"We're safe. No one is coming to the house."

"How do you know?"

"I had a dream."

"You were sleeping? There, like that, you fell asleep!"

"I was running down the street when two women in chadors stopped me. They had luminous eyes. They asked me why I was crying. I told them my house was about to be overtaken, and I was out searching for my son. Was he dead? They put a hand on my shoulder to calm me. They said, 'Don't worry, Amma, your family is safe. No one will destroy your home. You are sheltered, even those outside. Allah has provided your well-being.' "

I closed my eyes, relieved to be safe, even in dream.

"I don't want my son to die," she whispered, then covered herself again and hid her face behind the green fabric. Her shoulders shook in sobs. "*Ya* Allah, what you have shown me tonight! Forgive me, forgive me, and let me hold my son to my breasts again."

I slid over and we clung to each other, crying, and, for a moment, I felt like I was holding my own mother in the way I had always wanted, all that had come between us erased, if only for now.

Together, through the open shutter, we watched the early morning light overtake the darkness, and we heard the crackle of a distant loudspeaker being turned on.

"Allah *ho Akbar.*"

It was as though I was hearing the first words God had ever created. The first words uttered by mankind.

THE MEN KNOCKED at well past eight, each returning to his home and waiting like a stranger to be let in. We unlocked the bedroom door, the *divan* door, the front door, making our way out of the house in the same way we had made our way in, as anxious as intruders. The metal locks echoed in the empty rooms. Zeba slid each key into her blouse, pushing it deep inside the bra, as though to ensure we would never use it again.

The two men stood in the sunlight, clothes crumpled, faces worn, arms limp. They were each holding a weapon, a knife, a wooden cane. They threw them in the courtyard, just outside the front door, before filing in. They sat at the dining table and took turns in the bathroom to clean up. Last night's dinner lay before them, flies buzzing over it, close to their faces. One landed on Ibrahim's lips, but he didn't brush it away. It crawled about until I batted at it. Zeba and I quickly cleared the table.

Then the obligatory making of breakfast no one wanted, Zeba allowing me back into the kitchen. Milk boiled for chai. Finally, Feroz went to the prayer room and fell on the floor, on his stomach, weeping, falling asleep.

SAMEER CAME HOME after the second call to prayer, and the family celebrated quietly, the joy for our own survival muted on this eighth day of mourning. The drumming had resumed and pounded all around the house, hemming us in.

At the sound of his motorbike, the neighbors had wandered over, all, like us, still wearing the green clothes from yesterday. Seeing them, Ibrahim asked Sameer to remain in the courtyard. He explained to him that, yesterday, we had stood together like this, listening to a stranger tell us about our deaths, so now we would listen to his son tell us what had kept us alive.

My husband looked weak and haggard. His face dark from stubble, his hair standing up, the weaker leg shaking, barely holding him straight. There was mud on his boots. But without protest, he jerked the motorbike onto its stand and sat on it, long legs thrown in one direction, hands on his lap. He was trembling.

Zeba stood next to him, the length of her body against the length of his, perhaps to give him strength, and it appeared as though mother and son had become attached once more. She had brought out a plate of food and fed her son by hand, the rice and dal we had been unable to eat ourselves, without him.

I watched and listened from the doorway, half inside the empty house, half joining this odd little community. Once the gathering was quiet, without needing the urgings of anyone, he simply began his story. So fluid it came out, so full of life and detail, this tragic tale of what had occurred mere blocks from our home, just minutes from when the gang would have most evidently fallen on us, that I knew he had told this story before, if only to himself a thousand times.

PERHAPS IT HAD been two or three in the morning when he had witnessed their terror. The end of life as these two young people had known it. He couldn't be sure. He had not had the wherewithal to look at his watch.

He had not intended to be on the road so late. But earlier, while he was trying to leave the Old City, the back tire of his bike had blown. He couldn't find a petrol pump nearby that was open to fix it. Not knowing what else to do, he screwed off the tire and carried it onto a bus to downtown. There, outside the Old City, the bazaars were lit and people strolled, talking and singing and laughing. He'd had no problem getting someone to mend it. Then, the long bus ride back to the abandoned cycle. By the time he'd gotten the tire back on, it was dark. He recalled using the frail light of a streetlamp to screw in the bolts.

Even at that hour, the Old City was alive, voices pumping out of loudspeakers, each surging with the sound of a different *manjalis*, a different dirge, each at a different movement, wailing or chest beating, the sorrow overflowing the moment and reaching back hundreds of years. So the silence of the colony chilled him even more. Where were the drums for Ganesh, calling forth this god of protection?

He turned off the engine and coasted to the side of the road to take shelter under the trees where he and I had once stood, together.

He was at the top of the hill that dropped into the colony, and voices from below rose up to him. Screaming. A woman crying. Men laughing. The sound of flesh being beaten. Then a round light flickered. Coming his way up the hill. Not steady. But zigzagging. Out of control. He hid farther within the branches. A scooter moaned past. A man on it. Steering with one hand. The other folded against his chest. He was screaming. He was yelling out for help.

Sameer let go of his bike and moved forward. Then hesitated and stepped back into the shadows.

Down the hill, the woman had stopped crying. But the men were still laughing. He heard the breaking of glass. When he eased out of the branches once more, he saw headlights surrounding dim figures. They were rising and falling. Pushing at one another. Three bodies were on the ground, lying on top of each other, writhing.

What could he do? Around the three, others stood or sat on their haunches, heads thrown back now and then, an arm flung up to drink from a bottle. He closed his eyes and sat against the trunk. He would have to wait for this to be over.

A police jeep materialized over the crest of the hill and rolled past. Without sirens. He did not understand what was going on. Then he saw policemen leaping out. And the men on the street scurrying away, some into the woods. Except for one who remained on the ground, splayed in the middle of the road.

He grabbed his bike and began running with it, gripping the handlebars and running. He did not know where he was headed, just away from what he could not yet believe. Jeeps sped past him in the other direction. These with lights flashing and sirens wailing, at last announcing a guarding presence.

By one, he was spotted and caught. Held in jail overnight for questioning. He told them the truth. Told them what he had seen. Told them what he had just told us. And from them, the questions they asked, half serious, half dramatic—putting on a performance to show they were doing their duties—he gathered it was a young couple who was returning home from a late movie or outing. They were driving down the hill on a scooter when they passed the slow moving gang on motorbikes. They did not know to be invisible. So they were surrounded. Just like that. Rifle barrels were stuck inside the spokes of the scooter wheels. They toppled. Struggled. Somehow the man got to his scooter and rode to the jail-*khanna* for help. Screaming the entire way.

There had been eight members. All young men. All carrying weapons. Only two had gotten caught. And because the man on the scooter, the victim who had come to them for help, did not possess an ID to show them who he was, he was put in jail along with the others. For the police weren't sure yet which side he was on.

Sameer ended there, and we remained silent, as though waiting for more. But what more could we bear to hear? Then the plump mother, who had again left her daughters at home, gasped. With a hand over her mouth, she gazed about the gathering until her eyes fell on me.

"Beti!" she cried, then pushed through the group, and I stepped down off the stoop and into the courtyard with them. She held me as though I were one of her own daughters, her breasts pushing into me. Then she pulled back and examined my face a long while, seeing me, seeing her own flesh.

After she released me, the woman from across the street, the one whose son would have to try to survive here with a Hindu wife, folded me into her arms, and in this way, one by one, we held each other close, pressing body to body, feeling our heat, smelling our sweat, patting each other as a way of reassuring ourselves that we were still here, still whole. Men with men. Women with women. Then, finally, husbands and wives.

Sameer walked up and pressed his forehead to mine, eyes pushed shut.

AFTER I HAD showered and lain down to rest, Sameer came into the room and woke me. Taqi Mamu had just been over. He hadn't stayed long. He just wanted to make sure we were all safe. And he had brought a message. Something so terrible that Sameer begged my uncle to be the one who told me.

It was Henna who had been out there in the dark. Henna who had been raped. What Sameer had mistaken as two figures on top of a third had really been one man—then others—on top of Henna and her baby. Her pregnant body had been mutilated by the broken glass of a whiskey bottle.

It was Henna who had died.

DRUMS WERE BEATING in the distance. Sometimes growing louder, sometimes fainter, so that I thought one of the neighborhood Ganesh statues was being carried off, but then the beating would grow louder again.

Sameer and I were riding to Abu Uncle's, and at the turn onto his street, just at the corner of the main road, an enormous tent had been erected. On the outside, the shiny skin was red and blue, while the inside was the pale hue of an almond. Crimson and gold streamers were tied together and hung to make the sign of the swastika, denoting good luck. At the center of the tent, elephant-headed Ganesh, tremendous and majestic, sat on an ornate brass podium. His skin was pink, his crown gold, his neck and hands thick. He was wearing layers of jeweled necklaces that reached his oversized stomach. Around his feet, gold anklets. He sat cross-legged, meditative, powerful. The god of protection. The remover of obstacles. Where had he been last night?

Large speakers set up around the stage were blaring Telugu songs and prayers. Small boys lingered about the base, dressed in glistening shirts, teeth glowing white against dark skin. When Sameer and I rode past, they stared at us, expressionless.

We turned onto Abu Uncle's street, and the songs and prayers faded, along with those frightful faces. But as soon as he switched off the engine, I heard the distant drums, and thought of those boys' features grown into men's and wondered if this was what the murderers looked like. In that way, I realized that for some time to come, I would be looking into the faces of men, Hindu men, Indian men, men of all kinds, to catch a glimpse of what Henna had seen in her final moments. Six had gotten away!

"I can't come in," Sameer said. "I can't face them. Please try to understand."

When I didn't answer, he wiggled the bike so I would hop off, and I went and stood at the side of the road, just before the gates to the house. How was I going to face them myself?

"I couldn't have saved her," he said. "Even if I had gone to Hanif when he was calling for help, what could I have done? They would have killed me, too. You know that, right?"

I stared at him, not answering.

He shut his eyes and raised his hands to his scalp, fingers bumping up against his helmet. "Jesus Christ, Layla, you're right, I should have gone to help. I heard him shouting. All I had to do was step out from under that bloody tree. Show myself." He whacked his helmet with fists. "I watched her die, baby. I did nothing to save your sister. I did nothing but protect myself. I am a coward, Layla, hate me, hate me for being a coward, nothing else!"

I shook my head. "Nafiza's dead. Henna's dead. What's the use in hating?" Then I said, "I hate those men so much I feel nothing else. I'm overcome with hate. I can't even feel sorrow. Sameer, I want to feel sorrow. I want to feel Henna."

He grimaced, as though I was hoarding grief in some saintly way to keep from condemning him.

I said, "Not more than an hour, please. I can't take being here myself." Just as I was turning toward the gate, he lurched sideways at me and the motorcycle angled onto his weaker thigh. He grabbed my arms and shook me.

"Don't you see how many lives I have ruined!"

We struggled and the motorcycle shifted back and forth between his legs. Then I jerked away, and he lost balance. As the bike was falling, he leapt off. It crashed to the ground. He began stomping on the back wheel with his thick boots. Three, five, seven, twelve times. He gave a final kick then unstrapped the helmet and whacked metal against metal. The bike trembled, as though alive. Then he threw the helmet, and it hit the spokes and rolled to the middle of the road. He didn't pick it up. He marched to the boundary wall and crouched against it, hands in his hair, knees to his face. He was crying.

"I heard them, Layla. Don't you see? The police interrogated them in the next cell. They were laughing. They weren't terrified. They knew they wouldn't be punished. One of them was the son of such and such minister. They were just passing time until the call came to release them."

I picked up his helmet and stood before him, the weight of it in my hands. "Henna's dead. Nothing will bring her back."

He began tearing at his scalp. "I can't stop hearing their voices. They're echoing inside me. They were snickering at her body. They said her breasts were engorged, all juicy like mangoes—and just as sweet. Baby, they drank her milk!"

I dropped the helmet next to him. "It's not possible. She hadn't had the baby yet. Another three weeks." Even as I said it, I knew it could happen. The production of milk with the production of new life. The mother's milk not meant for such crimes.

"Fucking hell, this bloody country. Your parents were right to leave."

I looked about at the houses that were as familiar to me as Henna's. We had played together on this street. Marbles, kites, *gilli-dandol*. It was along this stretch she had taught me how to ride a bike. On the tar, we used her school chalk to draw those same designs we saw before the houses of our Hindu neighbors, diamonds broken into triangles, signs of luck and prosperity, fertility. Our play changing with the seasons. Then our bodies changed, and we were kept inside—hidden and safe from what? Now women were watching me from windows, curtains pulled back to reveal one eye, half lips, nose. I yanked off my chador. Let them see who I was.

"Jesus Christ, she was in the ninth month. The baby was whole when they sliced it out . . ."

I closed the gate on him.

INSIDE THE BOUNDARY wall, the house and its surroundings were quiet. I had expected crying, wailing, even screaming laments, so the silence shook me. The drums continued pounding in the distance, and I found myself growing to depend on the sound, the only thing reassuring me of my own continued existence. The world pulsed through me.

This was the city cottage Nana had moved into after Partition, when his *manzil* was overrun. He had divided it in half soon before dying, giving the front portion to Taqi Mamu and his wife, the back to Asma Kala and her husband. But after Ameera Auntie lost her fourth child here, the couple had shifted to another place nearby, thinking this land was bad luck. There, they lost four more. The last time I'd come here was when we'd picked up Henna for our excursion to Golconda. What had she told me then, hugging her pregnant belly as we stared off at the majestic tombs, that she feared disaster, Hanif's arrival bringing some sort of end. Indeed, the heart knew when it was driving toward its own death.

No one was in the front part of the house, and I thought the grief must have sent them all to Taqi Mamu's. But as I was about to walk there, I glimpsed the door curtain to Henna's room blowing in the breeze, as though waving to me, inviting me in. I walked slowly down the side yard, keeping an eye on the door, hoping to find my family, hoping they weren't there.

The door was open, and though no voices came from inside, I caught sight of Asma Kala's feet just below the swaying curtain. They were scratching at each other. I hesitated and stopped at the clothesline. Black fabric hung like flags of defeat. Among polyester pants and cotton saris, I found a sari-blouse I knew would fit me. It hung wrinkled and dry, the short sleeves reaching for the earth. They could have been wings. And the thing itself a dead and hung crow. I swallowed it in one hand and snatched it off, placing it next to my nose. Nothing but the smell of soap and sun. Angry, I pulled off all the items, clenching them against me, then holding them away. Like that, I brought them into Henna's room. An offering like no other. My final surrender.

Inside, the space was dark, the windows shut against the dying sun. The only sunlight that came in was a long strip that tumbled onto the floor each time the curtain blew back. Then it crept away, as though it had made a mistake by coming here. An air cooler was turned on in one corner and blew stale, warm air. The water inside had evaporated and not been refilled. The machine droned.

Abu Uncle sat on his daughter's bed, one leg pulled up, the other bent under him. He was wearing the white T-shirt and loose pajamas I knew he slept in, unable to dress for this day and what it had ushered in, the end of his life. His head was bowed, and I saw he was examining the pattern of the bedsheet, following the design with a finger, then making swirls and loops beyond it. He pulled the finger back and slid it over again. Then again. The third time I realized he was not following any pattern. The third time, I recognized the Urdu script. He was writing Henna's name, over and over. Writing her name with skin.

I turned away, toward Asma Kala, who was sitting far from him, on a chair next to the door. She was staring at her feet, slipping them in and out of her *chappals*, the kind her father had never let her wear, the toes rubbing at the heels. Even though my shadow fell across her, covering the whole of her being in darkness, she did not notice. Not knowing what to do or say—not even knowing how to address her without breaking down myself—I tried to slip back outside. My sandals skidded on the tile floor, and both she and Abu Uncle glanced up and raised their brows at me in greeting, in their usual way. Asma Kala even gave me a small smile.

"I brought in the clothes," I said, setting them next to her. Someone had moved all the chairs from the house into this small room and arranged them in a line against the wall, facing the bed.

"These are Hanif's parents." She raised her chin to point at the end of the row.

I was startled to find the old couple sitting quietly next to each other. They had chosen to be in the corner, under two closed shutters and next to the bathroom door, their bodies receding into darkness. Six chairs sat empty between them and Asma Kala. All of us were dressed in black but Abu Uncle. No matter the sorrows of the world, today I was mourning Henna.

I salaamed them and sat by Asma Kala, the pile of clothes between us. No one spoke. Like my aunt, I focused on my feet, not wanting to see how the room had been redecorated in preparation for the returning groom, the family's new life. Finally, I glanced at the old couple. The woman had draped her sari-*pallow* loosely over her head. She had a thin nose and dark circles under her eyes, not from this grief but from years of bad living. The father's features were more coarse. His cheeks pockmarked, the eyes deep set and moist. Every few minutes he leaned forward and coughed, his brows arching, his feet swinging under the chair.

I was meeting them for the first time, their faces alien to me, yet the two that had combined to make the one Henna loved, then the one that had formed inside her.

The light of a community had been blown out.

"IS HE STILL in jail?" My voice cracked, and I thought no one had heard it over the air cooler's barren wail, so I leaned forward and gazed down at the old couple.

"He is, Beta," his mother answered, her tone high, barely controlled. When she spoke, she leaned forward as well and peeked over her husband, down the long line of chairs at me. I stared at her feet, unable to take in her face. Her nails were orange from faded henna, the big toes glinting with silver toe rings. "What are we to do? Just now, before we came here, we stopped by with his ID card, but the police took it without releasing him. They wouldn't even let us visit him. How badly is my son beaten? I don't know. Are they allowing him to see a doctor? I don't know. *Hai* Allah, why did he ever come back from Saudi? He was better off there. Here, he was living in sin—I'm telling you, it's why he's being punished. They were together, Beta, during Muhar'ram! This man . . ." She shook a finger at Abu Uncle before scooting back in her chair.

My uncle spoke with his head bowed, still writing on the bedsheet. "They were so happy to finally be together, they didn't come out of this room for days; yesterday was the first time, and only because Henna wanted to bring flowers to the *durga*," Imams' shrine. "Her prayers had been fulfilled. They were safe in my house. The whole time, I had the servants place their food on trays and set them outside the locked door. My daughter was finally happy—what else mattered?"

The mother was startled and pressed her lips together. After a moment she leaned forward and spoke to me again. "He has a foreign card, Beta. From Saudi. So though he was born and raised here, they claim he's not an Indian national. They say he is a foreigner to his own country. And because he's a foreigner—maybe even a Muslim fanatic!—maybe he had cause to stir up all the trouble! Maybe this was the real reason he came back to India, using his wife's delivery as a ruse. These people are crazy! We've lived and died here for generations and still we are not allowed to consider it our home. Then, when we leave and try to make a better existence elsewhere, still we are persecuted. What do they want? Do they want us all to die?"

"That's exactly what they want," her husband finally said. "And they want to kill us themselves. *Ar're*, just today, as we were leaving the Chow-Rasta Jail-*khanna*, I looked up and saw an election slogan painted on the boundary wall. It read, 'Vote for me and I'll drive all the Muslims into the Indian Ocean.' My son inside for being beaten, his young bride raped and murdered, and I look up to see this. *Tho-ba!* It all makes sense to me now." He nodded at Abu Uncle, but my uncle had his head thrown up against the wall, gazing at the ceiling fan. Then his eyes rolled to the side and his jaw tightened, and I knew he was seeing something of hers. I didn't look. Hanif's father leaned forward and coughed.

Chappals scraped the ground outside the door. Taqi Mamu walked in. He glanced about the dark room then down the row of chairs at each of us, his eyes flat, not taking anything in. His hair was parted down the side, pushed back with a hand. It was greasier than when I'd seen him last, so I could not tell if he had oiled it or just hadn't bothered to bathe since all this had begun. A personal rite of mourning. He was half dressed, as though the news of Henna's death had caught him in an act that then felt too inconsequential to finish. He wore a button-down shirt over white pajamas. The string-tie hung between his legs.

"Why don't they just take Ganesh and drown him in the lake?" he asked the room. "For days, I've been hearing these drums. It's like they're sitting on my head and beating, reminding me what they've done to my child. For Allah's sake, when are they going to lift Ganesh?" When no one answered, he muttered, "I told my father we should go to Pakistan. 'India is my home,' he kept saying, 'India is my home!' What home? Even after they've stolen his home he says this is his home. Thoo!" He turned and spat, disgusted with us all. Then he bowed his head and announced, "I've taken the money. Just now, I phoned. I told them, two *lakh*, three *lakh*, whatever they want to give me for my land, I'll take it. No more fighting," he mumbled, backing out of the room.

"Poor Taqi," Asma Kala said, once he'd gone. "He's been pacing like that all day."

"He was very close to Henna?" the mother asked.

"She was a daughter to all of us. Taqi's wife never had kids. She became pregnant eight times and each time . . ." She turned down her lips and shook her head.

The mother clucked. "Some women just don't have children in their fate."

"She has severe diabetes," Asma Kala explained. "And his blood and hers don't mix. It was during a time when doctors couldn't do much."

I understood she was telling the mother that fate had nothing to do with it. It was a matter of physicality.

But the mother didn't understand. She clasped her hands, saying, "Oh, the poor woman. First no children, then diabetes. *Hai* Allah, you give us each our burdens. Let us not forget that during such times." She began reciting a prayer under her breath.

"Was the baby a boy or a girl?" I asked.

No one answered, and in the silence, the air cooler blew stale air at our faces.

Asma Kala began fingering the blouse I had taken from the clothesline. She opened her mouth, then closed it, then opened it again. "A girl," she managed to say.

I looked up at the wall to see what Abu Uncle had spotted. It was nothing more than a calendar. Not even a personal one with the name of her school or anything she might have had ties to, not even her bank. It was just a generic calendar she must have had one of the servants pick up from the corner store. But on it, under this month's heading, she had crossed out, in bold black ink, the days as they had passed before Hanif's arrival. Though now, looking at it like this, reading it backward, reading what we had not seen before, made it a countdown to her death.

I caught my breath and turned toward the parents. "How is it that your son was so lucky to have lived? They had motorcycles. They could have chased him. They even had rifles . . ."

"Shush now. Let's not talk of these things," Asma Kala said, sounding like Amme. "What has happened has happened. Kismet . . ."

"No, not kismet," I said. "God is not telling us to behave in these ways, to live like this, we are! Saying we are saving ourselves by killing each other . . ."

"You want my son dead!" the mother cried. "Isn't what has happened bad enough? Do you wish to be like one of those who tried to kill him?"

Her husband patted her thigh. "She's just a child," he said, trying to console her. Then he turned in my direction and stared at the space a few inches from my face, respectful that we were not related, not anymore, so he could not meet my eyes. He spoke in a calm voice. "Beta, we do not know much more than you about what happened last night, so we cannot tell you if Hanif left her because he truly believed he could bring help and save her. As my wife explained, the police would not give us any information, and we were not allowed to see our son. In fact, when we came here to pay our respects, we learned more about the happenings from your uncle than we knew ourselves. It seems your own husband was there. He is better informed than the rest of us. You should pose your questions to him."

"He did not come forth himself . . ." the mother began, but her husband squeezed her arm, strangling her voice.

I sat back and, through the chair, felt the strength of the wall. Last night, leaning up against it like this, I understood for the first time it was not impenetrable.

I now took in the redecorated room, the bright colored rugs over the tiled floor, a wooden crib next to her bed, the door that led to the main area of the house locked, a new *almari* (for him?) pushed before it, making this their private space.

I spoke to this room, "How was she mutilated? What did they do with the broken bottle? What did they do to her baby?"

"*Hai* Allah!" the mother cried, as though the violation had been made against her, the privacy of her body, so that, at first, I thought it was Asma Kala who had shrieked. "Can no one make her stop!"

"Why don't you go outside?" Asma Kala suggested. She crumpled Henna's blouse in one hand and hid it in the folds of her sari. "Go find your uncle. He is very torn up. First Nafiza, now this . . . this . . ." She spread open her palms.

AS I WAS standing to leave, Abu Uncle began tapping his chest with his three middle fingers. He looked up at me, his eyes glistening with tears. He said, "I had a heart attack. Did you know?"

Of course I did. His heart had stumbled when his daughter was returned home.

He said, "In my forties and already death . . ." he caught himself, reminded of Henna. Eighteen, the age in the U.S. when you become an adult and begin to figure out who you are, as an individual. By eighteen, my cousin had grown, gotten married, gotten pregnant, then died, all because of who she was. "Do you know why I had a heart attack?" he asked me.

I sat back down. He straightened and sat cross-legged. "You think it is because of Henna, I know. And this trip her husband made, Henna told others it was to reconcile. My daughter respected her in-laws so much, she did not tell even you, her own sister, the truth."

"*Hai* Allah, he's starting with this again." The mother turned to her husband. "Aji, are you going to listen to this again?"

Abu Uncle spoke over her. "It's our fault. I take the blame. We taught her how to be a proper woman, your *kala* and I. We taught her to be humble and obedient, respectful of her new family, attending to her husband. Do not voice disagreements. Do not talk back. Do not think . . ." his voice broke and his face crumpled into itself. He breathed in slowly and whispered, "Do not think of yourself." Old City ethics, rules governing each woman's life, ways to submit not to Allah, but to man. If my uncle had taught his daughter this, he had taught her how to survive, here; there was no need for him to feel ashamed. "When Hanif was gone," he said, "she did not once come home to visit. She stayed with his family to let us know she had accepted her new role. How were we to know what was happening? We thought they had no cause to make her unhappy."

"Aji, are you listening? Are you not going to stop him?"

"Not today, Kosar, not today."

The mother grunted and turned her face to the wall.

"After the two got married, Hanif did not want to go to Saudi. He wanted to get a job here and stay with his bride. A cousin of his even offered him a job in the bank. He could have become a bank manager. *Ar're*, what better news than this? But these two began protesting. The house is too small. There is not enough room. So I offered up my home. So big, so many rooms. How could your *kala* and I fill it? It was hers. All of this belonged to Henna. Your *kala* and I said we would occupy only one room, become like visitors waiting for our stay to end." He closed his eyes and knocked the back of his head against the wall, once, twice, five times.

"These two wouldn't let him. They wanted him to go and send rials home. We can't make a good living here, so beg money from our Muslim brothers. After two years, they wanted him to get a different contract for a different company, then another one. Like this, they expected the two to live out the rest of their lives. A few years, we thought, your *kala* and I, was sufficient to save enough to buy a house and car, make a good life here. We did not know he would have to stay there for good. *Ar're*, even these Muslim brothers of ours, these Saudi sheiks, think of us like servants, no better than the Hindu fanatics do here. Our own countrymen may be telling us to get out, but our own brothers are telling us we can't live among them, no citizenship is given, no visas to the workers' families, so the men must go there alone, sharing rooms with other men, their quarters partitioned off from the locals as though we are contaminated because we come from India, the husband not in peace, the wife not in peace. *Ar're*, why must the boy be forced to sell himself like this?" He stared at me with those deep-set eyes that could have been Henna's, that promise of redemption erased.

"One day he sent a letter to me. He said, 'Go see what my parents are doing to your daughter. Bring her back to your home. You have my permission.' Only because he wrote to ask for my help did we go." He patted his chest. "What my eyes saw I could never have imagined!"

The mother let out a grunt and shuffled in her chair.

"All her dowry gone. Sold! The car. The refrigerator. The water heater. The dishes. Even the *almari* in which she stored her clothes. Everything is gone. What these nawabs did not tell us, these *purana jageer-dars*," old landowners, "was that this man here, the one who is sitting now with his head lowered in shame, but only when it is too late and my daughter is already dead—gone with the rest of her possessions—is that he has a problem with his eyes. He is unable to see himself. He is still living as his forefathers used to live. Betting on horses. Going hunting. Playing cards. He entertains. He drinks alcohol. He is part of clubs. And because no one in his family has needed to work, he himself refuses. *Ar're*, the ancestral house was put up on mortgage and was about to be taken away, and still he would not take a job. Instead, they think up a plan to get their son married. Rather than use some of Henna's dowry to pay for the *walima* dinner, they paid off the house. By now, any man would bow and thank Allah for saving him from public shame. But, still, he does not stop. And this shameless woman, she keeps giving him my daughter's things to sell. The furniture. The pots and pans made of copper. Things that were passed down to your *kala*, then to Henna. And when there was nothing left, she began asking for my daughter's gold bracelets, her anklets, her necklaces, all her jewels taken. One by one."

"Aji, say something to him! Why must I listen to this?"

"And my daughter! Without protest, giving up her rights to this man. Her father-in-law! Not even her husband. *Ar're*, the day we arrive, we find her cleaning the floors and cooking because they have no money to hire a servant. And she's looking like one herself! No clean sari. No jewels. And these two sitting around her like the landowners they once were, when they no longer possess a thing! Not even the house! It all belonged to Henna. Paid for with her inheritance. Still she is wordless. When she sees your *kala* and me, she does not complain. It is only when she runs to throw up, and I ask if she is sick that I am told by these two that my daughter is pregnant." He clucked. "It is seeing her like this . . ." he stopped and thumped his chest. "The strain of seeing her gave me a heart attack. I have always been weak when it comes to that child. I brought her back. Yes, this father brought his daughter home. She did not come herself. She was not thrown out! These two were enjoying their comfort, believing I had given them my daughter to be a servant." He sighed and looked at the calendar again. "I do not blame him for leaving her to find help. The boy had no choice. Even when she was hurting at his own home, he called for my help." He paused, then his lips began moving as he said more, but nothing came out.

I turned to Asma Kala and found her staring at her feet again, one foot roughly rubbing the other as though trying to wipe something away. She looked up at me and shot me another smile.

I shouldn't have said it, but I did. "I don't agree with you. If he had loved her, he would have stayed. He must have known there would not be enough time to get help. He fled. He let her die alone."

"We shouldn't have come here," the mother cried, rising. She glared at Abu Uncle. "We have enough grief of our own. Why must we listen like criminals to crimes they think we've committed." She turned and spoke down at her husband's head. "We've done nothing wrong, I tell you, nothing!"

Her husband sat hunched, hands in his lap, head bowed.

She swiveled about and tried to meet Asma Kala's eyes, fists on her thick waist. "What daughter does not suffer, huh, what daughter! The girl was merely performing her duties, doing nothing more than what I did myself, nothing more than what you do even with all your servants. A wife, a daughter, must obey, it is all she can do, all that is open to her. If you do not believe this, why did you allow your husband to take Layla back to her in-laws? Why is she still there with that . . . that *man*?"

Asma Kala looked up at me, and the long stretch of light spread across her face. She had been crying for some time and her eyes were swollen and dark, her cheeks sunken, the body shrinking in on itself. The pause between life and death. The landscape of Amme's existence.

When tears began running down my aunt's face, I stood, not wanting to give her any more grief, and walked out into the remaining dregs of light.

IN THE SHADOWS of the neem tree, I found Roshan and Raga-be standing face to face, so engrossed in conversation that they did not see me until I was upon them. Then they turned in unison and stared at me with such surprise it could have been me who had died, then returned. When I joined them, Raga-be passed a hand over my cheeks and kissed the fingers that had touched me.

Then she opened her mouth to speak, but Roshan quickly said, "They buried her in the same cemetery as your grandfather. He took her in when she was three or four. This was the only family she knew."

So the divisions we drew in life finally erased themselves in death. I stepped forward to embrace her, but she moved back, her body going stiff.

"They wouldn't let me come to the funeral, Roshan. I would have been there."

She stared at something just beyond me, saying, "She came to me last night in a dream. It was at the same hour Henna was dying." Her lower lip curled up and slid into her mouth. She breathed slowly for a moment before she could go on. "She sat at the edge of my bed, crying. Just by my feet. She wouldn't say anything. I kept calling to her. 'Amma. Amma.' Finally, she got up and left."

VOICES SPRANG FROM the side yard, and we receded farther into the shadows to stand next to the hefty trunk. When our bodies had changed, confining Henna and me to this house, we would climb up this tree and stare out over the boundary wall, dreaming.

Asma Kala now appeared around the bend of the house. She was walking Hanif's parents to the front gate. Her sari had been wrapped in a clumsy manner so that, in front, the bottom edge rose above her ankles, while, in back, the fabric fell so low it dragged behind her on the dirt, wiping away her footprints.

Hanif's mother was nodding to something Asma Kala was saying, but when she caught sight of me, she jerked back as though I'd struck her. Her husband followed her gaze and stared at me with flat eyes. Then he took his wife's arm and led her outside. Not even a car or moped waiting to take them home.

"I have to see Asma *memsa'ab*," Roshan whispered, using the title from when she was still a servant, as though wishing to push back time. She broke free of us and walked in a steady line across the courtyard, her hands splayed before her to catch her if she collapsed.

My aunt was shutting the gate and did not see her coming. When she had locked it, she stepped toward Henna's room then stopped. I thought it was for Roshan, but then she leaned over the coconut tree and placed a hand high on the trunk, her skin the color of bark. Her legs gave out from under her. Just as she buckled, Roshan held her up from behind. She dug her face into Asma Kala's neck, sobbing. My aunt reached back with her free hand and patted Roshan's head as she used to Henna's. Like that, with Roshan still leaning on her, my *kala* bent forward and vomited clear liquid into the base of the tree. When she straightened, Roshan straightened with her, a child on piggyback, then my aunt bent forward once more. Finally, she spit and kicked dirt over her waste.

AFTER THEY HAD disappeared, a motorcycle's moan filled the air, and I headed toward the front gate, ready to go.

Raga-be stopped me. "The boy come already. I send he away. I say the child stay here tonight, the child must be with she family. He say he come tomorrow to burial. He get you there."

"I don't think they want me to stay, Raga. I'm only causing them more strain." Then I said, "Poor Nafiza, I had her thrown out, did you know? That's the memory of me she died with."

Her hunched form bent even more, and she startled me by letting out a loud laugh. "Me *jadu* work for you, *hahn*! You come to me, you tell me make so others believe you no touch before. Only touch by you husband. The world believe this. This power of me *jadu*." She shifted closer to me, her hot breath on my face. "This time, I bring you husband to you. Make him proper husband. I come to you tonight, *hahn*, Bitea?"

So, this was the real reason she had arranged for me to stay.

"No, thank you, Raga-be," I said, and she stepped back in surprise, her kohl-lined eyes like small circles on her face.

"What you say, Bitea! You trap-trap! What else help you? Nothing but magic!"

"I don't think your *jadu* will work on me," I said, then repeated what she had first told me when I'd asked her to perform the *jadu*. "I'm not fully Indian."

"No Indian! What you is if you no Indian, child! This grief talking, no me girl!"

Perhaps it was the grief. But at the moment it seemed that the only way to do away with borders was to start with the ones that had been etched in skin, splitting me.

ON THE NINTH of Muhar'ram, we buried Henna.

Taqi Mamu and Abu Uncle were among the men who carried her body on a wooden litter. Without a pause in their step, the men passed an end from one shoulder to the next. But when the cemetery came into view, Taqi Mamu handed his corner to someone else and stepped aside, and the small procession went on without him. After a ways, I turned to see him stick his arms out as he fell to the ground. Without picking himself up, he crawled to the edge of the road and sat staring ahead, his jaw moving as though chewing on something. People passed on foot or cycle or car and did not seem to notice him. Abu Uncle never once gave up his end of the litter.

She was shrouded in a white sheet. Her body had been cleansed for the final time, washing away the sins of this world. The women had cleansed Henna's daughter as well, washing her of her mother's waters as they would have done to commence her life. Then they enclosed her in Henna's arms. The one burial sheet was wound around the two of them, so that they were flesh to flesh. Pressed into one. The shroud, a new skin. Why was there no comfort in their joint departure?

When the procession entered the cemetery, the men went ahead to the burial site, while the women stayed back by the entrance. A tall, wrought-iron gate was the only thing separating the life rumbling by outside from the silence of the dead within. For now, we were enveloped in this silence, grateful for it. And grateful, too, that the entire Old City was in black. As we were in black. It was as though the whole of India was mourning these deaths.

Near the grave site, a police officer uncuffed Hanif's hands and he stepped forward. He was tall with wavy hair, and that was all, from this distance, that I could make of him. Abu Uncle handed him a shovel. For a moment, Hanif set his forehead on its handle, unable to raise dirt. But then the police officer elbowed him, and Hanif lifted his head and went forward. He dug the shovel into the ground, then placed a foot on it and dug even deeper. He pushed the earth aside. Only then did Abu Uncle step forward himself, and one by one, other men joined in, including Hanif's father. I had been told that once they were done, Hanif's soiled hands would be cuffed once more and he'd be taken away. His mother had not come.

The women had to stand apart while the body was being buried, and from where I was with Ameera Auntie and Asma Kala, Roshan and her daughter, we could only make out the dim figures of the men, their arms rising and falling as they dug at the earth, then pitched it aside. As the sun rose to the center of the sky, they deepened into the ground, losing ankles, calves, knees, thighs. Then they threw out the shovels, and hands from above grasped hands from below, helping them out.

The men surrounded Henna's body and lowered it into the hole, and I tried not to blink, tried not to miss anything of this final sight of my sister. This white angel of sorrow among us black shrouded souls. Then she was gone. The rise of her belly, the rise that was the child buried with her, the last thing to glimpse this wretched earth.

Once more, the men picked up their tools and created a mound I knew would flatten over time, becoming like all the others. The new dead joining the old. Somewhere next to her lay Nafiza's body, the cold dirt not yet warmed about it.

At last, the men set aside their shovels, and we stood, the men over her grave, the women by the gates, and, together, we uttered a final prayer.

There was nothing left to do for her.

ASMA KALA ASKED that I join her in visiting Henna's grave. From there, she wanted me to go to the *durga* and say our private prayers. I had gotten my period that morning, almost a month after the D & C, my body leaking blood as a rite of ancient cleansing, and though this made me impure in the eyes of Allah to be near the fresh grave, to enter any holy shrine, how could I refuse?

So I took my *kala*'s small hand in mine, the skin dry, the nails bitten short, the lifelines intersecting my own, and we walked together, leaving the others behind. Roshan thought it wise to keep her young daughter from sorrow that was not yet her own. And Ameera Auntie, who in grieving had worsened her diabetes, was now too weak to traverse this stretch of land, this path from the living to the dead.

We walked hand in hand, like mother and daughter, passing other graves, both old and fresh, small and large, the tombstones even with the land, and I whispered, "Salaam, salaam, salaam," peace, onto each one I passed. After a short distance, my *kala* let go of my hand and we went on like that, with her before me, steady and firm, and me trailing behind. The path was so narrow, the graves coming just to the edge, that I was scared to stumble and fall, so I carefully placed my feet where hers had left an imprint.

When we came to the far side of the graveyard, I saw Hanif was already gone and the rest of the men made the excuse of returning their shovels and picks and left us alone. Abu Uncle squatted under the shade of a nearby tree, his black-and-white checkered shirt smudged brown with earth. Taqi Mamu walked off alone and smoked, and when he was done, he looked about confused before he slid the butt into a pocket.

Asma Kala crouched next to Henna's grave and stared at it for some time. In a few days, she and Abu Uncle would have to return to place the cement marker with Henna's name and dates. But for now, my aunt simply passed her hand over the dirt, caressing her child through a mound of earth. Back and forth, back and forth, pebbles rolling away.

"Why did you have to be so insistent on going out?" she asked. Then she said, "We spoiled you too much." After that, she was quiet, her eyes measuring the length and width of the grave, as though ensuring that Henna was comfortable inside, not too squeezed in with her daughter. Then her hand closed on the dirt and clenched it, bringing it up to her face. She kissed it. Then opened her mouth and shoved the dirt inside and swallowed it. Then shoved and swallowed some more. Behind us, Abu Uncle began to cry. I looked away.

Next to my aunt's feet lay Nana's grave, and I stared at it, silently informing him that this was what was left of his hopes for the future. Just these three empty lives, my two uncles and aunt, then Ameera Auntie, Amme and me, three more. And I, the sole heir of their collective sorrow. I, their only hope. Then my eyes fell upon a miniature grave to the left of Nana's, just between him and Henna. It was a mere foot long, and above it, a small slab of cement. On it, swirls to the left. ABBAS. My brother. Amme's lost son. No dates inscribed for one who had died before living an age long enough to record. Dying at birth. Slipping from the nurse's clumsy hands and falling. Smacking his too-soft newborn head on the stone floor. And the cry for life became a startled hiccup and nothing more. For three days he bled from the nose, mouth and ears. He bled the same blood that flowed through me now. Accident or kismet? A child born only to die, and now he had found a playmate.

My legs buckled and I slouched next to Asma Kala, finally crying, finally touching sorrow.

WE WENT TO the shrine that Henna had visited the day she was murdered, when she had brought her flowers and prayers of thanksgiving for her husband's safe return, her family's long-awaited reunion. Allah rewarded patience, that was what was promised in the Qur'an, over and over, so though I had intended to go in and pray for her, I found I could not. I stayed outside the small one-room structure, listening to the family pray for peace—peace within themselves, peace without—and I told God that I disagreed with life. Like that, bit by bit, just as I had been bound by this existence, I was now breaking away. It was not enough anymore, blind faith.

Sameer found me awaiting my family in Abu Uncle's car, just outside the *durga*. He pulled up beside the passenger door, his gaze faltering, ashamed. He didn't get off the bike. We rode home without a word, lost to those we passed and to each other.

When we were upon the crossroads, he suddenly yelled, "There's the jail-*khanna*," pointing it out as though I'd not seen it a hundred times in a hundred different passings. It was no more than a square block, the faded cement boundary wall painted over brightly by this season's slogans. Passionate words that would be painted over themselves with the lusty faces of next season's film stars. And still Henna would not be returned.

Sameer stuck out an arm and the cycle swerved. "Wave to Hanif. Wave!" he cried, trying to sound sarcastic or untouched, but I could hear the pain in his voice.

A car jerked around us, and the front passenger thrust out his head and cursed Sameer. He was wearing a shiny orange shirt so I knew he was Hindu, just as he could tell from our black clothes, my chador, that we were Muslim. Sameer stuck his pinkie in his mouth and smacked it back out, a gesture of insult I did not know how to translate. We tailed the car around the curve of the *chow-rasta*, and just as I was growing nervous Sameer might lead us to danger, the car took the first right and zipped away. The struggle so quickly forgotten.

We continued straight until we reached the top of the hill that would drop us down into the colony. There, he pulled to the side and stopped. He didn't show me the tree under which he had taken cover, nor did I ask him to point it out. We sat in the last bright rays of the dying sun. Ahead, rambling down the slope were a few goats, a vegetable seller grasping his cart as it rolled ever more quickly before him, a *tho-bun* with a dirty laundry bundle on top of her head, her hips swaying side to side. At this time of day, on the ninth of Ganesh, there should have been more of a crowd, cheering and celebration. This was some sort of self-imposed curfew, news of Henna's death, as all such deaths, reaching the entire neighborhood. What was it that kept people away, the guilt that they could have prevented it? Or the fear that her ghost was lingering about, ready to enter any body that passed?

"Enter me," I whispered as Sameer whisked down the hill. I raised my arms over my head and closed my eyes, telling myself the air against my skin was really the pressure of Henna's ghost pushing inside. But even as I did, I knew it wasn't so. The borders of skin were as firm as the borders on any map.

Halfway down, Sameer switched off the engine and we coasted the rest of the way. I could now hear drums beating around us, and as we passed a dirt road, I saw a lorry carrying an enormous Ganesh. Four or five men in festive colored shirts sat in the back with their god. They were clapping and singing to him. We rolled on.

"Where did she die?"

He turned an ear to me. "Could have been anywhere along this stretch. I was too far to know." Whether or not he said that to protect me, I could not tell, and I began to examine the road, searching for signs of blood, of a torn sari or chador, of dried milk. I found nothing. Then I became so frightened that I would find something that I closed my eyes and pretended to be her.

It is dark and she is gliding. Her one arm wrapped around her husband's waist, the other resting on her stomach, on her baby. They are moving so quickly that hot air rises from under the wheels and she has the sensation, over and over, of her sandals flying off. So she curves her toes down to keep them in place. Ahead, there is darkness. Then figures emerging from it, coming into form in the frail light of the scooter. One, two, three, four. She sees only four. A group of friends. Just boys out having fun. Nothing to worry about, not anymore. Her husband has returned. She is having his baby. Together, they will create a future.

Then the first strike of the rifle's handle against her shin. At first, she is confused. Perhaps a stick on the road, a stick they have run over has flipped in the air and struck her. But then she feels it again, now against her shoulder, now her back, her neck, her crotch. She instinctively covers her belly. The bike is swerving. They fall. She falls. He rises and leaves. She watches him go. The men's motorcycle lights are pointing at her, they have encircled her and beyond that, all is darkness.

No, I would change it, as I was going to change so much else. Bring the invisible to life.

It is dark and she is gliding. She can hear the breeze shaking the trees around her, but she cannot see the branches. Every now and then a crow calls. Ahead there is no one, not even her husband. She is riding alone. The engine hums between her thighs, reverberates against her skin. Inside her, life trembles and sprouts. Outside, the wind blows through her chador, billowing it out and back, giving her wings. A nighttime angel. She soars, the small motorcycle light illuminating just the road before her, two feet, three feet, four feet, that is all. All else is hidden, but she is not afraid, not any longer. Though she cannot see it, she knows what is ahead. She trusts this road. She has faith it will take her home.

I DID NOT lock the bedroom door or the window shutters. There was no need. No one was at home. The family had gone to the Old City, to the evening gatherings, and afterward would attend the silent candlelight procession that would take them through the night and into the dawn of the tenth day, the pitch of grief.

He was sitting on the bed, face collapsed in his hands. I took the velvet stool across from him. The drumming tonight, the singing, the clapping, the celebrations, not for us.

"As your wife, I have the right to make demands of you," I said. "I demand that you make love to me."

He looked up at me, his eyes red, his face darkened from three days' growth. He had stopped shaving not for our saints, not for any convictions but the one he now held: he was a coward for staying hidden.

I stood and pulled off my chador, then my kurta, my loose *shalwar.* He watched me, saying nothing, though I could see the words in his eyes: he would communicate love today, in its true guise, without limits.

I challenged him. "If I am to stay here with you, if you are going to remain my husband, then you must provide."

He raised his chin, lips curled up in some defiance, before he stood himself and undressed. We stood naked in the glare of the overhead light, neither moving toward the other.

He said, "I was coming home from Naveed's house that night your sister died. I didn't sleep with him. I just let him talk."

I stepped past him and onto the bed, leaving the netting door parted. He climbed in and we sat on our knees, facing each other, still not touching.

He passed a hand over his forehead to massage the lines. "I thought that once I got married I wouldn't want to see him again." He swallowed before saying, "I swear, Layla, I never intended to hurt you."

"Put up your palm," I said, and when he gazed at me, confused, I took his hand from his forehead and raised it before me, then flattened my palm against his. "Whenever Henna and I were together and one of us was sad, we would set our hands together like this. I love her, Sameer, I'll always love her, how am I going to live without her . . ."

He clasped my face and lifted it up to him, finally gazing into my eyes, finally seeing me. "When Naveed revealed everything, I was so frightened . . . and yet so liberated. I should have let you go then, but when I got back to Hyderabad and saw my dad's face . . . all his concerns were about *you*—where were you, what had I done wrong, how had I failed you? And I couldn't do it, Layla, I couldn't tell him. It was easier to go back to the way it was, easier to erase it all. But now," he shook his head. "I could hide from everyone else, Layla, even from you who saw me—you saw me for who I am, in Madras, here, but I still couldn't look at myself, not until . . ." he stopped and licked his lips. "I didn't show myself, Layla. I could have, but I chose not to."

"You are not corrupt, Sameer, don't let them convince you of that. You are as stuck as I . . ."

"I want you to go . . . you are free to go. In your chador, you are invisible." He took his hands from my face and set them in his lap, staring at them a long time. Then he slowly withdrew the silver toe ring from his thumb and held it up between us.

"What about you? How will you make it here?"

He smiled and, for a moment, the tip of his tongue pushed through his front teeth. "This is what I can provide you, Layla. This is what your husband can provide. You mustn't ask me anything more."

I pushed back onto the bed and set my leg in his lap. He lifted my foot to his lips and kissed it, then pressed his forehead against it, eyes squeezed shut, hands trembling. Outside, drums were pounding, people clapping and singing. Finally, he stretched the silver apart, and, just as the women had done two days before our wedding, dressing me to be his bride, he slid it on my toe and cinched it tight.

THAT LAST NIGHT together, we slept pressed into each other at the center of the bed, legs entwined, arms wrapped around each other, in a way not even Nate and I had lain. By the time dawn azan rang through the skies, waking me up, he was gone.

I took his pillow and folded it over my ears, muffling all noise but that of my own slow breathing. I could smell the sour scent of his skin. Finally I rose and bathed. In the handbag, I found our completed immigration papers, wrinkled and torn along one edge from where his fingers had pinched them, confronting Naveed, confronting himself. What had he told me on the train to Madras, that he wanted nothing more than to escape lies, roles he could never live up to, his demon, not Naveed, not even himself, but the ghost they had made him into, here.

I opened his trunk and placed the papers on top, smoothing them flat on his jeans and button-downs, all his Western clothes. His dreams of making himself into something, if only himself. Then I unlocked the *almari* and found the bundle of money Amme had given me. Half had gone to Zakir's daughter, Sadia, and now I halved it again, winding the rubber bands around each, and set one alongside the immigration papers. Then I closed the trunk. If he wanted, he could still go to the U.S. It was the last thing I would provide him.

My passport and money, some jewels Amme had passed on to me, I slid inside the handbag. Then I dumped them out and grabbed the canvas bag he used to take to and from tutoring every day, strapped to his back on the motorcycle, stuffed with engineering books, and once, with Nate's letters. I put my things inside along with a change of clothes. I dressed in black, and by the time I had on my chador, Zeba came striding through the front gates. From the open window, I could hear her calling out for me even before she had unlatched the door.

I took a final glance about the room, the extravagant bed shaped into a peacock that Ibrahim and Zeba would now undoubtedly share, lying on top of velvet pillow covers Nafiza had sewn by hand; the *almari* filled with the silk saris and jewelry of my dowry, and the jewels passed on to me by Sameer's mother; and before the dresser in which Henna had slid Nate's letters, the velvet stool on which my new husband had sat on our wedding night, my kurta clenched between his fists, agonizing about Nate, what he must have known then he could never do himself. Then I saw it, right at the center of the bed, where he and I had been sleeping so tightly, splotches of red.

Menstruation blood, not of death, but of life.

IN THE CYCLE-RICKSHAW, we rolled up from the dead-end road, heading for the main highway, and I closed my eyes, letting some other rhythm carry me.

As we neared the bottom of the hill that would take me out of

Vijayanagar Colony, out of all that had been part of me, the driver began to slow, readying himself to dismount and push the rickshaw up, and the sky tore with the blasting of drums and music, frightening away the birds nested in the woods. Enormous, powerful Ganesh, the one who had been presiding near Abu Uncle's house, had been lifted and was being carried in the back of a lorry, his head held high under the weight of fresh flowers. Surrounding him, in the open back, were young men in wild flourishes of festive-colored clothes.

Following Ganesh was a caravan of cars and auto-rickshaws moving not much faster than our cycle-rickshaw, trucks on which loudspeakers were strapped to roofs, one song quickly folding into another, folding into a Telugu or Sanskrit prayer. From car windows, dark arms were flung out, jiggling in dance, some gripping sizzling sparklers, the flares like live wires under the gray sky. A sign of things that could erupt.

Groups of men strolled alongside the vehicles, dressed mostly in yellows and reds. They were drinking something from a bottle, they were passing it to one another, they were stumbling. Some had played earlier with colored dyes, and their faces and arms and shirts were patches of forbidden colors. The children who accompanied them were waving balloons that drooped on long sticks. While a few of the younger boys scampered along with their fathers, the older ones paused here and there alongside the road to light firecrackers. The sound like death.

I kept expecting someone to break a bottle. To come at Zeba and me, to stain our mournful blacks with the auspicious red of our own flesh. But no one did. Some eyed us with hatred and suspicion. Some turned the other way. Some didn't notice. And one old man with horizontal stripes across his forehead nodded at us, once, as a way of greeting, as a way of letting us know he had seen us in our sorrow, even from his joyful eyes, and we nodded back.

At the crossroads, the rickshaw took a right turn and headed toward the Old City, while the parade continued straight ahead, on its way to Tank Bund, the bridge joining the stray moments of our fleeting lives.

SHE TOOK ME to the flat roof of a building at the heart of the Old City, near the shrine the Qutb Shahi kings had built in the sixteenth century, the Badshashi Ashur Khana. The men's procession of self-flagellators was weaving its way through narrow back alleys, headed here to rest, and from the roof, we would be able to witness these final gestures of grief commemorating our martyred saints. All that had come before, all that was yet to come, carried in these very moments.

Around me, women were lined up along the two sides of the roof that overlooked the street the procession would take, the *durga* off to the corner. So many had come to marvel at this show of courage and sorrow that bodies were lined up one behind the other, an ever-moving mass jockeying to get in front, next to the cement railing, for a better view. And the ones lucky enough to be at the railing were flattened against it, torsos leaning over from the pressure of all that was behind. Up and down the block, for as far as I could see, women in black were crowded on roofs. I could have been looking at us.

In the distance, a rhythmic beating that, at first, I mistook for the drums I'd been hearing all these days. Then I realized it was the men's self-flagellation.

"*Hai* Allah! They've arrived," someone cried.

Zeba had been gripping my wrist to keep from losing me in this crowd, and she now shoved us forward, closer to the edge. She began yelling, "I have an American girl who must see these processions, please, Allah will reward you, let us though."

The women slowly parted and let me have a coveted spot. Then they closed in behind me, pressing me hard against the cement railing, the weight of their soft bodies a wall holding me up. I was captivated by what lay before me. The world, unobstructed and clear.

"Look! Look!" someone shouted, and a hand shot forward, pointing.

Across the way, just beyond a building, was the beginning of the procession. The men were making their way down the last bend of a narrow alley, their lengthy, circuitous journey through the Old City finally coming to an end. The women became quiet, and in the silence, the cry of a child. The mother tried to soothe him by smothering him to her flesh and, when that didn't work, she pulled out a breast and standing, watching the oncoming procession, let him suckle.

The men were reciting a prayer as they marched forth, and I now saw just how long the procession actually was. There were different groups, each group made of twenty or so men, in four or five rows each. The rows were far enough apart so that when the men self-flagellated, their weapons didn't strike those around them. Ten or fifteen yards behind the first group, another began. And it went on like this for twelve or fourteen groups. As long as a mile.

The first group now marched in and stopped in the middle of the road. The crowd that had amassed there, awaiting the procession, parted on either side of the men, a rippling of black. The leader called out, "Allah *ho Akbar*," and his group halted. The prayers stopped. In the silence, the self-flagellation began. Some men bent forward and struck themselves with chains or swords or whips made of five blades, others straightened and tore their shoulders with machetes; razors cleanly sliced chests, knives carved into foreheads. And just when I thought none was left, fresh blood spurted and dripped down faces and chests and shoulders and backs and onto pant cuffs, bare feet, the shuddering earth.

Finally the leader shouted out again, and the weapons came to rest, hanging loosely from arms, and as they marched on, the men's chorus began once more to rise under the gray sky. The street behind them stained as though bleeding itself.

The next leader brought on his group. They, too, stopped in the middle of the road and stepped neatly into the blood puddles left by the men before. They were heavier set than the first, their skin fair.

"Iranians, Iranians," the whisper went through the crowd.

I turned away and tried to catch a last glimpse of Amme's rambling house in the old walled city. But it was indiscernible from any other home. Just as we up here, in our black chadors, were indiscernible from one another. Sameer was right. I was invisible.

In the shuffle of the crowd, I released my hand from Zeba's, and slowly, moving with the rhythm of others' bodies, the thumping chests, the women's eyes gazing downward at the men, the men's eyes gazing upward, at Allah, I pressed back into the crowd. Another figure in black quickly took my spot next to Zeba, and for a moment, I stopped, silently wishing her farewell.

At the door to the roof, just as I was about to bound downstairs, I glimpsed Sabana standing alone at the center, the chador draped loosely about her, exposing her full face, the hair cut fashionably to her shoulders. Though it was not allowed, she was wearing makeup, her lashes thick with mascara, lips a pale pink. Still caught in some vision that had been projected onto the big screen, roles she'd taken up, hidden to herself. Her belly was as wide and round as Henna's had been the last time I had seen her, standing among what now seemed our own ruins. It didn't matter to me anymore, what Dad had done that night, choosing one, abandoning another. Indeed, if I was going to carry him now, inside me, inside any dreams, it would be the image of him boarding the plane, not leaving it all behind, but finally taking possession of his destiny.

I turned and rushed down the winding steps and pushed out into the narrow alleyways, making my way through the aching crowd, the rhythmic pounding of flesh like thunder under the gray monsoon skies. It was the sound of a heart breaking, coming back to life, surrender and union. I walked, I did not run. I walked through the winding alleys, listening to my sandals clicking on the cobblestone, the intake of breath. The canvas bag against my flat belly, holding a different life. Where would these streets lead me?

The wind rose, lifting up my veil like ravens' wings. Layla. Darkness. So I was. My body hidden and safe under the chador, belonging only to me.

ACKNOWLEDGMENTS

I WILL ALWAYS BE INDEBTED to the teachers at the University of Oregon, especially to James D. Houston for revealing the invisible, Ehud Havazelet for proving that "all shall be well," and Garrett Hongo and Chang-rae Lee for teaching me how to dance on the page. Three people who deserve special credit: David Mura, for helping me to embark on this journey, then undertaking the more difficult task of keeping me true to it; Alan Cheuse, on whose wings I took flight; and Bharati Mukherjee, a guide, a light, a master—how could I have been so lucky? Dr. Wade Smith of the NeuroICU at UCSF, thank you for helping to give me a second life. And thank you, Rona Jaffe Foundation, for enabling me to weave a narrative in that new life. I am also grateful to Mihail, who appeared like magic, then spun magic. My editor, Ayesha Pande, for her vision and unrelenting enthusiasm and support and giggles—I couldn't have done it without you! My agent, Eric Simonoff, patient friend whose faith never ebbed, taking me from there to here. Caring, generous Scotty, for his steadfast hand. Family and friends on both sides of the Atlantic for their prayers. Tim, without whose support this book would not be what it is. My two brothers, Zulfe and Jafer, who are my bookends. Naomi, noble friend. And my son, Ishmael, who shows me the miracle of each day.